ON THE WINGS OF THE MORNING

Anthony Reynolds

On the
Wings
of the
Morning

INKWATER
PRESS

*Scan this QR Code
to learn more about
this title.*

Publisher: Inkwater Press | www.inkwaterpress.com

Paperback
ISBN-13 978-1-62901-097-7 | ISBN-10 1-62901-097-9

Kindle
ISBN-13 978-1-62901-098-4 | ISBN-10 1-62901-098-7

Printed in the U.S.A.
All paper is acid free and meets all ANSI standards for archival quality paper.

1 3 5 7 9 10 8 6 4 2

For Norah
Daughter of the Prairie

1

RINGS OF FLATTENED GRASS – SHADOWS OF TEPEES SO RECENTLY ERECT – carpeted the coulee to the slopes beyond, charcoal smudges at their centres still smoldering.

Tom Dunbar had never seen such a sight. He had not known so many could be ready to fight. He felt threatened for the first time by these strange red-brown men, men he had only encountered in twos or threes or in small family groups. They were completely other, of that he was sure. But in their rough clothing of dried skins and discarded European garments they had seemed comical, not threatening.

He had heard tales around the night fires in this western wilderness of painted men astride swift, small horses, descending out of nowhere on some hapless settler family leaving them bloodied and scalpless. These stories came out of the American lands to the south. Not since the uprising around the Red River seventeen years before led by the Metis leader, Louis Riel, had shots been fired in anger between red men and white in Canada.

But tensions between the settlers who continued to stream in from the east, and the resident Plains Cree and Stoney tribes and their Metis cousins, had recently tautened like a bow. Riel had returned from exile in the United States, stirring up trouble once again. They were now marching towards what looked like a major confrontation with native insurgents who had raided several settlements and trading posts.

The march had broken the day before, at sunset, to eat – hard tack, dried beef, cold water. They were not carrying firewood and on this prairie no wood was to be had. The moon rose turning the grassland spectral silver. The company of some 300 regular soldiers and recruited militia formed up and marched on through the night, their scouts riding half a mile in front and on either side beating any bushes they came across to dislodge potential attackers.

The long hours of the night, the continuous murmur of voices, the shuffle of boots, the swish of long grass being parted by men advancing in four parallel columns, induced in Tom a mood of solitary reflection. This was a world away from his Scottish home, Abbeylane Farm, on the shores of the North Sea. He had known his Canadian venture would open many vistas, but he had never envisaged that it would involve going to war.

He had been recruited along with others to supplement government troops shipped out from the east to try to snuff out what looked like the beginning of widespread rebellion. After he had enlisted, they had all been required to give their commanding officer, Colonel William Dillon Otter, the names and addresses of their next of kin. He had given his older brother Rob's name, not those of his parents. If anything happened to him, he would rather have Rob inform the family in Scotland than some military bureaucrat.

Rob, on the farm in the valley of the Pipestone hundreds of miles to the east, would not approve. He was always cautious, missing out on life's opportunities. If Tom could not serve with Her Majesty's army in India, this was the best chance he would ever have to see action. Besides, he would show Rob he was his own man, that out here on the frontier he would not be treated as the younger brother. And he would return to Elphinstone with a good deal more money than he could make sawing lumber.

The weeks since he had signed up with Boulton's Scouts alongside his friend, Glen Lyon Campbell, had served up seemingly endless marches. First they marched the 135 miles from the South Saskatchewan River to relieve the beleaguered settlement of Battleford in the Northwest Territory and then, after a pause of a few days, this further march out to engage the Indians on their own ground. He feared that beneath the excitement of the coming engagement, he had few resources for a prolonged fight.

As dawn's light profiled the eastern horizon, they could see the abandoned houses of a settlement along Cutknife Creek. A small herd of cattle grazed along the banks of the stream. The early morning sky was a gentle blue while the low sun, already warm, cast long shadows before them.

And there in the low hills beyond were the Indians. Tepees had been erected but most individuals were gathered around open fires watching the advancing columns. At the sight of the enemy, adrenalin overcame the deep tiredness that had dogged Tom for several hours.

The column paused while its officers reconnoitered the terrain. Their tactics had to be straight-forward. The Indians held the higher ground affording them a clear view. There was no opportunity to feint an attack across the creek while others encircled the enemy by moving further down the watershed and climbing to higher ground. But they were confident any disadvantage from their exposed position and the fatigue from the long night's march would be offset by the Gatling gun.

This fearsome weapon had never before been employed in Canada. Invented in 1861, it had wrought awesome destruction during the American Civil War. Able to fire several rounds per second, it would surely sow panic among the ranks of the enemy, enabling the troops to pursue and pick off the fleeing Indians at random.

Bullets flew from two directions as they gained the other side of the creek. Two seven-pounder guns were quickly moved into position but it was discovered that one had been charged with the wrong sized ammunition and was immediately out of action. Now the other began to lob its shells into the midst of the tepees and fire pits. Women and children screamed and fled upwards towards the denser brush. The Gatling was pulled up the hill where its range could be more effective and the sound of its bullets spitting across the hillside brought a roar from the men as they raced through the scrub towards the Indian positions.

Tom was just downhill to the right of the Gatling when he saw a half-dozen painted warriors break out of the bushes and sprint towards the gun in an effort to overpower its crew. The officer closest to him shouted to the men to follow him against the Indians. They managed to cut two of them down with gunfire but their proximity to the Gatling demanded face-to-face combat if they were to block the attack. There was no time to reload their guns.

With their knives and hatchets, these wild men of the plains clearly had the advantage in a close encounter. Unencumbered by uniforms, with lithe bodies honed on strenuous exertion, the four remaining Indians hacked and slashed a bloody path through the larger number of troops. The crew of the Gatling gun and the other soldiers on the hill around this brutal skirmish could not rescue their comrades by firing at the enemy without hitting their own men.

Suddenly Tom's whole world became a screaming melee of grimacing faces and flailing limbs, knives slashing leaving bloody spray in their wake, rifle butts smashing into heads. Tom's immediate neighbour fell, his skull split by a feathered hatchet. As the warrior grunted to extract his weapon, Tom baulked. He had slaughtered many an animal, but had never taken a human life. Forcing his arms above his head, his eyes almost blind from the sweat and terror, he screamed and plunged the bayonet into the bare flesh between the warrior's shoulders. The latter stumbled to his knees. In the momentum of his effort, Tom fell across him.

Despite his grievous wound, the man managed to twist around and grab Tom by the throat while drawing his knife from the belt around his waist. Tom pinned the knife hand to the ground but the other's clenched hold on his throat cut off all air. Now it was a question of whether the wound between the warrior's shoulders would diminish his strength before Tom lost consciousness or whether Tom's hold on the knife hand would falter from lack of air. Suddenly the pressure on his throat eased, and the hand holding the knife lost its grip. Tom grabbed the knife and rolled away from the dying man's embrace.

The skirmish around Tom had subsided into the groans and

thrashing of the wounded. His body shook, his shoulders heaving as he tried to breathe. His eyes would not focus; such was the impact of the previous minutes' exertion and horror.

The six Indians were dead or dying but three of his comrades were crumpled in the grotesque repose of death. The battle raged around him. The Gatling gun once more was spitting forth its terror, raking the bush and occasionally finding its mark. From the forests above came the keening of the women like some heinous descant above the clamour of men and guns. The remaining seven pounder sought out the main concentration of the Indians and for a while it looked as though they were about to back off giving the troops the victory.

Then from the bushes and tall grass to the right, untouched by the Gatling's attentions, the Indians attacked in force, gaining a small ridge that protected them from fire and driving the soldiers in front of them farther down the hill in search of cover. The Gatling swerved to address this new threat but was ineffective against the outcropping stones of the ridge. The seven-pounder began to lob shells over the ridge, but then fell silent. Tom could see a huddle of men around the gun obviously struggling to restore it to working order but they began to be picked off by snipers and the rest had to take cover leaving it standing mute.

The Indians behind the ridge now began to move downhill clearly aiming to get behind the troops and cut any potential escape. Their advance having faltered, the troops sought what protection they could, uneasily awaiting orders as to what to do next.

Tom, still shaking, had no time to linger over the deadly encounter he had just been part of. He was told to move up the hill towards the still-flaming fire pits as part of a flanking effort to surround the Indians who it was assumed were still dug in there. Crawling, mostly on his belly, firing whenever he thought he saw movement ahead, he and his comrades gained the still standing tepees to find them abandoned.

The Indians had dispersed. From the heights they had gained, he could see they were now on either side of the main body of troops further downhill, using their snipers to thin the ranks of their opponents and squeeze them into breaking cover and retreating. As Tom watched, some Indians raised hats on top of poles wrapped in blankets. When a soldier stood to shoot what looked like an easy target, he in turn was picked off by a sniper. The clever ruse aroused in Tom mixed feelings of anger and admiration.

It seemed the number of Indians had grown, perhaps with the arrival of others alerted by the smoke columns Tom had seen the evening before. Some were only boys fighting with bows and arrows. Most had shotguns or old Winchesters which were ineffective past 200 yards while the soldiers had weapons that could hit a man at 800. But the Indians had the numbers with them and the skill of their snipers.

Returning to their unit was out of the question – the Indians had closed the line of retreat. There was nothing Tom and his comrades could do but watch the battle unfold.

Tom felt suddenly wasted as he lay in the deep grass, eyes riveted on the scene below. The adrenalin had evaporated and he trembled convulsively. The image reared before his eyes of that broad brown back, rent suddenly by his steel, its life blood spurting across his chest, smearing his hands. He retched violently, producing nothing but bile. But, then, the remembered horror was tinged with arousal, a tightening around his groin, a honeyed sensation coursing through his body, his mind sinking into that well of relief, the taut muscles relaxing. Could an act of carnage rouse his sexuality? He was well acquainted with his appetites; he remembered Kate and his torrid affair. But this crossed previous boundaries. He had taken a life and it now seemed, at some level, he had enjoyed the taking. The horror was now directed at himself.

A bugle blast broke the spell. It signaled retreat. He saw the Scouts attempt to retrieve the wounded and begin falling back towards the creek. The dead they left on the field where they had fallen.

Only the presence of men from the Battleford regiment occupying a sand bluff on the other side of the encircling Indians forced them to lie low and enabled the soldiers to scramble past with few casualties. Tom watched the retreat with alarm. He and his comrades were now on their own. The only escape lay on yet higher ground. Perhaps they could circle up and then descend past the warriors, finding their way to the soldiers' encampment under cover of darkness.

As they scrambled higher, they saw the troops gain the creek, cross it and move out onto the grasslands. Then to the sound of whooping war cries, Indians on horseback poured out of the bushes and across the creek to block the retreat. Here, finally, the Gatling gun proved decisive, causing horses and riders to pitch to the ground while others wheeled back out of the gun's range. The Indians fell back while the retreating troops torched the prairie to prevent their enemy from following. Rising flames and smoke signaled the end of the encounter. Tom and his companions were now on their own.

2

STONES, STONES, STONES. ROB WOULD REMEMBER THEM IN YEARS TO COME when a stone was as rare on the treeless plain as a Highland calf. Now they surrounded him – warm and pastel-shade in the summer's sun, cold and grey in the drizzle of winter. The house, the barns, the fences in the fields, even the poultry sheds were stone-laid, raised by worn hands in generations gone to clear the fields and build shelter.

Rob pulled the reins to move the horses closer to the fence along Greylocks, the largest and most productive field of Abbey-lane Farm set on the edge of the North Sea. The Dunbar family's land was ample, but he liked to use it all especially where it was so productive. He reined the horses in again to plough deep into the corners of the field. He would happily leave a wider margin for the stoats and larks to thrive in other fields but not in this one.

He had been on the land since just after day-break. It was the most peaceful of times. The strong, dark smell of turned earth mingled with the sharp odour of horse sweat. The shuss-crack as the plough rift the stony soil, the deep breathing of the horses as their lungs rose to the day's work, the gentle coo of the collared doves encouraging the reluctant sun, were all sounds that refreshed his soul. When he had had a restless night and had risen in a state of unease – as was often the case these days – a half-hour on the land with the horses was all that was needed to be right with the world again.

The sun had been up for well over an hour, yet mist still blanketed the valley of the Alewater Burn. It had rolled in from the sea overnight and now that treasured stream's edge, where he had fished since boyhood and loved to walk with Agnes, could be seen only in imagined memory. But the memory evoked a longing, a strange mix of joy and pain. He chided himself for indulging in stray sentiment. He could drop the reins and be at the water's edge within minutes.

But how much longer could he wander that stream? If the course of his life unfolded as he was now considering, there would be cause for that ache in the future.

The land was neither his nor his family's, though they tended it as if it were. The landlord lived in distant Edinburgh. His only connection, the four hundred and seventy pounds sterling paid to him on the first of January of each year. His father, Thomas, had leased the land when Rob was seven years old. The term of the lease: no less than nineteen years and no more than fifty-seven.

Most of the leases in his county had those time lines attached. Perhaps there was enough at the start to give a man the illusion that the land was his and therefore to be taken care of. But at the end there was a date that would ensure that it could not be passed on to future generations without negotiating a new arrangement. There was something quintessentially Scottish about those time lines – fair at the beginning but with a clear understanding that ownership was ownership and a man did not part with his property without getting its full value in return.

There was plenty of time left in the lease, except that the landlord had been raising the rent steadily over the last few years, not by much but enough to know that at some point, well before the fifty-seven years, they might have to look elsewhere. They had seen prices for their cattle and grain fall thanks to foreign competition.

Rob was now twenty-seven, the eldest of seven sons and two daughters. They were all of an age to pull their weight on the farm, easing the burden on their father and mother. Tenant farmers they were, but Scots blood and tradition defined the nature of their work, so they had prospered.

He had now ploughed almost a third of the field. The warming sun had begun to lift wisps of steam off the turned earth, solid in its rich, brown array, rolling like a gentle, motionless ocean. Sweat on his brow, a growl in his stomach: he would finish this row, unhitch the horses and let them graze by the fence line while he went in for a welcome breakfast. He could see his sisters, Hermione and Elspeth, making their way to the milk shed to provide fresh, steaming milk for the morning's table.

There was no sign of Tom as yet. He should have been up and about his chores well before this. His brother was a puzzle. He was a delight to be with but prone to moods and trouble. All the other siblings seemed to fall into the pattern set by their father, dutiful and reliable, with the occasional touch of humour to spark their conversation. Mind you, the young ones had not yet come into their own. Tom certainly had, and as he had grown through adolescence, he seemed less and less like a member of this family.

Rob had been awake in the small hours of the morning, turning over in his mind the choices he had to make when he had heard Tom stumble in to their room and throw himself on the bed fully clothed. The smell of the drink was on him. Rob pretended to be asleep. This was not the time to talk. As he rose in the pre-dawn, Rob had seen Tom lying where he had fallen. Tom's moods and choices caused knowing glances around the table these days but no one said anything openly about his behaviour. That was a matter for private admonition, not for discussion in front of the younger children.

Their father, Thomas, had taken Tom aside several times in recent weeks but had not made much headway in steering his son towards a different course. Isobel, their mother, urged patience. She, too, had an unpredictable side, a flare for mischief and a tongue that matched the spark in her eyes. Tom was the one closest to her in temperament, so she defended him and provided the space that still kept him tethered, however loosely, to the family.

Rob was well aware of these tensions. As he strode across Greylocks and through the farm yard, he pondered his own ambivalent feelings about his brother. Life would be smoother if Tom took off and found his way outside the farm. Yet he knew he should do what he could to help keep Tom within the family circle for they needed to support each other now.

Yesterday, his father had faltered. He was bringing a young heifer in to be bred. She was inexperienced and balked, knocking Thomas to one side. He had become dizzy, lost his balance and had fallen. Tom was quick to his father's side, calming the animal and leading his father into the kitchen. But Thomas could not focus his eyes or stand without holding on to the table. Isobel had him lie down, but for the rest of the day he was disoriented. The doctor urged rest.

So now Rob had an ailing father and a recalcitrant brother. It was no wonder he had been disturbed as he had hitched the horses that morning and sought the sounds and smells of the early morning to restore his customary confidence. Life threw these surprises at you, hurdles to surmount rather be deflected by. But he still believed the course he was considering for the future was the one to pursue.

He came into the kitchen silently and stood behind his mother as she removed bread from the oven. "Good morning," he said gently, not wishing to startle her. "How's Father?" He didn't touch her; one didn't touch, much less embrace another, save in exceptional circumstances – it was not the Scottish way. Love and affection were shown through the eyes and offered in the tones of the voice. Only on the most special of occasions did you extend an arm to touch.

"He remains abed," she answered, "but I'm sure he'll join us soon. Only a touch of over-tiredness. He'll be up and about again before we know it." Her cheerfulness could not hide the concern in her eyes. Mother had an indomitable spirit. Whenever others saw problems, Mother saw means of surmounting them. She seemed to know her way forward and carried the doubting along with her. She had been privy to Rob's wonderings about his future and was not about to let life's ordinary troubles prevent him from finding his way. He loved her deeply for this.

Rob settled into his chair, hot oats and steaming milk before him. Isobel took the seat opposite him. Rob took a big spoonful and chewed, but his thoughts had their own urgency and couldn't wait. "I don't know that I can leave with Father's health so uncertain," he said abruptly. "Perhaps I should wait a year."

"Nonsense.'" she replied. "He is still a strong man and every year you postpone this, leaves us one year less to start a new life for the whole family if that is what works out. Besides, it will be good for Tom to shoulder more of the responsibility around here. With you here he has less need to grow into manhood."

The family had talked a lot about their future in the past year. Big changes were underway in the world of farming. Prices for their grains and cattle had been dropping steadily. For the first time anyone could remember, markets were being flooded with cheap food from the vast lands of America. There, where land was free for the taking and soils had never been farmed, the settlers' costs of production were well below what farmers faced in the home country. Even with the expense of transportation across the oceans, they were underselling home-grown product and pushing prices lower. And now, they were even seeing meat, grains and vegetables coming in from Denmark at prices they could not match.

And farmers in Scotland knew only too well what the landlords could do. The Highland Clearances had become the feared means of squeezing out the little man. In the early years of this century, the Highland lairds had decided that running large herds of sheep on their vast, treeless acreages would produce better money than the paltry rents they were able to collect from their tenants. They used their power to change the laws and drive up rents, year by year, until the farmers could no longer earn enough from the hard scrabble land to feed and clothe their families and pay their rents. And so they were driven off to become a shifting, sullen work force for the grim city factories.

Thomas and Isobel thought their landlord, George Denholm of North Saint David Street in Edinburgh, was a decent man – he even paid them a visit every once in a while. They didn't believe he was cut from the same cloth that kilted the Highland lairds. Rob wasn't so sure. If he was so decent, why was the rent going up though he knew perfectly well that the whole of British farming was languishing because of cheap imports?

Rob appreciated his parents trust but he could not share it. Their attitudes had been fashioned in a different time. The world was changing and becoming a harsher place. If the Highland lairds who had the same word of God preached to them in the kirk Sunday by Sunday as the rest, could do what they did to their poorer neighbours, what would stop the Edinburgh landlords from doing the same thing. Money won out over morality every time.

They had to find a way out. Even if they could stay at Abbeylane, there were nine children. While the two girls might find farmers' sons with enough land to provide a secure life for them and their children, he knew he and at least four of his six brothers would have to find another means of livelihood.

They had seen some large notices in the *Gleaner*, the weekly that came out of the near-by fishing port of Eyemouth, stating that the new colonial government of Canada would pay the fare of qualified farmers who wished to take land in the western wilds of that country that were just opening for settlement. As much as 160 acres of land could be had free for each family if it was ploughed and sown within three years.

And then they had gone to a public gathering addressed by a returning delegation of Scottish farmers who had been sponsored to go out to the Canadian west. The tales they told were hard to imagine – unbroken land, free of trees and rocks, with deep, fertile soil, as far as the eye could see. A peaceful countryside as long as you did not travel too far west where conflict with nomadic savages was still possible. There was no shortage of water and a growing season that was much warmer than what they were used to in Scotland.

But it was not for everyone. They said that winters were severe and long. And the isolation, until more settlers came, was intense. But there were no landlords. With hard work and a readiness to accept the hardships, a man could earn a spread that was simply unattainable in the old country. It would be harsh, but freedom and prosperity were there for those with the will to grasp and work for it.

Rob had been entranced. He knew it was his chance to be his own man, never again to have to live with the fear that someone else might deprive him of the means to put bread on the table. And as he started to talk about it with his mother and then later with his father, it seemed possible that it might be the way out for the whole family. If he could make a go of it and establish a thriving farm in five years, then perhaps the whole family could follow and they could recreate a community of blood beneath the limitless skies of a new land.

As they talked together, it seemed more and more possible. But he shouldn't go alone. Tom would be needed at home on the farm, particularly as Thomas was showing evidence that age was draining his strength making the daily tasks on the farm much harder.

Their next brother, George, was not strong enough to take on a full day's work beside his father. And George was showing other disturbing signs. He would spend long hours sitting in the kitchen, engrossed in his own world, almost unreachable. The doctor had been consulted but could find no physical ailment. He had talked quietly to his parents about the possibility at some time in the future of George going to live in a new type of hospital, a place where those who could not function in the real world could be cared for and kept from harm.

So the next choice would be Peter, now a strong, young sixteen-year-old, much like Rob in his character. His presence would be sorely missed by his Mother, but he would be a perfect companion for Rob and together they could make a new life in America for themselves and perhaps for the whole family.

All this had been the subject of family discussion in the long evenings over the winter. And now it was coming soon to the time when decisions would have to be made. This was the content of the waking hours that increasingly disturbed Rob's nights. He was deeply excited at the prospect but also despondent with a sense of oncoming loss.

Many seasons might pass before he was again in the circle of his beloved parents and siblings. And while he knew it was not his own, he loved Abbeylane Farm, the Coldingham Moor to the west that bordered his world and beckoned as the sun slid behind it every evening. The gentle slopes that sheltered the farm led to the small valleys where the creeks fed into the lovely Alewater Burn. Those valleys hid so many memories, the joy of summer evenings when boys had nothing to distract them from wildly imagined games, repelling savage Norsemen as they sought to land their armoured ships upon a sacred coast or charging the arrogant Sassenachs bent on subduing the free-spirited Scots.

And then there was Agnes. Rob had never taken much notice of girls his age. His attention roamed to other things: the great draught horses, Clydesdales and Percherons, that hauled the goods wagons from one town to another; the new machinery – reapers, binders and rigs he could not identity – that he saw on the road traveling from one farm to another; the antics of the other young men and boys.

But now Agnes intruded into his thoughts many times a day. He was somewhat ashamed that these thoughts had become so emotionally charged. That did not sit well with the man he thought he was – steady, clear thinking, not vulnerable to impulse.

"You are far away somewhere," said his mother from across the table. He realized he had been sitting quietly looking at his no-longer-steaming oats for several minutes. He smiled. "Yes, I guess so." He took up his spoon with renewed focus.

Tom could be heard down the hall, singing to himself. He had a deep voice and used it so often that the family knew that if Tom was not singing, he was in one of his darker moods. His feet barely hit the floor in the morning before music of some sort was coming out of his mouth. The quality of the sound got better as the day progressed – in the early morning it could hardly pass for a credible tune. But it was partly the singing that made him so good with the beasts. It calmed them and seemed to give them a sense of being safe.

Tom looked surprisingly robust to Rob as he came into the kitchen, with just a bit of red in his eyes. "You were a long time coming home last night, Thomas," said his mother using his formal name as she did only to show some disapproval or concern. She was aware that he was keeping company with some of the rougher young men in the county and, unlike Rob, spent a fair amount of time in the pub in Reston. "Not to worry, mother," he replied. "When you spend your days in the company of cattle, it's nice to rub shoulders with your friends in the evenings. And the walk home under the stars is good for the constitution."

Rob knew there was more going on than a few drinks with his friends. Tom had a turbulent personality but had been more restless than usual in the last few weeks, finding an excuse to be up and away from the home right after supper and evening chores most nights.

Rob had been fishing in a secluded bend in the Burn just last month and had heard laughter and singing in the woods above him. When it was apparent that it was Tom and that he had a young woman with him, Rob had left off his casting and walked to the edge of the clearing. He was uncomfortable with his actions but justified investigating the scene on the grounds that loyalty to the family and its well-being required identifying anything that might disrupt that equanimity.

He had seen Tom with an arm around Kate, and he withdrew immediately, his face alight with alarm and confusion. Kate was the daughter of Roger Collins, an Irish hand who worked for the Cairn family three farms over. There was no doubt Kate was one of the handsomest young women in the county. She was also among the most forward, with a defiant spirit that matched the flame of her hair. Her parents had lost control of her and it seemed the only reason she remained under their roof was that her labour in the milking barn was needed to supplement the income her father's failing health could no longer ensure.

Rob had no idea that his brother was involved with Kate. She had been a fixture at the pub, but Tom was only one of a number of young men who bantered with her in a rather shameless fashion. If

Tom was alone with her, without either the company of his friends or any of her relatives, this could only mean that things had progressed much further than he dared imagine.

So when he stumbled home in the early hours with the scent of the drink on him, Rob could only anticipate that more trouble was to come. His brother had never talked about Kate or given any hint of a developing relationship. Tom, from an early age, had been a young man who kept much of himself to himself. There had always been shadows interwoven with the exuberance in Tom's personality and, of late, those shadows were becoming darker.

But this was not the time or occasion to intrude. He had to admit he was worried for his brother but also resented the ease with which Tom used his charm to get what he wanted. He wouldn't mind at all if Tom "blotted his copybook" and perhaps fell a few notches in the eyes of those around. It eroded the soul, that jealousy, and Rob knew it and squirmed with the recognition.

Isobel's voice broke into his reverie. "Here, it's already half-eight and you have not even begun your chores, Thomas. Get outside the both of you."

Rob held the door for his brother and then strode towards the horses in Greylocks while Tom disappeared into the barn. His father's fall yesterday had interrupted the breeding of the heifer but she was probably still serviceable.

With the horses back in harness, Rob returned to his reflective task, transforming the field, mottled by erratic spring growth, into tidy brown strips, expectantly awaiting the tiny life forms that would transform them into uniform, green, then golden rows of grain. His thoughts turned again to Tom and Kate.

There was no doubt she was a woman who excited a man's primal restlessness. It was the way she looked at you – her eyes unwavering, daring you to break with the expected and lose your restraint in her abandon. She as well as put your manhood on the line. By not rising to her defiance, your maleness was lessened, nay crippled, her look implied. He too felt the pull, something altogether other than what he felt for Agnes. Not something on which to build a life but perhaps

17

worth the foray and the fall. Yet, this was idle musing. He would not go there. He could not, no matter the urge came from deep within. He had launched his life on another stream.

His thoughts were broken by shouts from the barn. It was Tom, his voice raised in distress. He could see the bull, head down advancing on the fence in the pen but he couldn't see Tom. The heifer was standing agitated, unaccompanied in the same pen. Tom yelled again and Rob dropped the reins and raced across the field. He could now see Tom, on the ground, pinned by the bull's snout to the outer fence. The bull backed off but not enough to let Tom get free. Then he thrust again. Tom was trying to raise himself on the bull's head, to move his body up and over the beast's horns.

Rob grabbed a shovel, gained the fence and leapt it in a stride. Yelling, he struck the animal with full force on its rump. The bull paused in its rampage and turned, directing its attention to Rob, allowing Tom to scramble free. Seeing Tom free and mounting the fence, Rob knew he could not outrun the bull's fury but would have to rely on his agility instead. The animal was at him in an instant but missed by a hair's breadth as Rob side-stepped. By the time the bull had turned, Rob was at the fence and hoisting himself to safety.

He glanced at Tom who was laughing as loudly as his winded state would allow. Rob was irked. Did this man never take anything seriously? He had almost had the life pounded out of him and startled his brother into unaccustomed acrobatics, and it was all a joke. He clearly wasn't hurt and for that Rob was relieved. "Thank you, brother, you saved my hide," Tom said after the laughter subsided. "I guess it doesn't ever pay to be too casual or confident around that bugger, especially when he has a heifer in his sights."

"What happened?" Rob asked.

"I don't really understand," said Tom, shaking his head. "I was walking George to the heifer. He could smell her and was quick to anticipate action when something happened. I didn't have a rope through the ring because he is normally quiet, even in that state. Perhaps he got stung by one of those hornets. Whatever it was, he just roared and charged."

The two walked over to the stone fence by the orchard and leaned on it while regaining their wind and composure. "Sure scared the hell out of me," Rob said. "Next time you try bull fighting, just be sure you have a couple of clowns around to distract the beast."

Tom paused. "Well, I at least had one not far away," he chuckled. "I appreciate the speed you generated in getting over that fence. I'm afraid if he had had another chance to charge, I might have been rather hurt in the encounter."

This might be the time to intervene, Rob thought. Tom was finally pensive and his indebtedness to his brother might make him somewhat more willing to listen. Rob waited a minute in the companionable silence and then spoke. "I was fishing last week down by the big bend and I couldn't help but hear you and Kate laughing in the forest."

Tom looked up abruptly.

"I didn't know you were seeing her in that way."

"I'm not. We were just out on a lark. She's fun to be with, and besides, I don't know what business it is of yours," he added sharply.

"You're right, it's not. But she is one ready woman. Stares the pants off most men and I wouldn't want to see you find yourself with obligations you weren't prepared for, if you know what I mean." Rob glanced sideways to see what effect his words were having on his brother.

Tom's chin was up. "I can take care of myself. If she wants a piece of me, I'm only too ready to oblige. But as for anything else, she knows there can be no strings."

Rob sighed. "Well, if you must, be careful. But you are flouting family tradition that you only encourage a woman if you intend to treat her honourably. Mother and Father have a lot on their plate and they will be relying on you if Peter and I move off to Canada," Rob said holding his brother's eyes in a manner that he hoped would be seen as pleading rather than judging.

Thomas looked stung and then turned abruptly moving off to the barn without a word.

3

THE DAY OF THE CATTLE AUCTION DAWNED DARK, CLOUDS SCUDDING IN from the North Sea. The Dunbars had eleven head that had been well fattened over the winter. Hopefully they would fetch a good price for the tables of Edinburgh.

It was not a good day to be driving cattle cross country the few miles to the Fertile Hall in Reston, the site of the auction. This was Tom's job but in the threatening weather their father suggested that Rob accompany him in case the animals became unsettled. They started after breakfast, Tom on foot to be in closer contact with the cattle and Rob riding the gelding.

They were a third of the way there when the weather turned. Dark clouds towered above. The wind picked up. The cattle lowered their heads in the face of the storm and plodded on. Rain began to whip around them and Tom had to use his staff to whack their rear ends to keep them moving forward. Then a resounding crack as lightning lit the blackened sky, followed a few seconds later by the roar of the thunderclap.

The cattle were off, terrified and stampeding, down the road until the fences gave way to open crop land where they wheeled into a freshly sown field and kept going. Rob rode after them while Tom went to the farm house to make his apologies and round up additional help. At the back of Rob's mind, he realized that it was the farm where Kate's father was the hired hand, but the thought hardly had time to form as he tried to keep his eye on the cattle through the driving rain.

Some minutes later when the small herd had run into a gully

and had started to calm down, Tom appeared on horseback with Kate riding her own steed alongside. Rob was somewhat annoyed but did not say anything under the circumstances. With the wind blowing hard, the thunder clouds would likely move off to the west removing the danger that further lightning could panic the animals again. They decided to wait out the worst of the storm.

Rob dismounted under a large elm. Tom and Kate rode off down the gully and took shelter under a grove of trees. Rob kept his eyes steadily away from them. He had made his position known and he did not want to be further involved.

He loved watching the great movements of the clouds. Such high drama was unfolding above his head. Mountains formed and were shredded moments later – layers moved in different directions, the higher, a white, billowy texture, the lower, dark and solid as a clay bank. Flickers of lightening continued to bejewel the clayed mass. The thunder turned to a low growl. The cattle crowded together by the stream, calming each other by their shared presence.

Rob prized being out in this ancient landscape where the beauty of nature clothed the centuries-old passages of man. What dramas might have been enacted in this little gully? It would have been a perfect place for an ambush. Would the clans have battled here? Would they have sought to tempt the English to a clash of arms in the meadows around while kilted, hairy warriors waited under these trees to rush their flanks?

Rob knew that Tom would have loved to be alive then. He would have relished the blood-lust for battle, the chance to pit your manhood against that of the enemy and at the end taste the exhausted exhilaration of victory. Rob would have been ready to do battle too, if need be, but more in sorrow than in anger – he knew in those days the sword had to be used to protect and hold what you held dear. But he would not have relished using it as he suspected Tom would have.

They were such different men. He envied his brother's impetuous nature and wished he had more of that recklessness in his own make-up. It would make him a more interesting man, he thought, give life greater vigour.

But there was a void in Tom, a restlessness that nothing seemed to still. He was always the odd man out. When the family was together in some common effort or activity, Tom was rarely among them. And he had become increasingly furtive, avoiding sustained interaction with any of them. Certainly, whatever was going on with Kate probably contributed to this distance. Tom had always been guarded with those he should have been close to. But in the pub or on the street with casual friends or strangers, he could be spontaneous and charming. Still, there was always a hint of performance about him in these situations, as though he was standing back and watching himself play a role.

The storm had abated and they should be off with the cattle. But Tom's focus was elsewhere. Rob could just see Tom and Kate leaning together against a tree. So much for impetuousness – it could get you in trouble. He would get the cattle moving and Tom would catch up at some point.

He did, a mile or two down the road. He was on his own, a bit of a guilty smirk on his face. Rob said nothing and the rest of the journey passed uneventfully. The auction house was on the outer edge of town, a low wooden building with stone-fenced corrals at one end. He was concerned to see that there were a large number of cattle already in the pens. He hoped the number of buyers would be sufficient to keep the prices decent.

Prices had been depressed for some time. It had been reported that the Americans had found a way to dry their beef enabling them to ship large quantities across the oceans. This did not compete with fresh beef for the consumer market, but it gave governments a means of stockpiling supplies for their own purposes, principally to feed their armies. There was not much of a market for that in Britain, but the European states had been big buyers of beef for their armies, particularly the French and the Germans who seemed to be getting ready for yet another contest of arms. British farmers had benefitted in the past from European conflicts and the demand for meat they generated, but now this market had virtually disappeared.

They moved their animals into an empty pen. The delay caused by the storm meant that they were well down the line. Many other cattle would be on the block before their turn came. But experienced buyers spent considerable time walking among the pens and viewing the condition of the livestock so if their animals stood up well to scrutiny, they might not be too affected by their lower position. And looking at the other cattle, Rob knew their herd looked better than most.

Inside, the most active bidders ringed the fenced circle where the cattle were to be shown while others sat on raised tiers behind them, each in plain view of the auctioneer. The building hummed with talk, neighbours taking the opportunity to test their ideas about the markets, about the state of their animals, about politics. Most lived on fairly isolated farms and an auction was as much a social as a business occasion. A few women were present, some who continued to run their farms on their own after the passing or departure of their mates. But mostly there were men.

Tom moved off to talk with his friends and soon there was a small crowd of rather rough young men about him. Laughter ensued. Rob saw William Runciman sitting on the other side of the ring and quickly cast about to see if his daughter, Agnes, was present. No sign of her. Rob did not want to meet Runciman on his own so turned to his immediate neighbour, a man he had not seen around the district before.

He was a young Londoner, it turned out, employed by a wholesaler in Edinburgh and here to learn the cattle trade in Scotland. His sister had married the son of the firm's owner, hence his privileged position. He had directions as to what to buy and for how much but Rob judged he was inexperienced. He wouldn't say much about prices in other parts of the country, either because he was keeping his cards close to his chest so as not to give a seller an untoward advantage or because he simply didn't know. Rob judged it was the latter.

The auctioneer mounted his pedestal and the first cattle were prodded into the ring. A fine half dozen Aberdeen Angus, their coats a black sheen, their ribs well-padded and haunches rounded. Good looking cattle.

"What am I bid for this fine selection of healthy hooves from the Craig herd?" the auctioneer began. "We'll start at thirty-five Pounds per beast. Who'll give me thirty-five? Alright, thirty? Then twenty-five? I have twenty-five, who'll give me thirty? Thirty. We're going for thirty-five. I have thirty-five. Who'll give me forty? forty? Alright, thirty-eight? Thirty-eight? I have thirty-eight. Now forty? Forty? Going once at thirty-eight. Twice. Three times at thirty-eight Pounds to number seventeen."

Rob was pleased at the prices. His English companion looked disappointed. He had not bid on this lot but from his countenance he clearly was surprised at the prices they fetched.

The next lot came in, lowing intermittently. They were not as robust and as they were mostly Holstein steers, the buyer would get a lot of bones for the available beef. They went for twenty-two Pounds per animal, but that was not surprising. And then the lots came in one after another, each attracting the price the remaining buyers were prepared to pay. Generally, these were on the low side.

Finally, Abbeylane's animals were next. Rob did not indicate his ownership and he noticed his neighbour join in the bidding. It started at twenty-two. The young Londoner came in at twenty-eight. It went to thirty. A well-known Edinburgh buyer pushed it to thirty-four and it seemed to stick there. Thirty-four going once, thirty-four going twice. The Londoner came in at thirty-six. The other buyer raised it to thirty-eight. And there it stayed. "Thirty eight going three times to Mr Forke with number twenty-three."

Rob and Tom exchanged wide grins across the ring. That was a decent price. Their father would be well compensated for his labour and investment. Rob told his neighbour that they were his cattle and thanked him for his participation. The young man looked surprised but pleased. "Good looking stock. Do you have any more?"

he asked. 'Oh, in a couple of months' time," Rob replied. "Then perhaps we shall meet again," the man said.

Rob saw Tom leave his seat in the ring and went to join him but as he was leaving the building he saw Agnes arriving in a carriage with a sister. He recollected that the Runciman cattle had not yet been on the block. He paused and watched the two young women go into the auction house. Agnes had not seen him. He went over to Tom.

"Well, this is cause for a few pints." Tom proposed that they head to the Red Lion in Reston on the road towards home. Rob agreed that a drink or two was merited but he did not want to go immediately. "I'll join you briefly," he said, "but first I have some other business to attend to." He blushed slightly. He could see that Tom noticed but thankfully said nothing.

Back in the arena he took a seat where he could watch Agnes and her father but not be too conspicuous in so doing. He noted the easy way she had with her father so unlike many young women of her age. Her father talked with her continuously, seeming to comment on the various characteristics of the animals being led through the auction process. There was obviously humour in their exchanges. In the lulls between the bidding, others would come up and join them for a few minutes. She was always warm and welcoming, it did not seem to matter what age the visitors were.

At one point she seemed to have spotted him. He thought he had caught her eye looking at him, but if that was so, she swiftly turned her gaze away. And then he saw the same thing again a few minutes later. She had been looking at him, even in the midst of the bustle of the auction and the presence of a number of people around her. Did that mean something? Was she attracted too? His breath came a little quicker. But she must have realized that he was looking at her too. Best to be up and away before he embarrassed her.

The Red Lion was on the other side of town. He had mounted the horse and arrived there before he had noticed the distance, his thoughts bound up in that arena and that one spectator. Tom was seated with five other young men, most of them his steady companions. Their interaction was customarily raucous, with Tom, as

25

usual, the instigator. Rob did not want to dash the warm reverie he had been enjoying so took a seat at the other side of the room where he was not easily viewed from Tom's table.

But he could see Tom and as his reverie subsided, he found himself watching his brother. Tom was relaxed and performing for his friends. His face was expressive, fully engaged in the interaction with those around him. Rob felt the contrast with his own solemnity. He so often could not find the words to say what he felt or engage in the banter that was the common medium of exchange among his peers.

It wasn't that he did not care or preferred his own company. Indeed, he felt strongly for his friends and family and enjoyed meeting strangers, often finding qualities about them quite swiftly that made him want to get to know them better. It was just that he was not as quick to be able to express that. Would Agnes take to someone who seemed slower, more bound up in himself, or to put it plainly, dull?

His reverie had evaporated. He downed his pint, went over and told Tom he would fetch the money for the cattle, and headed for the door. It was best to put these thoughts of Agnes far from his mind. There were dozens of young men of her acquaintance with far more to offer than he had. Again he found himself envying Tom's ability to access warmth and pleasure in the company of his friends and his attractiveness to women that led to pleasures of a different sort, pleasures for which Rob found himself increasingly impatient.

Enough. He shook his head as he saddled the gelding, swung up on its high back and headed back to the auction house. There was no point dwelling on this. He was what he was and he had to get on with the tasks at hand. Besides, he had different adventures ahead of him, paths that offered challenge and excitement where personal affability was irrelevant. He deliberately turned his mind to contemplate the prospect of Canada.

At the auction house he went directly to the owners' stall. Activity had wound down and he joined a small queue of buyers and sellers concluding their money matters. He kept his eyes down, determined not to distract himself by seeking out Agnes.

When he arrived home an hour later, the post had come and in it was an official-looking letter with a Canadian stamp. He had written enquiring about emigrating to Canada under a program encouraging British farmers to populate the western prairies. He was surprised at the amount of material in the envelope and took it quickly to his room to read in private.

There was a long article, rather poorly printed, quoting people who had emigrated earlier – "the soil's depth and tilth is unlike anything seen in England..." – "we would never in two lifetimes have been able to acquire so much good land back home...." – "markets take all I can produce". And much more of the same. It was too encouraging, surely there were drawbacks. He scanned the rest of the material but found no mention of any.

Finally, there was a letter describing the money he could receive for his passage and the journey across Canada if he met the qualifications – sixty-five dollars for the first and twenty dollars for the second for each person. That would certainly help.

He heard his mother and sisters preparing tea and took the papers down to show them.

"Take a look at this, Mother. It sounds too good to be true. They say that there will be 160 acres for each man or head of household which he would own free and clear as long as he ploughs and seeds it and builds a house within three years," he said, skepticism edging his voice.

"I'm not saying that they're lying, but I am sure there are a great many hardships to encounter before you can be up and running."

"Of course," replied Isobel, "there is nowhere in this life without hard work and hurdles. The question is will you be farther ahead with that hard work there than you would be here? And will there be opportunity for your brothers to get out from under the control of the landlord? If there is, then you should chance it."

"But what about us, Mother," said Hermione. "Won't we be going too?" Thomas walked into the kitchen and took his place at the head of the table.

"There'll be none of us going until Peter and Rob have had a chance to see the place for themselves and get a good farm started. I don't think any of the rest of us should be thinking of moving for three years, perhaps five," said his mother.

"Och, in five years down the road, these old bones won't want to be going anywhere," said Thomas. "I'd rather lay them down in my own sod than in some distant wilderness. This is for the young. I'm not saying don't do it. There is no real future for you here, lad. But if you go, I'm afraid it is going to be the break-up of the family."

"No more of this mournful talk," interjected Isobel. "This is a great opportunity. Sure, it'll break our hearts, but it will be the fulfilment of you, Rob, and of your brother, Peter. We will miss you dearly and will think of you many waking moments of every day. But we will find joy in what you accomplish, and if the Lord wills it, we will all be together again, there or here." With this Isobel motioned them all to sit, give thanks and eat. Peter joined them and Rob passed him the papers which he read silently. "That's a fair pile of money they'll spend to get good farmers out on those lands," Peter commented. "What do they call them – the prairies?"

"Well, we are going to have to make a decision soon," said Rob. "The early summer's the only time to make the passage. I would not want to be on the North Atlantic in the wintertime. And we will need to get there in enough time to find us some work before the winter sets in. I doubt we will be able to find the land we want until the following spring."

Peter looked across at him, his eyes alight. He was honoured to be entrusted with this role by his family and so pleased to be valued as a companion to his brother, Rob. Being the third son, it had been hard to establish his own identity, particularly when Rob had shown such steadfastness in the family and Tom had been such a colourful character. This was his chance to show what he could do. He loved his mother for her strong support for the venture. He knew how much it must cost her to send two of her sons so far away. But she was ever the game one.

Chapter
4

THEY COULD SEE THE SMOKE AND FLAMES RACING ACROSS THE GRASSLANDS to the southeast from the prairie fire the retreating troops had started. It was now apparent that their line of retreat had been cut and the only way to avoid capture was to find refuge in the dense bush farther up hill. They would have to move with the utmost care as the warriors were milling about on the hillside below and the women who had fled from the battle would be returning to the camp, the remnants of which lay around them.

Tom hurriedly conferred with the other four men and they decided to split up, as moving together would certainly attract attention. A ridge some 200 yards from the camp would be their target, providing sufficient distance to hide them for the night. It was possible the Indians would break camp and depart in the morning.

As Tom crawled forward he could still hear a wounded horse screaming down by the creek where the Gatling gun had stopped the Indians' charge. A shot rang out and the scream stopped. He could hear the guttural shouts of the men as they tended to their dead and wounded. Some had started climbing the hill towards the encampment but they were preoccupied and not looking for enemy troops.

Soon he could not see his comrades. To his right there was a dip in the ground where the foliage was particularly dense. Tom moved swiftly into it. He was conscious of his own heavy breathing and tried to restrain it. The depression stretched almost to the ridge but at the end of it there were some ten yards of open ground. Any movement across that would certainly be spotted.

29

He reached the far end of the cover but by this time the voices of the returning warriors were near. He could not move further and had no idea where the others were. Then there was a shout from one of the braves who was walking above the encampment. He could just see the man through the foliage raise a hatchet as if to strike. Three of the warriors ran to join him and the skirmish that followed revealed one of Tom's comrades cowering on his knees. All eyes were on the encounter and Tom knew he must use the distraction to cross the open space.

He succeeded unnoticed. From his new cover he watched the braves beat their captive and drag him into the camp where he was lost from view. Now the warriors would certainly scour the area looking for other soldiers. They started shouting to their comrades below who bounded up the slopes and the search was on.

Within minutes they had found two more and the terrified men were pushed, stumbling down the hill into the camp. That left only Tom and one other undiscovered. Tom could hear men clambering up the ridge. He hid his pale face in the dirt and prayed that the thick brambles under which he had sought refuge would discourage a close encounter. Footfalls drew nearer, paused while a grunted exchange took place, and then moved away. His fingers ached with the panic that coursed through his body. How was it possible that he had not been seen? He began to breathe again and lay still for what must have been well over an hour.

Light was beginning to fade and the sounds and smells of a meal being prepared in the encampment reminded him that his last food had been hard tack and water the night before. He could now see the fires below and watched as more tepees were erected. It looked as though the Indians were preparing to stay beyond the night that stretched ahead of him. One of his comrades was still out there in hiding. He had no idea what fate had been meted out to the three others who had been captured.

The search seemed to end as the Indians moved towards an area where some bodies lay and now he could hear the sounds of wailing. He could just see men coming up the hill carrying the dead and laying them, side by side, before the largest tepee. He counted fourteen in all, one of which was certainly the warrior he had slain with his bayonet. The women now gathered and the wailing rose to a high-pitched keening.

The drums took up the lament and the women's wail flowed into their beat. The gathering dusk moaned with the primal mourning, sounds so alien to his ears and yet at one with the ancient hills around. He shivered where he lay, less from the cooling winds than from being so alone amidst such threatening grief. He knew this was the time to move, to get as far from the encampment as possible while there was still sufficient light. But he was immobile, held by the power of an ancient, alien ritual being enacted before him.

He struggled to break the trance, recalling the sight of his comrades being dragged into the camp, and forced himself to move. Crouching below the sheltering bushes, he crawled, avoiding branches that might break or stones that could be dislodged alerting the warriors gathered below. He had covered perhaps some 200 yards before he realized he had left his rifle behind in the bushes where he had stopped to watch the bodies being brought into the camp.

His first impulse was to return for it. It seemed his only security. Yet, he realized that one gun would provide him no escape should he be found and might in fact provoke a fatal encounter with his captors. He could also move much faster without its encumbrance. His only hope was to avoid detection.

After what seemed like hours, he judged he was about a half mile from the encampment and in the dimming light could see no sign of human movement. He could now run half-crouched, still seeking the cover of trees and bushes. He stayed on the hill but could see Cutknife Creek following the contour of the hill in the valley below. The light was fading fast with the western horizon showing only a tinge of yellow before the pale blue that shaded into the deep dark of the coming night.

He made his way down to the creek and drank deeply. Suddenly, exhaustion overwhelmed him. He knew he would have to cross the open grasslands under cover of darkness but he no longer

31

had the energy even to ford the stream. He found a dense clump of prairie willow on its banks and decided to sleep for at least a few hours before starting across the prairie. The drums and chanting had faded into silence.

He startled awake, his nerves on high alert, his mind in utter confusion. He had no idea where he was or how he had got there. Gradually the memory of the previous hours returned. Then he heard it again, the sound that had grasped him deep in his sleep and yanked him back into consciousness. It was the short, throaty murmur of human voices, Indian voices. The sky was shading light. He had slept far more than intended. They were coming closer, along the creek. He dared not move but feared that the evidence of his passing in the trampled grass would be all too clear.

They had spotted the trail. The voices increased in intensity and came towards him swiftly. With a high pitched yell, they were upon him, hatchets raised.

Tom had time only to stumble into a crouch and shield his head with his arms. Seconds became timeless as he waited for the blow to fall. The willow branches cracked around him as the braves circled, loudly disputing what to do next. Suddenly he was kicked forcefully and sent sprawling into the bushes. Then a hand grabbed him by the jacket collar and hauled him to his feet.

Three brown men, naked to the waist, their faces streaked with the remnants of yesterday's war paint, hatchets and knives poised, surrounded him. The largest of them grabbed him by the hair, forcing his head down and brought his knife swiftly up to his head. Tom braced for the excruciating pain he was sure would descend when the man sliced into his scalp. Then with a stark shout another of the men gripped the assailant's arm and a short, sharp skirmish ensued in which Tom was momentarily forgotten.

The intervener seemed an older man, one who claimed authority over Tom's assailant and the younger backed sullenly away while a third warrior took hold of Tom, twisting his arm sharply behind his back. The older two conferred briefly and directed the younger to search the area, perhaps for weapons Tom might have been carrying. While this was going on, the two continued to talk and arrived at a decision. They gestured to Tom to start walking in the direction from whence they had come.

Tom had no choice. Though unharmed, there was no way he could outrun the Indians, having had no food for more than a day. He stumbled to the creek and started walking back towards the site of yesterday's battle. Apart from pushing him roughly from time to time to assert their dominance, he was able to walk relatively freely and within half an hour he was directed up the hill towards the now visible encampment.

As he climbed he could not help but see several of his crumpled comrades undisturbed where they had fallen yesterday, grotesque in their death embrace. The Indians had removed all their own dead, leaving the corpses of their enemy to the crows and foxes. He was not close enough to recognize any but reflected that the retreat must have been precipitous to cause the Scouts not to retrieve all their dead. But it was also evidence that they would be back for they never left a comrade unburied or unblessed at the grave side.

His captors shouted as they neared the camp and other braves came running forward laughing, grabbing him by both arms and dragging him the last hundred yards to the large tent where the night before he had seen the Indian dead arrayed. He was pushed inside, forced down on his knees, a hand grabbing his head and thrusting it down. But not before he spotted his three comrades in a corner, alive and able to exchange a flicker of recognition.

The older of his three captors addressed the four soldiers in harsh tones, in Cree and incomprehensible. The Indians then left but through the walls of the tepee he could see two standing guard.

Tom looked up. "Are you alright?' he asked his companions. "Bruised and hungry but nothing worse – you seen William?" one asked referring to the missing soldier. "Not a sign," Tom replied. "Any idea what they plan to do with us?" "None," came the muffled answer. "You eaten anything?" "Yeah, got some pemmican this morning but nothing else."

Fear and hunger diminished talk. The sun on the walls of the tepee turned things uncomfortably warm. The noises outside the tent were the sounds of a normal day – women talking, children running and shouting, most of the warriors away from the tents, perhaps hunting. The shadows of the guards unmoving on the tent.

Drowsiness overcame apprehension as the day passed and the men slept. They were wakened by the sound of horses riding up to the tent. Men dismounted and the entrance flap was thrust aside. Five warriors entered led by a tall man, his head adorned by a set of buffalo horns and plumed feathers. Over his bare torso hung a pelt of fox fur with a wide black belt around his waist. He was clearly in the lead and shouted in Cree at the huddled soldiers. The monologue continued for several minutes. Then a sixth man stepped forward. He had entered the tent shortly after the warriors and from his dress he did not seem one of them. Instead he wore the mixed garb, Indian and European that many of the half-breeds favoured. He began to translate.

"You are prisoners of Fine Day, warrior chief of the Plains Cree. He tells you that the soldiers have killed some of his best men and he is very angry. He says many of his young braves desire to kill you in revenge. He would like to please them but the great chief, Poundmaker, must be spoken to first.

"If you try to escape you will certainly be shot. He says he will be taking you to Poundmaker's camp soon. But if your soldiers return and attack again, he will turn you loose for his young men to hunt down. Those are all the words he speaks."

The man moved to follow the warriors out, paused, and turned back to the soldiers. "You must do as Fine Day says. He is an honourable chief but you are in great danger from others. You will be taken to Poundmaker tomorrow. It is up to the great chief and he will decide what to do with you.

"If he wants to negotiate, you may be saved. If he wants to keep fighting, you will be seen as a burden and be disposed of. The only prisoners the Cree keep are women and children. When they fight, they expect to win or to die and they believe any warrior entering battle makes the same choice."

He stared for a few seconds directly into Tom's eyes and then left.

The sounds outside the tent diminished. Large flies buzzed in the heat around its walls seeking a means of escape. One of Tom's comrades shouted to the guards and when one of them stuck his head through the flap, the soldier made it plain that he had to pass water. The guard grunted and motioned him outside. The others rose as well to do the same but were abruptly turned back. Moments later the soldier returned looking relieved and the guard indicated another could come out.

When Tom's turn came, a docile sight greeted his eyes. Dozens of tepees had been erected and most had fires burning in front of them where it was evident that an evening meal was in preparation. He could smell the roasting meat and his hunger pangs became acute. There was no sign of the battle that had taken place the day before. A few of the women shot sideways glances at him.

The guard gestured that he should relieve himself directly at the side of the tent in full view of the activities around. Only the urgency of the pressure in his bladder enabled him to do so. He closed his eyes and imagined he was in some isolated place. He could hear women's laughter but completed the task in hand and returned to the tepee.

By now the pain in his empty belly was excruciating and he felt himself trembling from lack of sustenance. His comrades looked dejected; fear and hunger were taking their toll. None had the energy to talk, and what was there to talk about? They could only hope that the nature of the skirmishes between the government's forces and the rebels elsewhere were such as to cause Poundmaker to want to sue for peace. Then they would have a chance of surviving.

Otherwise, they had heard what the Indians had done at the massacre at Frog Lake where two priests had been shot, their bodies hacked up and tossed piece by piece down a well. The government agent, Thomas Quinn, a Sioux Metis, had also been shot by Big Bear's men along with four or five other unarmed men in a frenzy of blood-letting. They had no idea what other atrocities had taken place but their imaginations worked overtime in the afternoon heat.

The day slipped into evening without any sign that they were going to be given food. Then, as the dusk dimmed to darkness, the tent flap was thrust back and a guard entered with an old woman. She was carrying part of the roasted hind leg of a deer and placed it carefully in front of them, avoiding any eye contact. The men's' faces reflected their surprise and relief. Having no knives, they paused in some confusion. Then one picked it up and using his fingers, ripped flesh off the leg and passed it to his neighbour. The leg quickly made the round, once, twice and then again until there was only cream-coloured bone left.

Bellies replenished in part, the men sank into fitful slumber. The noise in the camp died. Flames played on the darkened walls of the tent. Subdued drumming commenced in the distance accompanied by guttural chanting. Some of the soldiers stirred when drumming broke into their consciousness but were quickly lulled back into sleep. Dark circled the encampment and within an hour, all was silent.

Tom wakened sometime in the dead of night. Through the silence, he could hear the distant yelping chatter of coyotes and the cries of unknown night birds. The moon must have been full for the tent was diffused with a pale, ashen light.

It was all so completely alien, so foreign to everything that gave him comfort, to everything that was reassuring. He thought of his room in the house in Abbeylane with its view of the gentle, familiar hills, of his dear family who would be sleeping in the rooms around him, of his brother, Rob whose body would be stretched out on his bed beside him, his torso rising and falling in slow rhythm.

He raised his head to look through the eerie light at his comrades sprawled in sleep, looking not unlike the dead he had seen on the hillside the day before. And he felt utterly alone, wholly at the mercy of the unknown. And as is wont to happen in those isolating hours of darkness, the terrors and regrets of the daylight hours assumed an urgent, fearful dimension of their own.

He now had the lives of two, no three, on his account – Kate lost to wanton disregard, and her child – his child – caught in the backwash. And now the red man, younger than he, taken amidst blood and arousal. Could he come to terms with the man he had become? Yes, he had made choices and each choice, regardless of its consequence, revealed to him more of who he was.

The gentle innocence of family memory, an existence hard but love-laden, belonged now to another world, to a life to which he could never return. He loved those with whom he had lived, but he had been straining as long as he could remember against their assumption that he shared their Scottish forbearance and charity. He wasn't necessarily proud of the fact, but he could find little taste within himself for a life of constrained virtue. That had led him into alien and lonely places but it also served up adrenalin-charged experience. And in the ghostly light of the moon-filled canvas, he felt every fibre of his being alive.

In the midst of this reverie, he must have fallen asleep again. It was the sound of horses and riders arriving that wrenched him back into daylight consciousness. The flap was pulled back and four half naked warriors, their faces adorned with fresh paint, entered before the soldiers were even able to sit up. They gestured the men out of the tepee.

Outside were two more Indians holding a number of horses, unsaddled save for ropes around their chests behind their forelegs. It was made plain that they should mount the horses, no simple task without stirrups or saddles. Tom grasped the rope around a chestnut mare and slowly pulled himself on her back. The others stumbling, followed his lead while the Indians scoffed at their awkwardness. One of the men did not have the strength to pull himself up until one of the warriors grabbed him by the back of his coat and half lifted him aloft.

The Indians followed, leaping with ease, one hand on the rope, onto the back of their mounts. Each grabbed a rope that secured the soldiers' horses and wheeled about heading out of the encampment. The soldiers, faces still showing the dregs of sleep, followed holding desperately to the rope around the beasts' chests. Heads poked out of the tepees as they thundered past towards the open grassland.

There was no sign of Fine Day. Were they being captured by the angry young men the chief had spoken of the day before or was this the party that was taking them to Poundmaker's camp? Tom could not tell. The braves were certainly young and their paint made them look angry indeed. But with each of their horses tethered to one of the braves' and with all their energy being required just to stay erect on the horse, they had no option but to hold on and be carried away.

Once down the hill and onto the grasslands, the lead warrior reduced his pace to a trot. There were six in all, one leading each of the soldiers and two riding either side of the party. They were heading west with the sun just beginning to breast the horizon behind them.

They rode silently for what seemed several hours, moving northwards towards low, dry hills. The soldiers by now had become accustomed to the bareback nature of their mounts and looked less disconsolate. The sun was warm and the deer meat of the night before had given them a reprieve of energy. The experience was almost becoming pleasant.

Then, as they descended into a gully, the Indians brought the party up short. On the ridge above appeared the heads and then the bodies and horses of some two dozen other warriors, who came charging down the edge of the coulee, whooping war cries, and heading straight for their captors. The latter were clearly confused and milled around shouting to one another but before they could group into a defensive position, the charging warriors surrounded them, their horses galloping in an ever closing circle.

No shots were fired. When the circle had closed tightly, one of the strangers began shouting to Tom's captors and a furious exchange took place, the intruder clearly demanding that the prisoners be surrendered to his men. The demand was resisted and for many minutes it looked as though violence would determine the outcome. Then the lead intruder forced his horse through the crowd and grabbed the rope holding Tom's horse. His comrades followed suit and the soldiers found themselves being led by the intruders, galloping up the edge of the coulee while their former captors watched them disappear over the crest of the hill.

5

THE NEXT DAYS PASSED SLOWLY FOR ROB. HE HAD SET THE COLDINGHAM
Fair as his conscious horizon and though his head told him
there was little point in looking forward to seeing Agnes, his spirit
dictated otherwise and his spirit usually trumped his head. He had
been thinking of her a great deal.

They had been in the same county for years, had gone to the
same school until Agnes left at age twelve along with most of the
other girls. That was the age when the teaching of domestic skills
alongside their mothers was the role society prescribed for a farm
girl. He had then seen her rarely – at the county fair in the autumn,
driving to town with her father behind the horses. He had not seen
her in church. Her parents were Methodists while Rob and his
family attended the Baptist church in Eyemouth.

It was at a community gathering last autumn that he had suddenly seen her in a new light. He guessed she must now be almost
20. He hardly recognized her – now tall, long of arm and slim of
waist. Her auburn hair carried high on her head, showing an elegant neck and jaw-line. He found it difficult to take his eyes off her,
but knew he must or risk embarrassing both of them. He found
himself, against his better judgment, walking the fairgrounds in
such a way as to keep her not far from his sight. He stole glances
for the rest of the day.

The daily tasks of the farm, mucking out the cows, piling stones
back on the fences where they had been knocked down, repairing
mortar on the stone buildings, traveling to town to order the spring
seeds, seemed to drag the time not quicken it.

The day had finally come and the whole family, rigged out in two carriages, made their way to Coldingham. This was the opportunity to compare notes with neighbours, to see what the local government agent had to say about new methods of cropping or breeding, and for the women to make up for long, lonely hours of labour on their farms by endless conversations with each other. And though the men were inclined to be somewhat more taciturn they still enjoyed vigourous, and for some, ribald, exchanges with their peers.

For Rob, there was only one focus to this fair. He amazed himself at how little interest he had in the new-fangled machinery. He had a passing interest in some new varieties of grain that were being shown, one of them called Red Fyfe that had been developed in Canada, produced a particularly hard wheat and made an excellent flour.

But he was distracted. He kept looking for Agnes. Even though he was now all but committed to going overseas, as much for the future of his family as to fulfil himself, he thought perhaps her high spiritedness might in fact mean that the challenge of a new land would appeal to her, would make him more attractive to her. But how could he think of courting her when he might be off in three or four months and not be back for four or five years? Even if she took to him, how could he expect her to wait that long? Questions, questions and doubts.

"Steady on," he told himself. "One step at a time. The future will unfold, if not one way, then another."

Rob walked towards the cattle barn where the beasts were being readied for the afternoon's show ring. The Guernseys were at one end of the barn and there was Agnes along with her father and a sister. "No more sneaking around," he thought to himself. "Just make your way down there and start a conversation."

"Good day, Mr Runciman, Julia, Agnes," he said with a nod. "Those are fine looking animals you have there." He was trying to sound as casual as possible. "When does the judging start for the Guernseys?"

"Why, young Dunbar. I hear you did rather well at the auction a fortnight ago. Got near the top price at the event. I wanted to talk with you and Tom afterwards but you disappeared," Runciman said. "That bull of yours seems to sire sturdy offspring. Would you be willing to lend him to me at some point? For a price, that is."

The young women, seeing the turn the conversation had taken, moved behind the stalls talking and laughing quietly. Rob was relieved to find a subject of mutual interest that did not require small talk. The men continued discussing the merits of the animal, the difficulty of handling him as he was somewhat high-spirited. Rob said his father would have to be consulted about price but was sure an arrangement could be made.

Agnes emerged from the stall and smiled briefly at him. He plunged in, "Agnes, I saw you at Mr Gladstone's meeting last month. You seem to have quite an interest in politics," he managed to say. "What did you think of what he said about the Irish situation?"

To her credit, Agnes did not appear surprised that he would ask her opinion on such a topic. "Oh, I thought his comparison of their situation with ours was fairly provocative. But I guess he is right. You can't have a double standard for people living in the same country, or, for that matter, for people living anywhere. It's just not right." A forthright response, thought Rob and just as he was about to extend the conversation, she blushed, averted her eyes and, seeming to become flustered, excused herself. "I have to ready the other animals," she said quickly and fled, awkwardly to the other side of the barn.

Rob was taken aback and for a moment stood uncomfortably, watching Runciman get on with his tasks. "Well, I'll speak to my father about the bull. And good luck in the show ring," he managed to get out.

"Don't let that young filly disconcert you," Runciman said. "She has a good mind and an able tongue, but she did not show either in the best light today. Good-day to you and thank you."

Rob could not figure it out. Why was she so lively with others but seemingly tongue-tied with him this morning? He so wanted to engage her in conversation. There was much he wanted to talk with her about. But why had he been so foolish to start out with politics? Perhaps that had intimidated her, though he doubted that was the reason given her well thought-out response. Was it just that she was not interested in talking with him? That might be the cause, but he knew that she had been raised in a family where good manners were important and one did not end a conversation so abruptly regardless of what you felt about the other person. Something else must be at play. Could it be that she was as attracted to him as he was to her, and her emotions got the better of her? Or was he just engaging in wishful thinking?

His thoughts were confused and disconsolate as he moved across the fairgrounds in search of his family. Yet for all his disappointment, he knew he was powerfully attracted. He would not let this setback divert him, at least not yet.

His father and Tom were in the machinery pavilion engrossed in examining a reaper, a horse-drawn contraption with twelve-foot twin blades out the side, held up at the far end by a wheel. As the wheel turned it moved the blades across each other, catching and cutting the stalks of grain. It would make swift work of cutting a field and save endless hours of the shoulder-aching labour involved in scything.

"We might buy one of these," said Thomas. "If we lose Rob and Peter to Canada this summer, we have to make big changes in how we work. I think we have enough left over from the auction sale last month to afford it. I'll talk to your mother and see what she says." He moved off to find the rest of the family.

When his father had moved out of earshot, he turned to Tom. "How is it that young women are so at ease around you?" Rob asked jokingly of his brother. "Whenever I try to engage them in conversation, they flee in distress. You have to give me lessons, brother."

'Your problem is lack of practice," said Tom at once, almost as if he had been waiting to be asked. "And because you do not do it enough, any young woman you engage thinks you are seriously considering her as a wife. And that gives them a fright. With me, they know I am not serious, so they relax and enjoy the game. That gives me the advantage. I can see what they are made of and whether they will keep me amused or just turn into a duty-bound biddy, trying to control my every whim."

"Well, you've got something there," Rob replied, taken somewhat aback by the thoroughness of his brother's insight. "I'll start watching you more closely to pick up the finer points."

"Isn't that what you're doing already?" remarked Tom, laughing. Rob blushed, looking a little uncomfortable. "Oh, I wouldn't say that. Just a bit of older brother snooping. Got to keep you somewhat on the straight and narrow," Rob replied with a wink.

They moved towards the show ring but when they reached it, Tom continued walking. The Guernseys would be coming up soon so Rob took a seat. He had hardly seated himself when he felt a hand lightly on his shoulder. Turning, he saw Agnes standing in the row behind him. "I just had to apologize for being so rude in the stables," she blurted out, her eyes wide and moist. "I don't know what came over me. It was very childish. May I sit down?"

Rob was speechless, his emotions roiling. All he could manage was a wide grin. "Of course, please do!" He couldn't collect his thoughts. Fortunately he didn't need to because Agnes filled the gap. "You must be fully engaged in the farm with your father. You certainly brought some great animals to the sale last month. My father was quite envious. How do you manage to get the steers so well finished? They almost looked as though they came from beef rather than dairy stock."

Rob relaxed. Great, here was a subject he could get into with no difficulty, so he started to detail the feeding program they had adopted following a course Tom had taken at the agricultural school in Edinburgh. She was clearly knowledgeable and participated fully in the exchange, asking questions and making observations. They were so engrossed they did not notice that the Guernsey competition had begun and it was only when a great round of applause broke their concentration that they looked into the arena and realized that it was her father receiving the ribbons for best animal in its class.

Agnes was on her feet cheering. "I'm so sorry, I must go down and see him," she said. "I'll come back soon."

"I'll come with you," he said, and then realized he needed to trail a bit behind her. It would not do to rush down in her company. They had not established the kind of relationship that permitted that type of closeness. He followed discreetly, but the emotions he felt were anything but discreet. In fact, his spirit was soaring. He found himself, to his astonishment, trembling slightly. What a wonderful few minutes! He had never been so happy. He would have gladly spent the entire day on those seats just talking with her.

He paused at the ring-side to collect himself and restore, to the degree he could, the calm he felt was appropriate. He watched as she ran to her father, embracing him warmly. Such a public display of emotion was rarely seen. Clearly, this was a family free of the social constraints that kept most others at arm's distance from each other in public. Rob loved the warmth and freedom he saw in that relationship.

Rob walked over to Agnes and her father. "I'm not sure you need that bull, after all," he said, smiling. "Perhaps we could take payment in one of the daughters – of that beautiful winner," he quickly added, not wanting any chance of misinterpretation.

Agnes finished a few words with her father and turned to him. "I'm famished. Would you like to see if we can find some lunch?" "Most gladly," he replied and as they walked away he could see her father looking at them and smiling.

After the encounter with Agnes at the fair, Rob decided that the way was open to pursue his interest. But he would now have to take a more formal route and seek her father's permission to call on her – that was just the way it was. His people had evolved this ritual to protect the reputation of young women from random provocation. A young man who had the courage to pass that test was deemed to have sufficient interest and decency to be allowed to court the daughter of a respectable household.

But Rob, wanting to be sure that he had not misinterpreted

Agnes' natural warmth for something more, decided he would first enlist his sister, Hermione, to sound her out.

Hermione belonged to a young ladies' group that went on supervised excursions to broaden their range of interests and Agnes had also joined the group. Hermione was now sixteen, Peter's twin and of an age to understand these things. He talked to her one night, stammering and flushed. Would she help him? Would she quietly enquire of Agnes whether he could come to call some time? "Mione" was delighted to be a trusted intermediary. She adored her brother and was very fond of Agnes.

When word came back that she was willing, Rob knew that now he must speak to her father. Young men did not just turn up at the doorstep of a young woman's house without the parents being informed.

Rob, reluctant to call unannounced at the Runciman house, found more reason than usual to visit the town and to linger there, so much so that it attracted his mother's attention. He did not want there to be any unnecessary suspicions in the family, so he confided in her as well. Isobel beamed and her mischievous streak added a conspiratorial air to the enterprise that Rob thoroughly enjoyed.

One day, at last, his patience was rewarded when he saw William Runciman tie his horse to the post before the dry goods shop. He followed him in. "Sir," he said. "May I have a word with you?"

Runciman turned, eyes lightening as he recognized Rob. "Yes, young man, what can I do for you?"

"If you would be approving, I would like to come some afternoon and call on Agnes," Rob managed to say without faltering.

"Well, would you now. Thank you for asking, but I believe that depends on Miss Agnes' wishes."

"I have reason to believe that she would welcome it, sir," he found himself saying, knowing immediately that he was being too forward. He hastened to explain. "My sister, Hermione, and Agnes belong to the same young ladies' excursion group. They have had words."

"Have they now," said Runciman, a smile creasing his eyes. He was clearly enjoying the young man's innocent awkwardness.

46

"Well, in that case, you may come on Sunday afternoon next, shall we say at four? You may stop and have tea with the family."

That was not exactly what he wanted. But he knew that the way into a possible relationship was highly structured. He would have to endure the polite conversation of the parents and the giggling stares of the younger children before he could spend time alone with Agnes. That was the way it was if you wanted a relationship to get off on the right note. And it was only appropriate, he knew, for if the friendship were to blossom into something more serious, he would be joined not only with a young woman he admired but with her family as well.

6

TOM HAD SEEN IT ALL SO MANY TIMES BEFORE. ONE OR TWO NEW THINGS to discover – a new binder or a more efficient plough, seeds that promised fuller crops with less chance of being levelled by disease, a different feeding program that promised better finishing for the cattle. These could be easily checked out in an hour.

They were not showing any of their herd so the care and grooming of the animals that usually kept him occupied was absent. The full day stretched before him and he was bored. Not many of his friends turned up at the fair – it was not their scene. Too predictable and staid. Too many of the people who by look or gesture made it plain that they did not approve, people just like their own relatives whose attitudes and very lives they found stifling. So they stayed away.

Tom recognized that he occupied a middle ground. He was not yet in open rebellion against his parents. He loved them too much to openly hurt them. But his restlessness was building. So he sought out those who already had thrown over the traces. Being in their company enabled him to savour the whiff of defiance without having to pay the price for it.

All the talk in the family of Rob and Peter heading off to Canada did nothing to slake his disquiet. All he saw ahead of him was dutiful labour; made even more burdensome by his father's failing strength and his brothers' pending departure. And he had picked up hints of the real reason for his father's choice of Peter to accompany Rob and not himself.

He was, of course, older and could therefore carry more of

the responsibility at home. That he didn't mind. It was the notion, never outwardly expressed in his presence but evident in the attitudes of his father, that the added responsibility would rein in his rebelliousness and pull him closer towards the dominant family mold. Only his mother showed signs of recognizing that this agenda could also be seen as a trap. She had quietly argued that Tom should be the one to accompany Rob, that the challenge of the Canadian venture would be the best way for him to work through this stage of his life. But Thomas was adamant. He did not want his son out from under his supervision until he showed evidence of the maturity which, whatever his other endearing characteristics, was so far lacking.

As Tom stood leaning on the barrier around the show ring, these thoughts coupled with the absence of anything around him of compelling interest, drove him deeper into the black anger that had lately been following him. He knew that by nature he was quickly dissatisfied and usually dismissed these turbulent feelings as just part of life. But, of late, those feelings had taken on a harsher edge and he found himself wanting to strike out, at what or whom he was not sure. Perhaps, just at the way his life was turning out.

There had been stories in the weekly paper that the army had launched a recruiting drive to augment its presence in India. Lately there had been posters up in the village that offered terms that were pretty attractive to young men who succeeded in passing the entrance tests for military service. He had never considered that option because of the demands of the family farm. But he was now of an age to make a claim on his own life. He was his own man and he did not need to conform to the expectations his parents had of him.

Yet he knew that were he to leave now, he would imperil Rob's venture to Canada, and if he waited until Rob had left and took off then, the work load might force his parents to give up the farm putting the future of the family at serious risk. This he could not see himself doing. That was the trap he saw himself in. He closed his eyes, hoping his anger would subside.

"Well, if it isn't wee Thomas, carrying the burdens of the world on those manly shoulders again." He heard a familiar voice, laced with irony, and felt a hand on his thigh.

"Oh, Katie, where did you come from all of a sudden," Tom blurted out, relaxing immediately. "I had just about given up the day for lost. Let's get out of here."

"I'm with the old man. Cairns are showing their Angus and we've been preparing them for the ring. I thought I would have seen you in the barn but only saw your brother passing through and mixing with William Runciman and Agnes. Has he something going there?" she asked.

"Not that I'm privy to. But, you're finished? Can we clear out? I have the rest of the day free."

Anticipation began to rise as he felt her hand still on his thigh, moving closer to the groin. "Ay, let's go. I'll not be missed for a while and by the time I get back, they will have forgotten they missed me," she replied.

They went out over the back fences so as to be seen by as few as possible. A wood stretched to the riverbank and they quickly found a footpath. As soon as they were out of sight, he spun her around and pulled her roughly to him, feeling the fullness of her body meet his. He was in a hurry and his mouth was hungry as it met hers. It didn't matter to him that he rose erect. He knew she was not one to be startled by such. In fact, she responded by inserting her hand between their bodies and pressing hard.

He broke away. "Let's move farther in," he murmured. "Too close to the edge." They stumbled off the path and through the bracken, making for a clearing they knew part way to the river. Reaching it, she held him by the waist and pulled him down. He loosed his belt as he fell and awkwardly yanked down the impeding garments. He knew he was coming quickly, probably because of the pent up anger and emotion he had wrestled with earlier. He knew she liked to linger, to let the tension build, but he thrust into her, repeatedly, until the explosive relief drained his desire along with his anger.

They lay quietly, side by side, she facing him, her fingers tracing the outline of his face and neck. "Oh, Kate, I'm feeling so down. I love the farm, but I've been working it so long, I just want something different," Tom said. "I wish I could get away from all this, go somewhere far away, push myself against the unknown and see what I'm really made of."

"But what about me? Do you want me far away as well?"

"Och, no. You know I don't. I want you with me. We could go together to Australia. Or I could join up and go to India with the army, but then you could only come if we were married and I hear they don't allow you to marry until you have served in the ranks for five years." Tom sat up, his face flushed, grabbing his knees.

"But then, what would happen to the farm? We don't make enough for father to be able to hire someone to take my place. And on his own, with only the younger boys, he couldn't make a go of it. So I have to put my life on hold so that other people can get on with what they want to do," he finished angrily

There was silence. Kate rubbed his back. Moments passed. Quietly she said, "You want something different, something new. I have something new for you, something that will make your life different."

Tom turned and looked down at her.

"I'm carrying your child."

"What? Are you sure?" He leapt up and faced her. "How do you know it's mine?" He immediately wished he hadn't said that. But it was a fair question.

"You bastard," she said. "So you think I have been sleeping with all your grubby friends."

"No, but..." he stumbled for words. "How long have you had it?" He recalled noticing that her breasts had become enlarged with blue veins evident where there had been only pale, soft skin.

"I think about four months. And there's no doubt it's yours. Whatever your impression, no one else has had me in the last six months."

"Och, that's just great. Now I'm truly hemmed in," his eyes showed panic growing. "What are you going to do about it?"

51

"What am I going to do about it? You think you're the one that's hemmed in. What about me, it's my body that is being taken over." Her eyes now brimmed with tears.

Tom knelt beside her. "Oh, Katie, Katie, I am sorry. I should have taken precautions. We'll figure something out. You haven't told anyone else have you?"

"No, you're the first, but mother is beginning to get suspicious. She keeps asking me questions. It's bound to come out sooner or later."

"Have you thought of getting it fixed? I'm told there is a woman in Reston who does it on the quiet." Again, he wished he had thought before he had spoken. Taking a life, even before it was born, shattered everything he had been led to believe was honourable, even if the act by which it had been conceived was anything but. "No, we can't do that," Tom continued. "We have to find another way."

"We couldn't even if I wanted to, which I don't. I'm too far gone. It would be too risky. Besides, it's your child within me. I want to bear your child, Tommy. You may think that everything we have been up to in the last few months was just a lark. But it isn't for me, not anymore, and it hasn't been for some time. I love you Tommy and I want to birth your child."

She suddenly looked vulnerable. The defiant, devil-may-care woman now appeared soft and in need of protection. Tom felt compassion along with remorse. But he couldn't affirm what she so clearly wanted to hear. He stumbled to his feet. "Come now. We should get back. I need time to think," he said. "Try to keep it quiet until we have had time to consider what to do. Above all, keep your mother at bay. If she suspects, nothing will stop the whole county from getting the news."

He suggested that they walk back to the fairgrounds separately. "When will I see you again?" Kate asked hesitantly as she gained the path.

"I'll find a way to get to you in the next few days," Tom replied.

As she disappeared through the trees, Tom decided to go the

opposite way, down to the river and approach the fair from the other side of the town. It wouldn't do to have them emerge from the forest a minute or two apart while it was evident that she had been crying. He hardly saw the path in front of him. The panic he had first felt now returned in force, displacing any hint of the earlier compassion.

Whatever she said, it had been a lark for him, a distraction, and an outlet for his boredom. Her brazen, flaunting manner was what had drawn her to him, made her an object to be conquered. She seemed so independent, defying any man to subdue her or make her vulnerable. It was that defiance, that challenge which provoked his lust.

Her coarseness, garbed in defiance, intoxicated him but now the image crumbled. Clothed as she now was in vulnerability, his feelings for her turned to revulsion. He knew he did not love her and did not see that he ever would. Now shame replaced the panic as he breeched the riverbank. His earlier anger at having his options foreclosed by his family responsibilities now turned to fury directed at himself. He couldn't go back to the fair with this hanging over him. He set his gaze towards the long walk home.

In the days that followed, he withdrew, occupying himself with work with the animals and around the barn. He barely noticed his family's growing concern about his mood. His responses let them know plainly that he did not want to talk, did not want to let anyone close to him. He didn't sing anymore, a sure sign to his mother that something was amiss.

His turmoil engaged him in constant internal deliberation. Sometimes his sense of obligation and compassion had the upper hand. She was scared and for the first time he saw her defenseless. And, after all, there was a child – his child – in the balance as well.

He was not the first in this situation and the community decreed that marriage was the only option. Unless a girl had very obliging parents, there was no place she could turn to for support if the man abandoned her. Tom knew enough about Kate's father to be sure that he would refuse to carry another mouth on his meagre income.

Perhaps, in time, he would come to love her or at least develop a working partnership. Yet, he could not shake off the feeling that marrying Kate would close so many doors that he had longed to go through. And how could he live day after day with a person he did not respect, a woman who had spread her legs for how many men he could not imagine, and could well do so again once her current vulnerability had passed. But for the sake of obligation, a virtue that dominated his family and community, and for the sake of the child, he might just have to accept this alternative.

Other days he bridled fiercely at the circling constraints. It surprised him how quickly what had been a lustful intoxication had become pitiless disgust. He felt repelled by the mental images of her, the very images that only days ago had roused him. He felt baffled by this about-turn in his emotions and he knew enough about himself to realize that these emotions could be expressed violently and she would be the object of that violence. On these days he couldn't give a damn for obligation, whether to her or to his parents and the farm. On these days he sought the company of the least savoury of his friends and the relief that drink provided from the black anger.

And now a week or more had passed since he had last seen her. He knew he had to come to a decision and see her again before her mother realized what had happened and the world around him became aware of their predicament. He determined he would ride over to Kate's place.

He knew he could not marry her. Perhaps he could enlist his mother's help in finding a home where she could live until the baby was due and then find an orphanage where the child could be placed. It would cost him all that he earned on the farm and then some, but it was a small price to pay instead of mortgaging the rest of his life.

She was pruning trees in the orchard when he approached and looked up tentatively and expectantly. She wanted to run to him but something in his manner gave her pause. Dismounting, he looked her in the eye. She smiled but he looked solemn and her smile faded. "Let's walk down the back lane," Tom said. He wanted to be well away from prying eyes.

"Kate, sit down please. I've come to a decision," he said. He had thought it all out, rehearsing many times the words he would use, trying to be gentle but firm, so there could be no misunderstanding. But when he opened his mouth, his words were lost in the dejection he already saw on her face. "I've been thinking of, of.... little else," he began, "I want to do the right thing......I will help and support you 'til the baby is born..."

Her eyes filled with tears. "But I cannot marry you, Kate. It wouldn't be fair to you, now nor in the long run. I cannot marry you unless I love you. You don't know me Kate. I'm afraid of what I might do to you if there was not real love between us."

She turned quickly from him and stood, fully erect, her shoulders back and when she faced him once more there was fury on her face, the defiance had returned but this time it was a fire of a different sort.

"You pitiful, wee snot. You think you can just use me whenever its suits your craving, and then walk away and dump me with whatever baggage you leave behind.

"Well, young Tommy, my name may already have been dragged through the mud in this county, but yours and your hypocritical family will be sneered at before this is over.

"And were you thinking that I would be happy to submit to being your wife, to be picking up after you and doing your bidding the rest of my life? Not on your sweet ass, laddie. I'll find a way to shuck this burden, but not before you've paid the full price." With her jaw extended, she tossed her head as though it were a weapon directed at him and strode off into the orchard.

Tom was so shaken at this display of rage he stood motionless for some minutes. By the time he had gathered himself together, she was gone. All that was left was to return to his horse and leave.

Why had he not approached the matter the way he had planned?

If he had been able to say that he would help her and the baby get on their feet before he mentioned anything about not being willing to marry her, she might have seen that it was for the best. But by blurting out that he didn't love her, he had as good as ended any discussion. It seemed that her feelings for him had been deep and his abrupt rejection had the expected result.

There was no way now to keep the matter quiet. He knew he had to warn his parents about what was coming and seek their advice, his mother's particularly. He knew his father's reaction would be one of shame and fury, not on account of the family's reputation – he laid little store in such things – but because of the muck-up he had made of his life and the damage he had caused the lives of others, not to speak of a sense of responsibility for the unborn one that his father would surely feel.

Should he speak to Rob first? Get his help in broaching the subject with the parents? No, no need to submit to his older brother's pained indignation. He had to face the music and face it alone.

Before dinner that evening he told his parents he wished to talk to them alone, once the younger children had gone to bed. His manner was such as to cause considerable apprehension in their eyes and during dinner the exchanges were more subdued than usual. Tom went out to the barn as soon as the meal was over and suggested to them that they follow him there when they thought it appropriate. In the meantime he sought the warmth and comfort of the animals as he readied them for the night.

His mother came out first. "Thomas, remember your father's condition. He is not as strong as he has been. Are you sure you want to say whatever it is you have in mind?"

"Mother, he will come to know anyway. I want to tell him myself, but I will do it gently," Tom said.

"Should we ask Rob to come out as well?"

"No, I want this to be with just the two of you."

Thomas came into the barn. "Father and Mother, please sit down." Tom was trembling. "Mother, Father......I have some bad news. Kate Collins is four months pregnant and claims the child is mine." His eyes were hooded, defensive. "Everybody knows she sleeps around. But she says its mine and she plans to blame me publicly. I know it could be but there's no way to be sure."

There was silence.

"I guess you've known for some time that I've been going the way I want to, without regard to your views. I'm not proud of that, but..."

His mother began to moan. "Tommy, Tommy, why did you bring this upon yourself? Why do you reject us? This will change everything. What will we do? What will we do?"

Thomas was silent, staring straight ahead, not at Tom but into the recesses of the barn. Minutes passed with only the sound of Isobel weeping and rocking.

"You've no choice, Thomas," his father said, his voice forced and breaking. "Marriage is the only decent thing to do. And we should arrange it as soon as possible to spare the babe any more shame than it will already face."

"Father, I won't do that. I don't love her and I can't spend the rest of my life with her. I've already told her I won't marry her"

"You should have thought of that before you went and got her with child," was the angry response. "Now you have to come to terms with the consequences."

"Thomas, please, let us take time to think." Alarmed by his anger, Isobel had gained control of herself so she could intervene. "There are so many things to consider. We know so little of her family. And they are of the Catholic faith so there could be no marriage in a church." She took a breath. "But above all, we have to consider the best course of action for Thomas, for Kate and for the child. And it may not be a marriage."

Thomas sat, his body slumped, drained of life. Tom too was silent, his eyes on the ground. Then he said. "Father, Mother, I am sorry to hurt you and the family, to disappoint you. But isn't this what you expected? I have never been able to measure up to what you want. The best thing for me to do is to move away and get on with my life on my own."

"Thomas, this is enough," his mother said. "Come into the house. We will think on these things and we will not speak of them to anyone until we have had the time to ponder," and she abruptly rose and walked out. His father sat longer, his countenance stirring, looking as though he had other things he wished to say but the words did not come. He rose slowly and without looking at Tom, followed Isobel.

7

ROB HEARD THE NEWS THE MORNING AFTER TOM HAD INFORMED HIS PAR-ents. His brother told him as they were mucking out the cattle and it did not come as a surprise. He had feared this would be the end result of Tom's rebellion. Now he was ashamed that he had hoped for such a comeuppance. If anything, he was angry with himself that he had not intervened more forcefully when he had seen the signs.

A pall of sadness and uncertainty had descended on the family. The prospect of his visit with Agnes provided a glimmer of joy over what were several very grim days and finally Sunday came. So there was both sadness and anticipation as he took the road to the Runcimans in the early afternoon. He hoped that the ride would give enough time for the sadness to recede so he could truly savour the visit.

He was not looking forward to sitting in the parlour making conversation with her parents but if he was lucky, the afternoon might end with the two of them being able to take a walk together.

He marveled at the range of feelings he was experiencing. Never before had he been so entranced by another person. Never had he felt such kinship, even though the time they had spent together in their whole lives could be counted in minutes. He smiled ruefully to himself. What an unexpected gift. This was something to handle gently, something to cherish. And he couldn't help but contrast what was happening to him with Tom's experiences over the past months. He was amazed that the same urges could have such different outcomes.

These musings made the ride pass quickly. The Runciman home sat at the end of a long drive, treed with grand oak. William Runciman was a tenant farmer just like Rob's father but the approach to the residence was akin to that of a laird's estate. This did not help abate Rob's nervousness. He was afraid that the reticence of his tongue would once again give him cause for embarrassment. He conjured up in his mind the warmth that Agnes had displayed towards him as they ate lunch at the fair and he felt himself relax somewhat.

Norah Runciman, Agnes' mother, was at the door. She smiled warmly and ushered him into the parlour where William Runciman rose to greet him and offered a chair opposite. Agnes was nowhere to be seen. Runciman shortly began a discourse on Prime Minister Gladstone and the proposals he was putting forward with respect to Irish Home Rule. This was a topic Rob was well acquainted with, given his high admiration for Mr Gladstone who was their local member of parliament. But Runciman showed little interest in Rob's views, seeming to enjoy the opportunity to have as a captive audience a young man who was obliged to listen respectfully.

The monologue continued for many minutes, Runciman noting that Gladstone risked having his party side-lined by the electorate if he made too much of the Irish issue. "But surely, Mr Runciman, one either has a point of principle or one does not," Rob managed to say. "If British lives are being lost in the conflict there, is it not important to come up with a clear alternative to the Conservative's policy?"

Norah joined them with a trolley of tea and an array of breads and scones. "Now, William, that's enough of your politics, I want to hear about Robert and his family," she said directing a warm but admonishing glance at her husband. "You and Tom are now grown men and the younger ones are coming on rapidly. Do you see your future with Abbeylane Farm or will you and at least some of the others be seeking a living elsewhere?" Norah had a reputation for being direct and to the point.

This was getting quickly into an agenda that Rob wished to avoid. He had decided he did not want them to know of the

Canadian venture until he had had a chance to deepen the relationship with Agnes. How could he expect her to wait the five years for him unless she was sure that she wanted to be with him for life? "Yes, of course, it's a problem," he admitted. "I think Tom and I are committed to agriculture and Father has not been too well of late and will need some of us by him for some time to come. We still have over 30 years on the lease and that land is very productive.

"But I am sure some of the younger ones will want to get into other trades," he continued, breathing more easily now that he had passed over the tricky part of the answer. "Peter seems keen on farming, but James and Richard show a great love for books. Maybe they will go on to get a training as teachers or go to work in Edinburgh with a publisher. We're not sure what the future holds for George or the girls."

But Norah wanted greater detail. There was still no sign of Agnes or the other children. Clearly this was turning into a gentle interrogation to discover the measure of this young man. Rob responded to her questions as openly as he could, realizing full well that they at some point must hear about the Canadian venture and would also likely hear about Tom's dilemma.

Thomas looked bored and in due course told his wife it was time for Agnes and the other children to join them. Norah showed no sign of being diverted; she too clearly enjoyed having the direct attention of this earnest young man. The Runcimans had no sons so this was a pastime to which she was unaccustomed. "Yes, in a minute or two," she replied. "Tell me more about your brother, Thomas. He is a fine cattleman, I hear, but I don't see him often at social events with the family. I suppose he has his own set of friends." Rob detected an inflection here that indicated she may be aware of Tom's wanderings.

Rob paused not knowing how to redirect the conversation but William came to his rescue. "Now, Norah, that's quite enough. What Thomas does is really none of our business. Please go and get the children." Norah obliged, rising slowly. "But I want to hear more about your dear mother and father when we get back."

Agnes entered first. She had dressed for the occasion. Her eyes were lively and she smiled broadly in Rob's direction. He rose and took her hand briefly in greeting, his feelings so stirred he could not utter a syllable and was sure his face had become embarrassingly flushed. She quickly sat and attention was diverted to the scrambling of the younger ones to be the first through the door, their eyes all fixed on Rob.

He remembered little of the conversation that followed, broken as it was by the logistics of tea and biscuits being served and the lively interruptions of the children. This was clearly a household that did not hold with the idea that "children should be seen and not heard." While the conversation touched on many subjects, he found he had overcome his reticence and partook freely in its ebb and flow. The more he experienced the interaction within this family, the more he liked what he saw.

At long last, Norah said, "Robert, perhaps you and Agnes would care to go for a short walk in the orchard?" Did he hear a special emphasis on the word "short"? It was the custom concerning these rituals that in the early stages of a courtship, and in some cases throughout it, a family member would accompany the young couple at a respectful distance. But here the orchard was so close to the kitchen windows that observation was easily afforded.

"Yes, that would be lovely," Rob said, realizing that he seemed over eager.

He helped Agnes into a light coat as the late afternoon had brought a chill to the breeze. And then they were on their own. Agnes broke the awkward silence. "I'm so glad you came to call. Not easy to step into this gaggle of a family."

"They're a sweet bunch," Rob replied. "I like the easy way everyone talks to each other. You are fortunate to have such warmth in your family. I am equally lucky, but there are so many of us Scots who are reserved even in the bosom of our families. We seem to be far freer with our friends. And that goes for the parents as well as the children."

"Perhaps that comes from the bleakness of our climate or

perhaps the hard times our ancestors suffered," Agnes mused. "And I don't think that the Scots way of looking at religion helps much either – too much emphasis on hell fire. It gives righteousness a pretty grim cloak."

Rob turned the conversation towards Agnes' life. They talked about what she hoped to do in the coming few years, about her interest in politics and the admiration they shared for Mr Gladstone, about a recent excursion her young women's group took to Edinburgh. It did not take much to elicit lively conversation from her, only a few well-placed questions. She was clearly her father's daughter.

Rob wanted to broach the matter of their relationship, to ask her if he could see her regularly, if she would be open to spending considerable time with him. That would signal the beginning of courtship. Simple friendship was not possible in their social circle; you only spent significant time with someone of the opposite sex if you were contemplating a long term relationship, sanctioned of course by marriage.

"Agnes," he began hesitantly. "I would like to see you more often. I think we have much in common and I greatly enjoy the privilege of being in your company. Do you think you could see your way clear to accepting an offer of courtship?"

He looked directly into her eyes and was relieved that the words had come out simply without being addled.

"I should like that very much and I would accept," she said without hesitation. "I, too, have thought of you often in the past weeks. I should enjoy the opportunity to get to know you better."

She took his arm.

The rest of their conversation, engrossing and ranging as it was, was lost to Rob's memory, so elated were his spirits. She seemed the easiest person to talk to he had ever met. Thoughts and words flowed between them as comfortably as the coming together of the palms of two old friends.

With the shadows lengthening in the orchard, Rob knew it was time to return to the house. He had not been at all conscious of observing eyes, but he had nothing to hide so was indifferent to whether or not they had been watched. Norah was the only one around when they came in. He thanked her graciously for the afternoon, took both Agnes' hands in his and bade farewell. Norah's face was calm but her eyes shone – not however enough to match Agnes'.

Chapter
8

Isobel had earlier asked Tom to accompany her on a walk to Alewater Burn. They passed the first many minutes in silence. Then Isobel turned to him. "Tom, I do not want to tell you what to do. You are my son but you are also a man and as such free to live your life as you wish. But I don't want anger and frustration to be what drives you. That can only lead to dead ends."

"You're the only one who at least tries to understand me," Tom replied. "All I get from Father is judgment. Disappointment is written all over his face. He wants me to be another Rob, and I'm not.

"I'm already at a dead end. I can't be what you want me to be. Of course, I love you and the rest of the family. But I'm so hemmed in by what you expect of me, by all the unspoken assumptions expecting me to see the world as you and Father do. And I don't. I'm tired of pretending. I want to be what I am and not to have to make any apologies for it."

"Tom, you have every right to go your own way. And if that means moving out, you will have my blessing, though I will miss you terribly." There was silence; all that could be heard was the fall of their footsteps which grew more evenly matched as they passed alongside the burn.

"You and I are a lot alike. But I made my choice a long time ago to be your father's wife, and don't regret it. But it meant that I fitted my life to his. You are free to make your own choices, but now, because of choices you have already made, you are responsible for the child, if not its mother. Choices lead to consequences, but if you run from consequences, you spend the rest of your life running."

"I know I have made a mistake, but I will not marry her just to keep up appearances," Tom said vehemently.

"I'm not asking you to," Isobel responded gently. "But you and we as your parents have to come up with an alternative. Remember, we are now talking about a child who is of our flesh and blood. And neither you nor I will rest easy for the balance of our days if we abandon that child."

They walked on in silence. "Will Kate want to keep the child after it is born?' Isobel asked.

"I don't think she will go through with it. I think she will try to have it aborted," Tom replied.

"Lord, have mercy!" Isobel exclaimed. "In that case we have to move fast. We have to find a home where she can live until the birth. And we will have to be responsible for her expenses until the child is several months old."

"But what happens then, if she doesn't want to keep it?" Tom asked.

"I don't know."

On their return, Isobel found Rob and asked him to come with Tom into the barn where they found Thomas. The news of the possibility that Kate might seek an abortion spurred Isobel to insist that the men focus on an alternative.

Tom wanted the child placed in an orphanage until an adoption could be arranged. Isobel could not agree. Orphanages had a poor reputation and there was no way, if the child was in the care of an institution, that they could protect it from being adopted by a family who was only looking for cheap domestic help.

She proposed that they attempt to arrange the child's adoption themselves and, until then, be its legal guardians. She doubted Kate would wish to keep the child, and even if she did, she did not want a grandchild of hers being raised in that environment.

Thomas, looking wan and dejected, interrupted her. "Isobel, my dear, this isn't realistic. How can we at our age take on to care for and rear a babe? You've raised nine already and we're both tired.

If we lose Rob and Peter to Canada for five years, we're going to be stretched as it is without taking on to raise another bairn."

"Father, I don't think we should let the Canadian plan influence our decision about the child." said Rob. "If it's right to take the child, we can put off a decision about Canada for a year to see how the family fares in this new situation. What is important is to do the right thing for each other now, and let the future unfold as it will." Tom gave Rob a long look.

"Thomas, this is going to be hard on you," Isobel said taking her husband's hand. "An infant brings noise and disruption, something we both know is harder to take as we grow older. We know the boys will willingly take on more of the work of the farm. And I believe that Hermione and Elspeth will relish the chance to help me care for the babe. It will do much to enhance their womanhood. Elspeth will be leaving school next year and with Hermione now at home, the load in the household is in fact lighter than it has been in some years. They will rise to it, I know they will."

Tom stepped back from the others and turned away. Isobel could see that he was weeping. Was it from shame or remorse, she wondered. Or did his tears flow from the realization that this child of his issue might not be lost to anonymity or to the hard-scrabble world of Kate's family. The prospect gave him relief for the first time in days.

9

As SOON AS ROB REACHED HOME HE KNEW SOMETHING WAS AMISS. ISOBEL'S eyes were rimmed in red. Tom was looking desolate. Thomas was nowhere to be seen. His first thought was that his father had had another bout of fainting.

"Jim Collins was here an hour ago raising a storm," Tom explained angrily. "He insists that I marry Kate or he will bring the wrath of the community down around our heads. He was not ready for any discussion on the matter and he gave none of us a chance to present an alternative." Tom's fingers clenched and unclenched at his side. "He has given us until tomorrow evening to agree."

Despite her appearance, Isobel spoke calmly. "I think your father has gone to the barn. There is no point in talking more of this without him." In silent agreement, Rob and Tom followed her, where they found Thomas standing at the far end of the cow stalls facing the wall. "Thomas, I want you to join me and the boys. We have to come to a decision together," Isobel said clearly.

Isobel spoke. "Now let's just collect ourselves. I still think what we are considering is the right way for the child, for Kate and for Tom. But we have to get Jim Collins to listen."

"How do we get through to the Collins?" Tom wondered.

"Well Thomas, you first owe Kate's parents an accounting," said Isobel. "You need to seek them out and let them know how profoundly sorry you are for leading Kate on and misusing their daughter. That needs to be done before we consider anything else. Leave the question of responding to his ultimatum about marriage until that is done."

Tom paled but nodded his assent. "That'll have to be done by tomorrow, God help me. But what about his threat to spread the news abroad if we do not agree to a marriage? I can handle the looks and the shunning but, if he doesn't change his mind, he is going to blacken the name of the family as well."

"I think this family can withstand anything Jim Collins throws at us," said his father slowly. "Yes, there'll be talk, and it may be hard on the children and we will have to explain things carefully to them.

"But we can face down the rumours by being open about the facts when that is called for. Tom made mistakes," he continued gathering momentum as he spoke. "He has acknowledged them and is taking responsibility for the results. We are not denying anything or blaming anyone else. That, in my view, will make short work of the chatter. It is about time that this community admitted its humanity and proclivity to sin. Too much righteousness and not enough honesty around here – in my opinion."

"Well said, Father. I agree," Rob declared. "Let's see how things turn out when Tom speaks to the Collins." There seemed nothing more to add. With that, they gripped each other's hands momentarily but just as they were leaving the barn, Rob stopped them. "This may be as good a time as any to tell you. This afternoon Agnes Runciman agreed to allow me to court her."

Broad smiles erupted. Even Tom looked pleased. "That is news to lift the heart," said Isobel putting her arms around Rob. And the two men, each in their turn, grabbed his shoulders and pulled him close.

Tom knew that the best time to find Mr and Mrs Collins on their own was the evening. That meant he would have to go tonight. Rob agreed to cover his evening chores.

The Collins were still at table when he knocked on the back door. Kate was not with them. Collins opened the door, his face darkening. "We were expecting you, Dunbar." Mrs Collins got up from the table and moved to the sink.

"May I sit down," Tom asked hesitantly, his eyes not able to meet those of the older man.

Collins gestured a chair. "I won't offer you tea," said Collins, "for I don't suppose you've come to engage in any small talk."

Tom paused, taken aback momentarily by this abruptness. He looked at the woman who gave no indication of being ready to join them.

"Mr and Mrs Collins, I wish to say, first of all, that I am grievously sorry for the dishonour I have inflicted on your daughter. I was not raised to behave that way. I accept responsibility for my actions and for the results that have....have flowed from them. I have done Kate and the two of you a great disservice and I am deeply sorry."

Collins' mouth hung partly open, his belligerence fading. It was as though he could not comprehend what Tom was saying. His wife had stopped her fussing at the sink and stood looking at the wall. Tom could hear her sniffling. It seemed that Collins' anger had been deflated.

It took Collins a moment to collect himself. "That's all very well, Dunbar. But what about the future?" he asked resuming his hostile tone. "You are going to take care of Kate and the child. We depend on her to make ends meet and with a child hanging on her hip she is going to be useless around here. Words are fine but a marriage is what I want and money to make up for the work she was doing before. That's all I want from you and your privileged family. If you're not prepared to give me that today, then I see no point in talking!"

Despite his intentions to remain calm, Tom was angry. "Mr Collins, I am not ready to give you an answer. I need a more time."

"Dunbar, I am not an educated man like you and your lot. But I know two things. My family has been dishonoured by the likes of you who think you can take whatever you want and someone else will pick up the pieces. And you have made us poorer.

"Only a marriage can fix the first. But even so, your family owes us something big for the work Kate will no longer be able to do. And that's a fact. You take that back to your prosperous hearth and let me know when we can expect the money and a date for the marriage."

There was no point in lingering. "Mr Collins, I will give you an answer shortly. Maybe we can have a decent conversation at that time."

"You can talk whenever you want as long as I get what's coming to me," said Collins, his eyes defiant. His wife remained at the sink, her back to the two men. "Good day, then," said Tom.

Chapter

10

ROB KNEW NOW THAT THERE WAS NO HURRY TO TELL AGNES ABOUT CANADA. The whole scheme might never come to pass if the adoption of Tom's child became reality and the resulting work in the family required that he and Peter stay home. At any rate, the decision was far from imminent and for this Rob found he was greatly relieved.

His greatest interest, now, was to pursue his burgeoning relationship. Perhaps they might even marry before they made a decision about going to Canada. He was certain that whatever hardship awaited them in establishing a new life in the wilderness, life would be much more bearable in the company of this woman.

So while the situation with Tom saddened him, his overall mood was one bordering on exhilaration. The fact that Agnes lived an hour's ride distant meant that to spend any time with her took at least four hours out of a day. Thus his opportunity to do so was limited, mostly to Sundays. However, as the pace of work on the farm ebbed and flowed, he did his best to break that pattern and make the journey to Norfield Farm in the middle of the week whenever possible.

It was a mark of the esteem in which he was increasingly held, as well as the trust they had in their daughter, that her parents made no move to chaperone their time together. And for many weeks, anyone observing them would have taken them for brother and sister enjoying an afternoon together. There was so much to talk about, so much to enjoy, and just being with her and finding himself engrossed in her animated conversation gave him a great sense of satisfaction. He felt life had taken on a larger and nobler dimension. He remembered a phrase his mother had used about "the cleansing power of a new affection" and concluded that that was how he felt – cleansed, renewed.

He discovered that they shared an interest in fishing with a fly so he would bring his gear and she would borrow her father's rod. She knew the best spots on Eve Water that flowed not far from her farm and had an able arm to put the fly within feet of where she intended. They cast the pools together and when she had a hit, she could play it with considerable skill. He loved the excitement when one of them had a dancing trout on the line but he found he enjoyed even more observing her lovely profile from the other side of a pound, the graceful way she drew the rod over her head, the fixed intent of her face as she looked for clues on the water's surface, the smiles she would cast from time to time in his direction.

It was, in fact, some weeks before he found his sexual energy being aroused by her presence. Once, on a walk, she had stumbled and in moving to prevent her fall, he had drawn her body up against his, and held it there. She did not resist but responded by putting her arms around his waist, turning her face towards him and kissing him on the mouth. She lingered and a spasm rippled through his lower body. He gently released her. She was flushed but did not seem in any way embarrassed. He just smiled and kept her hand in his. As they walked on, their bodies moved closer.

Following that, when he had not seen her for some days he found his newly aroused sexual fervour troubling. His imagination seemed to power his longings even more than her presence. For the first time he began to understand how easy it would be to take the path Tom had taken and he had to remind himself of the insight he had had early in their relationship about the difference between cherishing and using. He wanted to protect her and their relationship from the pall that he was sure the latter would cast.

On these occasions he knew there were scriptural passages that had been made familiar to him by his parents' daily readings with them as children. He would find his Bible, which in recent years he had not often opened, and look up those selections. "The fruits of the Spirit are love, joy, peace..." They gave him the assurance that he could wait until his relationship with Agnes had been grounded and blessed before God and their families before he gave his sexuality full rein. And after the turmoil his imagination had triggered, he found a calm that surprised him.

In the days following his visit to the Collins, Tom became increasingly morose. The conflict in his mind was not resolved and he was not at all convinced that the solution his mother had suggested for the future of the child would be acceptable to Kate and her parents. He had a portent that these matters could never be resolved as simply as his mother had hoped. He was sure there was yet a greater debt of grief to be paid. At times he thought the only way out was to agree to a marriage. That would spare his parents the burden of caring for yet another child and would to some degree placate Jim Collins and his wife.

Yet when he contemplated a lifetime with Kate, the black anger that had been his companion returned. He had seen village men who had taken a wrong turn and sought relief in drink. Their apparent isolation from their families, their inability to shoulder manly tasks, their surrender to drink-induced stupor, made him cringe. He knew himself enough to know how readily that could be his lot. Marriage to Kate would solve nothing. And it would be perilous for the future of his child. The sooner he closed that option the better.

The opportunity to do so arose quickly. He was in town to consult about an ailing heifer when he saw Collins across the square. Should he broach the issue in a semi-public place? It might constrain the nature of Collins' reaction which he was certain would be violent but it could also quickly bring the whole conflict out in the open. It would come out anyway. He decided to seize the occasion.

"Mr Collins, I would like a word with you," he said approaching the older man. "Would you care to accompany me to where we can talk privately?"

"Anything you have to say to me can be said in public," said Collins. "I only want to hear one answer from you, Dunbar. If it is not what I want, then the whole town will hear of your shame anyway."

Tom reddened. "Mr Collins, I cannot marry your daughter."

Collins took a step back and looked as if he was about to strike Tom. Tom moved forward, placing his hand on Collins' arm.

"Mr Collins, hear me out." In his anxiety, Tom was speaking almost at the top of his voice. People stopped and stared. "I will support Kate until the baby is born and for some time after."

Collins struggled to be free of his grasp, his face contorted. He tried to respond but choked on the effort. "We will provide you compensation for Kate's lost income," Tom continued hastily. "And I will make arrangements to support the child until it is of age. But, Mr Collins, Kate and I have no basis for a marriage. It would destroy her and me."

Tom thought Collins was having a heart attack. His body shook as he staggered to find his footing. With wild eyes, he turned on Tom flailing with his fists. "I'll kill you and your like. You think you can despoil a man's daughter, the light of his life, and then cover up the damage with money and kind words." He was shouting and trying to land blows on Tom who, being younger and considerably taller, managed to deflect the worst of the damage.

A crowd was gathering. Tom managed to keep Collins at arm's length, refusing to engage physically. He looked around wildly at the people approaching to view the fracas, hoping to see someone who could act to calm Collins. "Please, Mr Collins. This is going nowhere. We have to talk this out. Mr Collins."

Tom saw James O'Brien, the town grocer and Collin's co-religionist, join the crowd and then move swiftly to Collins' side and grasp him by the shoulder. "Jim, calm yourself. There'll be no fighting here. What's the trouble? Come with me into the store and we'll sort this out." O'Brien's firm hold subdued Collins but the man held his ground.

"Good people of this town know this: this man, Thomas Dunbar, took advantage of my daughter for his own pleasure and distraction, my only child, marked by beauty and innocence. And now that he has despoiled her and left her with child, wants nothing to do with her, abandons her and his child. And he and his family claim to be Christian people!"

A few of the younger men in the crowd snickered. A mother quickly hustled her children away from the scene. Most of the crowd stood stunned at the public display of accusation and shame. Tom stood, eyes to the ground, his face ashen. O'Brien turned Collins by the shoulders in an attempt to move him away from the crowd.

"Dunbar, you and your lot have it coming to you. You'll not get away with this behaviour. There are ways of dealing with the likes of you." Collins kept shouting as O'Brien almost dragged him across the road and into the grocery. All eyes were on Tom.

But Tom had had enough and turned to cross the square. Before he reached the other side, however, he was joined by a grey-haired man.

"Mr Dunbar, I know your father and I can see you are trying to resolve a most difficult problem. If you will permit me, I would like to speak to Father Chisholme. I am a member of his congregation which the Collins attend from time to time. Perhaps he will have advice and counsel that can contribute to a solution."

"That might be of assistance, Mr----Mr----?"

"James," said the man. "Clifford James. I understand your predicament and it is not for me to judge. But the way we have traditionally dealt with this kind of situation by forcing an alliance between unwilling partners does great damage to any children that may be the issue. Would you be prepared to talk with the priest about what you and your family are offering Jim Collins?"

"Yes, of course," said Tom, relief flooding over him. Help from any quarter was welcome. "Thank you for your offer. How can I be in touch with him?"

"I see him later this evening. Perhaps we could meet tomorrow. I will suggest to him that you might join us in my law office above the municipal hall tomorrow at two."

Tom made his way back to the farm, his mind crowded with the public scene that had just unfolded. He felt he was tied to a runaway horse. His face burned, his eyes smarted at the public shame forced upon him by Jim Collins' intemperance. Yet he knew he had brought it on himself by his own impetuousness at broaching the issue in the square. His calculation had back-fired, but at least the issue was coming to a head. And the intervention of Clifford James might offer the one solution that would bring Jim Collins to the table.

He felt an urgent need to inform his parents. There was now no question that his affair with Kate and its aftermath would be on the tongues of all the gossips in the county within the day, tomorrow being market day. They would have to prepare the children for the stares and snide remarks they were bound to meet. He would also need his parents' advice about the prospective meeting with the Catholic priest.

That evening, after the children had retired, Tom recounted the afternoon's events. Despite her concern over his public shaming, his mother welcomed the possibility of an intermediary and suggested that Thomas accompany his son to demonstrate the family's support, both for the young man and for the course of action they were proposing.

Thomas looked dubious. "Clifford James is an honourable man, but I never thought I would have to turn to a Roman cleric to help rescue one of my family from the consequences of sin. My Baptist forebears will be spinning in their graves."

"Thomas, this is full of discomfort for us all," Isobel said gently. "But you have often said that we need to rise above our differences to achieve greater things. There could be nothing more important than finding the right thing for this young woman and this child. Father Chisholme, I hear, is a thoughtful man. He will surely have compassion for those caught up in this situation."

When Thomas and Tom met Clifford James the next day as had been arranged, they found that the priest waiting with him. James offered his study for the three men and excused himself.

"Reverend Chisholme, it is good of you to see us," Thomas began. "Perhaps you know already about the sorry development that has involved my son with the daughter of Jim Collins."

Thomas' brow was moist with perspiration but his voice remained firm. "Tom, here, has told his mother and me about how this came to pass and has expressed regret for his errant ways. And he has been to visit Mr and Mrs Collins to apologize to them for the dishonour he has brought upon Kate and the family. Miss Collins is with child."

Tom was staring at his hands clasped before him while his father spoke, his knuckles white. He raised his head and looked the priest in the eye. "Father Chisholme, I have gone against the teachings of my parents, and I have asked forgiveness of my family and the Collins.

"I take responsibility for what has happened and I will not turn away from helping Kate and the child, but I see no basis on which to enter into a marriage with Kate Collins which seems the only thing that will placate Mr and Mrs Collins."

The priest listened quietly. "My son, I can see repentance written across your face. But now we must address the innocent. That child enters the world wholly sinless even though conceived in sin. It must be given every chance for a normal life surrounded by a loving family. Is there no possibility that you and Kate Collins could together provide that loving family?"

Tom found himself moved by the priest's manner. He had not known what to expect – perhaps hostility, perhaps judgment or at least a lecture on his waywardness. He paused, weighing again the debate between duty and reality that had raged in his mind for the last two weeks, between doing what others thought should be done and what he knew were the limits of his capabilities.

"Father Chisholme, I have spent hours pondering that question. If I felt there was a chance to create that, I would embrace it. But I see no basis for that relationship and if I agreed to it now, I know I would only be condemning Kate to a marriage of convenience that was loveless. That would destroy her and impair the child's chances in life. The alternative will be harder to achieve but in the long run will be better for everyone."

Tom described what he and his family proposed to offer in place of a marriage.

Chisholme got up and strode to the window, standing there for some minutes. Then he turned. "I will ask to see Jim Collins and his wife but they are people with almost nothing to fall back on. They feel grievously wronged and it doesn't help that they are generally shunned in this county because they come from a different place, a different culture. Though they occasionally join us for Mass, they have little capacity to handle life's crises. It will not be easy to turn their minds."

"Thank you, Reverend," said Thomas. "Thank you, Father," said Tom.

The Dunbars heard nothing from the priest or the Collins in the days that followed. But they met everywhere the evidence that they were the subject of widespread talk – eyes averted, quiet conversations begun when they appeared, nods in their direction. Tom chose to stay around the farm. Rob had told Agnes the day after the confrontation in the square so that she would hear it from him before the rumours reached the next county. Norah Runciman asked forthrightly for an explanation. So far, those who had had the courage to broach the subject directly with a member of the family had seemed to appreciate the way they were dealing with the situation.

Three days later, Clifford James appeared at the farm. He looked grim, asked to speak to Thomas alone. He was ushered into the parlour by Isobel who offered to make him tea but this was politely refused. Thomas entered the room and James asked him to close the door.

"Kate Collins perished last night," said James. "Something went wrong with the pregnancy. The doctor was called late in the evening and spent most of the night there but there was nothing he could do. She had developed septicemia, an infection in the blood and died before dawn."

Thomas lowered himself slowly into a chair, his face a portrait of shock. "Oh, the poor woman – the child – what a loss!"

He sat quietly for a while. "I feared we would face a grievous outcome, but not one such as this. The wages of sin really are death. My poor son. This will be devastating for him. I must speak to Isobel. She will know what to do."

"I am sorry to be the bearer of such terrible news but you needed to know immediately. I will leave you now. Father Chisholme is at this moment with the parents. Perhaps he will call here on his way back to the village." Clifford James quietly excused himself and left.

Thomas stayed alone in the room, desiring to share the news with Isobel but lacking the physical strength to get up and find her. A minute later the door opened and Isobel came in of her own accord. "Wife, we have a terrible development. Kate has died and the child with her. Poison from the pregnancy." Isobel began to weep. "What will they do? Kate was their only child. How can we ever make it up to them after this tragedy? Oh Thomas, I cannot face the world after this!

"How is Tom going to handle this? He has been so brave and open up to now, but this blow could cripple him. Does he know yet?"

"No, Clifford came straight to me. Reverend Chisholme is over at the Collins now. He might come here on his way to town. We must get to Tom before he arrives. I will find him."

"Are you alright?" Isobel asked. "Should I accompany you?"

"No, let me deal with Tom alone for the moment. He will need your advice and comfort after he has had a chance to absorb this news."

Thomas got up and walked slowly through the kitchen and then out towards the barn where Tom would be engaged in the morning chores with the cattle. He found him in the loft pitching hay down the chute.

"Tom, I have something to tell you. Come down here, son, and sit by me."

Tom looked surprised at his father's manner. "What is it, father?" he said as he found a seat on a hay bale.

"Thomas... Kate died last night. There was a problem with the pregnancy, something wrong in the blood and it poisoned her. The doctor was there but could do nothing. She was dead by dawn."

Tom collapsed, his head between his knees. Harsh sobs shook his shoulders. All the manliness and fortitude he had displayed in the previous weeks as he came to terms with his situation, abandoned him. He cried as would a child. Thomas moved beside him and gently put his arms around his trembling body. This was an uncharacteristic gesture but the circumstances called for action not words. He just let the spasms roll through his son.

Gradually Tom became quiet. The only sound in the barn was the shuffling and murmur of the cattle. They sat there in silence for many minutes. Finally Thomas said, "I will leave you now, boy. Take as long as you need. Your mother and I will be waiting for you in the house when you are ready. We will stand by you through this."

Tom did not appear for the rest of the day. Shortly after noon the Catholic priest came by. He confirmed what Clifford James had said. He told them there was little anyone could do for the Collins at the moment. They needed time to process their shock and grief. No date had yet been set for the burial. Chisholme asked after Tom and told the Dunbars that he would come back later and see him. He was clear that Kate's death had in no way brought greater calumny on Tom's head in the eyes of God and that he sought only to give him comfort.

Thomas and Isobel both found themselves strengthened by the priest's presence and told him how much they appreciated his help. They asked him to help determine how best they could support the Collins in their grief. "You must know there is nothing you can do to ease their pain. They must themselves find their way to their loving Father to find their ability to forgive. Until that happens they will continue to be consumed by anger. But you could pray for them at this time. Please pray and pray earnestly."

Chapter

11

ROB HAD LEFT THE FARM DIRECTLY AFTER BREAKFAST BEFORE CLIFFORD JAMES had arrived with the dread news. He wanted to spend as much time as possible with Agnes. The day was bright and brisk and as he travelled the road his spirit sang. He found himself thinking of all the hitherto unknown aspects of Agnes' character that were now being revealed to him and how much he relished the disclosures. They were going to ride down to the sea and spend the day exploring on horseback the coast north of the estuary by Ayton Castle.

It was early summer and the gentle hills were garbed, the trees with their leaves still a light and fresh shade of green. The generous force of nature was all about him and he marveled at its ability to renew itself year after year, to reclaim and repopulate areas that man's depredations had temporarily laid low. Perhaps the mounting joy in his own spirits brought upon him by the love of the young woman was of a substance similar to the burgeoning growth visible all around him. He thought again of his mother's phrase, "the cleansing power of a new affection".

Agnes was waiting for him seated on the front steps of the house. She ran to embrace him as he swung off his horse. "Oh I have missed you these last days," she said. "I have thought of you and the family so often, and particularly of poor Tom. How is he faring?"

"I don't know where he gets the strength," Rob answered. "Almost everyone now knows what he did, and yet he faces people with his head up and a frank account if he is queried. Mind you, he is not going into town unless he has to, but he does not shy away from people when he meets them. He acknowledges that he

82

has been at fault. Of course, some people see the only outcome being a forced marriage but most seem to accept the view that this is no solution unless the marriage would have come without being forced by a child in the offing."

Agnes went into the house to collect a picnic hamper and say goodbye to her parents. Norah followed her out. "How is the family faring in the midst of this scandal?" she asked.

"Mother, this is not a scandal save in the eyes of those who would make it one," said Agnes sharply. "It is a tale of human error but also of redemption, at least for Tom if what I hear is correct about the way he is conducting himself."

"Well, I think your parents are saintly in their willingness to adopt the child until Tom has the ability to care for it on his own," Mrs Runciman continued. "But what chance is there that the young woman and her parents will willingly surrender it?"

"We do not know as yet," Rob replied. "The Reverend Chisholme, their parish priest, has undertaken to be an intermediary. But we have not heard what progress he has made. It will not be easy."

"Please let your parents and Tom know they are in my prayers," Norah said as the young people readied their horses to leave.

They quickly found the path down to Eve Water which they would follow to the sea. The stream was some 15 feet wide by this time, tumbling over the rocks where it ran shallowly and then sinking quietly into graceful pools alive with myriad forms of life below the quiet glass. Occasionally the water swirled as a trout or salmon lunged at a fly that had lingered too close to its surface. Rob noted the pools where the fish seemed most active and made a mental note for their next excursion on the river.

They reached the estuary well before noon. The low tide exposed the gentle slope of the shingled beach and Agnes gave her horse, which had been straining to canter, its head. Rob joined in and they raced across the strand, Agnes – her long hair streaming behind her – managing to keep well ahead of him. A rocky promontory brought the horses to a slower pace and their riders laughed at the joyful exertion.

The North Sea, whose customary greyness reflected the oft-clouded skies and the muddy waters of its estuaries, today shone blue and sparkling. The town's fishing fleet had headed to sea before dawn and was long gone but several schooners as well as a coal-laden barge could be seen less than a mile off the coast. The horses picked their way over the rocks to the promontory's summit which afforded a broad view of the coastline before them. They decided to head for the small harbour at Netherby before finding a sunny, sheltered place for the picnic lunch.

Agnes spread a cloth across the sand just behind a dune which provided some shelter from a light breeze. Out from the basket came a generous array of breads, cold sausage and early summer vegetables from the Runciman garden. Rob's stomach growled in embarrassing anticipation. He had not eaten since before sunrise and the cool, refreshing air as well as his high spirits conspired to give him a healthy hunger.

Stretched out on the sand, warmed by the bright sun and graced by the beauty of the young woman opposite him, Rob could not imagine being happier and more content. They had seen a good deal of each other over the past several weeks and Rob was certain that this was the person with whom he wished to spend the rest of his life.

The nature of her warmth and response gave him every encouragement that she might share this sentiment. He now thought that he could begin to share with her his hopes about starting a new life in Canada. With his parents offer to adopt Tom's child and the additional work this would likely mean for the rest of the family, it was clear that the Canadian venture would have to be postponed so a long separation from Agnes no longer seemed likely. There was every chance that they could get married before leaving together for Canada. He had decided that this would be a good day to tell her about his hopes.

Agnes was in the midst of telling him of a recent visit to Edinburgh to explore the possibility of taking courses that would enable her to get a certificate to teach junior grades in the county school.

"I am happy at home, but mother does not need as much help as she used to and I think that I would really enjoy a new challenge. My two greatest loves are people and books and both those would be satisfied by teaching."

"What type of courses would you have to take to qualify?" asked Rob.

"Well, I left school a year or two before you did but I can make up the difference in a few months by taking a concentrated school-leaving course at the teachers institute in Edinburgh. Then there would be courses in teaching methods, curriculum organization and understanding how children learn. If I took these courses consecutively I believe I could qualify within the year. But it would require living in Edinburgh full time. And that I would find difficult, especially now that I have found you." She looked at him smiling broadly.

"Perhaps, then, I should tell you something about what I am thinking about the future," said Rob.

"Yes, it's about time. I was wondering if you would ever get around to it," she replied looking at him mischievously.

"I have hesitated," he said, "because it might involve a somewhat dramatic change from what I have known all my life. And I didn't want to alarm you unnecessarily. My family and I have been talking about Peter and I going to Canada to explore the possibilities of farming there."

Agnes' expression altered abruptly. Suddenly this happy exercise of sharing hopes for the future while surrounded by the sand and sun of a languid afternoon became threatening. "Are you truly serious? Have you set a time to depart? What about us?" she asked, her face clouded with apprehension.

"You can see why I hesitated---yes, we're serious. A few months ago we had thought that Peter and I should go for a trial five year period to see if we can make a go of it. Then perhaps the whole family would follow. But now, with Tom's baby on the horizon, everything is on hold. So there is nothing imminent but it is a real possibility in the future." Rob shifted on the blanket so he could more fully watch her face as he spoke.

"You know that with nine of us children, the prospects for my family here are very limited. And our landlord has been steadily raising our annual rent. We still have many years left in the lease but we are getting squeezed with declining prices for our produce and increasing costs. In the Canadian west it is possible to acquire 160 acres for each family, free and clear, with the only requirement that the land be cultivated within three years."

"Do you mean that you could actually own the land yourself, no more landlords?" asked Agnes.

"No more landlords," said Rob, his voice becoming animated. "Can you imagine standing on a spread of that size with the whole thing below your feet belonging to you and your family? That could never happen here, not in several lifetimes. And we are told that the available land has great fertility, has never been farmed before and is virtually stone free.

"Mind you, life would be very different there." Rob looked over the water and the wheeling gulls. "All the comfort of known places and loved faces would be behind. And the winters are severe, months of cold and deep snows. It is not for the faint hearted. But the summers, we are told, are gloriously sunny and warm, not like our clouded and tepid climes and the growing conditions excellent, assuring one of steady crops, year after year."

Agnes was silent. Rob noticed her change of mood, wanted to comfort her, to assure her that whatever he did he wanted her to be at his side. But he could not say that, not yet. While he was certain of his feelings for her, to be able to move beyond courtship to a contractual undertaking required steps he had not yet taken.

"I do not expect that we will be looking at a date for at least a year and by that time we will both know better what the future holds. In the meantime, should you decide to go to Edinburgh I want to spend as much time with you as possible before you leave."

"What do you think about the possibility of my taking those

courses?" she asked. "I wouldn't be able to get home often if I want to complete the requirements within a year."

"By all means you should do it," Rob said firmly. "Whatever the future holds, that training will hold you in good stead and it will enrich your life. The year will pass quickly and I will be able to come up fairly often. I have cousins living in the city with whom I can stay. And it would be a welcome change to take in the life of Scotland's premier city and to do so with you as guide and companion."

The apprehension seemed to have lifted. The possibility that many months would pass before decisions had to be taken about Canada and the prospect of shared adventures in Edinburgh restored Agnes mood. They finished their lunch, returned to the horses and spent the rest of the afternoon in a leisurely exploration of the coastline.

On the way home in the late afternoon, they decided to rest awhile on the banks of Eve Water and enjoy the richer tones of the diminishing sun and the lengthening shadows it cast across the landscape. The flowers of early summer reflected their colours more deeply in the changing light presenting a panorama rich in form and shade, the stillness broken only by the occasional drone of insects or a gentle splash in the river as a fish or a frog sought nourishment.

Rob took Agnes' hand and motioned her to a grassy incline, stretched himself full length and with his eyes beckoned her to do the same. She nestled close to him as he let his arm find her waist. She leaned over and kissed him. He responded intensely feeling again the surge within his body. He took her head in his hands and returned the kiss but this time with more vigour than ever before.

He wanted to roll over onto her, wedge himself between her limbs and let his feelings have full rein. It took all his restraint to pull away, hiding, he hoped, the fact that his manhood was erect and ready. But not fast enough for he found he was already spent. He sat up quickly, his breathing sharp.

"Och, aye, I'm sorry. I go too fast. Forgive me." He was flustered and embarrassed. If Agnes suspected anything she did not show it. She took his hand. "We will have plenty of time," she said softly.

They sat quietly for a long while watching the glory of the dying day. Then wordlessly they mounted their horses and turned towards her home.

Alone in the dusk heading for Abbeylane Farm, Rob found himself profoundly happy and yet shamed that he had let his ardour lead him into action that may have disturbed and embarrassed Agnes. Still, she showed no sign of embarrassment. Was it naivety on her part or simply a loving understanding of the perils of intimacy? She was the daughter of the farm so it was not likely a question of naivety. She had been dignified and open, neither leading him on nor recriminating. It was as though she understood, and as though there was nothing to forgive. What an amazing woman.

When he opened the kitchen door he knew immediately that something had dramatically altered. His mother turned towards him, her eyes red-rimmed; his father sat despondent at the table. "Kate is dead and the babe with her," was all his mother could say. Stunned, Rob took a seat beside his father. "What has happened?" he said in a whisper. Thomas told him what they knew.

"Where's Tom?" Rob asked after his father had lapsed into silence.

"I don't know. He got the news in mid-morning and hasn't been around since. I imagine he is out on the land somewhere trying to come to terms with what has happened," said his father.

"Rob, will you try to find him?" asked Isobel. "I think that now he needs you more than any of the rest of us. He has ridden such a roller coaster the last weeks. His emotional resources will be drained dry. I'm afraid he might do something unwise."

"Don't worry, Mother. Tom has a lot of strength. But I will certainly find him. But perhaps I could have a bite to eat before I head out."

It was dark before Rob finished his meal. He had no idea where Tom could have gone but he knew a couple of places where his brother had liked to wander when he wanted to be by himself. He headed for the first, a hillock the other side of Greylocks field from which you had a view of the valley and river beyond. But he was nowhere to be seen around the hillock or on the paths leading to it. So he headed down to the river, a partial moon providing sufficient light.

A couple of hours later he still had found no sign of his brother. He decided the best course of action was to sit on the front porch of the house so he could intercept him on his way in. He must have dozed for he heard nothing until he felt a hand on his shoulder. Looking up in the darkness he could just make out Tom. He rose silently and embraced him. Then, taking his elbow he led him towards the barn.

In the light of the lamp, Tom's face reflected the anguish of the past hours. 'Tom.... We cannot comprehend God's purposes. Father Chisholme was with her before she died. We must trust that she and the unborn babe are at peace."

The dam Tom had been manning all night cracked and in the safety of his brother's presence, he allowed himself to weep. "Och, the poor wench, the poor wee babe. What have I done to them? How can I ever forgive myself? I will never be able to put this right with her parents."

"No, you will not and your grief will be deep but there is no room for more guilt," Rob said with all the feeling he could muster. "You have done everything that you thought was right and this tragedy could not have been foreseen."

They sat together a long time. "It's almost dawn," Rob said. "You need to sleep." Tom nodded. They rose and moved quietly into the house and into their room. Neither shed their clothes as they slumped onto their beds. Tom was asleep in minutes. Rob could not stop thinking about the day's happenings and lay watching the light creep across the fields outside and into his room. A day of contrasting emotions, a tangle of events. Finally, he slept.

It was late in the morning before Rob awoke. Tom was still sleeping. The house was quiet. Rob stripped and washed himself quietly in the basin in the room. The cold water braced his body awake and overcame some of his tiredness. He grabbed some bread in the kitchen and went outside.

He had to get back to the work of the farm. He saw it as a refuge from the emotional turmoil of the past days. They were fallowing the southern-most field and it would be time to plough the weeds under that had grown up over the spring and early summer. He went into the barn to hitch the draft horses. The sounds and smells of the barn helped restore a sense of normalcy to his mind. He wrestled the plough on to a wagon, walked the horses into position and led them down the line of trees to the fallowed field.

The next couple of hours passed quickly. The swish and click of the plough as it sliced the earth, the clop of the plodding hooves rang a familiar rhythm freeing his mind from the need to think. His satisfaction came now only in the form of the increasing ripples of soil arising to his right and left as he and the horses strode back and forth across the landscape. And that was enough. He needed no further justification for existence.

The sun climbed across the top of the sky. He was two-thirds finished but now his thirst was intense. He halted the horses at the top of the field, unhitched them and led them to the small brook that formed the southern boundary of the farm. He let them drink downstream while he scooped water over his face and shoulders and drank deeply. He pulled some cheese, cold sausage and bread out of a day sack and quieted the rumbling in his stomach. Then he dozed awhile in the sunshine.

Finishing the rest of the ploughing seemed to take much longer. He began to be restless. The whole picture had now changed. There was no longer an infant to be brought into the family. There would no longer be a reason to postpone the decisions about going to Canada. What would that mean for Agnes and himself? And what would happen to Tom? Would he be able to stay on the farm, to stay in this community after all that had happened? Too many questions and only time would supply the answers.

When he returned to the house in the late afternoon he learned that Father Chisholme had been there and that he and Tom had walked off together across the fields. Tom had not yet returned. The funeral for Kate would be held in two days' time at the Catholic church. His family would attend but he doubted Tom would be able to.

He welcomed the noise and laughter of the younger children. Solemnity never subdued their spirits for long. The two little boys raced each other around the kitchen until told to move outside by their sisters. The girls were clearly carrying more than their share of the household's chores given their mother's preoccupation with the state of her third son. George, as usual, sat by the window scarcely engaged in the events around him. Peter and his father were undertaking Tom's customary chores with the cattle.

Tom and Chisholme did not return until after supper. The latter did not linger, paid his respects to Thomas and Isobel and left. Tom was quiet, ate his dinner and went to bed. No one queried the nature of his afternoon with the priest. Rob and his parents lingered awhile in the parlour after the rest of the family had gone to bed. They decided that the three of them would go to the funeral and would leave Tom to make up his own mind. Too much had happened in the last days to make any other decisions.

Chapter

12

THEY HAD BEEN ON HORSEBACK FOR HOURS, THE SUN NOW GLARING DIRECTLY overhead. Tom's thirst was immense and his will to stay erect on his mount fading. Their captors kept a steady canter. With no sign of man or habitation on any horizon, Tom feared he or one of his comrades would crumple and fall off the fast moving horses, inflicting who knew what injury.

Abruptly they came to the edge of a coulee, its presence invisible behind a slight incline and began to descend. There, at the bottom, among tall cottonwoods, stood an encampment, perhaps half a dozen tepees with as many horses tethered behind them. The tall, finely muscled brave who was clearly the leader among their captors, shouted and the flaps of the tents opened and several dozen people emerged.

The nature of their tepees with their markings seemed quite different from those of the Cree who had first captured them. Perhaps these people were of a different tribe with an agenda other than that of Fineday and Poundmaker. That would explain the violent confrontation that resulted in their transfer.

They were gestured off their horses, given water and some pemmican and were then tied in a line to a horse. It was evident that they were now going to have to walk to their final destination. The warriors on horseback were joined by two families who packed up their belongings and tied them to poles behind two horses and joined them on foot. The rest remained at the camp.

They followed the snaking ravine for a couple of miles and then headed up over its side onto the open prairie. The mounted men led the way and several rode perhaps a quarter of a mile out on either side. Progress through the tall grasses was slow and the small party was silent, solely focused on the journey. It was now clear to Tom that these were not Cree. Their language was quite other than the guttural intonations of the Cree and Ojibwa that he had been accustomed to in Elphinstone. It was somehow softer; its individual words more pronounceable to the English ear and tongue.

They walked all that day, and the next, breaking for the night only when the sun had departed, using the light of the long dusk to set up camp and eat, the soldiers eating the same fare as their captors.

Most of the band ignored them with the exception of one of the families. The couple were elderly and were accompanied by two young women who could have been daughters or granddaughters. These women did not seem to follow the pattern of avoiding contact, eye or otherwise, with the soldiers. They were curious and the older one, who seemed especially spirited, took the opportunity to smile and linger slightly longer than was required when giving the men food or water. Tom noticed her watching him on occasion.

On the third day of walking, they approached a ridge of low hills and on a plateau in their midst saw a large assembly of tepees. Rising dust soon revealed a dozen horses galloping towards them with men astride their backs. Shouts of recognition identified these as fellow tribesmen and the traveling party was escorted into the midst of the encampment while many others crowded around pointing at the soldiers and exchanging animated comments. The soldiers were herded into a large tepee and placed under guard.

But the atmosphere in the camp around them quickly changed. Tom could hear heated exchanges taking place with the conflict seeming to be between their younger captors and the older men resident in the camp. Some hours passed and then a young man – not one of those who had captured them – entered the tepee. He was alone but seemed confident. To their surprise he addressed them in broken English.

"My name Ohiteka. You now in Lakota camp. Sitting Bull our

93

great chief but he not here. We come to this place few years past after fighting American cavalry. They not cross the line and Canadian police allow us to stay. But we must be at peace. Our young men do not like to be at peace when Cree brothers fighting your soldiers. So they take you. Elders angry with them. We talking what to do."

With that, he turned and left but soon after three women came into the tent bringing food and water, this time roasted meat, perhaps deer or antelope, and flat bread. One was the young woman whom Tom had noticed watching him. Once again, she made a point of singling Tom out for a nodded exchange, handing him the prepared food before distributing it to the others. Tom hoped his comrades had not noticed.

All was now quiet in the camp save the normal noises of people going about their evening's preparations. Dusk gathered and the men waited but their relief was evident. For the first time in days they sensed that they might get out of this alive. Then, just as they were falling asleep, they heard people approaching the tepee. The flap was opened by the young man they had seen earlier in the afternoon. With him were two old men, chiefs or elders judging from their dress and the deferential manner by which the young man treated them. Their presence was such that Tom instinctively stood up. The others followed him.

The chiefs sat and began speaking in their flowing tongue. They spoke for a long time until finally stopping and looking to the younger man. He began to translate.

"The chiefs say big mistake made. Lakota have no quarrel with Great Mother across the seas and her police. Some young men very angry with all whites because of big war with American soldiers. Many our people die so we come north across the line to find safety. Great Mother says we can stay but must live in peace with white man. That we wish to do.

"Our great chief and medicine man, Sitting Bull, has returned to American side of line with many our people and he say we must fight no more. But some young men do not understand. They hear

94

stories of ghost dancing, ceremony that makes man able to stop bullets and so give Sioux nation victory over American cavalry. They want to bring ghost dancing here. They take you prisoner to show our people they have power over whites."

He stopped and gestured to the older men to continue. They spoke for several minutes more and then the translation started again.

"We have said if young men want battle, they must leave this encampment and this territory. You are not now prisoners. You are guests and we take you back soon to police post. Until then, we take off rope and our people treat you as respected guests of tribe. You will live with our people until we leave in day or two. That is what the chiefs say to you."

The soldiers were still standing and the young translator knelt down by one of them and began untying the rope. One of the chiefs shouted and two other young men came in and helped free the remaining soldiers. Tom and his comrades could not believe their good fortune but held their relief in check, not knowing what kind of behaviour was acceptable in the presence of the chiefs. As the latter rose to go, however, Tom stepped forward and asked the young man to translate his words.

"Respected chiefs, we thank you for your words. We, too, want to be at peace. Surely there is enough room in this land for both our peoples. We will tell our chiefs that a mistake was made and that no harm was intended by your people."

When he had translated, the young man told the soldiers to follow him and led them to three other tepees in the area where they were greeted by the men in each tepee and ushered in. To his surprise, Tom found he and another soldier were directed to the tent of the young woman who had been particularly solicitous over the last three days. He and his comrade were gestured to sit down and food was immediately presented. When they finished what was before them, more was pressed upon them which they gladly accepted given the lack of food for the previous six days. Again, when finished, more was offered but they could eat no more.

With the soldiers actually in her tepee, the young woman

seemed to be a good deal more reticent to engage. But Tom look the lead indicating by gestures his name. She seemed to understand and responded by pointing to herself and saying, "Wynona". By the same means Tom asked the names of her parents. She smiled and, pointing to the elders, shook her head. Tom assumed that there must be some custom that prevented her from mentioning her parents' names.

Wynona began to speak, surprising Tom with her knowledge of English. "You soldier?" she asked. "No, I am farmer,' Tom replied, not knowing how much she could understand. "From where?" she asked. "My home is Scotland but I look for land to farm here." "This land very good," Wynona replied.

'You wife?" she asked. "No," said Tom. "But someday I hope." He thought she blushed but then remained silent. Tom decided to ask in turn, "You have man?" She quickly looked him in the eye and said softly, "Also not yet."

By mutual consent, something seemed to have been established and any further words now seemed pointless. Tom felt his energy quicken. He glanced sideways at her. Her facial profile was indeed beautiful. Unlike many of her people, her face was not round and full but somewhat angular with fine cheekbones. Her long black hair hung loosely curtaining a sculpted neck. Like her people, she was tall, only slightly shorter than he. Her legs, when he glimpsed them, were strong ending in feet that he thought were beautifully shaped. He found his being stirred again. It was so long since he had been close to a young woman, certainly not one who seemed accessible and yet beyond imagined reach.

Fires were now burning low and the camp was quiet. On entering, they had seen that skins had been placed on the other side of the tent from the family's sleeping arrangements and the mother gestured to the soldiers that this was where they were to sleep. Tom's colleague immediately lay down, fully clothed, against the wall of the tent. Tom took off his boots and lay down, his back to his comrade. He watched through half-closed eyes as the family prepared to sleep and noticed that Wynona placed herself on the outside of the family bed, closest to the centre of the tent.

As he contemplated the coming sleep, Tom felt the warmth of sexual anticipation. He allowed his imagination to create a scenario where he felt the smooth beauty of her skin, drew deeply on the mixed scent of smoke and sweat that her body emitted and contemplated her hands caressing him. With that comfort he surrendered to sleep.

He was startled half-awake by the presence of someone lying down beside him on his right, away from his sleeping comrade. The tepee was infused with a pallid light, the moon shining through its skin walls. He could smell her scent and as he struggled to gain consciousness, realized what was happening and found his body instantly alert. She lay still, her face inches from his. Slowly she placed her hand on the side of his face, stroking gently. Tom had to check a groan as his suppressed desire rose within him. He reached over and slid his hand under her deerskin garment, finding in reality the image he had contemplated only hours earlier.

Now he was faced with a dilemma. She had made clear that she was available and wanted him, but with all the others sleeping around, and not knowing what was permissible in the custom of her people, did he dare continue to the point where there would be no stopping until the process of passion had worked itself to fulfilment? And what if others woke and saw what was happening?

He did not worry about his comrade fast asleep on his left. He was sleeping so soundly that nothing would likely awaken him. And if he did stir and notice, Tom was quite able to handle the jousting that would come the next day. But if her father or mother discovered, what would the consequences be? Might it imperil the chances of freedom that seemed to be within their grasp? Could he risk this for his comrades?

He did not have a choice. It took all the restraint he could muster to withdraw his hand and push her gently away, slowly shaking his head. He did not wish her to believe that he did not want her. With everything in his being, he did. So he leaned over and kissed her gently. He then shook his head again and gestured that she should go. She rose quietly and without looking at him, returned to her sleeping place.

It was a long time before sleep took Tom. Perhaps it was the potency that could accompany mid-night emotions, but Tom had never felt such longing even at the height of his infatuation with Kate many months before. It was certainly profoundly carnal, plumbing the ripeness of his manhood. But there was also something exquisite about it, a sense of the ethereal, of warmth and dignity. He lay there watching her, wondering how someone who was so other, so alien to all he had heretofore known, could evoke such feelings. The sexual arousal had faded but in its place he found himself immensely happy.

He was next aware of the sounds of morning and when he opened his eyes, the family had left the tepee and the camp was bustling. His neighbour slept on. Tom rose, found his shoes and went out into the early morning. Wynona's mother tended a fire by which flat bread was baking on poles. The young woman was nowhere in sight. The older woman did not acknowledge Tom and he quickly wondered if she had been aware of the night's events. His comrade emerged, the dregs of sleep on his face. The woman offered them the flat bread.

Soon after the father appeared in the company of the young translator from the day before. He asked them to accompany him to the other side of the encampment where the other soldiers had been assembled in the presence of the chiefs. There they were informed that later that day, a party of warriors would accompany them to the police post at Fort Walsh west in the Cypress hills. Tom's fellow soldiers could not contain their delight but Tom found his feelings suddenly mixed. The power of his emotions from the night before shadowed his consciousness. They had such force but in the light of day would they retain their urgency? If he was to leave immediately, how would he ever know? Would he ever see Wynona again? Could he ask to stay on for some time? Would this be seen as deserting the ranks?

As they walked back to the tent, Tom was captive to his thoughts. No, he would have to go. This was likely only a head-strong impulse brought about by the extremity of their last days and the long period he had been without the close presence of a woman. He had to get back to his regiment if he was to be paid for his service and then make his way somehow back to Elphinstone. Rob would be aware now of his absence from the mill and he had to make it back to the farm before the start of the harvest.

The accompanying braves including the young man, Ohiteka, who had translated for them, had gathered and provided horses for the soldiers along with provisions for the journey which was expected to take two days. Still no sign of Wynona. There was no way for Tom to know whether his rejection of her the night before had caused such humiliation that she would not enter his presence again. Then just as he was mounting his horse, she came around the tepee and looked straight at him. Her face was pained but quiet. And then she smiled – slightly, tentatively, but definitely. He looked back at her and his face creased into a wide smile. He paused. And then they were off.

Chapter

13

THE DAY OF THE FUNERAL CAME. ROB AND HIS PARENTS ATTENDED. AS expected, Tom could not face this stark reminder of his misadventures. The three of them found a pew at the back of the thinly attended church. It was impossible not to pass by the Collins but their faces were vacant and impassive. They showed no sign of recognizing the Dunbars. Father Chisholme led the simple service, not a funeral mass. He spoke of the unfathomableness of God, how profound were both his love and his purposes and of the gift of sin forgiven by the death of Christ on the cross. He acknowledged also the presence and the sanctity of the unborn one in Kate's womb, a being also beloved of God. Rob found the service serene and potent in its healing possibility.

Rob tried to be available to Tom in the following days but had decided not to crowd him. The work on the farm resumed its customary rhythm. It was some days later when they were repairing fencing on the southern fields that Tom started to talk about his afternoon with Chisholme.

"We spent a long time walking without saying anything to each other. I was glad for his company and that he allowed that silence to continue for so long. In a strange way it seemed to build a bond between us.

'Then he said to me, 'Tom, life is a story of mistakes made. The mistakes are not nearly as important as how we react to them."

Then he went on to say that the God he worshiped was always present. He was there when the babe was conceived, not condemning us but grieving, grieving because the child was being made in an act not of enduring love but of abandon.

"And he said He was there when its mother fell victim to the poison that ended her life and the life of the child." Tom stopped, his voice faltering. It was some minutes before he resumed.

"He said that the God he knows does not intrude in human lives to protect them from the consequences of their actions but is alongside us, suffering with us."

Rob was deeply moved. There was a new dimension to his brother. These experiences had matured him. Rob almost envied him his pain and the lessons he had learned first-hand from it.

Tom resumed. "I would like to believe Chisholme. I wish I could walk away from life's mess. And there are days when I know that I could if I was prepared for the other half of the bargain."

"What do you mean by that?" Rob asked.

"This God stuff always ends up backing me into a corner, taking away my freedom. I wasn't prepared to give up my freedom in a marriage to Kate. And I'm not prepared to hand it over to God just to ease my conscience." With that, Tom turned abruptly and walked away.

When they returned to the house, Isobel told them that Father Chisholme had come by on his way to town and had said that the Collins had suddenly left to return to Ireland, terminating their employment and did not intend to come back. There was nothing further that could be done for them; that chapter had closed.

Rob knew now that he would have to reconsider his immediate future. He had been delighted with the prospect that he and Agnes would have more time together; perhaps even time to marry, before he headed to Canada. Now he began to question that. Was it fair to take her to an unknown wilderness where life could be exceedingly harsh, where he knew not what kind of employment he could obtain or what precarious living conditions he would have to endure? And would not the company of a wife, no matter what joy and comfort it might bring him, severely constrain his ability to forage for the work he needed?

And could he now put off for another year the possibilities of his whole family beginning a new life in Canada so that he could spend more time with Agnes? With each passing year his parents would have greater trouble adjusting to the change. It was just not his nature to put gratification before duty. Besides, Agnes seemed eager to undertake further studies in Edinburgh. Even if he delayed his departure, he would see little of her.

So as day followed day, much of each spent alone in the fields or on the ride to town to fetch supplies, he found himself increasingly persuaded that the time to go was sooner rather than later. It would have to be well before the autumn storms made passage difficult and enough time to find work before the Canadian winter set in.

Then one morning he awoke with the awareness of something that had been before his eyes for days but had not been recognized. It was obvious that Canada offered a way out for Tom, a way to distance himself from the tragic events of that spring.

Though he had scarcely admitted it to himself, he had been aware that leaving the farm in the company of Peter would put welcome distance between himself and Tom and allow him to grow more fully and confidently into his own identity without comparing himself to his gregarious, younger brother.

Since his blossoming relationship with Agnes he had felt a good deal less vulnerable to comparisons, a good deal happier in his own skin. But being forced into close quarters with Tom over an extended period was not something he relished. He wondered if he had the heart to propose this alternative.

He was preoccupied with this question as he descended the stairs to do the morning chores before joining the family for breakfast. He found his parents alone, the younger children still abed and Tom somewhere else. Isobel and Thomas had obviously been talking intently when he joined them. They broke off their conversation. Then Isobel turned to him, "Have you been thinking again about the possibility of going to Canada this year?" she asked.

"Yes," he replied. "I have thought of it a great deal and with the events of the past few days, it seems as though this may be the right time to go."

"But what about your relationship with Agnes? We do not want you to jeopardize that," his mother said.

"I have thought of that, too," Rob said. "I now know that I want to marry Agnes and I believe she would accept a proposal. But I do not think it would be wise to take her with me while we explore the situation in Canada. It would expose her to unknown hardships and would hamper the flexibility we would need to find work and survive. Besides, she has plans to study in Edinburgh this next year."

Isobel looked at her son. So strong, so thoughtful, so dependable, she thought. Agnes would be so fortunate to have him as a mate. Surely she would wait for him.

"Oh, Rob. I am so glad about you and Agnes," she said going over and putting her arms around him. "Have you asked her yet?"

"No, but I shall have to do so swiftly if we follow through with these plans," Rob replied. Then Isobel paused and looked at Thomas. He made no move to speak so she continued. "Would you consider taking Tom with you instead of Peter?" Isobel asked carefully. "I cannot see how Tom can remain on the farm and in this area. It is just going to be too difficult for him. Peter will be greatly disappointed, poor boy. But I think it could be the saving of Tom. In the face of his disappointment and loneliness, he could easily pick up with the same crowd he was with when he first got involved with Kate. If he joined you, a whole world of possibilities would open to challenge him."

Rob was surprised at the way their thoughts had moved in parallel, but now that he heard the idea spoken aloud, he suddenly felt resistant to it. "I was so looking forward to having Peter's company," he said and he got up from the table and walked over to the windows looking out over the expanse of fields as they rolled down to the North Sea.

"But I guess you're right," he continued in a voice that held no enthusiasm. "Perhaps you should ask him if he wants to go."

"No, Rob, I think you are the one to invite him to accompany you," said his mother. "But only if you are fully comfortable with that," she said looking him directly in his eyes. She knew that the divergent nature of her two oldest sons had always set them somewhat against each other.

"I can see it is the right thing to do," Rob said, trying not to let the heaviness he felt show in his voice. "I will ask him. But we must talk to Peter first."

Peter was crestfallen but he was cut from the same dutiful cloth as Rob and though he was young, immediately saw the difference it could make in Tom's life. When his parents pointed out the increasing responsibility that would be his on the farm with his older brothers away, and the fact that they all hoped to follow Rob and Tom in a few years, he found it easier to walk away from his disappointment.

It was decided that Rob should be the one to raise the possibility with Tom. If Isobel or Thomas put the issue to him, they were afraid he might interpret it as a rejection or a doubting of his ability to overcome current circumstances.

Rob wanted his proposal to appear a casual thought and so waited for an opportunity that evening when he joined Tom in the barn to help with the day's closing chores.

"Brother, what would you think of coming to Canada with me?" he asked. "Instead of Peter?"

Tom had his back to him, shovelling silage to the cattle. He stood abruptly, turning to face Rob. He paused. "Do you think that's possible? What about the farm? Wouldn't Peter be terribly disappointed?"

"I'm sure he would but he can rise to the challenge of taking a lead in running the farm. That would do a lot for him. And he can follow with the rest of the family before too long."

Tom was silent for several minutes, then grinned suddenly. 'Och, I would love to do that. There's nothing left for me here save my duty to the parents. Do you think they would approve?"

'Well, let's ask them. I would welcome your company, your

strength and your humour as we face whatever the wilderness may throw at us," said Rob. "Together, we could get an operation up and running in no time so the parents and the others can join us in a couple of years."

"But what about Agnes?" Tom asked. "Aren't the two of you moving towards a permanent relationship? Are you thinking of going soon?"

Rob outlined his thoughts about his future with the young woman and his view that they should leave for Canada within a few weeks. As the reality of this proposal began to register with Tom, Rob could see his eyes brighten and his shoulders lose their sag. "Och, that would be wonderful. And that would solve many a problem," he said almost to himself.

And then Rob suddenly felt apprehensive. Here he had almost committed himself to an early departure without any consultation with the person who was becoming the most important in his life. His face clouded. "Look," he said, "I have let this run away with me. I have not even mentioned the possibility to Agnes. I can't commit to anything until we have spoken and until I have given her time to consider. And if we did decide to go this summer, I would have to propose marriage to her, which is what I want to do anyway, but that will require the necessary preparations with her parents." As he spoke he could feel a growing sense of loss and panic.

"Tom, let's talk to the parents and, of course, to Peter. Let's keep this between the five of us until I have had time to talk with Agnes and we have had the chance to consider together what the right course of action is for us."

"Of course," said his brother. They walked back to the house.

That afternoon, after the three brothers and their parents had discussed the possibility of an early departure, Tom decided to walk the valleys and river banks of his youth. He took a fly-rod with him. His mood swayed between exhilaration and a pensive sadness. The prospect of the Canadian venture roused his blood. For the first time in several months, his horizons lifted, he could see beyond the shadows. Here was a chance to start over again, to go where no one knew of his past, to embrace risk and hardship and recover his belief in himself. It was a liberation that made his heart lift.

But as he gazed at the low hills, the gentle flow of the valley that ended in the blue ribbon of Eve Water, he could feel how much of himself belonged to this gracious landscape, lived in so long and yet seemingly unblemished. The marks that men had made, the fields in the valley bottom that climbed tentatively up the slopes, the houses widely dispersed on the ridges with their hedges and gardens, did not wound the natural world around them. Each complemented the other, showing all in their best light. Of course, distance hid the rough edges which were only too evident as you approached the habitations. But from this viewpoint, all seemed harmonious. He loved this land and he knew that the price of liberation meant it would be his only in memory.

The pain he felt at this prospect was physical. He sat on a hillock overlooking the quiet stream, his vision now blurred by tears. He knew the bill had to be paid. It was his best option but the pain was no less because of that. He let himself weep and then relaxed into the strange peace that sorrow serves up. He found comfort that the emotional turmoil of the last weeks had not drained him completely. He could still feel deeply in the presence of the beauty of the land and its incipient loss.

"Och, that's enough," he told himself and grabbing the rod he strode down to the river and until he reached a large pool just up from the estuary. The river entered it at a narrow stretch, bubbling over rocks, a spot where trout often lurked waiting for the water to deliver varied edibles.

He approached the pool carefully, knowing the range of the fishes' vision would be quite wide in the quiet waters. He selected a place behind a slight ridge near the water, casting his line first into the rapids above the pool so that the fly would be carried into the quiet waters. No action. Then he began working the pool, placing the lure so that it would drift under the overhanging banks opposite.

The water boiled as a fish struck. Tom sharply raised his rod sharply and the beast was hooked. Seconds later it was running hard downstream towards the estuary. Tom kept a gentle pressure on the line, not wishing to give the fish enough slack to shake the hook. Then it leapt, twisting its tail across the waters. A dance of beauty and of death.

But it still had plenty of life in it and Tom had to scramble along the bank to avoid running out of line. Then it turned again and raced back towards the pool with Tom reeling frantically to prevent the line getting tangled on underwater obstacles. As it approached Tom could see the size of the animal and let out a yelp of surprise and delight. If he could land it, it would be a real prize, a larger fish than he had ever had on a line before.

Now he had to try to exert greater control on the fish's movement. He had to increase the drag to wear it down. It jumped several more times but each leap was less than the one before. Many minutes passed in this mortal contest with the man's prowess matched against the beast's adroitness and cunning. Then he saw the flash of its side and he knew the game was climaxing. Minutes later, Tom was able to work it into the shallows and up on the rocks close to shore.

As he reached to grab it, the fish let loose one last burst of energy, flapping vigourously in the shallow water. Tom had to pin it with his foot before he could loop his finger under the life-giving gills. The fish was his and he marveled as it slipped out of the water and was lifted on his outstretched arm. Here was a prize for the whole family, a final gift from these beloved hills and waters, perhaps even a portent that he could look forward to a future of abundance. He turned for home, his rod in one hand and the fish held by his fingers over his shoulder.

Chapter

14

ROB WAS OUT AND ON THE ROAD BEFORE DAY-BREAK THE NEXT SUNDAY AND arrived at the Runcimans' shortly after they had finished breakfast. There was church to be attended to before he and Agnes could have time together. He had not seen Agnes' parents since before Kate's death and he was not relishing her mother's expected inquisitiveness. But the only reference was an easily answered inquiry as to how Tom was faring. He was of course invited to stay to lunch which passed pleasantly enough though Agnes shot him several concerned glances, noticing his preoccupation and lack of the spontaneity which normally characterized his interaction with the family.

The early afternoon was sunny and warm and the two of them decided to walk along the river. Agnes took his arm. "My dear, I've been thinking much about the future," Rob began. "The way is now open to go to Canada sooner than we had expected. And I believe that Tom should come with me rather than Peter. That would provide him an opportunity to start again, to leave the tragic events of this spring behind."

He felt her hand tighten on his arm. She looked straight ahead. "However, the most important matter in this decision is you and our relationship." He stopped and gently turned her to face him. "I love you. I want to marry you, if you will have me.

"Before you answer, and you needn't rush to answer, there are two more things I must say. First, I have not yet spoken to your parents and I must do that before anything can be official.

"And secondly, I cannot see how we can be married before I

108

go to Canada. What I mean is, I cannot subject you to the uncertainties and trials of Canada until we have established suitable employment and habitation. Life will be rough and hazardous in the Canadian west and I do not want to put those I love most, you and my family, at risk until I am certain that a better life awaits us there than what we have here. We shall have to wait until I return."

Agnes walked forward alone and sat on the river's bank. When she turned to him her face was both expectant and clouded. "With all my heart and being I will marry you. But I want to be there beside you to share the risks and labour of establishing a new life. I could not bear to lose you to an unknown world. Rob, let us go together."

"But what of your wish to follow courses in Edinburgh this next year?" Rob asked.

"That utterly pales against the prospect of being with you as your wife."

Rob walked over and drew her up into his embrace. "Thank you, thank you," he said as he brought her face forward into his and words were lost for many moments.

He loosed her. "I will speak to your parents this afternoon. Let us take time to consider the question of when we marry. Their views, too, will be important."

Her face lost its clouds and broke into a beautiful smile. She put her arms around his neck. They embraced again and held each other. Arms entwined, they turned back towards the house, only returning to holding hands when they reached within its view. Agnes said she would attend to the horses in the barn leaving Rob free to find her parents. He watched her cross the yard. She turned to him just as she entered the barn, her face alive with happiness.

Rob had not expected events to move so swiftly, but his relationship with the family was such that he did not feel overly nervous about the task facing him. He entered the kitchen door to find Norah by the sink. "I wonder if I might have some words with you and Mr Runciman," Rob said. She gave him an expectant look, as she wiped her hands on a towel. "Of course, go into the parlour. I will fetch him."

William Runciman had clearly been napping, his face sagging from mid-day sleep. Norah would not normally have interrupted his slumber but her curiosity would brook no delay and she hustled him to the parlour where Rob sat waiting. He settled himself into a chair and smoothed his hair with his hand. "Yes, young man. What is on your mind?" he asked.

"Agnes and I have seen much of each other the last few months. I have come to care for her deeply. I would like your permission to propose marriage to her," Rob said in his customary straight-forward manner.

The parents looked at each other, exchanging slight smiles. "We have been expecting this," said Runciman. "And we would be very happy to see such a match. But what do you plan for the future? Do you now intend to stay to help your father on the farm and then, as the eldest son, succeed him in assuming the tenancy?"

"That is uncertain," said Rob. "You know that we have been long considering exploring a future in the Canadian west for the whole family. We do not see enough of a future here for all my brothers and sisters. I had planned to go ahead along with Peter to see first-hand what the prospects were."

He went on to explain why an early departure along with Tom now seemed the right course of action.

"So when would you wish to marry?" asked Norah.

"That is a matter we would have to consider carefully. I would be very reluctant to expose Agnes to the harsh conditions of the Canadian west until we had the chance to establish a sustainable life there and that could take a couple of years. But it would be highly unfair to expect her to wait for me without formally making my intentions known. Hence, I would wish to propose marriage to her now and then, together with you and my parents, we could consider the matter of the timing of the marriage."

"And you are certain that you want to leave all that you have known to try to establish a new life in that wild and god-forsaken country?" asked Norah

"Yes, ma'am," Rob replied confidently. "Many others are now

doing it and the reports of what they find are encouraging. I do not see my future here subject to the whims of a landlord when it is possible to own land for oneself if you are prepared to work for it."

The Runcimans were quiet. Then Thomas rose, walked over to Rob and held out his hand. "I welcome you into our family, if Agnes agrees." Norah followed and kissed him gently on the cheek. "So do I, Rob," she said.

The decision had been made. After the mutual rejoicing at the news of Rob and Agnes' engagement, their parents had met with them to consider timing for a wedding. It seemed imperative to Rob and his parents that Tom be provided the opportunity to get away as soon as possible. That would mean leaving for Canada this year. And time was of the essence if they were to travel this season. They would only have three to four weeks to obtain a passage that would enable Rob and Tom to find work before winter set in. The implications were inevitable. There could not be time to arrange a wedding before they had to depart.

Agnes reluctantly accepted the logic of these circumstances. She would have relished going to Canada with Rob, the joy of the unknown, the risks taken, embracing all that was new and living it through the eyes and experience of her beloved. She had no fear, confident in the strength and wisdom of the man she had chosen. But she was also a traditional daughter, used to submitting to the judgment of her elders and in this matter of her marriage she was not about to risk dissension. Nor did she wish to stand in the way of her future brother-in-law having the chance to find himself again.

In the hectic days that followed, she was often over at Abbey-lane Farm helping the family prepare Rob and Tom for their journey. She found herself looking at Rob as he went about his tasks, relishing all the years they would have together. She had concluded that this period of delayed togetherness, of prolonged anticipation, made the future all the more enticing. After initial disappointment, her spirits rebounded and she was fully caught up in the excitement of the preparations for their departure.

They had managed to book passage on a ship called *The Buenos*

Ayrian out of Glasgow, bound for Montreal. It departed June 27 and would drop them in Montreal with enough time to get to Winnipeg, Manitoba, by train in early August. From there, they would make their own way west seeking the means to sustain themselves through the fall and winter, it being too late in the season to find land and crop it until the next year.

Tom could not believe his good fortune. For the first time in months he now woke as the dawn was emerging which, in summer at this high latitude, was well before five. He relished the resurgence of energy. The fog of apprehension and guilt had lifted. The day's tasks stretched out before him, simple and clear. He was singing again.

Isobel was making lists. Clothing would have to be made for the journey, also for the fierce winter that lay ahead. Clothing made of wool, long underwear next to the skin, wool pants, shirts, pullovers. And coats and jackets of sheepskin. The girls and she could cut and sew certain of the items but the tailor in Coldingham would be called on to make the pants, pullovers, coats and jackets.

No bedding would be provided on the voyage so the women made feather ticks and pillows. Tools were assembled – hammers, chisels, saws, a plane. Farm implements would have to be bought over there. Rob began collecting his personal items – two ties, both black, one wide and the other narrow – half a dozen coloured handkerchiefs – ink – oatmeal cakes – slippers – his Bible, the collected works of William Shakespeare and a *Life of Napoleon*.

A week before the departure, Agnes' parents decided to host a Sunday afternoon gathering, an occasion to formally announce the engagement of their daughter and to enable friends and family to wish her fiancé and his brother a swift and safe voyage. Their intentions were the best but when Tom heard of the event, he could not face a crowd. The memories were too raw and the mix of curiosity and sympathy he was bound to face affronted his sense of privacy. He did not want to spoil the event for Rob and Agnes, so he said nothing and when the family gathered that Sunday morning for the ride to Norfield Farm, he was nowhere to be found.

In their different ways, the family was coming to terms with the imminent departure of these two men. With very different personalities, they shed such a light on their days, strength and steadiness on the part of one, warmth and humour from the other. It is true that the twins, Hermione and Peter, as the eldest, after George, of the remaining children, would come into their own. Their personalities – no longer in the shadow of their older brothers – would fill out. But the void would persist for many weeks.

Any subdued thoughts were swiftly dispelled on arrival at Norfield Farm. It was apparent from the number of horses and carriages on the road that the crowd would be large. As they walked up the long, treed lane, William and Norah Runciman strode down to meet them, broad smiles on their faces. Agnes was not to be seen, likely occupied with the other guests.

"Well, this is a joyous occasion," William said, his arms spread wide in welcome. "I cannot think of a family I would rather have a daughter of mine join."

"Why, thank you," said Isobel. "You express our sentiments exactly. Welcoming Agnes as a daughter helps balance out the preponderance of men in our family." The Dunbar girls had been overjoyed that an older sister as bright and warm as Agnes would be part of their family. "And we shall have the great pleasure of having her around us as an almost-daughter-in-law while she waits for Rob to get established in Canada."

They moved into the garden and were engulfed by the attention of neighbours and friends. The women wore elaborate, flowing dresses, their hats seeming to compete with one another in the width of their brims and the variety of appendages hanging from them – so much so that it was often difficult to see the identity of the wearer. The men were dressed less formally, in smart jackets and pullovers with only a handful of top hats in evidence, most choosing bowlers or peaked, cloth caps. Only the children's heads remaining uncovered.

They raced around the garden with more than a few dogs in tow, darting in and out of the tables spread with cakes and sandwiches, always leaving with a swift handful of sweets. Agnes was busy with her sisters bringing plates of food out from the house.

When Rob first saw her, so lovely and gracious as she went about her work, he again felt the surge of feeling that he knew would have to sustain him over many lonely months, and perhaps years, in Canada. Yet he felt certain that they were going about their future in the right way. There was a time and place for everything. And waiting for it made it all the more to be cherished.

However, there was little space for isolated reverie as he had to respond to many comments and questions from the other guests. The women wanted to shake his hand and tell him how perfect he and Agnes were as a couple. The men were full of questions about the voyage, about their preparations, about Canada and their expectations. It was a long time before he was able to extract himself and seek out Agnes. William Runciman asked him to bring her up to the covered porch where he and perhaps others wanted to address comments to the crowd. He found her still occupied in the pantry where she swiftly embraced him before they made their way through the house to the balcony.

Runciman was already speaking when they arrived and was demonstrating his well-known facility with language. Rob felt distinctly ill at ease with the comments directed at him by his future father-in-law and the scrutiny of the up-turned faces of the crowd. He knew this was part of the ritual to be endured and he firmly grasped Agnes' hand and managed to smile slyly in her direction.

Then there was a pause in the proceedings and he realized he was expected to say something. This he had not expected. He hesitated and realized he was blushing red in his anxiety.

"Well, I guess all of you realize my good fortune," he started. "But I am sure some of you must also doubt my good sense to have the opportunity of marrying Miss Runciman and yet to postpone that happy day in order to try to survive the wilds of Canada. I have often doubted that choice myself. Put it down to a young man's folly if you will. But both Agnes and I believe this is the right decision.

"We are blessed to be able to take advantage of a continent opening up. I know our forefathers would have leapt at the opportunity to escape the heel of the landlord. So I do this for Agnes and for our children and for all those from my family or hers who wish to follow us there."

"Bravo, bravo," came shouts from the crowd. Rob held up his hand. "All I want to say, in addition, is to express my deep love and gratitude for this lady who stands by me in this decision. My brother and I shall return, owners of our own lands, and will celebrate together a great wedding feast."

Smiles and clapping broke out all around. Runciman stepped forward and as the couple was leaving the veranda, he quipped to the crowd, "Mr Gladstone will be very happy to see you departing for Canada, Rob. Otherwise I am sure he would worry that someone with your gift for oratory might give him a run for his money at the next Liberal nomination." There was more laughter and cheers as the crowd broke up.

The sun was moving towards the hills in the west when he and Agnes slowly moved to extricate themselves from the gathering. He had been invited by her parents to stay the night and he very much wanted unhurried time with her after the crowded busyness of the day.

They walked through the orchard down to the river. The midsummer air was redolent with myriad scents of growth, aromas earthy and warm, promising a bounty of beauty and provender. Rob grasped her hand and could not imagine a more perfect moment – the love and laughter of family, the admiration and envy of neighbours, the pervasive wonder of nature surrounding them and, above all, the devotion of this woman.

"Memories of this are going to stay with and comfort me in the months to come," he said "but I am going to miss you dreadfully. I guess the challenge of what lies ahead will prevent me from feeling too sorry for myself and regretting the decision we have made.

"And you, my dear, you must keep yourself fully occupied as well. You must take advantage of this time to relish all the learning available in Edinburgh. Who knows when you will ever again have the chance to access that kind of nourishment for the mind? You must stock up enough for us both so that the long Canadian winters ahead can be enriched by all you will absorb."

"Oh, Rob. What a dreamer," Agnes said with a tender smile. "Here you are, the tenant farmer's son, talking like some child of the landed gentry. But I love that part of you, a mind that always looks beyond the immediate circumstances, that sees the best in every opportunity.

"But when I am in Edinburgh I am not going to forget who I am – a daughter of the soil. Otherwise, I won't be much good to you on the open prairie in Canada. I suspect we will not have much energy for the finer things of life until we have put in quite a few years of heavy labour."

"You're probably right" he said with a sigh, their conversation tailing off as they walked into the fading light of the afternoon.

Chapter
15

THE DAYS OF PREPARATION HAD PASSED AND IT WAS THE EVENING BEFORE THE family would leave to accompany the men to the dockside in Glasgow. Isobel and the girls had prepared a splendid feast – a circle of lamb chops, a great roast of beef, chicken, duck and pheasant, early summer vegetables from the garden, new potatoes, broccoli, fresh young carrots and beets, scones and country bread and a rich apple crumble with thick cream for dessert. Isobel was determined that her men would board the ship with full stomachs.

The setting was festive and Isobel was determined to keep the mood in the same vein. There would be time for sorrow but the memories of their last hours together must be joyful ones. The younger children were filled with anticipation; it was almost as though they too were going on the long ocean voyage. Their questions about the ship and the risks of sailing on the high seas were endless.

Tom had gathered together all the printed material they had collected about the conditions that awaited them – sketches of Montreal, descriptions of the train-ride west, stories about Winnipeg and tales by those who had trekked west and found land. Tom's eyes flashed as he painted pictures of the scenes they would see and the people they would meet. Isobel found herself thinking that the old Tom was back, that the recovery she had long prayed for was underway.

As the evening waned and the amount of food consumed slowed the pace of conversation, Thomas rose at the end of the table. "Now, my dears, I want you all to come with me into the parlour. We are going to spend some time reading scripture and then we must all be off to bed. The morning will come early and we must be on the road before sunrise."

The solemnity of the event was marked by their entry into the parlour, a room reserved for only the most important of occasions and the children's mood changed to reflect it. Thomas took up the large, black family Bible. "I want to read at first from Psalm 139," he said and, finding the page, he read slowly,

> *"I can never escape your Spirit, I can never get away from your presence.*
> *If I go up to heaven, you are there, if I go down to the grave, you are there."*

The little boys looked on in wonder, their wide eyes absorbing the gravity on their father's face.

> *"If I ride on the wings of the morning, if I dwell by the farther-most seas,*
> *Even there your hand will guide me and your strength uphold me."*

Thomas was quiet and all seemed by their silence to be dwelling "by the farther-most seas".

By this time both Tom and Rob's eyes were wet. Sitting next to Isobel, Tom took her hand. "You are the people I love most in this world," he said. "You will travel with us every step of the way. We shall always carry you in our hearts with great thanksgiving."

Rob and Tom quietly rose and gave their father and mother each in turn a long embrace, then hugged their sisters and brothers. "Alright, all of you off to bed," said Isobel with forced cheerfulness.

There was no point in prolonging the moment; it had achieved all they wished it to. They turned and made their way to their rooms.

Rob and Tom said nothing to each other as they stripped and lay down. The lanterns extinguished, both lay silently awake. Sleep would not come to Rob. Despite the anticipation, he was in agony. All he was about to lose rose before him – this room with its cherished memories, the receding sounds of his beloved family as they settled in the tiny rooms around him, the hills he could see from his window with their hidden valleys that held the adventures of his youth.

He found his mind tracing all the contours of the farm, the furrows he had so often turned, the heat and dust of a high summer's harvest, the lowing of the cattle on a still, misty morning, the great oak by the stream under whose generous limbs he could spend an hour just absorbing the beauty of the valley beyond, and now the gracious, natural beauty of a woman, one whom he had never imagined would choose to spend a life with him.

All this he was letting go – for what? For a harsh, unknown land, for the uncertainty of strangers, for the perils of weather, beasts, men and for days of aching labour and loneliness. He had always prided himself on being resolute, calm in the face of difficulties, but now he was overwhelmed. He wanted to shout his pain, to turn the clock back to the days before he was even considering a move, to restore the familiarity, the stability of those earlier years when the biggest decision he had to make was which of the many tasks on the farm he would tackle first.

He must have groaned for Tom's voice came softly, "Rob, you alright?"

Rob lay silent before speaking. "I guess so, but I never thought it would be so hard to go. We are leaving so much behind." His voice caught. "I'll be alright in the morning." He forced his mind to review the hopes that had fuelled their decision to go – owning land, securing a future for his brothers and sisters, testing his manhood, carving out an abode in the wilderness for his love and their children, redeeming Tom's life. And slowly the sacrifices began to seem worthy and he slept.

They had picked up Agnes in the early hours of the morning, then taken the coach together to Edinburgh and the train to Glasgow. From there it was carriages from the station to Clydeside, the area along Scotland's largest river long famous for the great ships it built, ships that made Britain master of the seas, creating its far-reaching Empire of commerce.

119

As they approached the docks in mid-afternoon, the high masts of ships became visible, both those under construction and those taking on cargo for distant shores. The noise and activity were daunting, great drays stacked high with crates, shouts of anger or alarm, boys and men jockeying, pushing trolleys and carts, vendors hustling their wares, great buildings with smokestacks voiding black soot and here and there dispirited people waiting work or begging from other passers-by. They had visited Edinburgh but this was a far cry from the capital city's tidy streets.

It took many minutes for the carriage driver to find Rob and Tom's ship. As they approached, they could see three great masts and then a tall black smokestack sitting between two great round structures which housed paddle-wheels. It was *The Buenos Ayrian*, the ship that would transport them across the seas and its size was an immediate source of comfort.

It was due to sail in the early evening and was now loading its cargo. The family collected the men's cases from the carriages while Rob went to find those in charge of passenger entry. He was told where to place their trunks for loading into the hold and that passengers would be allowed on board in a few hours. They decided to take advantage of the time left to them to explore the dockyards further though Isobel was concerned that the younger children not stray and fall victim to the chaos of moving carts, cranes and horses.

It was a wholly different world that flowed around them; such crowds and such activity as they had never seen. People of all colours and races were dressed in ways that would never be seen on the country roads of Scotland, thrown up on this shore by the great ships that had carried them from across the world. Coarse-looking men hauled the cargo. They heard tongues they could not understand. All around were cases piled high bound for Bombay, New York, Sao Paulo; sheep and cattle sat penned awaiting shipment.

The children, wide-eyed, hovered close to their parents. Rob and Agnes were temporarily diverted from their sad preoccupation with the fading time left to them. It was a fitting introduction to the wider world that would be opening to Rob and Tom.

After an hour or so of walking, they spotted a crowded restaurant. It was time for a last meal together and Isobel urged the men to eat heartily before facing the ship's uncertain fare. No encouragement was required for the children after the appetite-stimulating action of the day. They lingered at the table as the only thing left to do was to return to the ship and see the men on board. Rob sat very close to Agnes, their arms and shoulders touching as though hoping to make permanent the memory of that physical connectedness.

At last the clock demanded their return. Back at the dockside, the family were allowed to accompany Rob and Tom on board to see where they were to spend the next twelve days. Isobel was disturbed at the crowded conditions that were evident in steerage – rooms with three double bunks, two up and two down, for a total of twelve people crammed in each, a dining area and lounge that was not much bigger than her own kitchen. They would not be allowed into the first and second class sections of the boat. Steerage passengers could access the lower decks, so there would be ample space to walk but living would be cramped.

"Thomas, we should have helped the boys with more money so they could have at least travelled second class," she said to her husband.

"Mother, there is no need to worry," said Tom who had overheard her comment. "This will be good training for conditions much harsher than this. We're heading to a frontier and we had better get used to the absence of home comfort. Besides, these close quarters will make for a better chance to get to know our fellow passengers," said Tom.

The ship's whistle blew three times, the signal that all non-passengers had to leave. Rob and Tom chose to get off the boat with them to say their goodbyes on the dockside. Isobel held on to her two men closely, her face contorted as she tried to suppress her grief. Thomas looked stern as he first shook their hands and then awkwardly put his arms around them. Each of the other children bravely kissed their brothers goodbye, the girls now openly weeping. Finally, Rob took Agnes in his arms, buried his face in her hair and held her a long time. "God be with you, my dear," she whispered to him, tears now tracing many a path down her face. They parted and the two men turned and walked up the gangway.

The ship's whistle blew a long blast. The stevedores unhitched the great ropes that tethered her, the smokestack belched and slowly the great paddlewheels began to turn. The ship veered away from the dock and moved into the mainstream. Rob and Tom appeared on the lower deck, arms raised in farewell. "We'll write often with all the details. And we shall see you all again, I'm certain of that," called Tom. Some of the family replied but the distance and the noise of the paddlewheels drowned their words.

Rob and Tom stood watching the shrinking figures on the dock until distance merged them with the crowd and they could no longer be distinguished. Rob set his face to the west, the widening river and the sea beyond, not yet visible but ever present.

He stayed for well over an hour watching green fields and villages slip by, sheep and cattle still visible, carriages on the road parallel to the river, the last signs of human activity they would see until they spotted the shores of Canada. The boat was beginning to roll slightly and he could smell salt in the air. Tom rejoined him just as they spotted the last headland that would bring Scotland to an end and launch them on to the Irish Sea.

Chapter
16

SUPPER THAT NIGHT WAS THEIR FIRST CHANCE TO MEET OTHERS TRAVELING steerage and a motley crew they were. The saddest were a couple with four children, none of whom seemed strong or healthy. They had lived in a tenement in Glasgow, the father earning barely enough to keep bread on the table. He had a brother in the Canadian west and hoped to provide a better future for his children, choosing the great uncertainty of the journey over the known certainty of life in a Glasgow slum. The little girls coughed continuously. Rob doubted they had the stamina to survive the trip let alone the harsh conditions on the frontier.

Another was a young bank clerk, pale and spare of limb, who wanted to farm in Canada. Rob could not see how either experience or physique suited him for the role. Tom got into conversation with a soldier who had recently returned from serving in India. He had a wealth of stories and Tom relished the future entertainment they promised during the long hours of the passage.

Supper was better than expected – beef, potatoes, thick chunks of bread, black tea. Rob spent most of the meal observing the interaction around him. He did not feel much like eating or talking, the ache of separation still acute. Tom, true to his nature, engaged in conversation and was soon the centre of a lively exchange with the other men, all of whom were caught up in the novelty of their surroundings.

Rob left the group to walk the deck, noticing for the first time the white caps of the waves hovering like restless ghosts in the increasing darkness. Then, though it was early, he headed for his bunk. He and Tom would share a lower bunk and had secured one against a wall that gave them some privacy. He had no idea who among the other passengers would be his roommates nor had he any intention of waiting to find out. There was insufficient light to read by so he took out his feather tick and pillow from the trunk he had in the cabin and was quickly asleep.

As he regained consciousness in the early light of the dawn, he saw for the first time the sleeping humanity around him. Tom was next to him and beyond lay the ten other men in varying, unflattering postures of sleep. The air was heavy with the night's odours. He moved swiftly to dress and get onto the deck and in the process woke his brother who joined him in escaping to fresh air. They could see land off to the left and concluded it must be Ireland's northern coast. The swells were larger now and Rob found he had to grab the bulwark at times to keep steady.

The morning meal was the same as the evening before but the beef was cold. Breakfast eaten, Rob recovered his life of Napoleon from his trunk and settled in for a morning's read on the deck as the small lounge was crowded and noisy. Tom tracked down the soldier from India to mine his adventures, remembering his own hopes of escaping the monotony of farm life by enlisting to serve the Empire in that far country. That seemed a life-time ago. His imagination reveled in the details of that exotic place.

Apart from the rolling of the ship, the day was highly pleasant, the sun bright on the waters and the slight winds surprisingly mild. Rob's mood remained reserved, processing inwardly the altered nature of his life. There would be time aplenty to make the acquaintance of his fellows. Reading about the small Corsican who single-handedly turned France and most of Europe on its ear, he concluded that the changes he was undergoing were insignificant in comparison to the whirlwind that had encompassed the lives of so many.

Evening arrived and it was delightful. The white caps had receded, the air remained warm and the sky was clear. He had never seen the myriad wonders of the sky shining with such intensity. From horizon to horizon the display was massive, but particularly the great belt of stars and planets winding across the sky in the

Milky Way. Here, on the open ocean, the grandeur was unbroken and immense. It made one feel small but at a deeper level, at one with an extraordinary mystery, at home in a vast universe.

Tom joined him as the evening wore on and the two of them sat on the deck, their backs against the bulkhead, quietly soaking up the spectacle. They were in no rush to return to the crowded bunk room and both must have fallen asleep. Rob was roused, he was not sure how much later, as the boat pitched heavily. The weather had turned abruptly. He woke Tom and both decided it would be prudent to return to their bunk.

By morning the storm had become much more intense. Several of his roommates had already voided their stomachs on the floor and the stench was foul. Staying in the bunk was not an option and the brothers made for the deck.

Now the sea seemed to be one solid white cap, the wind whipping the spray horizontally. The ship was both rolling from side to side and heaving stem to stern. Standing amidships seemed to expose them to the greatest movement. Tom suggested they retreat to the middle of the stern. There the rolling was minimal but the rise and fall of the stern was greater. Still, its timing was somewhat predictable and they could brace themselves for it. The great sails had been lowered and the paddle-wheels which were now the only means of propulsion spun noisily when the waves lifted them clear of the water.

They could only imagine what conditions would be like in the bunk room or the lounge and decided that the best place to ride out the storm was just where they were. Even if they died, it was better to die out here than in the stifling, stinking conditions inside. In time, several of the other men came to the same conclusion and joined them at the rail of the stern. By this time, Rob had lost what remained of his supper from the night before and had no desire to replenish his stomach. And so the day wore on, the density of the scudding clouds making the hours of its passage indistinguishable one from the other.

They had been told that the ship's average speed was about eight knots per hour but, with the sails stowed and the paddle-wheels often lifted out of the water, that speed must have been halved.. As the afternoon passed and the winds grew cold, the brothers were forced to take shelter indoors. They made for the lounge, there to sit on the floor leaning against the walls as the heaving of the vessel made perching on chairs impossible. No one was interested in food.

After a few hours, Rob decided to head for his bunk. But the odour in that enclosed room was so bad, he grabbed his pillow and tick, along with Tom's and returned to the lounge. There, at least, there was enough of a cross-draft to keep the air breathable.

The night passed fitfully. The next day was not much better as the storm continued to blow. If he and Tom were finding the passage so difficult, Rob wondered how others, more vulnerable, were faring. He had not seen the Glasgow family with their four pale children since the day the voyage began.

Finally on the third day, the winds began to abate and the men started to restore some order to their living quarters. The great waves generated by the storm lost some of their anger. They continued to approach in ordered progression but their predictability made the ship's roll more tolerable. Food was once again sought. Life resumed some normality for the brothers but it soon became apparent that this was not so for everyone. The father of the Glasgow family emerged to say that one of his daughters was gravely ill and needed the attention of a doctor.

For some years, British law had required that every ship carrying more than 100 passengers have a doctor on board. But as their passenger load was less, the only hope was that one of the other passengers had medical training. As no one in steerage had that advantage, Tom volunteered to enquire among the second and first class passengers. He returned empty-handed. The little girl had a high fever which had brought on convulsions. The brothers, having observed illness among their siblings and their animals, suggested that the parents soak sheets in cool water, wrap the child in them and attempt to bring her temperature down. The distraught father returned to his cabin grateful for the advice.

Later that afternoon the sound of weeping came from the room that housed the slum family. The fever was too advanced to be broken and had brought on another severe convulsion: the child was now dead. The precariousness of life, particularly on an indifferent sea hundreds of miles from help, now weighed on them all. It would be at least another ten days or more before they reached Canada as the storm had cost them at least two days of sailing. There was no option but to bury the child at sea, which, once explained to the mother, brought on another bout of pitiable wailing.

The next day, towards noon, the family emerged. The father carried the small bundle, wrapped in a sheet and placed it on the table in the lounge. The mother seemed shrunken, her hair disheveled while the remaining children hung around her skirts. As the steerage passengers gathered in the lounge, the ship's motors wound down and the forward momentum slowed. The captain had agreed to this as a gesture of respect. The persistent thudding of the engines that had been their constant companion for days went silent. Now there was only the sound of the waves around them and the creaking of the boat.

Rob had spent the morning preparing to say something that would give comfort to the grieving family. He turned to his mother's favourite psalm, introducing it saying, "We do not know why God puts such sorrow in our path, why He gives us the gift of a child whom we love so dearly, and then takes that gift away." The mother looked on, uncomprehending, perhaps unreachable.

He asked them to say the Lord's Prayer. A mumbled response came back broken by the sobs of the children. Then the father and Tom picked up the body and led the rest of them out onto the deck. The sea was calm, only a steady, gentle swell marking the passage of the waves' hills and valleys. The two men walked to the railing and lowered their burden by ropes the distance from the steerage deck to the waves.

The mother, now shaking with sobs, made as if to climb the railing and follow the sheeted object but was restrained by her husband, who held her tightly as the white being floated to the stern, the water overwhelming and beginning to submerge it. Rob turned to go back into the lounge followed by the rest of the passengers. The family stayed by the railing watching until their daughter could no longer be seen.

The following days passed without incident. Eleven days out, while the brothers were walking the deck in the evening, they saw a great white shape on the horizon. As the evening progressed, more and more of these ghosts of the night came into view, sighing and growling as the waves struck and moved their huge icy bulks. After a while the ship slowed to a crawl, it being too dangerous apparently to maintain customary speed through a field of icebergs. Fortunately, the night was clear and relatively calm making the presence of these menacing shapes almost benevolent. But there was always the risk of a berg lying so low in the water as to be barely visible, its vast underwater bulk ready to tear out the side of a ship.

The first mate happened by. "You're seeing something the captain says he has not seen in forty years of sailing," the man said. "You rarely see more than two or three of these cruel beauties at one time." Tom and Rob stayed on the deck, fascinated by the Arctic visitors, until the night was almost half through.

The next morning, waking late, they hurried outside to see the icebergs in full light. But their place had been taken by an immense sheet of ice that stretched to the horizon. The ship was not attempting to traverse it but seemed to be following parallel.

Later in the morning they heard that a major change of course had been required by this unusual phenomenon. Usually at this time of year it would be possible to pass into the Gulf of St Lawrence through the Strait of Belle Isle, that narrow passage between the up-stretched northern finger of Newfoundland and the coast of Labrador, but this was not to be. Instead *The Buenos Ayrian* would have to enter along Newfoundland's southern coast adding another couple of days to the journey, more days before they could get relief from the unrelenting sameness of their food and the crowded nature of their quarters.

Rob's interaction with the rest of the passengers had remained restrained while Tom had engaged most of them in as much conversation as each had been prepared for. He had struck up a particular friendship with another young Scot, Glenn Lyon Campbell, whose father, a retired Hudson Bay manager, was developing land in northern Manitoba. Campbell urged the brothers to join them where he assured them there would be lots of work that winter. Rob realized again that one of the great benefits of having Tom as a companion was his unending interest in other people. It was certainly going to smooth their way and assist them in getting help whenever they needed it.

Within a day of the ship turning course, they could see the coast of Newfoundland across the vast ice sheet but it was not until the ice had diminished and they were able to sail closer that they could see its characteristics. Great, high cliffs marked the edge, and beyond, rocky, barren hills covered only sparingly with stunted trees. It appeared hostile and forbidding like the most forlorn, isolated stretches of highland Scotland where nothing but bracken would grow. For the first time Rob began to wonder whether he had been chasing a dream. The cold wind, the ice and the barrenness of the shore eroded his confidence.

He walked the deck hoping the wind would dispel the gloom but his surroundings only deepened it. He finally retreated to his bunk and determined to engage Agnes in conversation, even if it was a one way affair, by writing his first letter. The letter would not begin its long journey to her until they reached port but it was the only way to unburden his soul.

He began cheerfully enough, sharing the sights and sounds of the preceding days but sparing the hardships of plain food and crowded quarters. Neither did he choose to tell her of the girl's death. No need to increase the anxiety which he knew Agnes and the rest of his family harboured.

But he could not avoid telling her of his disappointment with the first sightings of land on the other side of the Atlantic. He decided not to finish the letter until they were further on in the voyage and he had seen the banks of the St Lawrence River. "This whole journey has been embarked upon in faith – faith that we would find hospitable land on which to build our future, faith that we would have the common sense and strength to make our way into the unknown, faith that God would hold you and all the family safely in His hands until we return. Hence I continue in that faith.

"So while I miss you intensely and hardly an hour passes without your being in my thoughts, I remain resolute in the direction we chose. My heart is heavy at times, but that passes soon enough as I think of the challenges and surprises that lie ahead."

An hour or so of writing and he felt altogether different, almost as if she had been in the room with him. He folded the sheets carefully and sought out his brother.

They could sense the growing anticipation as the ship turned into the Gulf of St Lawrence and this vast, strange land began to unfold along the horizon. The ice had cleared and the seas were calm. To their south they saw more land, this time low hills, densely covered with endless trees. The ship was now traveling less than a mile off shore, close enough to see patches of land that had been cleared and here and there small cabins, and then larger wooden houses as villages emerged out of the forests.

Then as they gained entrance to the river itself, hills on both sides climbing the banks seemed to march on forever. By the dawn of the fourteenth day out of Glasgow they could see the high cliffs of Quebec City, its battlements standing guard, cannons pointing at them down river. Drawing closer, the city's tin rooftops gleamed in the morning sun.

That afternoon, east of Montreal, they stopped at a quarantine station where a doctor came on board. All the steerage and second class passengers were assembled on one deck behind a heavy rope and then, one at a time, were led forward to be inspected by the doctor. Some, judged to be sick, including the Glasgow family, were turned aside. They were told they had to disembark and spend time on a small island where quarantine quarters had been set up. The family, their faces dejected and fearful, seemed to lack the energy to question their fate and joined the others descending into the transfer boat with their few belongings.

The city of Montreal was surprisingly large with two and three storey buildings plentiful. The port, though smaller, had all the chaos and bustle of Glasgow. But everything was of wood – wood boats, wood buildings, wood sidewalks – and there was not a brick or stone to be seen.

It was well over an hour before they were permitted to disembark and directed to a low, log structure. Rob and Tom found themselves out on the street amidst milling crowds, gaunt horses pulling carts, wooden sidewalks and mud, mud everywhere spawned by the cold rain and churned by wheels, hooves and boots.

They unloaded their trunks against a building to protect them from the downpour. Rob sat on a trunk and observed the life surging around him. People were dressed in rough, rustic clothing, coarse wools, and rude cotton. Most were thin and pale, with the occasional dark-skinned individual, their faces surrounded by long black hair. Rob wondered whether this was the result of an arduous life and a harsh climate or inherent in their ancestry as most seemed to speak French. The cold, the rain, the mud and the stunted nature of the people reminded him again of his fears when he first saw Newfoundland's barrenness.

There were small inns around the dock area but also some houses with signs stating "Chambre a louer". They chose one of the latter and rented a room with one bed. The brothers offered it to Glen Lyon, who had decided to travel on with them, and found space on the floor using their coats and clothes as mattress.

The brothers found their spirits lower than any time since their departure from Glasgow. Perhaps it was the anti-climax of arriving at their destination when speculation was exchanged for reality. And the reality was unsettling – everything was rough and rustic, a far cry from the order and stability of home. It was as though survival did not allow for merit or quality. Beauty was sacrificed to function. In their limited interaction with the people of this land, they found them brusque and even hostile as though life had drained them of civility.

Propping themselves against the walls the three men considered their options. Glen Lyon was determined to proceed. He was assured of work and welcome by his father and had sufficient resources to make the journey in some comfort.

Rob and Tom counted their remaining money and realized they had just enough to buy passage back to Scotland. Perhaps that is what they should do. They did not yet know what train tickets to Winnipeg would cost so determined to make a final decision the next morning after visiting the station.

The next day dawned sunny and warm and the men made their way through the city. The streets were long and in the city's central area, paved with wood. All had names in both English and French. They noted a complete absence of the chimneys and factories that were a ubiquitous part of any Scottish city. They passed an enormous church, Catholic and French, that covered a good acre of ground. Stepping inside out of curiosity, they were amazed at its grandeur – ten-foot high candles and ornate carvings above its altar in striking contrast to the rough simplicity of the rest of the city.

It turned out the fare from Montreal to Winnipeg would be ten shillings more for each of them than the return passage to Scotland. If they proceeded to Winnipeg and continued to be disappointed, it would take many months' work to earn their passage back home. But Glen Lyon, who had spent his childhood in the wilderness at the various fur-trading posts with his father, encouraged them to go on saying that the life and the people in the west were far different from the sullenness they had encountered in this city.

Rob knew he could not return to Scotland without fully testing what the Canadian west had to offer. To do so would be to disappoint those he loved most and foreclose a freer life for them all. He and Tom agreed to buy the tickets and keep tightening their belts until they could secure work in Winnipeg or points further west. The next train left in less than twenty-four hours. Having been confined ship-board for two weeks and facing a further week of restriction on the train, they took the afternoon to climb the great hill above the city in the hope of regaining the fuller use of their atrophied limbs.

Chapter

17

IT WAS A SPECIAL TRAIN RESERVED FOR IMMIGRANTS. IT WAS SLOWER AND HAD fewer comforts than the regular runs, but was cheaper and left them with more money for food en route. There were no classes on the twelve cars as there were in Scotland – everyone was jammed in together.

Many of the windows had no glass so the hot smoke and soot often poured in, depending on the winds. The noise of the engine and the incessant ringing of its bell chasing dogs and horses and people off the tracks were constant companions of their waking hours and interrupted their sleep at night. Outside the towns, they were told that land was reserved for one mile on each side of the tracks to prevent speculators from profiting from its sale until such time as it could be auctioned off to real settlers.

Some of those on the train seemed to be prospective settlers from various parts of Scotland but by their dress and language, it was evident that many were from other countries across Europe – some Swedish, German, French – and then there were others whose languages were so strange their countries of origin could not be determined. Over time they discovered passengers who had been in eastern Canada for some years but had decided to move further west in the hopes of bettering their lot.

Rob saw nothing but trees until they came to an inland sea, so vast that it followed them for the better part of two days. And then more trees and large outcroppings of bare stone, until finally on the fifth day out of Montreal, the trees began to dwindle, the land opened up and the hills gave way to flat, treeless prairie where once again they saw settlements, fields yellow with wheat and green with corn, roads frequented by carts drawn by oxen or horses. The sight of this expansive farmland gave him the first assurance since they had first seen the bleak shores of Newfoundland that they had made the right choice. Towards late afternoon the train crossed a wood trussed bridge where two great, grey rivers, the Red and the Assiniboine, met and they were in Winnipeg.

The train slowed to a halt by a row of low sheds. Covered with dust, their faces besmirched with the shadows of soot, Rob, Tom and Glen Lyon descended onto the milling platform.

The urgent crowds, the mix of language and garb, the horse-drawn wagons and men straining behind carts reminded Rob of the Glasgow dockyard they had departed only weeks before. The hot afternoon sun brought to mind that they had not bathed since departing Montreal and finding a room and cool water became their first priority.

The principal street was the widest thoroughfare they had ever seen, sufficient surely for half a dozen carts to race side by side. To their further surprise they found it crowded with wagons drawn both by horses and oxen as well as individual riders and two wheeled buggies, as busy as any street they had seen in Glasgow or Edinburgh. In the summer's heat, clouds of dust rose behind the swift moving vehicles. This was a frontier town vivid with energy and growth.

Rob was not sure what he had expected but it was not this. Streets were lined with well-built wooden buildings, some three and four storeys tall. Here and there were stone edifices that would not have looked out of place in Edinburgh or even London. Banks, hotels, dry goods stores, clothiers, saloons, suppliers of farm machinery and equipment, grocers and ironmongers announced their readiness for commerce with brightly painted signs. The wooden sidewalks were crowded not just with the rough clothing of immigrants or farmers, but with the black felt hats of prosperous merchants and here and there the bouncing of long feathers perched atop hats of elegant women.

It was all fascinating and only their discomfort from the accumulated grime and sweat caused them to concentrate on finding accommodation. Enquiries at several hostelries along the way persuaded them they had to move towards the fringes of the town to find a room they could afford. They turned up a road called Selkirk and soon saw a good number of tents housing men and even families; though what these folk would do come the winter cold was anybody's guess.

A good half hour of walking found smaller dwellings, some of which advertised rooms. None had indoor washing facilities but they finally chose one run by an elderly woman with two young daughters. A walled courtyard at the side held a hand pump and provided a measure of privacy. They took turns at the pump stripping to their under garments while one stood watch at the courtyard entrance. Finally, clean and cool, they settled into a room with one bed, wide enough for two to share with one of the floor and considered their next step.

By this time Rob and Tom had barely enough money between them for a few days' provisions. Glenn Lyon insisted that they take some of his funds, assured that these would be returned as soon as the brothers joined him in the north. On the train they had learned that settlers who hired men for the harvest generally did not permit them to spend the winter as the severity of the climate inhibited farm work, so they determined that they would make their way north after some weeks and join their friend and his father clearing land during the winter months.

The task before them now was to find a meal and then obtain work for the immediate weeks ahead. Back on Main Street they found an establishment called the Davis House with long tables crowded with evening diners. They joined one where a lively conversation was underway between a man who was also a new settler and several others who seemed to be traders or drivers. Two of the latter, both smoking a strong blend which turned out to be red willow bark, were swarthy in complexion, dressed in blue coats with red sashes around their waists. Their accents were hard to place, a little French with a lilt of the Welsh, throaty but musical. They were describing how goods travelled before the railways and the steamers

"In de early days, travel to markets in de south was by Red River cart. Dese cart trains could be mile long and de sound deafening to de ears 'cause wooden wheels turned on poplar axles wit no grease."

These tall, bronzed men were Metis, offspring of the inevitable confluence of white adventurers, traders and Indian women.

The men's faces became more animated, reliving the days of their childhood. "In dose days, maybe six tousand carts go back and fort. At night, de carts dey form one giant circle and out come de drums and de fiddles and de prairie ring wit our songs and de shadows of our dancing, dey fly everywhere." His hands, which had never been still during the recounting, now flew into the air and then fell back onto the table.

"Dos days, dey gone forever wit de buffalo. Disappear before de streamers and de trains." Their faces reflected the loss more eloquently than any words.

"Where you from?" asked a burly man with a large red face turning to the brothers. Tom briefly recounted their month's journey. "Scotland, eh? Did you know that the first white men to settle these parts were Scots?" he asked rhetorically and with evident pride. "And my great granddaddy was one of 'em."

He told how the Earl of Selkirk, the great Thomas Douglas, who had journeyed to these parts with the Hudson Bay Company, had wanted the company to sell him the whole of the valley that the Red flowed through, an area five times the size of Scotland.

"The company turned him down flat. But that old Earl was not one to take 'no' lightly. So he persuaded his relatives and friends to buy up some 40% of the company's shares. With those in his pocket, he had the clout to get the company to part with the land he wanted. And so Manitoba began with Douglas and his settlers landing on the shores of Hudson's Bay at a place we now call York Factory in 1811.

"But the poor buggers," he continued shaking his head. "The

freeze-up came early that year and they were stuck on that God-for-saken shore all winter and would have perished to a man had the red man not come to their aid. Had my granddaddy not been young and stalwart, he would have left his bones by the bleak bay with the others."

Tom and Rob had almost forgotten their food, so rich was the conversation around them. It matched the vitality of the city they had noticed earlier and they spent what little remained of the day walking, absorbing the sights and sounds around them. At last, they returned to their room where they found Glenn Lyon had already booked passage on a steamer to a town called Portage la Prairie, eighty miles west of Winnipeg. From there he would join other travelers for the long journey up to the Riding Mountains. He would be leaving in the wee hours of the morning, so they bade him farewell, sorry to part company with this generous and knowledgeable friend.

The task the next morning was to find work. Their dinner companions had told them the best place to look was outside the General Store on Main Street and there they found a wide variety of signs seeking able-bodied men. The railroad needed them to lay tracks westward. House builders offered ten to 20 cents a day, depending on skill. But it was work on the farms that interested them most, providing the opportunity to learn from the experience of others in this new land.

One notice got their attention – a family named McKenzie was farming near Portage la Prairie. They were offering $10 a month plus room and board for work to the end of October. You could get to "Portage" by steamer along the Assiniboine River but that cost money they did not have and, in any case, they would learn much more about the land if they walked the distance. The route west was an old Indian trail that followed the north bank of the Assiniboine which settlers called the Great Highway or the Edmonton Trail. And so, at five o'clock the next morning as the day broke fresh and clear, they headed across town to the bridge over the Assiniboine and the trail westward.

18

OUT OF THE TOWN, THE TRAIL CROSSED FARMS ARRAYED IN LONG NARROW strips. Each fronted on the river giving access to transportation and water for irrigation. Some had been subdivided two and three times to provide land for sons and were as narrow across as one hundred yards – these, they learned, were called "farming lanes". Inland, the farms combined to form common pasture where stock could roam in the dry summer months.

The day was cool. They made excellent time in the morning but as the established farms dwindled, the land became a bog, soaking them well above their knees and making the going rough with the heavy packs on their backs. Those traveling the trail by cart did not do much better. Within the space of a couple of hours they came across 8 teams of horses mired in the mud.

Despite the toil, their spirits were high. They were headed west, finally off mechanized transport and on their own legs, overcoming the miles with muscle and for the first time feeling they could pit their worth against this raw and verdant country. By dusk, they estimated they had covered some fifteen miles and began to look for shelter. The evening lingered but the only human habitation they came across was a tepee some distance off the trail. At their approach, the women disappeared behind its flaps, the two remaining men watching them without moving. The brothers had seen the occasional Indian from the train or on the streets of Winnipeg but these were the first they had encountered at close quarters.

They tried making conversation but were met only with vacant stares. Rob gestured with his hand to his mouth hoping the men had meat to share and offered money. A solemn shaking of heads indicated refusal, their long, lined faces and scrawny torsos witness to their own scarcity. Rob put down his pack and retrieved a loaf of bread, offering this to the man closest to him. The man shook his head but a slight softening of his face perhaps hinted at appreciation. With no other means to communicate, the brothers turned and resumed their walk.

"I fear for these people," Rob commented. "They have lived on these lands for generations hardly leaving a trace of their passing. What chance have they to continue the life they are used to with so many of us crowding in upon them?"

"The sooner we educate them to our ways the better," Tom replied. "They're going to have to change or die."

"Don't jump to conclusions, Tom. From what we have heard, our people would not have survived on this continent in the beginning had they not been generous. We may find we still have something to learn from them."

The conversation died as the deepening shadows made finding a place for the night more pressing than winning an argument. A knoll of stunted oak offered them shelter after bread had stopped the hunger in their gut.

The following days offered easier travel, the land growing firmer under foot. Most nights they were able to sleep in settler barns on freshly mown hay. Somewhere along the way they made the acquaintance of the "greybacks", a particularly voracious species of lice and wished they had included a fine comb in their packs with which to hunt down and dispose of these fellow travelers.

They came across many others on the route, a few discouraged spirits returning east failing to realize their hopes on the open prairie. "T'isn't a country for such as are up in years," said a man about their father's age. He and his wife had been "swithering" as to whether to try for another year but could not face the coming winter. But most were heading west still pursuing whatever dream that sustained them.

They overtook another family, the Grahams, who were twelve

in number, traveling from Ontario where cleared land was now expensive, a hundred acre farm costing some thousands of dollars. Most settlers were reluctant to break the heavy bush when open land was still available on the prairie. Among the twelve were great grandparents, aged 99 and 101, sitting quietly on a cart, taking life as it unfolded. They would later learn that the grandfather had died a day before they reached Portage la Prairie and his simple cross joined the others along the trail.

On the fourth day they reached Portage, a few dozen dwellings and stores. In the centre of the town stood a handsome two storey granite building with windows as tall as one would find in a large town in Scotland. Some were obviously doing well enough to replicate the kind of structures that marked the prosperous back home.

After enquiring, the brothers learned that the McKenzie farm, "Burnside", stood at Rat Creek, a further eight miles west of the town. Further, they discovered that Kenneth McKenzie was not only a prosperous farmer but had been recently elected a member of the Canadian parliament.

They began to walk to "Burnside" the next day. The land lay prone to the horizon, as it had throughout the last four days, a narrow strip with the heavens immense and cloudless above. It was almost as if the sky possessed the land, favouring the winged creatures, while those dependent on legs and feet were relegated to inferior status.

Initially the brothers had thought the landscape dull. But as they walked, its subtleties became increasingly apparent. Bending willows dipped in the sloughs, dark green marked copses of trees where a depression in the land offered slight protection from the unceasing wind. The latter made its presence known in the undulating grasses and the alternating whine and shush of its blowing, strong and soft. Beauty was both in the grandeur, which first captivated the eye, and in the small details of life at your feet.

Colonies of small furred creatures scurried among the grasses or stood at the entrance to their burrows. Hawks hunted from their aerial abode, diving to the prairie below and ascending with some small creature struggling in their talons. And here and there a handsome black bird with a long black and white tail, strutted proud in its profile. And then, as they had walked the high bank of the river, a row of large grey birds with ponderous beaks, almost a third the size of their bodies, flew parallel to them. The birds flew in perfect formation, each the same distance from the other and their great wings flapping in unison. It was as though they had been drilled to perform.

"Burnside" welcomed them heartily when they arrived mid-afternoon. The large, motherly wife of McKenzie was clearly relieved to have additional hands to address the coming harvest. The men of the family and the hired hands were off working the land but she showed them to quarters above the stables where the brothers found beds made of strung rope on which they could lay straw and their bedding. She told them that the evening meal would be at half past five and that they could use the time before to settle in.

The house was a handsome two storey wood structure with a garden before and back. Flowers graced its front and a fenced area showed a fine array of vegetables, many of them ready for the eating. Around the yard rows of young trees would, in time, provide much-needed shelter from the blasts of winter. It appeared the family had been there for several years.

Rob and Tom were delighted at their good fortune. Within an hour they heard the men returning from the fields and were shortly joined by three bronzed young men, the occupants of the other beds in their attic. One was from Ireland and the others from Ontario. All had been with the McKenzies since planting time in the spring.

The young men informed them that they would eat the evening meal and then return to the fields for another two hours before the work of the day was done. Then tea would be served with "accompaniment" and all would turn in as the next day started very early.

As the brothers made their way into the kitchen of the main house they were surprised to see that all ate together around a long oblong table, McKenzie, his wife, two sons, a daughter and the five hired men. They appeared to be a religious family as the meal was begun with prayer. The food was plentiful – bread and sweet butter, beef, potatoes, beet root, stewed apples and molasses, all washed down with tankards of milk. McKenzie, a larger version of his wife, lively and forthright in his expression, was still very much the frontier farmer despite the role he now played in the capital, Ottawa.

He had come from the Highlands of Scotland some 30 years earlier and had originally owned land in the area which was now Portage. He had made some eighteen thousand dollars – a fortune – by selling his original holdings to speculators as the town expanded and moving west to the land he currently held. When he had first started he told them, a man could acquire as much land as he could plough a furrow around in a twenty-four hour period. McKenzie began at the stroke of midnight and having lined up a spare team of oxen, had stayed at it until he collapsed of exhaustion just prior to midnight, twenty-four hours later. He was proud of that initial two thousand acres and over the years had purchased much more. He and his accomplishments seemed larger than life to the brothers who saw in them fresh evidence of what this new land could bestow in exchange for hard work and a measure of good luck.

Now, however, the same rules did not apply. Raw land could be acquired free – but only 160 acres for each man or head of a family – provided it was ploughed and a habitation built on it within three years. But beyond that "quarter section", land had to be purchased.

The men were mowing hay and transporting it to low wooden structures for winter storage. The long cold months demanded that much forage be put away to sustain the cattle who spent the winter in the open but could not get enough nourishment on the open range.

Those with narrow river lots had to venture out on the prairie to cut their hay on unclaimed land. An intricate protocol governed how and when such hay could be gathered. To give every family a fair chance, a common day was picked before which no hay could be cut, but some tried to secure the best hay meadows by cutting a swath with a scythe around the meadow before the fixed day. Families would stay out on the prairie for the whole week, returning to their homes on Saturday night as there was no cutting on Sundays.

Anyone carelessly causing a prairie fire that endangered the supply of hay was seen as virtually a criminal. One year, he recounted, when fire destroyed one family's stacks, neighbours delivered one hundred cartloads of hay – such was the prevailing spirit of community among people who had risked everything to better their lives.

McKenzie's two boys were in their mid-teens and mostly silent around their father. The daughter, Elizabeth, was made of livelier stuff. She would have been close to twenty years of age, tall of stature, with striking red hair and was obviously her father's favourite. She engaged Rob and Tom in conversation without hesitation, peppering them with questions about their journey. Rob responded briefly but Tom warmed to the opportunity. The young woman, though not in any way forward, seemed to have little idea of how attractive she was to young men who were a long way from home and had had no female companionship for weeks on end.

Dinner finished, they followed the other men to a horse-drawn wagon that returned them to the hay fields in the gathering evening.

The next morning, Mrs McKenzie wakened the men by shouting from the stables below. The light from her lantern cast shadows across the room as she climbed the stout ladder to place it in the doorway. Rob reached for his clock on the floor – four-thirty. He couldn't believe it as he sank back on the bed.

"The man's a true Scot," he grumbled as he pulled on his clothes in the morning chill. "He's going to get every bit of work out of us that he can in return for our wages."

But the breakfast was generous – large bowls of porridge, bread, jams, more stewed apples with molasses, milk and tea. The McKenzies understood that to get the most out of their hired help, good food was essential. They were out on the fields as dawn was brushing the eastern horizon, working the mowing rig on the uncut meadows and turning the grass that had been cut the day before with a horse-drawn rake. McKenzie's horses were stalwart creatures, much larger than the Indian ponies that served to pull the carts on the road. Rob noticed that the horses were unshod, likely because of the absence of stones anywhere in the fields or along the trails.

Once the sun was high enough to burn off the night dew, the men turned to pitching the long rows of dried hay on to a wagon for transport back to the storage sheds. Several hours of this heavy arm and shoulder work were enough to show the brothers the price they had paid for a month of no labour with their bodies. When the women brought out buckets filled with food for lunch, they collapsed in the shade of the mowing rig, glad to give their arms a break.

The field they were cutting was not far from the trail and they had seen several groups of people heading west. Some travelled in wagon trains of 15 or more carts loaded with implements and hauled by oxen or Indian ponies, with their stock of cows, oxen and horses trailing behind. The wagons were usually covered with white canvas to keep off sun and rain. At nightfall, one or more of these groups would turn up at the farm. There they and their animals would be fed and housed in the barns for the night and then sent on their way with no money changing hands.

Sunday came and Mrs McKenzie extended an invitation to come with them to church. The brothers agreed, though the three younger men chose to stay abed. They rode the eight miles back to Portage where a sizeable crowd gathered in a white-washed, wooden Presbyterian church. The minister was a Scot and the brothers remarked that a finer sermon could not be heard in Scotland.

Following an excellent lunch, Rob and Tom had the rest of the day to themselves. Rob immediately retired to the loft to write home "a guidish screed" and began his letter to his parents and siblings. "Here are the two of us far away across the sea looking about to find a home for ourselves in a strange land who not over seven weeks ago had a home which could not be surpassed."

He quickly told them of their good fortune in finding the farm of a member of parliament though "what would any of our members think if they were sitting beside another member at tea to see him throw the dregs and leaves on the floor before getting another cup." He recounted the success that met the McKenzies efforts of many years. "They have no fear of the rent falling due and have nothing to pay; all that grows is their own. One can plough two and one-half acres a day with a good hock of horses, then just give it a scratch with a harrow, sow the seed and it needs no more til harvest time. The soil here has amazing fertility. They say you can plant and harvest for several years before having to fertilize. We have seen potatoes the size of your hand, weighing some four pounds. It returns many times over the labour you put into it."

Chapter

19

THE DAYS FOLLOWED ONE ANOTHER IN HARD LABOUR. THE BROTHERS SOON were able to keep up with the other men, relishing their recovery from the weeks of enforced idleness. They observed the land closely, noting the varying shades of the soil and which ones seemed to produce the heaviest crops. They sought every chance to engage McKenzie and his sons in conversation about what they had learned farming this prairie land

The brothers looked forward to their evening meals with the family. Conversation was lively and they could see how well-informed their employer was about events that went well beyond Portage and its environs. One evening he brought the news that there was likely to be conflict in the Northwest Territory. Towns had begun to form, paddle-steamers were plying the South Saskatchewan River and the railway was pushing into the southern part of the territory. The Metis farmers who had sold their lands or been expelled from the Red River valley following the rebellion some years earlier, had moved west and north and established new settlements. Some among them had allied themselves with the Plains Cree and the Salteaux Indians who were becoming ever more restive as more and more settlers moved into their territory.

Treaties had been entered into with several of the tribes, who, with the disappearance of the buffalo, had retreated to specific sites set aside for them and survived principally on provisions from government agents. Others had rejected negotiations outright, refusing to recognize any claim on the lands that had been theirs for a thousand generations. It was these groups who were aligning with disgruntled elements among the Metis and challenging Canadian authorities.

McKenzie had strong views on the subject. Large numbers of American Sioux had fled north of the border following a long campaign against them by the US Cavalry and it was thought that these Sioux were intent on making joint cause with the rebellious Cree. "Local authorities can no longer protect the settlers from these threats. It is high time Her Majesty's forces became engaged. If we do not act, we will find the American cavalry will act for us. I fear more the presence of American troops on British soil, in the long term, than I do the disruption of some wild Indians today."

Rob was curious about the arrangements that had been made with those who had agreed to treaties. Apparently, the land that had been reserved for them was a fraction of the lands they had once roamed. McKenzie said they had the right to continue to hunt on their old territories as long as those lands were not needed for settlement or farming. In that case it appeared the settlers' claims took priority under the treaties.

The parallels to the enclosures in Scotland were all too apparent in Rob's mind. "But don't you see that we are doing to them exactly what the lairds did to our fathers and grandfathers," he said hotly one evening. "They justified robbing thousands of their homes and livelihoods because they thought they could make a better profit from sheep than from rents. You want our government to do the same thing so that the prairie grass can be ploughed under and the land sown with wheat."

Tom took McKenzie's side. "Anything that can make the land more productive is justified in my books," he said. "These tribes have far more land than they need. Why should landless people like us be denied an opportunity so that some savages are free to chase buffalo hither and yon? The world is changing. Once we have shown them how to farm and helped them get a start, then we have every right to the land that is in excess."

Tom seemed to rest easy in the assumption that the civilization he represented could only benefit those it encircled even if their transition to it was highly disruptive. If that were so, then surely they should be doing much more to ease that transition. Rob welcomed sleep at the end of exhausting days as a means of quieting these thoughts.

The summer skies were now a relentless blue and the wheat that had been sown the previous spring was growing tall and filling out. With the first hay crop cut and in the barns, the brothers were tasked with breaking prairie that had not as yet tasted the plough. It was their first experience using oxen and they marveled at the strength and benign temperament of the beasts.

They were shown how to "break" the land by turning over the top two inches of soil in twelve inch strips and then "back-setting" it by ploughing between the strips to turn the undersoil to the top. It was arduous work but the oxen seemed tireless. Unbroken land had to be ploughed the summer or fall before it was seeded in the spring. And with the growing season relatively short, seed needed to get in the ground as early as possible.

The late summer came and with it the demanding task of reaping and threshing the huge wheat harvest. Horse-drawn reapers and rakes cut and moved the stalks into furrows. Then came the backbreaking work of gathering the stalks by hand into armfuls, tying them up and stacking them into stooks to dry thoroughly before being gathered onto wagons and carried to the threshing floor.

Their days began before dawn and continued as the hot sun rose in a cloudless sky and the dust rose from the machines and penetrated the scalp and every pore. Lunch was taken in the field in whatever shade could be found, usually under the machinery. In the late afternoon, the pump behind the barn that sourced water for the animals was off limits to the women and children while the men stripped down to wash off the fine silt before sitting down to supper. Exhaustion muted conversation and food was consumed quickly before they returned to the fields until the sun's setting made work no longer possible.

With the harvest coming to a close, the days becoming shorter and the sun weaker in the sky, the brothers began to plan their journey north. First, they had to make a trip to Winnipeg to pick up the trunks stored on arrival and to buy a pair of oxen and a cart. As time was short, they took a horse-drawn coach from Portage to Winnipeg.

Their most pressing errand, before the purchase of the ox and cart, was the retrieval of mail. Before leaving Scotland, they had discovered the address of the general post office in Winnipeg and told Agnes and their parents that they would be able to get mail at this address. The prospect of hearing from those at home was more pressing than the hunger that had been gnawing at their bellies since their arrival. The excitement at finding four letters was unbounded. Two were for Rob in Agnes' hand writing and the others for both of them, one from Isobel and the other from Peter and Hermione.

They fled the crowds down to the banks of the Red. Rob felt himself trembling as he opened the first letter from Agnes. Her tight, neat lettering spelled out exactly what he wanted to hear – that she was well, that she thought of him constantly and prayed for him nightly. She had enrolled in her courses in Edinburgh. "I travel with you so often in my mind's eye. I imagine I see what you see, smell what you inhale be it the fresh winds of the ocean or the rich odour of virgin forest. I live your every experience as though I were right beside you until I realize with sorrow that I cannot touch you anymore. And then I cry softly and hope my tears might be a blessing for you."

The second letter written from Edinburgh showed that the course work was filling the void his departure had left. Its tone was less fervent, the intensity replaced by the recounting of arrangements for her stay in Edinburgh – a description of her boarding house, of her initial impression of her teachers and fellow students. It was breezy and optimistic and though he was deeply moved by the tone of her first letter, he was equally reassured by the second that her life was moving on and that she was happy.

Tom was reading the letter from his mother, exclaiming and laughing as he digested the news. They had made another excellent sale of cattle at the latest auction. Peter had stepped up to the plate and was filling much of the void his elder brothers had left. Isobel was ever cheerful, ever encouraging. She said their father seemed in much better health and that even the younger boys were showing greater maturity, willingly taking on tasks that previously they had resisted.

Peter and Hermione's note was full of youthful questions and concluded with "put your arms around each other every night and imagine all the rest of us being there to bless and encourage you."

The brothers, having finished their reading, lay back on the bank in a state of high relief. A feeling of completeness, of being connected again, suffused their thoughts as they gazed at the clear sky through the high green branches of the surrounding Manitoba maples. Then the hunger pangs returned and they broke the reverie to address more immediate needs.

The next morning, they could hear the bellowing of the animals well before arriving at the auction barn. There was a rush of the familiar as they wandered amongst the wooden pens where scores of beasts milled about, the aisles thronged with potential buyers. The section with oxen displayed six pair and several single animals. Most looked robust with much work left in them. They favoured a pair, one largely cream-coloured with a brown patch on its face, the other mottled brown and white. Their names were Pete and Old Harry, according to their current owner.

The oxen did not come up for bidding until the early afternoon but the prices they went for were considerably higher than the brothers had expected, reflecting the demand for these beasts so well suited for frontier conditions. Rob and Tom ended up spending sixty-five dollars for the pair which was almost a third of their summer's savings.

A cart was procured next, then a camp stove, frying pans and nails from Ashdown's. They loaded these items and the trunks and were back on the Great Western Road by dusk. Conditions on the trail were much better than they had been two months before as the hot Manitoba sun had dried out the wetlands and the mosquitoes had vanished. They were back at "Burnside" two and a half days later.

The next morning dawned clear. They woke with the rest of the men at 4:30, ate a hearty breakfast and packed the wagon, Mrs McKenzie supplying them with a large quantity of food for the journey. The men had left for the fields before they took to the road.

The main trail west passed the northern border of the farm and they headed for the settlement of Minnedosa at which point the trail turned north. They could see low houses either side of the trail every mile or so. The sun was warm, the breeze cool and the trees turning a brilliant yellow; the brothers' spirits were high as Pete and Old Harry kept a steady pace westwards.

By late afternoon they were approaching Minnedosa when they came across a tent with a sign announcing the availability of food. From it emerged a man who said his name was Sewell and that he made his living cooking rabbit and prairie chicken for passing settlers. The price of the meal was twenty-five cents and the brothers decided to partake with the intent of querying Sewell about the territory as much as sampling his cooking skill. He warned them to watch for the weather which this time of year could change abruptly with bitter cold and even snow sweeping down from the north. Several travellers had been caught this time the previous year in such a storm and with the early coming of winter, their frozen bodies had not been discovered until the spring.

Thanking him for the warning and the food, Rob and Tom continued towards the settlement. There they found a warm bed, the best they agreed they had had since leaving Abbeylane, with a feather mattress below and tick above and a full breakfast for $2.50 each. But the following morning the temperature had dropped substantially and the sky was a slate grey. Their host urged them to remain in Minnedosa in case a storm materialized. They chose to continue north as the trail was well marked and there seemed to be a settlement every few miles but decided to don winter clothing – a woollen shirt, a pair of woollen drawers and trousers and over them, duck pants. "Now let's see what the weather throws at us," said Tom in playful defiance.

The trail was well established but it passed terrain pockmarked with hundreds of small ponds that would make farming difficult. Their destination for the night was the settlement of Beautiful Plains which would give them seventy miles in the two days since leaving Burnside.

Within the hour the wind began to blow, sharply increasing the cold and then the snow came. At first it danced lightly around them but it rapidly thickened and as the wind picked up speed, it was driven almost horizontally into their faces, stinging as it came. Not many minutes passed until the landscape around was coated in white making the trail difficult to discern from the surrounding land. They quickly marked its direction in the distance seeing that it passed close by a thicket.

As the trail only seemed to change direction to avoid obstacles, they decided that after the thicket they would continue going straight. They could still see where the passage of carts and people had flattened the vegetation creating a small dip in the landscape that was now entirely snow covered. The oxen, heads lowered against the driving snow, fortunately seemed to sense the trail's presence and plodded on. There was no alternative but to continue forward in the hope that out of the looming darkness of the sky and the curtains of white that now whirled around them, some form of shelter would emerge.

It was too cold to ride in the cart. Walking was the only way to generate warmth but their boots quickly became frozen and it felt as if their feet were encased in iron. In the distance, as the wind shifted, they could hear the prairie wolves howling but all else was as silent as death. Were there not such a thing as hope in the human breast, how dark would be the path of man, Rob thought to himself.

They must have continued this way for a couple of hours, and the snow which was now up to the knees of the oxen, had wiped out anything that distinguished the trail from the surrounding landscape. The danger of finding themselves lost in a white desert was now grave. A patch of trees loomed up out of the white and they made their way to them. In their shelter, they placed the cart astride the sweep of the northwest wind and unhitched the oxen and tied them to the leeward side of the cart. Wrapping themselves together in their bedding, they stood between the beasts to keep warm, their backs to the gale.

Rob had never thought of the oxen as anything other than a means of transportation and ready labour. Now as he leaned against Old Harry's broad side and rested his arms on his back, he saw why these great beasts were so valued on the frontier. Their strength and placid nature warmed him and gave him the assurance that they could survive the night ahead. He pulled his arm out of the bedding and rubbed the beast's neck.

They had to keep moving their legs during the night to maintain circulation so they decided that they would take turns dozing while the other remained awake. If they both slept, they feared they might never waken. For the first time since they left Scotland, Rob was fearful for their survival. Even in facing the brute forces of nature that the sea had thrown at them, he never doubted that they would get through. This threat was far less dramatic but infinitely more sinister.

As he strove to keep awake while Tom dozed, Rob evoked his fondest memories of Scotland; first and foremost the face of his beloved Agnes, calling forth the texture of her hair, the profile of her chin and neck, and this warmed him. Then he envisaged each of his family, seeing them seated at dinner or riding to town in the wagon. Next he forced his mind to walk through all of Abbeylane's fields, imagining their look from one season to the next, the quiet barrenness of winter, the furrows unfolding as the plough broke the spring ground, the tiny shoots of green that emerge above the furrows, so brave, so hopeful, the rippling waves as the maturing grain caught the wind and imitated its passing.

With a fierce buffet of wind, he was brought back to the desolate world around him, the endless, cold plains, indifferent to man and his memories. He had to keep at arm's length the terror that they too would be discovered in spring, their bold venture frozen by a heartless climate and young men's rash ignorance.

It was time to waken Tom who was standing at his side up against the animal. He put his arm on his shoulder and shook him. No response. Rob grabbed the shoulder and shouted into his ear. Tom mumbled, shifted his weight and slowly shivered into consciousness. He was very confused. Rob suggested they walk around together to get their circulation flowing and be sure he was awake. Tom was very lethargic, very close to sleeping again. Rob decided it would be too risky for him to sleep and that their best chance was to keep each other awake until the light of dawn enabled them to assess their options.

Rob began recounting the memories of their old home that had given him comfort earlier in the night and then he challenged Tom to see who could remember the greatest detail of their home and farm. The device worked. Tom rose to the occasion and became more animated as each detail was described. "What in God's name are we doing in this desolate wilderness? How could we have been so foolish to leave behind all those cherished places and people?" Tom growled. "We should leave this desert to the red man. No wonder he has no time for the finer things of life, trying to survive this abomination."

Rob was determined to keep fear at bay, but with no idea of how far the night had passed and how long they would be trapped in white blackness, he did not want to fall asleep and never wake up without saying some things to his brother. "Tom, we share the same flesh and blood and I want you to know that I love you."

Tom was taken aback. "Och, yeah, I love you too."

"Tom, there's something I want to say just in case we don't make it. I've ---- I've envied your ability to mix so well with folk, to always find the right words. There have been times when I have been jealous of you because you had what I wanted. At those times I did not wish you well and took pleasure in your difficulties. If we don't get through this, I want to ask your forgiveness for such an ungenerous spirit."

Rob did not know if the tears he shed were from the cold or the emotions that surged through his body. Tom turned to him, "Oh Rob. You're such a fine man. You don't know the number of times I wished I had your strength and your peacefulness. We are quite a pair but we have been there for each other in the past and here we are again. We are all each of us has right now." He reached over and held Rob in his arms. The bedding they were wrapped in fell off with this exchange, but they let it fall and held each other for what seemed many minutes.

"It's blasted cold. If we don't stop this slobbering, they'll find us in the spring a pair of frozen statues," Tom said and reached down to pull up the protective wrapping.

They were silent and then Tom began to sing, slowly at first.

I have heard the mavis singing his love song to the morn.
I have seen the dew-drop clinging to the rose just newly born;

Rob joined him in the sentimental, old ballad to Mary of Argyle, the pace quickened and the volume rose.

But a sweeter song has cheered me at the ev'ning's gentle close
And I've seen an eye still brighter than the dew-drop on the rose.
T'was thy voice my gentle Mary and thine artless winning smile,
That made this world an Eden, Bonnie Mary of Argyle.

"Well, this God-forsaken spot has never heard anything as sweet as that," said Rob, sensing the power of the music to lift their spirits. "How about this wondrous song:

The Lord's my Shepherd I'll not want
He makes me down to lie,
In pastures green he leadeth me,
The quiet waters by."

And Tom joined him, his base voice resounding over the stillness. And so the last hours of the night passed, neither man sleeping, but talking together and taking turns to pick loved songs. At long last the eastern horizon began to shade grey. The snow stopped and as the light illumined more of the sky they could see the deep prairie blue returning to it.

"Och, the sun will be our ally today and we will find our way to some habitation," said Tom hopefully. The snow was deep but not impassable. The trail, however, was invisible both ahead and behind though they knew the direction from whence they had come. "If I were the first to cut this trail, I would proceed directly ahead," said Rob. "We are just going to have to risk it. At least the visibility is good and we should be able to see any settlements."

They hitched the oxen and Tom walked in front leading them. But this was the first time they had been exposed to a prairie sun that was reflected back from a snow canvas. It did not take long for their eyes to begin to water and to burn. They had to bring their headgear low on their foreheads and squint into the glare. Then they noticed that the oxen were suffering even more from the snow blindness. Their eyes became enlarged and emitted a stream of water. They stopped and pulled an old shirt out of their pack, tore it into two strips and tied them to the oxen's horns so that their eyes would be shaded.

Then they saw a pair coming toward them, a woman riding a small horse accompanied by a tall man on foot. As they approached, they could see that the woman was Indian and the man possibly Metis. Both parties were eager for information. The Metis was half Scottish, introducing himself as Canning. The woman watched them from her seat atop of the horse but said nothing.

The two had left Beautiful Plains yesterday, but sensing the power of the coming storm, had spent the night in the barn of a homestead a mile or so behind them. Canning assured the brothers they would receive a warm welcome should they want to recover from their night in the open. After they had left, Rob commented to Tom, "The mix of Indian and Scottish blood produces a fine breed. You can see the wild blood in his veins by the look in his eyes, but a more civil and pleasant fellow you could not wish to meet. He has the mark of nobility about him whether from his white or red blood."

They soon spotted the homestead far enough off the trail that they would have easily missed it in the blizzard. By the time they reached its door, both brothers were weak from hunger and the effort needed to wade through the snow. Their knock was answered by a young man, clearly startled by their appearance. He pointed to where the oxen could be tethered and where feed could be found and then told them to come back in while he made some food.

A fire in an open chimney hearth was boiling oats and frying smoked bacon when they returned. As they hastily shed their outer clothes, the young man, Thomas Wilder by name, asked if they suffered any frostbite. Noticing their confusion at the meaning of this term, Wilder asked whether any of their extremities were numb and both brothers realized that they could not feel several toes.

Wilder hastily went outside and collected snow in a pail, added water and instructed them to immerse their feet. This seemed mad to the men, but he assured them it was the only way to reverse the process safely. Within minutes, Rob and Tom were in excruciating pain as their feet began to thaw.

Wilder gladly agreed to their request to spend the day and next night with him so they and their oxen could regain their strength. He clearly relished the company. On their departure the next day, Rob offered Wilder payment for their food and lodging. The man refused.

They passed through Beautiful Plains a couple of hours later but saw no need to stop. Their destination for the night was the village of Elphinstone on the banks of the Little Saskatchewan River. From there they were less than a day's travel to Glen Lyon Campbell and his father.

The Little Saskatchewan, when they reached the low hills overlooking it, was no more than a frozen stream. The village nestled on its northern bank and consisted of a Hudson Bay trading post called Riding Mountain House, and a new saw mill and grist mill. The two mills were powered by a giant stationery steam engine, standing black and alien on the banks of the stream, belching clouds of white smoke and making an ungodly clatter as they approached. This time of year its giant belts were powering the grist mill. As winter lessened its hold, the engine would run the saw mill, cutting the winter-felled timber that arrived in the spring on the swollen Little Saskatchewan. The mill had been built by a Scot, a Mr Iredale.

They later learned that this monster had been cast and constructed on the banks of the Clyde in 1851. It was then transported by ship to the shores of Hudson Bay and carried miraculously by boat through the myriad rivers and lakes of the wilderness down to Fort Ellice from whence it had been hauled across country by a train of three pairs of oxen.

If anything demonstrated the determination of the Scots to profit from the resources of this wilderness, the saga of the steam engine did this.

Tom and Rob stayed only long enough to replenish supplies from the small general store and enquire about the route to the Campbells. They were directed to follow a dirt road that skirted Kesk-oo-wee-ne-we, a large reserve of Ojibwa Indians. Three hours later, cold and tired from the long days of travel, they arrived at the Campbells' quarter section of land, its entrance marked by the faded insignia of the Hudson Bay Company, a flag with the Union Jack in the upper left-hand corner and the letters HBC resplendent on a red background. Robert Campbell, Glen Lyon's father, had been chief factor for the Swan River District which included Elphinstone. He had worked for the company for decades, opening up the Yukon and establishing posts before retiring to Elphinstone in 1871.

Young Glen Lyon came bounding out of a large log building to greet his friends, ushering them into the warmth of the cabin and introducing them to his father, an old but still vigorous man. The cabin had two storeys and they were showed up a wooden ladder to a large upper room warmed by the rising air from the iron stove below. Over hot tea, Glen Lyon plied them with questions about their journey, his eyes wide with the horror of their night in the open between the flanks of the oxen. "You can thank those beasts for saving your lives," he told them. "We would never have been able to conquer the wilderness but for the patience of the ox and the knowledge of the red man."

Campbell father and son were pleased with additional help. They were clearing land with the intent of ploughing and seeding in the spring. They would cut rail fences and haul excess logs to the Little Saskatchewan that ran through the neighbouring quarter section. The addition of the oxen was a signal advantage and they offered the brothers together a wage of forty dollars a month plus room and board for their labour and the use of the oxen.

The weather remained clear but cold. Snow lay on the ground, the trees retaining most of their golden leaves though each day more fell to be hustled by the breezes into little piles of fading yellow. Harnessing the oxen in the morning under the blue sky and setting out through the forest with the early winter sun accentuating the colours, the brothers' spirits were high. Evenings did not last long, perhaps enough to consume a page or two of Napoleon's life or the dense prose of a Shakespeare play before sleep made further reading impossible.

Rob set about to write his parents. "This land has the old country beat. No muddy boots, wet feet, no slush and sleet one day and rain the next. Just a steady frost and clear skies day after day and night after night until the ground is locked hard and the rivers and lakes are solid ice.

"I can boast, and not without sufficient reason, for being honoured with a noble sized proboscis. But in Manitoba it becomes a question of whether such a possession is an advantage. In summer it offers extensive domain for the mosquitoes to work upon and when winter, with its biting breath reigns supreme, my poor nose becomes a victim to Jack Frost."

They had not been three weeks into their work when Glen Lyon came riding out to where they were cutting, panic in his face. His father had collapsed in the field behind the cabin and he needed one of them to ride to Elphinstone to fetch the doctor. Tom climbed on the horse behind the young Campbell and the two of them set

160

off back to the cabin. Rob turned the oxen and followed as quickly as possible. When he arrived, Tom had already left for help and Rob assisted Glen Lyon in carrying his father into the cabin and making him as comfortable as possible. The old man had lost consciousness but was still breathing. There was nothing they could do but keep him warm and wait. But to no avail. Before Tom and the doctor returned, old Mr Campbell had stopped breathing.

Chapter

20

THEY BURIED THE OLD MAN UNDER A LARGE MANITOBA MAPLE SOME TWENTY yards behind the house where the ground had not yet frozen solid. Had he died a month later, they would have had to keep the body in the barn until spring once again made the earth able to be breeched.

The winter's work still had to be accomplished. Glen Lyon kept his mourning to himself, redoubling the energy he applied to cutting trees. The brothers were glad to be there to support him. Tom and Glen Lyon manned the axes, felling the aspen, stripping the branches while Rob bundled them and hitched the piles with rope behind the oxen and hauled them the mile or so to the frozen Little Saskatchewan.

Christmas approached and Glen Lyon became more talkative again. With his father gone, and no other close relatives in the vicinity, he began to question his commitment to the land. His inheritance gave him enough to consider several options, one of which was to return to Scotland and go into business for himself. The more he talked of this, the less interested he became in cutting wood in the silent cold of northern Manitoba.

In the middle of December, he suggested that they travel to Elphinstone to take advantage of the scene that the village would create over Christmas. He told the brothers that he would make up his mind during that time whether to return to the land and finish off the winter's cutting or throw in the towel and head for Montreal to catch an early boat back to Scotland.

Slate grey skies and blowing snow greeted them on the morning they set off for the village, Glen Lyon on his horse and the brothers behind Pete and Old Harry. The snow was unbroken, the trail being marked only by the cleavage in the trees. It lay almost chest deep for the oxen but as the days had been so cold it was relatively light and could be broken with ease. The world around was cold and hostile, devoid of colour. Dark clouds in the northwest reminded Tom and Rob of the night they were trapped in the blizzard and they knew they must keep the oxen moving at a rapid pace. Elphinstone was only fifteen miles south but these conditions would require a full day's travel.

They had the promise of accommodation in the loft above the general store run by George and Martha McIntyre, friends of old Mr Campbell. That held the certainty of consistent warmth from a generous wood stove that was stoked twenty-four hours a day in the store below. Dark had fallen before they saw the glimmer of light from the village.

Martha greeted them with warm enthusiasm and showed them where to shelter the animals in the adjacent barn. A large, homely woman clearly practiced in the ways of taking care of cold, hungry men, Martha hustled them into her kitchen and had them digging into large bowls of steaming meat and vegetables. Exhausted from the day's long, cold journey, the men stumbled up to the loft to shift the bales, boxes and barrels and make a temporary living space.

Christmas was a mere three days away and the next night the community was gathering in the Hudson Bay factor's home to begin the season's celebrations. Martha assured them they must go, that the music and dancing was just what they needed to banish the cold and shyness from their solitary lives. It took little persuading. Having been away from crowds for many weeks, the men waited until they could be sure the party was well under way before venturing up the hill to the large, well-lit house.

The sound of fiddle music preceded their arrival. Lamps glowed, their rays illuminating dozens of male faces, the air pungent with smoke, roast meat and sweat. The floor boards thudded as heavy boots attempted to keep pace with the racing instruments. No one paid them the slightest attention as the three men scanned the boisterous crowd. The factor's wife and a younger woman, perhaps her daughter, carried food in from the back rooms. They seemed to be the only women in attendance but then as Tom shouldered his way through the crowd he could see three young women sitting together at the other end of the room. All the dancing, at the moment was being done by the men, either singly or in pairs.

That, however, did not last for long. Within minutes, the three women were on their feet accompanying the younger men in a lumbering polka. None of the faces in the room were familiar. Most, judging by their clothes and the state of their facial hair seemed to have been in this back country for some time. Here and there, brown faces identified Metis and a few Indians. The Metis, resplendent in their sashes and buckskin vests, were among the most energetic dancers, displaying a grace and ease that was noticeably absent from the white men. The Indians stood silently around the edges of the room, looking on.

Tom counted the crowd – all told there were twenty-six men and the three women, not counting the factor's wife and her helper. Little chance, he thought of obtaining any female company that night. Glen Lyon obviously knew a number of men in the room and he was soon on the floor partnering with a couple of them as the dancing gained intensity. Tom grabbed Rob's arm and pulled him into the crowd and the two of them picked up the rhythm, awkwardly at first and then with greater ease as they relaxed.

The music stopped and someone called for a reel. The crowd lined up on both sides of the room, pair by pair, with the three young women, now joined by the other two, blushing pink with exertion. The caller took his place beside the three fiddlers and the melee began. Round and round they danced, sometimes connecting with their opposite partners, at others working their way up and down the lines, arm by arm. Any formality or hesitancy evaporated amid the mirth and exertion.

The reel was followed by another. This time Rob had the good fortune of securing one of the young women as his partner.

Dark-haired and olive-skinned, she reminded him immediately of Agnes, and as he caught her round the waist and spun her, she brushed close to him with eyes alight with laughter. Rob was immediately aroused. It had been so many months since he felt the surge of this attraction. The reel done, he managed to keep her with him for a slow waltz and he allowed himself to relax into the sweet warmth of her presence. Before the dance was over she was looking directly into his eyes, not something that young women of Rob's acquaintance normally allowed themselves to do.

Liquor was flowing but Rob had not imbibed. He did not need other stimulation to enjoy the hinted sexuality the young woman proffered. As they danced, Rob yearned for the sensation of a feminine body with its gentle curves nestled close against his own. He sensed that this would be available; all he would have to do is make the first move. The music ended but before he could suggest anything, a red-bearded stranger interposed himself with a forceful "It's my turn now" and Rob found himself standing alone at the edge of the room. Afflicted by what he had just contemplated, Rob left the room and walked into the night.

He sat on a fence by the barn. The night was clear but not cold. A full moon cast deep blue shadows across the glistening snow. The horizon of forest stood black against the night sky. He had to think. He had come so close to doing what he had said he would never do; betray Agnes for the thrust of sexual adventure. Clearly, the long months away from the woman he loved and the absence of any overt erotic expression, laid him open to misadventure. As he contemplated the stark beauty around him with the noise of the party a distant backdrop, he found the turmoil receding. He was learning things about himself that he had not been open to before, perhaps better understanding how similar he was to his brother – and how little cause he had to judge.

His reverie was interrupted by loud shouts from the house as the front door opened and two men burst out, in the midst of a brawl. One appeared to be Metis. Other men followed forming a rough circle around the combatants coarsely egging them on. The sickening thud of fist striking human flesh turned Rob's stomach. Now the men were on the ground, rolling in the snow, each seeking a lethal hold.

Suddenly there was a high pitched yell and the factor's wife broke through the circle of men, shouting at the men on the ground and kicking them. Whether it was their surprise at her boldness or the sheer moral force of an older frontier woman, the men broke off and were each grabbed by a bystander. Rob saw Tom and Glen Lyon as the circle broke up and the rest of the men drifted back into the house. He motioned to Tom and told him he was heading back to the store for the night. Glen Lyon decided to join him as the fracas had erased the joyful exuberance of the evening. Tom opted to stay on.

On the walk back to the store, Glen Lyon told Rob that one of the men had come on crudely to a woman who turned out to be a sister of the Metis. It had quickly escalated well beyond flirtation and the Metis had intervened. Glen Lyon said that most of the conflict on the frontier arose from the scarcity of women.

The days over Christmas and the New Year were difficult for Tom and Rob. Strangers around were friendly and being quickly recognized as civil young men and friends of Glen Lyon, they were invited into the hospitality of several families in the village. But their thoughts were thousands of miles away, amidst the gentle hills of lowland Scotland, knowing exactly what their parents and siblings would be doing as each day advanced. It was the women in a family who preserved the traditions, and Isobel had loved repeating the beloved rituals, season after season.

In Scotland, Christmas was quiet and for many it continued to be a working day. In the brothers' household, activity centred on family and church. The rooms would be brightly decorated with candles, fir boughs and holly and a tree adorned with strips of the tartans from the ancestors' clans. The Christmas Eve meal would be a large venison stew followed by shortbread and a black bun, a heavy cake thick with fruit and spices and drenched in whiskey, though not enough to alter anyone's state of mind – Isobel saw to that. After dinner, all would climb into the carriage for the long dark ride to a church service so solemn and slow that most of the children would be asleep well before it ended and would be carried out to the carriage bundled in heavy blankets.

Their festive times began a few days later and spilled into New Year's or Hogmanay. Tom, with his dark hair, was a popular choice for "first footing", the custom of being the first to cross a threshold in the minutes after midnight on New Year's Eve. If the first across was dark haired, that was a sign of good luck. If blonde, that signified bad times ahead, a superstition dating to the days when Norsemen would rape and pillage villages on the east coast of Scotland. Much food and drink would be consumed in those early hours of the New Year and gifts would be plentiful for the young.

The brothers took part in the events of the season – a Christmas Eve service in the factor's house, a festive dinner with their hosts, the McIntyres, on Christmas day, but with little pleasure. Only when New Years was celebrated in the sawmill, the largest building in town, did their spirits lighten. Glen Lyon left before the New Year to close down his father's house in preparation for a return to Scotland

Between Christmas and New Year's they managed to secure employment with a Mr McDonald who had a contract with the Hudson Bay Company to cut twelve thousand pine logs over the winter. Rob would get thirty dollars a month for him and the oxen while Tom took in twenty. They came across a large, broken-down cabin that had been the company's first trading post on the river and negotiated with Mr Audy, the company manager, to make it habitable for themselves and several other company employees. Thus, they could live rent free for the winter.

There was little contact with the outside world and letters arrived only once every three weeks. Rob's torment at the dance had brought home his vulnerability. For a long time he had relied entirely on the rigours of hard work and the novelty of his changing surroundings to ignore his emotional needs. If he was to remain loyal to Agnes, he had to do something to still the restlessness that had recently been awakened.

He turned to the books at hand, and despite the exhaustion from the nine to ten hours of outside work that daylight allowed, he determined to spend his evenings with his works of Shakespeare and his Bible. The two fed different segments of his spirit and the contentment he had known returned.

Rob's other source of comfort were the letters he regularly wrote home. It was, for him, as though he was in conversation with them. "We wear moccasins. They don't freeze like boots," he wrote Agnes. "When actively employed you get into a fine glow but to stand idle is a bad policy. The air though cold is sufficiently bracing and is a most potent incentive to physical exertion. A constitution nursed upon the oxygen of our bright atmosphere makes the possessor of it feel he could toss the pine trees in his glee. For character and a daring reckless spirit whose delight is to be surrounded by difficulties, this is the life.

"The work is most pleasant; out in the morning to see the sun clothing the tall pine tops in its golden light and hear all the day the merry calls of the teamsters and the cracking of the great trees as they fall before the keen blows of the axmen. There is plenty of joking going on and too often not very pleasant language engaged in."

He decided to describe in detail the nature of their activity to his father and mother. "First the choppers cut down the trees and then the sawyers cut them into twelve, fourteen and sixteen foot lengths. Then the swampers take off the branches and help the skidders collect them arranging them on a sled in lots of thirty to one hundred logs. Then the teamsters with their sleighs take them off to the creek where they wait until spring break-up to be floated down the river to the Hudson Bay fort, twenty miles away."

But life was not without danger. Felling trees in the wilderness was a work filled with hazard, not the least of which was that any serious injury left a man days away from the attention of a doctor. Driving down a hill one morning the oxen ran away. Rob rushed to their heads trying to hold them back by the ropes on their horns. He fell between them and was dragged down the hill under their feet. Somehow he was not injured despite the momentum of the downward rush of a sleigh full of wood behind them. He emerged with bruises and his casual confidence shaken.

In the late winter a traveling party from further west brought disturbing news. Metis settlers were once again restive at the constant westward flow of European settlers. Some of them were joining forces with Indian tribes who were refusing to sign treaties. It looked as though violence might once again break out on the prairie between the white man and the red. The Indians and Metis were far more numerous than the European settlers and without the arrival of troops from eastern Canada, further settlement in the west could be made very difficult. There was talk of recruiters arriving to enlist local men to form a militia.

By late April with the daylight lengthening and the weather warming, the brothers decided to head south. Travel would be much easier before the melting snow turned the trails into rivers of mud. They would try to find land while there was still time to break the ground and get a crop in. Good land was apparently still available south and west of Brandon, a village some fifty miles west of Portage.

Old Harry and Pete once again proved their worth, hauling the brothers and their few belongings down the long, snow-laden route. Harry, with his wide, patient eyes, provided the steady and loyal tread that overcame all but the occasional snowdrift. Pete was more temperamental and easily distracted, shying at deep shadows and prone to wander when the path opened up. But he was strong and pulled more than his weight and Old Harry calmly held him to the course. Rob mused wryly on the similarities between the paired oxen and he and his brother. Because of that he had a deep affection for them both, with a clear preference for Harry. Wherever they found night-time accommodation, Rob would take care to ensure the animals were well sheltered and fed before the men turned in.

They approached the village of Brandon six days later. No sign of habitation was visible, the prairie stretching to the horizon until suddenly the prairie floor opened to a large coulee and there along the river's banks sat several dozen decent-looking houses, warehouses, stores and a police detachment. Brandon was already a hub supplying the wagon trains that ferried settlers to the west and a market for the produce from farms already established.

Both men felt their spirits rise as they sought out the supplies and equipment they would need to break the prairie. At the general store they bought a John Deere Prairie Queen plough – robust enough they were told to break through the deep sod. They needed seed – wheat, barley, oats – and tools – a couple of axes, a two-man saw, hammers, nails and rope. The cart would be piled high.

It was time to replace Old Harry and Pete's shoes – not an easy undertaking. They had been told that, unlike a horse, if you lift the foot of an ox to reshoe it, the animal would topple. But the local iron foundry had an ox stall, a strong wooden frame and a wide canvas strap which was passed under the animal and was then lashed to the frame. A winch could then lift the animal so that the strap took most of its weight and a foot could be lifted for shoeing with no danger of the beast falling.

Harry took to the contraption without batting an eye. But Pete balked, his eyes rolling in fear. It took both brothers and the farrier to manhandle him into position and they had to winch him right off the ground to immobilize him sufficiently.

Their tasks accomplished, the brothers decided to take advantage of the local hotel to spend a final night in a decent bed and use the evening to ferret out all the information they could about the surrounding land. They had already learned to avoid the light-coloured, sandy soil that was found on the ridges as it would produce stunted crops and hold little water. The best soil was what the locals called "gumbo," heavy and black, having been laid down millennia ago.

Land that was somewhat sheltered from the fierce northwest winds of winter with access to sufficient water to get them through dry summers was what was needed. But they were advised to stay away from the American border. The war between the US cavalry and the Sioux people had forced many of the latter, hungry and hostile, into Canada. While some were settling peacefully under the protection of Canadian authorities, others were trying to use their Canadian refuge as a base from which to continue raiding in the United States.

The second day past Brandon, Rob and Tom came across a wide valley with low treed hills to the south that appeared promising. The river was wide with the spring run-off. Rob, grabbing a shovel, walked beside the oxen stopping to dig through the sod every hundred feet. The soil seemed rich and black. But the level land was only a couple of feet above the wide sloughs on each side of the river. Higher up, where there would be less danger of flooding, the soil became yellowish and the early grasses were sparse. Also, there was no protection from the winter winds.

They had to move on. On the morning of the third day they were still following the river but the land now lay well above it and there were low ridges to the west and north. They halted the oxen and though it was early in the day, decided to make camp and thoroughly explore the surrounding country. South of the river, the land rolled gently away and everywhere they dug they came up with rich, black soil. On the other side of the river, the earth was not quite as promising but had sufficient black tilth as likely to be productive. To the west, the land between the gentle ridges harboured sycamore and poplar providing wood for construction and fire. While still high with the spring floods, the river ran slow and therefore deep, holding out the possibility of water through the dry months.

Rob felt an increasing assurance that this was where they would make their life. Though it could not be more different from the rolling, stone-walled fields framed by the rolling grey of the North Sea that marked the land of their youth, this would be the land that would give their lives sustenance and security. And with time, as neighbours arrived and homes, barns, gardens and trees gave greater shape to the expanse around them, they would perhaps come to cherish this as much as they had the landscape of Berwickshire.

By late afternoon, the men returned to the cart and the grazing oxen, affirming to each other that they had found what they were looking for. As the sky was dimming, they decided to spend a leisurely evening around the fire enjoying the first of what would be thousands of nights to come. After a meal of fried salt pork, warmed beans and bread washed down with cool water from the river, they settled in to watch the western sky create another masterpiece. Rob suggested that it would be fitting to close such an evening with a reading from scripture and he chose the passage Isobel had read to them in the parlour the night before their departure from Abbeylane.

'I can never escape your Spirit; I can never get away from your presence.
If I go up to heaven, you are there, if I go down to the grave, you are there.
If I ride on the wings of the morning, if I dwell by the farthest seas, Even there your hand will guide me and your strength uphold me.'

Rob rose from the fire and stretched. As his brother joined him, he reached out, grabbed his shoulders and hugged him. They rolled out their bedding and within minutes were asleep.

Chapter

21

THE NEXT DAY, JUNE 1, DAWNED COOL AND CLEAR. THE BROTHERS' EXCITE-ment at finally putting the plough to their own land made for a quick breakfast. They rounded up Pete and Old Harry, drove the cart with the plough to within fifteen feet of the river bank, and hitched it to the oxen. Rob grabbed its handles, dug in his heels and Tom stood on the end of the blade to drive it beneath the surface. With an exultant shout that startled the two old beasts, Rob released the plough. Rarely had he felt such a thrill – in fact, it reminded him of the first time Agnes had allowed him to kiss her. They had begun the first of tens of thousands of furrows they would slice through the black soil on their own land.

They had learned the art of breaking soil when they worked at Burnside. The ground was free of stones but after ploughing for an hour, Rob decided he had to go back over the ground to ensure the sod was fully cut free. It had grown undisturbed for thousands of years and only reluctantly let loose its hold. Once done, Tom took over to break the next area. Looking back, they could see the transformation. Moist strips glinted in the sun like black gold, rich with promise. The brothers pressed on.

Once about half an acre had been broken they turned to back-setting which helped rot the sod and bared the soil for the seeds to be sown. This third pass was much easier and as Rob ploughed, Tom followed his left arm around a pail of barley seed, his right spraying an arc of golden semi-circles over the welcoming earth. As he strode, his hand plunging into the pail, he caressed

173

the smooth, flowing grain feeling it as sensuous as a woman's hair. He smiled at the memory and his pace quickened.

After lunch, Rob returned to breaking the next section while Tom headed for the trees to the west to cut firewood. The sound of his axe must have carried a distance for suddenly he was aware of two red men on horseback galloping towards him. Rob was out of sight on the other side of the trees. Tom had no weapon other than his axe, but he stood tall waiting their approach. One of them slid off his horse but did not appear hostile. He began talking in his own tongue, clearly wanting to engage Tom. His words were urgent and he gestured widely to the south. Tom was at a loss as to the meaning of the encounter. Not wanting to appear distant, he pulled bread out of his pack and offered it to the man but he put up his hands, remounted and with a final guttural admonishment, rode off the way he had come.

The next morning, pleased with the progress of the previous day, they were hard at work with plough and seed. The day seemed exceptionally warm and they broke off at mid-morning to cool off in the river when the Indians from the previous day turned up again accompanied by three others. Rob mounted the river bank and greeted them warmly with a few words of Cree he had picked up in Elphinstone. The leader of the group abruptly raised his head and began talking rapidly but the sounds were not those of the northern Cree. He dismounted and walked over to the ploughed land, got down on his knees and inspected it closely. He then addressed Rob and Tom with angry words and gestures. It appeared he was either confused or angry with what they had done to the prairie grasses.

The brothers were at a loss as to what was transpiring but Rob was determined to look neither afraid nor hostile. He answered back, explaining to them what he and Tom were doing, smiling and gesturing as he did so, knowing full well they he could not be understood. The Indians were equally at a loss and after another round of comment, got back on their ponies and rode off.

It was evident that there must be an encampment not far from

174

their site. "We must find out more about these people," Rob said, "and we must find someone who knows their language and can help us with some basic phrases."

The next two weeks were fully occupied with breaking, back-set-ting and sowing with an occasional excursion to the river where Tom, being an excellent shot, secured duck to vary their diet of salt pork. With some fifteen acres now sown, five with barley and ten with wheat, Rob suggested it was time to go back to Brandon to register their land. They had encountered four or five groups of settlers seeking land and thought they had better get the 160 acres they each could claim registered before others began to encroach on the land they wanted.

Arriving in Brandon late on the second day of travel, they went straight to the post office. Three letters had been forwarded from Winnipeg and Rob quickly slit open the one from Agnes. Her classes in Edinburgh were coming to a close. She still had another four months of courses to take in the autumn, but she was increas-ingly anxious to be with him in Canada. She had a cousin in Edin-burgh who intended to emigrate and she proposed foregoing the rest of her schooling and leaving with him in the late summer and asked if Rob could meet her in Montreal.

As they made their way to the land registry office, Rob found it difficult to focus on the task at hand. Her proposal stirred strong emotions, keen anticipation at the prospect of her joining him so soon and yet grave concern with so much still to do. He would far rather have welcomed her to a reasonable dwelling and sufficient food to weather the severe winter that would break upon them so soon after her arrival.

The procedures in the registry office took the rest of the day. They had not realized that certain 640 acre sections had already been allotted for the provision of local governments and railways, even as far from established settlements as the land they were claiming. The Canadian government was granting private investors large tracts of land in return for their stake in the railway. The land Tom wanted east of Rob's claim had been so allocated. He could provisionally claim another area due south of his brother's and confirm it later once he had proven its worthiness. Tom agreed and they signed the documents giving them ownership.

Visiting Brandon gave them the opportunity to write home again and they had much news to share. Tom began the letter:

"Dearest ones, here we are on the land that we think will be home and hearth for years to come. It lies along a lovely small river that affords fish and game. The horizon stretches in all directions. The land is rich with potential and over the last few days we have ploughed some fifteen acres and planted wheat and barley. It is a joy to look over those rich, brown acres and know that the crops they produce will no longer have to be shared with a landlord.

"We are of one mind that this is the place for us. We are isolated, the nearest town, Brandon, being more than a day's ride to the east. This is such a vast land. But we are sure to have neighbours before long. There are almost as many families moving west in their carts as you see on the roads of Berwickshire during the autumn harvest fair."

For Rob, work on the new homestead was always accompanied by thoughts of the old. "How I used to enjoy my walks down by the familiar Alewater when the leaves were putting on their greening tints. And what I would not give to be there today. On a ramble down by the Witches Knows and across by the Gala Law to view the pleasant land with its rustic beauties, its well-ordered fields and woods, its hills and dales, and added to all, the grand old ocean with its restless tide bearing on its waters the commerce of the world. Days of the past, yet how sweet to think of possessing memories of hallowed beauty.

"But you must be assured that we are happy and well and believe we have finally found the perfect spot where our own land will provide for the rest of our days. It does not yet possess the beauty of Abbeylane, but it will be our own and its air is fragrant with freedom."

It was by now too late to return to the trail west, so they headed for one of the three boarding houses in town with the intent of picking up needed supplies in the morning. Rob knew that he would have to decide immediately about Agnes' suggestion so that he could reply before leaving Brandon. He had steeled himself to a long absence and was comfortable with the composure he had achieved. Her letter threw this into turmoil. he found the specter of his loneliness rose again. It was all he could do to think straight. He told Tom the choices he faced and then headed out to walk the river to clear his head.

It was a soft summer evening. Horses, some with riders, others pulling carts churned small clouds of dust on the town's one street. Children rolled hoops and in the distance he could hear a mother calling her own home to supper. The general store, the blacksmith and the few other shops had closed for the day. The saloon seemed to be doing a healthy business judging from the various modes of transport lined up outside.

He was at the edge of town within minutes and continued down the coulee, along the banks of the river, still high with the spring runoff. Trees were now in full leaf, their green showing clean strong tones. Birds abounded, far more than could be seen on the open prairie. The lip of the prairie above the coulee seemed to move as the wind teased its grasses. There was a wild beauty to this land, one he was feeling increasingly at home in.

He loved Agnes too much to subject her to the harshness and uncertainties of the coming months. He would reply encouraging her to complete her studies and, provided he could get a dwelling and storage sheds built this summer and secure sufficient harvest to provide the funds needed, he would return to Scotland in the autumn, marry her surrounded by family and return together in the spring. Tom would be able to go back with the oxen to Elphinstone and work the winter. Perhaps by the autumn, they would have neighbours who could keep an eye on the farm.

By morning he had his reply ready for Agnes, and, handing it to the postmistress, set his sights on the return journey, recovering some of his earlier composure. While he had been writing, Tom had procured fresh supplies of dried beef, salt pork, vegetables and bread, along with more seed and a supply of oats for the oxen. The work ahead of Pete and Old Harry would require more sustenance than could be had from prairie grass alone.

Heading west felt much different on this return journey. Instead of facing the vast unknown plain, they were heading home to a stretch of land in which they had already invested sweat and toil, making it their own. The long hours passed rapidly for there was much to stir the imagination. Rob contemplated where he would erect a dwelling. There was a slough close to the river with a good bank on its south side and the higher ground beside it would be ideal for a house from which most of his land could be readily viewed. The prevailing winds seemed to blow from the northwest so he would place its door and windows south and east. Further excavation could probably turn the slough it into a excellent watering place for animals.

By late afternoon they were looking for a site for the night. They came upon several Metis freighters, their oxcarts already circled with a fire bright in its centre. One of the men beckoned them in and the brothers decided to welcome the company. It was a chance to mine the knowledge of these plainsmen.

The Metis might also be able to tell them about the Indians they had met on their land. He described the encounter to a man named Alphonse Dumont who suggested that they might be Lakota Sioux from south of the border.

Dumont explained that quite a few Sioux had crossed into Canada to escape pursuit by the US Cavalry. He said that they did not have specific lands set aside for them but roamed freely for the moment across the southern part of the territory. Alphonse did not know the Sioux language but took Rob to meet a young Metis who had had dealings with them. Rob spent the rest of the evening picking up elementary phrases in Lakota, the language of the Sioux.

With the dawn, the brothers hitched their oxen, bade goodbye to their companions and headed west. Their first priority in the weeks that followed was to break and sow as many acres as possible before the drier days of summer set in. They managed to plant a further fifteen acres, giving them thirty which they judged was about all they could harvest given the equipment on hand.

Their next task was to sow a garden – potatoes, carrots, cabbage, beets – crops that could be stored to see them through the winter months and then other vegetables for summer eating. Since they had been living in their tent for the seven weeks since Elphinstone, it was time to build something sturdier that would provide protection for the winter months.

Large diameter trees on the plains were rare so most settlers started out with sod houses. The heavy prairie sod was ideally suited as building material. The brothers headed to an unbroken area and there cut a twelve inch strip, slicing it every eighteen inches to create a sod block. These they piled on the cart and hauled to the gentle rise south of the slough. Two days' work produced the outside walls standing eight feet at the entrance and sloping two feet at the back, steep enough to shed the rain. They framed two windows on the south side and another on the west using poplar saplings to hold up the sod. Then they cut more poplar saplings and laid these side by side to form the roof, placing a layer of sod on top.

The shelter complete and moderately weather-proof, Tom set about building rough chairs, a table and two bed frames also out of poplar. Being early summer, the grass was not long enough to gather to make mattresses so they placed their extra clothes on the poplar rails and made an acceptable bed.

Their homestead, although still provisional, gave Rob some pride. He wrote almost daily to Agnes in a continuing letter so he would not lose the images of these early days. "Think of breaking up the sod, fresh from the hands of the Creator, where nature has grown prairie grasses and flowers in abundance, where the buffalo has roamed for ages and where the red man was master of all he surveyed. Soon the wild prairie will be robbed of its wild and lonely grandeur and instead will be seen the broad fields of golden grain and herds of lowing cattle."

Much of the early summer toil was now complete and the

brothers thought it wise for one of them to return to Elphinstone to secure paid work until the harvest. That way they would have a reserve of cash should anything happen to the crops. Tom clearly showed preference for the adventure and they returned to Brandon so he could buy a horse to ride north and an iron stove for the sod house. He promised Rob to keep him abreast of his travels and they bade farewell until mid-September.

It was the first time that he had been alone for an extended period. In the initial days, Rob found himself unhinged. Old Harry and Pete provided a living presence, and as the nights were now warm, he took to bedding down outside near them, just to hear the sound of their breathing. But he became used to the solitude, and became much more attuned to the details of prairie life all around him. The land they had broken and sown was now awash in green shoots, the barley, wheat and oats demonstrating by their vigour the richness of the soil beneath.

Physical work gave structure to the days. He ploughed a forty foot strip around the shelter. Prairie fires could arise almost sound-lessly and sweep with frightening speed across the unimpeded land-scape spurred by the constant wind. He had heard tales of settlers losing everything before the onslaught and some had even forfeited their lives. A fire break put open soil between the sod house and the grasslands and gave enough space for him to be able to lead the oxen to safety, provided he could control their panic. And he could lead them into the slough should a fire storm leap the break.

Then he needed to find sufficient wood to take Tom through the winter while he returned to Scotland. There was precious little dead and dry wood in the thickets along the river. He knew that any poplar he cut would be green and provide little warmth. There were a few sycamores that promised more warmth for the work involved, but he would have to fell, cut and split them and hope that the summer would be hot and dry.

He needed also to construct a barn to shelter the oxen in the coldest months and provide protection for the crops they were to harvest in case they were not able to transport them to sell in Brandon should winter descend early.

On clear days, he occasionally saw smoke from the fires of what he assumed was the Indian encampment south and west of the river. He had not been visited again by its inhabitants and decided it was time to make their acquaintance and try the few phrases of Lakota he had picked up from the Metis lad. Riding the cart behind Pete and Old Harry would give him a better presence than arriving by foot. It might also give him some protection should that be necessary.

He was perhaps a quarter of a mile from the encampment when he spotted three horses and riders start off towards him. Rob recognized one of the older men who had visited previously and stopped and waited for them. *"Hau, kola*"* he shouted as they approached, *"nituktetanhan hwo?**"* The old man slowed his horse to a trot and answered, *"Itokagata wikoti.***"* The three approached the cart and Rob stood, smiling broadly. The old man continued talking but by now Rob was well past any understanding. Then they motioned him to follow them back to the camp.

The camp consisted of some dozen tepees, with women, children and dogs, making a pleasant domestic scene. The men dismounted and went to the largest tepee, opening its flap and beckoning Rob to come in. Seated by a small fire was another elderly man who judging by his garb was likely the chief. Two women quickly brought buffalo robes from the corner, placed them by the chief and signaled Rob to sit. Having prepared for such an event, Rob removed from his satchel a fine silver hunting knife he had purchased in Winnipeg and gave it, handle first, to the chief. The latter looked pleased, accepted it and began speaking rapidly. Rob smiled, pointed to his ears and shook his head. "My English, very

---

*   Hello, friend

**   Where are you from?

***   Southward village

181

small," said the chief. "My Lakota also very small," Rob answered. "My name Rob Dunbar."

"I have English name also," said the chief. "English name, Old John." He then turned and spoke to one of the women standing by. She left and returned minutes later with a much younger Lakota. "The boy name Ohista. He speak much English."

The young man nodded towards Rob and spoke, "I study in church school in America. Now I translate sometimes when we talk police or soldier. I can help chief understand."

Aided by Ohista, Rob described his journey across the seas from Scotland and explained what he and his brother wished to do. A long, leisurely conversation ensued. He asked the chief what his people called the river that ran beside his farm. Old John replied, "*Shandyhookawakapa*" which Ohista translated as "river of the stone pipe." Roasted meat was brought in by the women and then a dozen or more other men joined the group and sat silently listening to the exchange between Rob and Old John.

This band was part of a much larger group of Sioux who had fled across the border four or five years previously. Old John said that they had been part of the Sun Dance alliance between the Sioux and Northern Cheyenne peoples. Their great chief, Sitting Bull, had had a vision in which he saw many American soldiers falling from the sky. This meant, he said, that a great victory was in store for his people.

The Sioux had been living in the Black Hills of the Dakota, Wyoming and Montana territories which were promised them in an agreement with the Washington government. But miners had found gold in the territory and the government wished to move the Sioux out by offering money for their land. Sitting Bull refused the offer so the US army moved in to force removal.

Old John and some of his warriors were with a combined Sioux-Cheyenne group in a village by the Little Bighorn River that was attacked by a detachment of the Seventh US Cavalry under command of a Major Reno. He said that their warriors greatly outnumbered the cavalry whose detachments, commanded overall by

General George Armstrong Custer, were separated from each other by considerable distance. The first shots were fired in mid-afternoon. By nightfall, the cavalry were defeated, Custer was dead and any surviving soldiers in panicked retreat.

But their victory seemed only to cause the government to increase its efforts to defeat the Sioux. After more battles, some Sioux leaders surrendered while Sitting Bull and about three thousand of his people crossed into Canada. Old John said that he and his people had accepted to be governed by "the Great White Mother", and to live in peace with both the settlers and the tribes on the plains, but that the Canadian government had turned down their efforts to secure their own land. So they had to follow the dwindling buffalo and seek a living from whatever was available on the land they roamed. But now that more settlers were coming, it was becoming much harder to survive. His people were often hungry.

Rob did not know what to say in response to this tale of war and hardship. But the similarity of their situation struck him and he told them that he too had been forced to leave his land – perhaps they could help each other build a new life in this new territory. He told Old John that if ever they needed help in their negotiations with Canadian authorities, he would be ready to assist. The chief looked at his sitting men and spoke at length.

Ohista interpreted, "The chief says, 'This white man a friend. No warrior must harm him. Perhaps he help us. We help him. It is good to have such neighbour.'" With that, Old John waved his hand and Rob knew the meeting was at an end. When he reached his cart, he found two buffalo skins rolled up under the seat.

Some days later, two families of settlers arrived late one afternoon and asked if they could pass the night close by. Rob welcomed the company and joined them round their fire as the long prairie evening drew to a close. They were fellow Scots from the town of Crieff in Perthshire. One group consisted of two brothers, McIvor by name, and their aged father. The other was a man and his wife, George and Molly Milligan, and two sons in their early teen years. Both families had left for the same reasons as Rob and Tom, increasing rents and lower prices for their produce. As the evening progressed and the talk became freer, Rob realized that he could do no better than persuade these people to take land in the area.

The next morning, at his suggestion, Rob accompanied the men as they explored the surrounding land, testing the soil and looking for a location that would offer some protection from prevailing winds and the threat of spring floods. By evening, they had decided to take the land along the river to the west of Rob's farm, beyond the gravel mounds. It now being late June, the prospect of harvesting a successful wheat crop before the killing frost was poor but they decided to risk putting in a crop of oats to provide winter feed for their animals and a large vegetable garden for themselves.

Rob continued his work, delighted with the sight and sound of his neighbours pursuing the same. The long days of sun and warmth were transforming the land around him. The grain he had sown added its rippled waves to the surrounding prairie grasses as the winds played across the land. The vegetables had to be thinned and the potatoes hilled.

By mid-July he was cutting the grasses with his scythe, testing again the strength of his shoulders and arms and wishing he had the horse drawn cutter they used at Abbeylane. The days continued clear and hot, and the aroma of the newly mown hay brought back sweet memories. Within the week he was able to rake the hay, gather it in the cart and store it in the sod shed he had alongside the house.

Tom had returned to Elphinstone. He knew the town and many of its people had become acquaintances and friends in the course of the previous winter. And he was certain he could find employment at either the gristmill or sawmill.

He was not disappointed. Most of the young men whom he had worked with the previous winter had dispersed either to find their own land or to work others' farms. Mr Audy, the Hudson Bay

Company manager, was delighted to give him a job at the gristmill and he returned to the shanty he and Rob had helped rebuild the previous winter, joining five other men, two of whom he knew already.

In the course of time he learned that his old friend, Glen Lyon Campbell, had not returned to Scotland but had instead had headed west, supposedly to return to the Yukon where he had spent his childhood. Occasionally, they heard news that boded ill for the settlers further west in the Northwest Territory. The possible alliance between displaced Metis and those tribes who were refusing to enter into treaty with the government seemed to be solidifying. There was a rumour that Louis Riel who had led the first revolt against the Ottawa government some dozen years ago, was back from exile in the United States, and fomenting further trouble.

The work was good, the pay steady, and on his free time he and a couple of friends would take to the woods or lakes in search of deer or geese to supplement an otherwise predictable diet. There were a higher proportion of women around than there had been last winter, though the men still outnumbered them five to one. But Tom's natural charm meant that he was never at a loss for their company at the dances held every couple of weeks. While drink was available, its cost meant he partook sparingly. Others were not so inhibited and the dancing usually continued until the morning light, with Tom staying to the end.

It was after one of these extended nights when Tom woke close to noon and stumbled out of the shanty that he saw Glen Lyon approaching on horseback. But he hardly recognized his friend garbed as he was in uniform. Tom gave a whoop of delight as Glen Lyon swung down off his horse and the two men grasped each other by the shoulders.

"Where have you appeared from and what's with this attire?" Tom asked. "It's a long story," Glen Lyon said with a grin, "but have you any food? I haven't eaten since last night." "Of course," Tom replied and while Tom cooked up some beans and salt pork on the shanty's stove, Glen Lyon regaled him with his adventures since they had last seen each other after Christmas.

While traveling in the Northwest Territory, Glen Lyon had learned in Fort Edmonton that the government was shipping soldiers out from eastern Canada and actively recruiting militia in expectation of confrontation with Riel and his Metis and Indian allies. Glen Lyon had been offered the rank of colonel in a brigade called Boulton's Scouts and he was now enlisting other men for the expected skirmishes.

He was certain that with the professional soldiers from the east and the militia drawn from the ranks of the settlers who knew the local land, the coming battles with the insurgents would be over quickly. The government was offering considerably more on a monthly basis than Tom could earn at the mill.

Despite how pleasant life was in Elphinstone, this was an opportunity not to be turned down. It was not just the money – though that was attractive – but the chance to act out a long-held dream of taking up arms for the Empire. And here it was being offered to him on a plate by one of his close friends. There was no debate. He was sure Rob would not approve, but he was far away and there was no way to consult him before making his decision, even if he had wished to, which he did not. His only concern was whether he would be able to make it back to help Rob with the harvest in late September. Glen Lyon was certain that this would be possible. He was convinced that the engagement would be over in six to eight weeks, by mid-September at the latest.

His boss at the mill was not pleased. Interest in the expedition was rather widespread and the loss of labour threatened the viability of the mill. He tried offering Tom half again as much as he had signed on for. But Tom was determined. Glen Lyon went about his business in the town and among the neighbouring farms. They agreed to meet in two days.

22

Wagon trains continued to flow westwards. At first, one would see specks on the eastern horizon, like white birds nesting on the endless green. As the hours passed, they would become steadily larger, the animals and wagons more distinct. Some would pass by with no more than a wave while others stopped seeking information. If it was close to the end of a day, they would ask if they could spend the night along the river. Rob always accommodated them, allowing their animals to graze on the open prairie and sharing what food he had if they needed it.

Many were new settlers from other central European lands – Hungary, Germany, Russia – with their limited English and alien ways. Rob warmed to them all and was generous with information. The more settlers that came, the quicker they would have a railway, local schools and towns that offered a wider variety of goods and services.

The summer's work proceeded apace. He dug a root cellar in which to store vegetables and other provisions for the winter. He hoped that sufficient warmth would penetrate from the house to keep food from freezing. He had been eating the first spring vegetables from the garden for a couple of weeks – lettuce, young carrots, beets – a welcome addition to the diet of porridge, dried beans, bread and salted meat. He hoped that Tom might have a chance to begin a wooden house during the winter months when he was away in Scotland.

It had now been six weeks since Tom had left for the north and as he had not been back to Brandon he had had no news of him, nor any further word from Agnes or the family. Though well provisioned until the late summer when he would return to the town to sell what produce he could, he became increasingly restive for news. The McIvors were making the trip and Rob decided to accompany them.

Much as he enjoyed his solitary life, its days filled with work whose progress gave him much satisfaction, he found himself looking forward to meeting other people. His first stop, as always, was the postmistress in the general store. The joy of receiving letters was immense, a living contact across the endless wilderness and oceans with those he loved. It never ceased to amaze him that correspondence sent across such distances actually arrived.

The letters from Agnes were opened first. She had clearly been disappointed with his proposal that she delay her departure until he could return that winter and they could cross the ocean as a married couple in the spring. But she accepted the wisdom of it and dearly hoped he could get a passage early enough so as not to be caught in the north Atlantic in the dangerous winter months. She would be finished her courses by Christmas and would be back living with her family shortly after he arrived, with plenty of time to prepare for the wedding. Rob counted off the months, only four or five, before he would once again hold that lovely being. He had taken the letters down by the river and lay back on the bank allowing his contemplation of that moment of reunion to linger.

The next letter broke the reverie. It was Tom's note informing him that he was headed west with Boulton's Scouts for the confrontation with the insurgents. Rob's first reaction was alarm at his brother's action. If he became a casualty, their whole undertaking could be imperiled. Then he realized that the greater likelihood would be delay in getting back. He would have to get the harvest in alone, a herculean task, and would not be able to leave for Scotland in his brother's absence.

The joy he had felt moments before turned to exasperated rage. His mind raced. This man was totally unthinking, unreliable. He only pursued what was immediately in front of him, with no thought for the consequences for others. How could he be so impetuous?

The old anger rose up, a mix of indignation and jealousy at the effortless manner Tom charmed his way to get what he wanted. He seemed always to be spared the consequences of his choices while others paid the price. Rob thought that these feelings had faded as a result of their dependence on each other over the past months but apparently not. They were as intense as they had ever been.

He returned to the general store to pick up a short list of provisions – coal oil for the lamps, two barrels of spikes, and an extra set of harness for the oxen, an adze for shaping wood, tea, sugar, and flour. The McIvor brothers arrived just as his purchases were being tallied. Rob was now in no mood to linger or seek out others in the town and told them he was heading home early.

But now he did want to find out all he could about the insurgency in the Northwest Territory. He went to the largest boarding house in town – those passing through might have the most knowledge. When he asked the clerk if anyone from the western territory was staying, he was told that three men from Fort Edmonton had booked in the night before. A description of them and a short walk down the main street was all that was required to identify them.

Their information was based on rumour and told him little that he did not already know. It was said that several groups of Plains Cree and Salteaux had rejected proposals that Canadian officials had put to them in the most recent treaty discussions and it was feared that they might be preparing to forcibly resist the advance of the settlers. There was widespread hunger among these peoples because of the scarcity of the buffalo. This could well lead to raids on outlying trading posts and settlements.

His anger receded as the steady pace of the oxen measured off the miles and despondency took its place. He contemplated another year without Agnes. He would not dash her hopes until he was certain Tom would not make it on time but this was a strong possibility. As he continued to consider the situation he concluded unhappily that perhaps it was time he and Tom went their separate ways. He was tired of the emotional toll of frequent disappointment and he would be happier operating on his own. He would help Tom build another house on the land he had registered. They could help each other as neighbours but he could no longer count on Tom as a partner.

A double weight of sadness burdened Rob in the days to come. The crops were encouraging, the grain beginning to head out and the vegetables showing by their size the benefit of the long hours of sunlight. But the pending rupture of his relations with Tom and the receding hope of seeing Agnes in the next few months, took much of the joy out of the long, hot days.

There was some consolation in his growing friendship with the McIvors. Seumas and Dewar were younger but shared his attentiveness to the tasks at hand. Rob was forthcoming with suggestions and help as they set about building a shelter for themselves and their father and breaking the prairie in preparation for next year's sowing. As they had only a few acres of oats to harvest, Rob was hopeful that if Tom did not return in time, the brothers would be able to give him a hand bringing in his wheat, barley and oats.

Chapter
23

Tom, his comrades, Ohiteka and his Sioux companions were on the trail heading west. The late summer days were shrinking but the sun still shone warmly, its burnished rays enhancing the yellow-tinged cottonwoods in the coulees and the tawny spread of the fading prairie. The nights had turned cold.

The first day on horseback, he thought of little else than what might lie behind the muted smile that had passed across Wynona's absorbing face. That she had shown herself open to him and that he had backed off from exploring the moist fullness of her availability, made the remembering poignant and painful. He had been so long in the company of coarse, guarded men. To have denied himself a journey into that warm gentleness leading to intense fulfilment and relief, he now deeply regretted. He wanted her scent of smoke and sweat and leather, the sharp cut of her features, her long, lean limbs, the play of awareness and humour in her eyes.

His horse stumbled and almost fell, jarring him back to the dust and hot sun and the pounding of cantering hooves. They had been riding for perhaps four hours. They were headed to a fort from which the Northwest Mounted Police guarded the American border. It was there that the great chief, Sitting Bull, had negotiated safe entry for his people fleeing the American cavalry. For the Sioux, this was the place that represented Canadian authority.

It was some two day's ride to the west across territory that was not well known to their Lakota companions. The latter kept a wary eye out for signs of other riders on the open prairie. They stayed off established trails, choosing instead the open grasslands.

Occasionally, one of the Lakota would prod his horse into a gallop and speed ahead to check some upcoming coulee or thicket. They did not want to be drawn into conflict.

Once in a while they came across signs of the herds of buffalo that had wandered the plains – earthen depressions left by the beasts where they had rolled in the spring mud to rid their coats of lice. Late the first afternoon they had seen the prairie covered with bleached bones, the huge rib cages now forlorn and empty, mute among the grasses. Only a great hunt would account for such slaughter. Toward evening, they spotted a small herd of antelope, diverting several of the Lakota. Roasted meat that night marked a successful pursuit.

They smothered their cooking fires before night fell, the better to remain undetected. Tom and his comrades shared their few blankets to preserve warmth while the Lakota slept singly on the other side of the smoldering embers.

The next day they were up and off just as the sun was breaching the eastern horizon, each with chunks of cold meat from the evening's antelope. The landscape remained unchanging. Tom was in awe of these endless grasslands. His world had become horizontal save for the massive, roiling clouds that occasionally marked storms on the horizon, diminishing the prostrate plains below. Such limitless land, so much potential for all those in the old world who lived on rented land, at the whim of ancient bondage. Yet, the red men who roamed the plains were thin and hungry, seeking only to harvest what nature provided. Their half-starved faces were all the argument Tom needed that what he and other settlers did in breaking the soil and planting crops was justified.

By early afternoon, he could see what looked to be forested hills on the western horizon. Within hours the flat prairie had given way to rolling grasslands with these hills looming close behind. The Lakota led the party north along the edge of the rise, coming shortly to a trail that led up a narrow valley. At its end the trail climbed through the forest, its tall conifers reminding Tom of the treed hills that lay to the west of the farm in Scotland. Did this mark the end of the prairie expanse or was it an island in the seas of grass?

They were climbing quite steeply now. Reaching a ridge and a break in the trees, Tom could see in the next valley a number of white-plastered buildings surrounded by a high stockade of upright logs, bleached grey by the sun. The Canadian flag flew from a high mast. There were a number of tepees standing outside the stockade and people going about their business. This was clearly their destination, the fort that quartered the Northwest Mounted Police.

The forest had been cut down about a quarter of a mile around the fort and as they broke out of the trees riding towards the stockade, they saw several men quickly mount their horses, wheel through the gate and ride to meet them. They were a striking sight in their red tunics and white helmets. They appeared unarmed.

The Lakota motioned to Tom and his comrades to ride in front of them, accompanied by one of their number who could speak some English. They were soon within shouting distance of the officers. Slowing to a trot as they neared the police party, Tom quickly identified himself and his comrades.

"We are members of the militia, and were serving with Boulton's Scouts under Colonel William Dillon Otter," Tom said as the men reined their horses in around them. "We became isolated in an engagement with the Cree at Cutknife Creek. We were captured by Chief Fineday's men and held for several days after the battle." Tom detailed the rest of their adventure as the men listened attentively.

"You are welcome. I am Corporal Daniel McKenzie," said one of the officers, a tall young man who, judging by his accent was of Scottish descent. He rode over to the Lakota, "Hau. Wowahwa.'" Then to the soldiers he said, "Come into the fort and bring your Sioux companions. You can stay here until we get word about your regiment. The deputy superintendent will want to talk with you to learn what he can from your experience."

---

*   Greetings, peace

As they rode towards the fort, Tom asked McKenzie where his family came from in Scotland and was delighted to hear they were from Berwick, just up the North Sea coast from his parents' home. "Well, we should have a thing or two to talk about," said Tom.

Approaching the gate, the Lakota held back. Tom and McKenzie went back to talk to them. They said they wished to set up camp outside the fort. In the absence of their chief, they could not discuss any questions with the police. Though their people had been assured safe passage in Canada, it was evident they were still wary of white men in uniform. The Lakota waited while their white companions dismounted, retrieved their few belongings and handed over the reins of their horses.

Tom turned to Ohiteka, "Please do not leave until we have had a chance to speak to you again." He nodded and the Indians rode back towards the forest.

Tom and his comrades followed the officers into the fort. They were immediately struck with how orderly everything was. The long, low buildings seemed newly painted and Tom could see a large vegetable garden towards the back of the compound. The principal offices of the fort were directly ahead, with stables and storehouses on one side and residential quarters on the other. There were several women about including a couple of white women. Other police officers were engaged in grooming horses while off to the right behind the stables several police and a couple of Indians had horses in a coral, obviously in the process of breaking them.

McKenzie showed the men to a dormitory, invited them to settle in and then to come to the main office to meet the deputy and join the other men for an evening meal.

Tom could not believe this turn of fortune. Convinced on two occasions that he would not return from this military engagement alive, he was now among his own people and surely would be able to find his regiment, collect his back pay and return to the farm. As he and his comrades stripped off their clothes behind the residence and washed off the encrusted sweat and dust of the last days, he felt himself begin to relax. Jocular banter erupted among the soldiers, the first sign of humour in many days.

Dinner that night was a feast, so long had it been since Tom and his comrades had eaten food cooked on other than a camp fire. The deputy superintendent told them that the rebellion had all but come to an end. There had been a pitched battle with the insurgents, both Metis and Indian, near the Batoche settlement, which the Canadian military had won. Louis Riel had been captured. There were rumours that both Poundmaker and Big Bear were negotiating surrender.

The latest they had heard was that most of the Canadian military had regrouped in Prince Albert though some were still in the town of Battleford. The superintendent did not know where Boulton's Scouts were. He suggested that Tom and his comrades wait a few days and then join a party that was expected from Fort Edmonton which would proceed to Regina and then on to Winnipeg. He was certain that once they reached Regina they would discover the location of the Scouts.

Tom asked whether they might make a gift to their Sioux companions for journeying with them to Fort Walsh. This was readily agreed to. Tom also wanted to find something that Ohiteka might take back to Wynona, something to indicate to her that his interest was not simply a product of his isolation. But he had no money to buy anything.

After dinner as they walked the compound in the fading light, he fell in beside McKenzie and asked if the superintendent might advance his party money to meet their needs on the journey east. He was assured this would be forthcoming the next morning. The next challenge was to find something appropriate in this isolated outpost where it appeared only the barest of essentials were available. He decided to explore the loft above the administration building where he was told traded goods were stored to exchange on occasion with the Indians. Mentioning that he wanted to purchase something as a special gift to the Lakota family who had taken him in, he asked McKenzie permission to access the storeroom.

Once up the stairs, he was astounded at the profusion of fur hanging on the walls – luxuriant pelts of fox, wolf, lynx and bear, their fur catching the sun's slanting light. He had no idea that the fur on these animals could be so redolent of health and vigour and so pleasing to the eye and touch. Where, in the middle of the prairie, could these beauties come from? Likely the forest clad hills around the fort, this rich island of diversity set in the ocean of the plains.

His eye caught the glistening bronzed pelt of a fox, perfect from head to tail tip. That was what he would give Wynona, something that as a child of the prairie she might never have seen. But it would surely cost him a good several weeks' pay and he was unlikely to have that amount of money available. He would have to confide further in McKenzie and see if the prospect of romance could best the fiscal caution his compatriots were famous for.

McKenzie was delighted. There was so little opportunity for the graceful things of life in this secluded place that he readily backed Tom's intent and arranged for him to buy the pelt at a price much reduced from what Tom had expected. He gave Tom the address of his headquarters in Regina as the best place to forward payment for the loan.

The next morning Tom and two others left the fort on horseback to find the Sioux in their forest encampment. They returned with Ohiteka and two horses to pick up bags of flour and sugar to take back to his people. The young man stood tall and solemnly nodded his thanks. Tom then handed him the fox pelt wrapped securely in burlap and asked him to take great care of it and give it to Wynona from him. Ohiteka's eyes widened slightly and for an instant he looked intently at Tom. Then he caught himself, returned to his customary demeanour and nodded slightly. Tom held out his hand, "Thank you, friend. I hope our paths cross again."

The next day dawn broke in a threatening manner. Huge, black clouds massed on the western sky above the hills and by early afternoon, snow had begun to fall and the wind blew. By nightfall, they were in the midst of a roaring blizzard, the snow flying almost horizontally, propelled by the gale.

The next day was no different. The Indians who were camped around the fort were now seeking shelter within. The dining room was opened to house them. Tom and his comrades could do little but play cards and contemplate their future. Finally on the third day, the storm abated but the snow stood several feet deep in the square and piled much higher against any barrier to its flight. McKenzie sought him out to tell him that any travel would be impossible until the snow melted or at least until the sun and wind had formed a sufficient crust on it to give horses a chance at a decent footing. It was now nearing the middle of October. There was no way Tom could get home until November at the earliest. That would mean Rob would be left to bring in the harvest alone. He doubted his brother would leave the farm until he returned and that would rule out a journey back to Scotland this winter.

As his situation became apparent with its implications for him and for Rob and Agnes, Tom's regrets began to mount. While the events of the last weeks had been beyond his control, his decision to enrol with the Scouts was his alone. But it was too late for regrets and there was no way to let Rob know where he was and when he might return. Communication in this wild country was hostage always to distance and the weather.

Standing at the window of the dormitory, looking out over the bleak, white world, he hoped Rob would forgive his foolishness. He ached for Rob's disappointment, for his prolonged separation from Agnes.

Chapter

24

THE DAYS GREW SHORTER AND THE GRAIN WAS HEADING UP BEAUTIFULLY. This first harvest looked to be more than Rob had expected, the plants showing by their size and vigour the richness of the black soil beneath. He contrasted this with harvests at Abbeylane, where the plants seemed half as tall and the kernels not nearly as full.

His excitement mounted each morning as he strode into the fields, seizing handfuls of kernels and rubbing them to assess their readiness. He had come to terms with the fact that his brother would not be around for the harvest. As the days passed, he became more and more worried about Tom's whereabouts. He considered traveling to Elphinstone to try to pick up his trail but he had left it too late. The harvest would be overdue by the time he got back with the grave risk of heavy rains or frosts decimating the returns of his months of heavy labour.

Then one day a party traveling from the west to Winnipeg stopped for the night. They had come from Prince Albert in the Northern Territory and had news of the unfolding insurgency. Rob asked them about Boulton's Scouts, the regiment Tom had said he was joining. Yes, they had heard that the Scouts had been in a fierce fight with insurgent tribes southwest of the city and had lost a fair number of men killed or missing. They had no knowledge of the names of any individuals. If the battle had taken place some weeks before, perhaps there was a letter for him in Brandon from Tom or some information from the regiment about Tom's condition.

Rob could hardly concentrate on anything other than finding out what had happened to his brother. He calculated he had about a week before the barley would be at its peak for harvest with the wheat and oats following some days later. He had already talked to the McIvor brothers about the help he would need in Tom's absence and with the extra hands they offered, the harvest could be completed in a week. He had just enough time to get to Brandon and back before the heavy work began.

And the trip would be timely. He and the others had shared their food supplies with the Lakota and they were now short on salted meat, sugar and other items. The three families compiled their requirements. They also gathered what vegetables they could from their gardens, the sale of which would augment their funds.

Young Seumas McIvor wanted to come along. Rob welcomed the company on what would have been a long, lonely ride filled with increasing anxiety about Tom. They left before dawn the next day in order to reach the town by nightfall.

His first stop, as always, was the post office in the general store. It yielded letters from Agnes and his parents but no letter with a Canadian stamp. His eagerness to hear Agnes' news was dimmed by the frustration at hearing no word from or about Tom. He now had to face the reality of informing Agnes that he could not return this autumn and that it would be at least late next spring, after planting, before he could think of journeying east to sail to Scotland.

He left McIvor to negotiate the sale of their vegetables with the manager of the general store while he headed to his quiet spot down by the river. He again found the old anger welling up, the fury against Tom for always seeming to act without regard for others. But this time these emotions were mixed with dread that somewhere out on the trackless plains, his remains might be lying exposed to the wild beasts and birds. He must find some way to contact Canadian military authorities. Someone somewhere must know what had happened to his brother.

But now he must write to Agnes so that the letter would begin its journey to her before he left Brandon. He must tell her he could not come as planned but avoid the fact of Tom's disappearance. He could not alarm his parents before he had definitive information.

199

"My dearest," he began. "I have just received your last three letters and feel you are here right beside me as I sit on the banks of the river in Brandon to send you my news. I am exceedingly well and healthy. The work of our summer looks as though it will return wonderful rewards. The grain is heading up beautifully and we will start the harvest within the week."

He went on to describe his work over the past weeks, the completion of the house, the well, winter shelter for the animals, the arrival of his new neighbours. He mentioned Tom's journey back to Elphinstone once the spring sowing was done.

"But now I have some sad news. I was so hoping to be able to free myself in time to travel to Montreal and set sail for Glasgow by mid-September so that we could spend the winter months together and arrange for our wedding. But it is now clear that that is not realistic. We will be done our autumn's work and preparations for the harsh winter too late for me to get to Montreal before the season's shipping comes to an end. For reasons you will understand, hardly a ship dares brave the north Atlantic come November.

"This gives me much grief. I had so counted on being in your lovely presence within a few months. While I now have great confidence in the success of our venture here and the fact that we can provide a full and free life for ourselves and those of our families who choose to join us, I am not sure, had I known the deprivation of heart and soul that this venture has entailed, that I would have had the courage to embark on it at the beginning."

He assured her that he was certain that once the spring ploughing and planting was complete, he would be able to travel east and be in Scotland no later than early July. That would give them time for a summer wedding and a return in time for the harvest in mid-September.

He folded and sealed the letter and then turned to write his parents. It was very difficult to account for his days while saying so little about Tom. They would surely wonder at the paucity of his information but he could not mislead them. He tried to make up for this by describing in detail all that they had accomplished in the last number of months on the farm and his genuine confidence in the success of their efforts. He had to tell them as well of his inability to return to Scotland in the autumn and assure them of his return right after spring planting.

By the time he had finished, the long summer dusk was fading and he made his way with a heavy heart back to the boarding house. Young McIvor was buoyed by the prices his vegetables had received, ample to pay for tomorrow's purchases. The mistress of the house had saved supper for them, after which they were quickly asleep in their quarters.

There was nothing left to do the next morning but purchase the supplies needed and head west. But as they were weighing out the flour and sugar, the post mistress suddenly appeared at Rob's side to tell him that there was another letter that had been overlooked the previous day. This had a domestic stamp but the address was in a hand he did not recognize. He took it, excused himself, and went out to the store's front porch where he could read in private.

He knew immediately that it was an official letter from the military. He quickly glanced at the signature at the bottom of the page. It bore the name of Colonel William Dillon Otter, commander of the Boulton's Scouts. Rob read:

"We have been informed that you are the next of kin of Thomas Dunbar. On July 23 of this year, our regiment in which Mr Dunbar was a volunteer engaged a band of insurgent Cree at Cutknife Creek in the Northwest Territory.

"In the course of the battle, Mr Dunbar and several of his comrades became separated from the regiment. On our return following the battle to retrieve our dead, Mr Dunbar's body was not among them. It is assumed that they were made captive by the enemy under Chief Fineday and subsequently removed from the site.

"I want to assure you that the government's forces are doing all we can to track and recover the prisoners. The rebellion appears to be coming to an end, and we are confident that in the coming negotiations with their leaders we will be able to secure the release of all prisoners.

"In the meantime we will inform you as soon as we can of any news concerning Mr Dunbar. Respectfully, Colonel William Dillon Otter."

Rob leaned back against the rough logs of the store's exterior and took a deep breath. This was some relief. There was a chance that Tom was alive and perhaps even at this moment back with his regiment. Rob quickly found young Seumas, shared the news and asked him to complete the purchases while he wrote back to Colonel Otter. He thought about revising his letter to his parents to inform them of the development but decided against it. It would only cause them great anxiety. Far better to wait until he had more definitive news.

His letter to Otter requested that any further news be addressed to Mrs Bracken, the postmistress in Brandon, an arrangement with which she was only too happy to comply. In this way, mail could be forwarded with travellers heading west.

The journey home passed rapidly. Rob's hope that their venture might now get back on track was returning. His disappointment about the postponement of the wedding faded somewhat with the anticipation that his brother might be alive. The relief also displaced the anger with Tom's impetuousness. He might still want to revise their partnership but he would much rather have his brother alive and living in close proximity than end up as bleached bones under vast and indifferent skies.

The next days quickly passed and one evening he called at the McIvor's and told the brothers he thought the harvest could begin in two days hence. Rob collected their hand scythes and honed the three instruments until they were sufficiently sharp to peel a fine shaving from his fingernail.

That evening he sat in the long dusk looking westwards towards the retiring light, watching gentle winds leading the barley in a celebratory dance of life and abundance. The evening was silent save for the occasional rustle as sharp gusts tossed the mature kernels about.

Rob felt a deep connectedness to this land, land he had altered with sweat for the first time since it had been laid down millennia ago. It gave him a humbling sense of significance and power, having ploughed up one long, balanced, undisturbed story and imposed the first of the many chapters of his own tale. Gazing at the fullness of the stalks that waved before his eyes, he felt gratitude for the eons that had built and preserved this soil and an imperative to sustain its treasure.

He knew this could not be done by simply cropping it year after year. He had heard tales of some settlers who had taken virgin land but because of ignorance – or more likely poverty – had not restored the nutrients their crops had extracted. And so, within a few years, the crops became stunted and yellow and they had upped stakes and moved on. Behind them the soil eroded and disintegrated before the wind. Many thought nothing of this as fresh open land seemed endless in this country of abundance.

But Rob knew that by impoverishing the land, they impoverished themselves. The wasteland might be left behind but the act of wasting eroded self-respect. Family and community could not be built by running away. His father and mother had poured their life's energy into the land at Abbeylane, even though they were only tenant farmers. They held their heads high because of it. He would do the same – and had even more reason for the land belonged to him. It was his inheritance from earlier eons to be held in trust for generations yet to come.

The next morning, dawn had barely nudged the eastern horizon when Seumas and Dewar were at the door eager for the day's work. The sky appeared somewhat overcast; welcome protection from the hot sun as swinging the scythe would be arduous work. They made their way to the barley and decided to work by splitting the field in thirds and advancing parallel to each other. A light dew moistened the stalks but they remained firm enough to topple swiftly before the honed steel. Rob felt the muscles of his upper arms and shoulders rise to the work, fully energized by the joy of reaping his first harvest.

They bantered back and forth enjoying the cool of the morning, the thrust of the blades against the stalks and the vigour of each other's company. But as the sun rose behind the thin cloud cover, they needed all their energy to maintain the momentum and conversation died.

Breaking after a couple of hours, they decided to begin gathering the mown grain into bundles and stacking these. About a third of the field had been cut, but they needed to give their shoulders a rest. Armfuls of the barley were pulled together and roughly tied into swathes with a handful of stalks. These were then stacked upright in groups of four or five into stooks to finish drying and facilitate later threshing into the back of the wagon.

The work was grueling. Though in prime condition from the summer's labour, the constant stooping, gathering and carrying pushed the men to their limit. After the dew dried, dust followed their every movement. They broke for lunch and gathered by the well where they stripped and poured cool water over aching limbs and then collapsed to dry in the sun.

By nightfall, they had finished the scything and could look back on scores of stooks marching across two-thirds of the field. The balance they left to gather and stack in the morning. The brothers returned to their father. Although he had told the young men that he could finish the field on his own in the morning, they had insisted on returning to complete the job. Rob grabbed cold ham bought during the recent trip to Brandon, ate it with bread and fell asleep on the rope-strung bed, fully clothed.

The weather remained warm and Rob judged that the stooks should stay in the field for a couple of days to ensure that the stalks were dry enough to release their kernels with minimum threshing. That would give them time to recuperate before the next operation. Checking the state of the wheat and oats the next day assured him he had at least a week before scything could begin on those fields.

Two days later, Rob hitched Pete and Old Harry to the wagon and headed to the stooked barley. The McIvors returned and they spent the day traveling from stook to stook, lifting the swathes high and beating them against the sides of the wagon to free the columns of kernels, then spreading the empty stalks on the ground.

As the wagon filled, they unloaded it in a long, low pile at the back of the house. While the brothers returned to threshing in the field, Rob took a hummeller, a square frame holding a dozen parallel metal blades fixed to a short wooden handle. This he stamped sharply down on the piled barley to break the beards from the kernels. He then made his way back to the wagon to assist with the ongoing threshing.

This took the whole day. The final step of winnowing and bagging the barley would have to wait for the next day. Rob realized that it would have been wiser to thresh, hummel, winnow and bag the grain from half the field so that the operation was completed in one day. By threshing the whole field, the unwinnowed barley was open to the dew and perhaps rain over night which would threaten its quality. He had forgotten how long the process took as the threshing they had done at Abbeylane had been mechanized several years before his departure.

He used a long wooden shovel the next morning to toss the grain high in the air, the kernels falling to the ground while the incessant wind swept away the chaff. By the day's end he had cleaned and bagged some eleven sacks of barley, each with weight that required his full strength to lift. He slept that night with a deep sense of contentment.

In the few weeks that followed, Rob and the brothers worked their way through the fields of wheat and oats. The prairie weather held bright and cool, the dry winds keeping the stalks brittle, facilitating scything and threshing, and sending the winnowed chaff spinning out across the now empty fields. He had over forty sacks of wheat and twenty-three of oats, in addition to the barley, much more than he could take to Brandon in one trip. He would need to hold some back for next year's seed and most of the oats would be required for winter feed for the oxen. Some of the wheat he would have milled in town for his winter's supply of flour.

It was now early October and the huge cumulus clouds that had been growing across the skies in recent weeks were beginning to turn a deep grey, a harbinger of winter weather. And still no news of Tom. He found himself slowly coming to terms with the possibility that Tom might never be found, that he had come to a lonely end at the bottom of some coulee, victim of the anger of the red men whose lands his people seemed determined to usurp.

With the harvest in, he could make the journey to Elphinstone or better yet, to Regina in the west to meet with the military face-to-face. But a journey of that nature would take more money than he had on hand and traveling with the ox-cart would lead him into the weeks when winter storms might break. He would need to have a saddle horse. He decided to journey first to Brandon to sell his grain, then buy a horse there and procure provisions for the journey.

But on a sudden hunch he decided to visit his Lakota neighbours – perhaps Old John or some of his people would have word about the conflict. The next morning he left early and reached the camp as the sun was just above the horizon. He could see the cooking fires from a distance and when he arrived in the camp, the young man who spoke some English saw Rob arrive and made his way over. Together they walked to Old John's tent. The old chief was still asleep, wrapped in his buffalo robe.

Old John's women folk welcomed Rob and beckoned him to sit and partake in their fried bannock and dried meat. Old John emerged in time and quietly joined the circle. They talked of the weather, the group's effort to hunt and gather sufficient food for the cold months ahead. The party they had sent to the police head-quarters earlier in the summer had returned with supplies of flour, salt and dried beef, enough to provision them while the men pursued the late summer hunt and the women gathered berries and harvested their small gardens.

Rob then told Old John about Tom's journey to Elphinstone and his decision to join the military expedition. He spoke hesitantly, carefully, realizing that Old John might not be inclined to answer the questions of one whose brother had decided to join a war against his people. He said that he had heard that Tom had perhaps been captured by the Cree and was still missing. He asked John what he knew about the current state of the conflict and whether they had heard anything about white soldiers being held captive.

Old John was silent for a long time, looking into the far distance across the prairie. Then he spoke. "We have heard something. We have Sioux brothers who live many miles west. None of our Sioux are involved in fighting the Great Mother's soldiers. But some of our young men are restless. It has been told that a party of them saw white soldiers being taken as captives across the plains by a party of the warring Cree. Our young men were many and they decided to seize the white soldiers, perhaps to hold them for ransom.

"But such action goes against our agreement with the Mother's police. So the elders in this camp made white soldiers guests and some days later took them to police camp. That is all I know. The names of the soldiers are not known to me."

Rob's mind raced. There was just a chance that Tom was in that party. Rob asked if John knew which police camp they had been taken to. The chief shook his head but the young man who had been translating said he had heard that it was called "Walish".

It was now imperative that he make his way to Regina. He wanted to turn around and head right back to the farm but he knew that custom required that he linger and spend the rest of the morning hours with Old John and his family. As the sun climbed high in the sky he took his farewell. It was now too late to leave for the town until the next morning. He loaded the wagon with half the grain and made ready to depart before dawn.

He reached Brandon by late afternoon and went directly to the warehouse of John Holmes, a buyer and shipper of grain. The golden beams of the late afternoon sun reflected warmly through the spiralling dust of the warehouse where sacks of grain were stacked eight feet tall. Wagons were being loaded for an early start the next day for Winnipeg. Holmes came forward and greeted Rob warmly. His men loaded Rob's cargo on to a scale while Holmes opened one sack each of the wheat, barley and oats, rubbing the handful of each type of grain assessing its quality with a practiced eye.

"That's fine product," he told Rob, "but prices are not the best this season. Plenty of competition from the American prairies. The best I can give you is fifty-six cents a bushel for the wheat, forty-eight for the oats and fifty-two for the barley. You would have done better if you had held back until the late winter. By then prices are usually higher."

With the weighing done, the two men retired to Holmes' office where he handed Rob $176 in cash, more money than he had had in hand since he left Scotland. Despite the lower prices, Rob was feeling highly pleased as he made his way to the familiar boarding house. He hoped he might still find some dinner available despite the late hour.

Next morning he headed to the general store to enquire who might have horses for sale and to stock up on the provisions needed for the trip west to Regina. As he walked down the town's only street, he noticed a group of men on horseback descending the sides of the coulee from the west heading for the town. Something about them made him linger, watching them closely. As they approached the street a few blocks north of where he stood, he was sure one of them resembled Tom's profile. He started to run, and as he got closer, to shout.

The man spurred his horse to a canter, barely drawing up beside Rob before leaping off. The two men fell into each other's arms. "Oh, Tom, you're safe. Oh, thank God." Rob pushed Tom's shoulders back so he could get a look at him. He noticed immediately his brother's features were lean, his face reddened by the sun and wind. "What happened to you? Where have you been all these months?"

"Oh, I have much to tell you," Tom said. "Let me get this horse taken care of and then we can talk." The other men in the party approached and Tom introduced his brother. They made their way together down the street to a livery stable. Tom took down a small saddle bag, handed the horse over to one of the other men and told them he would be back in an hour. He turned to Rob and the brothers walked down to the bank of the river.

The initial emotion of surprise and relief had faded. Tom's face was set and he did not look directly at Rob. He was clearly finding it difficult to talk. "I didn't expect to see you here," he said. "I have had an extraordinary adventure."

They sat on the grass as Tom spoke rapidly, engrossed in his story but showed no sign what his prolonged absence had cost his brother. Rob sat silently, his relief that his brother had returned safely giving way to anger at what Tom's decisions had cost.

"Didn't you think of the risks involved in joining the Scouts, the possibility that exactly what has happened might happen, or worse? You must have known that there was no way I could return to Scotland as planned unless you were here?"

Tom did not look at him.

"Tom, you had a responsibility to me, your first responsibility. I depended on you. And you let me down. So I have had to put off my marriage to Agnes and had it not been for the willingness of some new neighbours to step into the breach, we would have lost most of our crops. You could not help getting captured, but you walked into that danger with your eyes open and your brain shut. And you don't seem to care what happened at my end."

"Of course I care," Tom shot back angrily. "I don't need you to tell me I made a mistake. Of course I'm sorry. But it was a chance to make a lot more money than milling wood. How was I to know it would turn out this way? I was told we would be done and back in Elphinstone in six weeks, plenty of time to get back for the harvest."

But Rob's fury would not abate. "But you damn well weren't back. You have no idea the grief you have caused – my fear for what might have happened to you and the deep disappointment about not getting back to Agnes. You've taken things too far one time too many, Tom. I've come to the point where I don't want to have to rely on you anymore." He knew he was saying things that could wound their relationship but his frustration was too great.

Tom was startled at the force of his brother's anger. But his last comment triggered Tom's resentment, always close to the surface, of his older brother's dominance

"That's alright by me. You seem to have survived without my being around. So you can just keep at it. I'll stay here in Brandon and get winter work. I don't need you standing in judgment. I've made my own way the last three months and that suits me just fine." Tom got up angrily, turned and headed back to the livery stable.

Now it was Rob's turn to be startled. He had not expected this outcome. But he had meant what he said and if the consequences were that they ended their partnership, then so be it. Rob was too upset to consider what this would mean right now. But there was no need now to buy a horse or the extra provisions he had come to Brandon for. He had the cash from the grain sale in his wallet. Some of that rightly belonged to Tom, so he followed him catching him just before he reached the stable.

"Don't be an ass, brother. Come back to the farm and we'll sort this out," he said. "Besides, I sold some of the grain and part of this money belongs to you."

Tom turned on him, "Keep your money. I don't need it. And I don't need you shadowing me and telling me what to do. I told you I am staying here, and that's what I will do." He strode into the stable.

Rob went back to the boarding house to hitch up the oxen for the return journey but decided to wait a day to try to figure out a way to bridge the chasm that had opened in his relationship with his brother. He fed the oxen then decided to climb the coulee and walk the prairie in an attempt to regain his composure. He noticed heavy dark blue clouds building on the eastern horizon. Not a good sign.

He thought back to the day when his mother suggested that Tom join him on the journey to Canada rather than Peter. He knew then that the possibility of a conflict that could sabotage their endeavour but the argument about giving Tom a chance to start again had won the day. As he thought of the past year, he could see that the tensions between them had never really gone away but had been kept in check by the challenges of survival that confronted them. And while there were many days when he enjoyed his brother's company and admired his eagerness for adventure and his openness to people, he was increasingly aware that Tom chafed at the position of leadership Rob had assumed.

Perhaps it was for the best that they spend time apart. With the harvest in, most of the season's work was done. The long winter months stretched ahead and the prospect of their sharing that small house with too little to keep them occupied did not bode well. Tom could make money staying in Brandon and Rob's friendship with the McIvor brothers would assuage his loneliness. The passage of time might bring Tom to the realization that they had to find a way to work together if they were to build an alternate future for the rest of the family. But would the parting of their ways further delay his return to Scotland to take Agnes to wife?

He returned to the town to seek out Tom, express regret for his angry words and let him know that whenever he wanted to return to the farm, he would be welcome. But he was nowhere to be found.

25

Tom had been in Brandon for several weeks, though he was frequently on the road between the town and Winnipeg. He had found work with John Holmes, hauling grain by wagon train to the railroad in the larger city. But the work would only hold until the harvest had been delivered and by the end of November he knew he would be again looking for work.

He had not talked to Rob since their heated exchange. He had written his parents telling them he had found winter work in town but said nothing of his military adventure or of his conflict with Rob. There was no way he could adequately convey what was happening in his life and any attempt to do so would only generate alarm and parental intrusion. He didn't need that. He was his own man and wanted parental concern no more than brotherly guidance.

The railway was heading west. On one of his last hauls to Winnipeg he had seen a posted notice advertising jobs to build station facilities in Portage and Brandon over the winter. He applied immediately and by early December he was part of a crew of fourteen constructing a station in Portage.

Life was pleasant. A good job, a steady wage and a comfortable bed were a welcome contrast to the turbulence of the recent months. In the long, dark evenings when he had had enough of male company, he thought increasingly of Wynona. How had she received that fox fur? Did she think about him with the same pained pleasure her image conjured in his spirit? Would he ever be able to track her down? Should he try to do that as soon as spring made travel across the plains possible?

Christmas was approaching. Memories of family ties were powerful and he could not let that season pass without returning to Pipestone. He had made his point with Rob and his return to the farm would perhaps signal a different relationship. He would only stay for the festivities – whatever they might be – and then return to Portage.

A week before Christmas he was able to join a wagon train to Brandon. The weather was cold but the snowfall had been light and the roads remained passable. But once in Brandon, he could find no one heading west. Travel had come to a halt as families prepared for the season. Tom decided his best option was to buy a good horse. He would need a strong one to take him into the Northwest Territory in the spring in his search for Wynona's people.

It took a day to find a willing seller with an animal to match Tom's requirements. It was now December twenty-second. As Tom mounted the coulee to pick up the trail he saw ominous clouds across the western horizon. Black clouds this time of year meant only one thing – white snow and plenty of it. In any other circumstance, he would have turned around immediately and waited out the storm in Brandon. But there was no telling how long the storm might last and the trail could well be impassable for days afterwards. He prodded the horse to a canter.

All went well for the first hours. The threatened storm held off. The trail had been well travelled and he could see it clearly ahead of him. It felt good to be back on this land, land he and Rob had often travelled across. The horse was responsive and with the path well marked, needed little direction. So it was some time before he noticed the wind had picked up strength and was now blowing from the northwest where the clouds were their blackest.

He could see the storm coming down upon the land ahead of him obliterating the few trees whose dark shapes broke the empty white desert. It was as though a dirty, grey curtain had fallen across the land. As he rode closer it was less like a curtain and more like the billowing waves of a great storm-tossed sea.

Within minutes the storm engulfed him. He could now see

barely a couple of feet in front of the horse who now had lowered its head and reduced its pace to a walk. Tom knew that within minutes any sign of the trail would disappear.

Apart from the fact that he was surrounded by white emptiness, the temperature was not that cold and once the storm had landed, the wind died back. He pressed forward knowing that his only option was to proceed in the hope that he might find shelter. He spurred the horse to a trot. The snow was dry and light and though it was now almost to the animal's knees, it did not yet encumber their progress.

He estimated that it must be about noon. If they were still on the trail, they should shortly be coming to a small coulee with a stand of cottonwood along the bottom that would offer some protection. The anticipated coulee did not arrive. Tom's anxiety mounted. Was his timing off or were they completely off the trail? If the snow became impassable or the temperature dropped before they found shelter, they would not be discovered until spring, if then.

The horse showed surprising resolve. Tom had lost any sense of direction but the horse kept moving steadily forward. Perhaps he sensed something Tom did not. With no other option, Tom let him lead. He was getting badly chilled. He decided to dismount and walk but resisted the urge to take the halter and lead. If the beast knew where it was going, Tom would walk alongside. He was not drowsy and as long as he could keep his circulation going, was not likely to succumb to sleep. But he had to keep panic at bay, and that was much harder to do without a companion.

He must have walked for at least an hour and was warmed through but decided to keep walking. It was reassuring to be walking beside that warm animal, his hand on its shoulder. Riding it up top was lonely and, in these conditions, passive. He had chosen the horse well and knew that if they survived, they would be bonded.

The snow kept falling heavily but did not accumulate. It was so dry that the wind blew it like mist across the surface, drifting only when it came to an obstacle of which there were few. Tom could tell by the dimming light that the evening was approaching. He halted the horse and pulled some dried meat out of the saddle bags. Still no sign of accessible shelter though he noticed the dark shadow of a grove of trees every once and a while drifting by in the shadows. But his instinct was to stick with the horse's lead rather than divert to find shelter.

Fatigue was setting in. He was afraid of exhaustion and so decided to mount the horse. Night descended rapidly but still the animal plodded on. He had lost track of time and several times was jolted awake when the horse stumbled or broke stride. He knew he must keep awake and began to sing, startling himself with the strange sound of this frail human voice in the midst of the vast, white cold. At first it was the bar room ballads, the more suggestive the better, to pry open his memories and bring to life the images of friends from what seemed another life.

The ballads held little comfort now. He turned to the hymns his parents had sung every Sunday evening in that stone house sitting high in the fields above the North Sea. "I need Thee every hour,"---"Blessed Redeemer". He knew the words by heart. They tumbled out of him and he was warmed; the panic subsided. They rode on through the night.

He was awakened by a change of pace as the horse had slowed down. Out of the snow and the dark emerged strange shapes. They were tall and snow covered – several on the left and the right. Too wide for the straggly trees that survived on the plains. They looked like the tepees he had seen at Cutknife Creek. He must be delusional, his mind replaying that trauma.

The horse stopped and pawed the ground. He tried to spur it forward. It would not move. The shapes were still there. He dismounted and led the horse towards one of them. Yes, beneath the covering of snow, they were tepees. He was immediately afraid. What if he had survived the storm only to find himself once again captive?

A dog barked, the sound muffled through the snow-laden tepee; then another, followed by a chorus. Someone threw back the flap on the nearest tepee. Two men shrouded in blankets emerged and shouted something he did not understand. Caught between fear of the dark strangers and terror of the desolate emptiness he had just passed through, he found himself shouting, "Hau. Wowahwa." From somewhere in the muddled recesses of his mind he had recalled the Lakota words for "Greetings. Peace be with you", words he had learned from Corporal McKenzie at Fort Walsh.

The men grunted a response and came across the few yards to the horse. One of them took the bridle and turned to his colleague speaking in an animated fashion while pointing to the horse. The other motioned to Tom to dismount which he did with difficulty, his limbs rigid from the cold and time over-long in the saddle.

The tepee slowly glowed orange. Someone had lit a fire and he could see shadows on its walls. One man took the horse, the other beckoned him into the tepee. Tom brushed the snow from his clothes and followed.

A woman was fanning the small fire. She did not look at Tom. The Indian motioned for him to sit close to the flames. The second man came back into the tent. Tom slowly took off his coat and heavy gloves, rubbing his hands and face in the increasing warmth. The two men sat opposite him, looking at him intently and began to talk in their language which seemed to Tom to be Lakota, the language of the young warriors who had accompanied him to Fort Walsh – Wynona's people.

He spoke to them slowly, "I am Tom Dunbar and my brother is Robert. We have a farm on Pipestone Creek, Shandyhookawakapa. I became lost in the storm."

The men looked on uncomprehending. Then one of them got up and left the tepee. The woman said something and passed bread and dried meat to the other man. He passed it to Tom who nodded thanks and quickly began to eat.

Soon after the second man returned with a much younger man, the night's sleep still heavy on his face. The three spoke for a while and then the young man turned to Tom and said in English, "We know your brother. He a good man. He live not many miles away. My name Ohista. When storm stops we take you to farm."

Tom felt his body relax and immediately drowsiness was upon him. But the conversation continued with one of the men speaking excitedly to Ohista, pointing to Tom. Ohista asked Tom where he had obtained his horse. The horse, it turned out, had belonged to this man and he had sold it several months previously to a passing traveler. The latter must have resold it to the man in Brandon from whom Tom bought it – so that was why the horse had such a clear sense of direction. Tom broke into a wide grin and explained the events of the last day.

But now he could hardly keep awake and the men spread a buffalo skin and some blankets next the fire and beckoned him to lie down. He did so and quickly lost consciousness.

The tent was suffused with a dull light when he awoke. He was alone save for the old woman sewing on the other side of the fire. Tom lay quietly enjoying the warmth and the peace of his surroundings. When he stirred to get up, the woman rose and left the tent. Within minutes Ohista returned and asked Tom to come and meet Old John, the chief.

Outside the sky was grey but the snow had stopped. They walked across the encampment to the largest tent, and Tom bent to enter, following Ohista. It took some moments for his eyes to adjust to the dim interior but the he saw a group of older men seated around the fire. He looked at each carefully, none of whom he had seen before until he came to the last man in the circle. He instantly recognized him but could not place where they had met.

One of the men spoke in Lakota. Ohista translated. "I am Old John, chief of this camp. I am very glad that brother of my friend found our tepees in storm. Your brother helps us much. You are honoured guest and later we take you to brother's farm. First you eat well."

Tom hardly heard what the old man said, so absorbed was he with trying to recall where he had met the other man in the circle. The chief then spoke to three women who came forward with food.. The three had their eyes downcast but as the youngest handed Tom a chunk of roast meat she quickly looked him in the eye.

It was Wynona. Without a doubt.

His heart leapt wildly. He fought to conceal his emotion. Then the old man was her father, the man who had taken him into his tepee when they had been released from the young warriors. How could this be? Why were they here? His mind raced, keeping pace with his pounding heart. It was difficult to eat. He had to look at her but could not. He tried to think of ways to keep the conversation going. He asked Old John when he had last seen Rob. By this time Wynona's father was looking at him intently.

He finally spoke while the young man translated. "We know you. You are soldier and you stayed my tepee far away some moons ago. My people took you to Fort Walsh."

There was much murmuring around the fire. Ohista looked to Tom for a response. "That is correct. You were very generous to me and my comrades. We went to Fort Walsh but a big storm kept us there many weeks. Finally, I could leave and made my way to Brandon. How is it that you are here so far from your home, you and your daughter, Wynona?"

"That is fine," replied the old man. "We talk later."

Tom now felt free to look over at Wynona and smile. Her face was flushed but she did not look up.

Tom's head was swimming. First the good fortune of having been delivered to this encampment, then finding he was not among hostile strangers but friends of his brother and now the woman he most wanted to see turning up to serve him roasted meat. He was suffused by a mixture of shock and wonder. His efforts to sustain a conversation died amidst the grunts of men consuming their food.

He was told that when they had finished their meal, Ohista and some others would escort him to the farm. Outside the tepee, he asked Ohista how it was that the old man and her daughter were here, miles away from their home encampment. Ohista informed him that the wife of the old man was the sister of Old John's wife and that they had come to prepare for the marriage of Old John's son. And would they be staying for some time, Tom wanted to know? Yes, he said, the ceremony would happen when the snow

218

melted but the winter was a good time to visit as there was little work to be done in the camps while the snow ruled the land.

Tom was determined to find a way to talk to Wynona before they set out for the farm. He told Ohista more about his previous encounter with the family and asked if he could take him to the old man's tepee so that he could pay his respects to him and his wife.

"You go inside and talk. I get horse ready for travel," Ohista said as he left him at the parents' tepee. Tom hesitated, not knowing how to make his presence known. Then he used again the only Lakota words he knew, "Hau. Wowahwa." The old man opened the flap and looked out. His face broke into a smile. "Hiyu" he said, and beckoned him in.

It took moments for his eyes to adjust to the dim interior but as they did, he was transfixed by a luxuriant bronze fox pelt hanging on the tepee's wall directly in front of him.

Chapter
26

It had been a long, lonely autumn for Rob since his altercation with Tom. He kept the sadness muted during daylight hours with the labour needed to stock wood and food for winter. The earnings from the grain sales in Brandon had paid for dry goods. The garden proffered copious amounts of food and he stored all he harvested. You never knew when a crisis might make extraordinary demands – a call for help from Old John's people, or a pitiless blizzard might send lost travelers stumbling through the white desert.

The root cellar in the basement came into its own, filled with potatoes, carrots and turnips while onions hung from its beams. Corn, dried on the cob in the hot sun of late summer, lay stacked on a long wooden shelf along with several dozen orange and dark green squash. Sacks of flour, milled in town from his wheat, also stood on a wooden platform off the earthen floor.

After John Holmes had advised that prices were likely to be higher in the spring, Rob stored the oats, barley and wheat not needed for himself or the oxen. He built an addition to the stable, setting four inch aspen logs vertically into the soil and chinking them with a mixture of gumbo and straw. He piled the sacks of grain well away from the walls so that he could observe any rodent activity.

Labour numbed his emotions during the day but the evenings were harder. Once he had fed the oxen, eaten and cleaned up the dishes and there was nothing else to occupy his hands or his mind, the heaviness would begin. He had never felt so alone. It was though his small room was closing in, relentlessly, suffocating him. When he looked out the windows he saw nothing but empty blackness. He tried fighting it with recollections of that other life, a house crowded, splendid with the murmur of loved voices. But that only inflamed the anguish of loss. He began to doubt even the existence of Agnes, as if she were only a story he had read or a tale some passing traveler had told in a dark night many years ago.

Weeks passed in this divided state. Some evenings he sought relief in the company of the McIvor brothers and their old father. Out would come the cards and he would gain some passing relief in the slip and slap of games that had been forbidden in the Baptist home of his parents. But he was poor company and after a couple of such evenings, he turned down other invitations.

Christmas loomed, compounding the sense of isolation. He could not endure that season alone. If Tom would not come to the farm, he would go to Brandon and find him. Even Christmas at the boarding house would be a happier prospect than sitting by himself in the cabin. At least he could go to church and that might lift the dark murk that encompassed his days.

A day or two was all he needed to find Tom if he was in Brandon at all, so on the morning of the twenty-second he awoke early to hitch the oxen. Darkness fell early and he wanted to be sure to reach the town in the daylight hours. Outside, the morning was unusually dark and he noticed giant cumulus clouds turning the western horizon black. In the minutes it took to feed and harness the oxen, snow began to fall so heavily that he could no longer see the cabin. Clearly, this was no day for a journey. The only option was to wait out the storm and hope the trail would still be passable once it had passed.

Disappointed though he was, the very act of deciding to break the pattern of the last weeks seemed to lift his spirits. There would still be a chance to make Brandon by Christmas. Rob decided to use the day to write Agnes and his parents, letters he would mail from town.

He had not written since he had found Tom. His letters, particularly those to Agnes, had always been an outlet for his emotion. That spontaneity now had to be reined in. He did not want to reveal the split with Tom – so much of what contributed to his state of mind could not be shared. Writing the letter to Agnes was not the release he had hoped it would be and what he wrote to his parents was even more stilted. Frustrated at the end of the day, he tore up both letters, fed the oxen and the storm having abated, went walking the land.

The wind was still whipping the dry snow across the prairie, at times lifting and twirling it into unusual shapes. He walked southwards over the land Tom had registered for his farm, heading for a substantial copse of trees that stood on the farm's southern boundary. This was the site Tom had chosen to build a house, which they would have started on that autumn had he been there.

As he strode towards the trees, the wind gusted strongly and out of the blowing snow Rob suddenly thought he could see a building in the thicket. Startled, he strained his eyes to see more clearly and as he did so, it seemed the building was consumed by smoke, a cloud darker and more sinister than the white snow swirling around the copse.

Rob broke into a run, trying to understand what his eyes saw but his mind denied – an ominous sense that he was seeing a sinister shadow. He shook his head, fearing the stress of the previous weeks was unhinging his judgment. Suddenly a burst of wind pushing the snow before it completely obscured the trees. Rob pressed on through the blindness and when it abated, he was at the edge of the copse. The trees stood as he knew they would. There was no building standing there. Baffled, he turned back towards his own land.

The next morning, the trail was obliterated by the snow but with the sky clear and the route so well known, he was confident he could follow its general direction. The oxen were strong enough to plough through the dry snow so he hitched them again to the wagon and headed towards Brandon.

As Tom and Ohista headed away from the camp all he could think of was that bronze fox pelt and what its presence on the tepee wall could mean. He had not seen Wynona again though he had spent a few minutes of wordless pleasantries with her parents. He judged it bad timing to seek her further at that point. But she was there and would be for some time, or so Ohista had said. This would change his plans for the winter.

He felt a rush of anticipation course through his body, lifting him in the stirrups and causing him to prod the horse to a canter. The landscape shone, its gleaming white neighboured by the azure of the sky above. He had energy to burn, sufficient to surmount any obstacle. He would make his peace with Rob, but it would be peace on new terms, no longer the younger brother waiting for the elder to initiate or approve.

He wanted to meet Rob alone so he thanked Ohista and bid him goodbye but when he reached the house, it seemed abandoned. The snow around told the tale; through the footprints between the cabin and the barn ran wagon tracks and two sets of hoof prints extending beyond the yard and disappearing over the small rise east. So little wind had disturbed them it was apparent they were at most hours old.

He opened the door, dropped his saddle bags and got a fire going in the hearth then headed out to his horse. He would make much better time than the oxen and wagon. His elation returned. He was his own man again. He had cut the sibling bonds. He had a wad of bills from his militia pay and construction work. But above and beyond all these, the woman who had fired his imagination the last long months was close by.

They flew across the prairie, horse and rider seemingly one in their exhilaration. It was with a certain disappointment that less than an hour out from the farm he could see the wagon on the horizon. Now he had to collect his thoughts to set before Rob the reason for his return.

The original motivation, to visit for Christmas and then return to Brandon, no longer sufficed. He could say he had earned sufficient money for his needs until the summer and no longer wished to stay in Brandon. But that was unconvincing. A better reason would be to propose that they use the quiet winter months to fell the wood needed to build his house, taking advantage of the snow to haul it to the site in the copse of trees he had selected. That provided the best cover to pursue his relationship with Wynona, the thing that now gave meaning to his life.

When Rob heard the horse galloping across the plains, he had turned with some alarm. With relief and surprise he leapt from the wagon as Tom's horse drew close. "I was on my way to Brandon to find you," he called as Tom came within hailing distance.

"And I was on my way to Pipestone to find you," Tom replied, sliding down from the animal. They looked at each other warily but then Tom advanced grabbing his brother's extended hand. Both relaxed. Tom recounted the adventures of the last two days and his meeting with Old John and his people. He said nothing about Wynona.

"Well, this will be yet a fine Christmas," said Rob. "Let's get back to the farm."

Tom gave Rob high praise for the progress made on the homestead over the previous nine months. He was delighted with the provisions stocked in the root cellar. "It looks like you were expecting me," he said with a grin. He was equally surprised at the quantity of grain stored next to the barn. "That should bring in enough cash to more than pay for new equipment in the spring and your journey to Scotland."

They ate. Tom settled his things. Rob did not question his intentions. In time, they would be clear. He was just happy to have the hostility that stamped their last encounter, gone. Late in the afternoon, Seumas McIvor appeared in the doorway to invite the brothers to share a roast goose on the eve of Christmas.

Some days after that happy Christmas feast, they were in the valley cutting aspen along the shores of the Pipestone. Tom had made his intentions clear about building his house but had said nothing about the real reason for his continuing presence. He did not want or need Rob's approval and a disclosure seemed to imply just that. As the days passed he became increasingly impatient to return to Old John's camp but could think of no reason to propose a visit on his own.

Then, just before noon, Ohista and two other young men rode up to the farm. Rob hailed them. They said that the Sioux visitors from further west wanted to talk to Tom. Police had raided their home camp and had arrested some of the young men on suspicion of raiding across the American border. The young warriors had been taken to Fort Walsh and were being held there until they could be tried in a court in the spring. The elders claimed the young men were innocent. Would Tom be prepared to tell the police that the way he and the other militiamen had been treated demonstrated the elders' authority over the younger men and their good faith?

This was a long shot. They seemed to believe that a white man's word, any white man's word, carried weight with the authorities. And even if he spoke with the police in Brandon, there was little chance of his message getting through to their counterparts in the Northwest Territory. But he was willing to try and this was the excuse he needed to go back to Old John's camp.

Rob was keen to go as well as he had not seen his Lakota friends for some months. But Tom knew his brother might suspect the real nature of his interest in the Lakota if he accompanied him, and proposed that he return alone immediately with Ohista so as to be back before nightfall. The two of them could then undertake a longer visit in the near future. Rob seemed puzzled by the urgency of Tom's insistence but let the matter drop.

Wynona's father and several other elders assembled as soon as Tom and Ohista arrived. It seemed that troubles were increasing for the Sioux. A number of Sioux had decided to return to their homes in the United States, where they would invariably resume their conflict with American authorities. Canadian police were monitoring all movements closely and suspected that the young warriors were part of this militant movement. Two of their tribesmen had ridden across the winter prairie to request that the visiting elders return home as soon as possible.

This was going to put an end to any prospect of time with Wynona. He was in conflict. He knew he had to try to explain how little he could do to help but he wanted, above all, to encourage the family to remain. He assured them that he would go to Brandon as soon as possible and provide a formal statement to the police. He would try to get assurances from the government that all Sioux who wished to remain in Canada could do so without harassment. But even as he said these words, he was conscious of how grandiose they sounded and how inconsequential his voice would be. He was merely trying to diffuse their alarm for reasons of his own.

It shamed him to see how readily they accepted his words. Wynona's father said he would remain with Old John to await the outcome of Tom's intervention. Tom excused himself from the circle and told Ohista that he would travel back to the farm on his own. Left alone, he walked through the camp in the hope that he would see Wynona. She was not outside her parent's tent nor was there anyone inside when he opened the flap.

He walked further and then noticed a group of women returning from the thicket carrying firewood. He managed to position himself casually across their path and as they approached, he saw Wynona among them. He crossed the open space so his presence would be seen. She lifted her head, their eyes met and he nodded his head slightly. The women then continued towards the camp.

Tom's heart galloped. He hoped that his gesture would encourage her to return to her tent in the expectation that he would meet her there. He walked around the camp, approaching her tepee from a different direction. No one was around but he could see fresh footprints in the snow leading to the entrance. He stood just outside and gently called, "Wynona".

Riding across the prairie an hour later, Tom had never felt so complete, so happy. Wynona's welcome had been instantaneous. The passing of months seemed to have stoked her longing as much as his.

She had quickly pulled him into the tepee. Through the impediment of heavy winter clothes, they probed the contours of each other's bodies. It was all Tom could do to control his urge to lift her deerskin garment and move immediately to consummation. It was only the immediate tension in her shoulders as he began that caused him to hesitate. She drew back slightly and then slowly stroked his face, her eyes alight.

In the onrush of emotion, he had told her he loved her that he wanted to be beside her for the rest of his life. What of his words she understood he did not know but she looked at him and said, "Wynona stay Tom".

The sound of footsteps in the snow alerted them just as the flap was opened and Wynona's father entered. Startled at first, the old man's face quickly relaxed. He sat on the far side of the tent without looking at Tom and began to sharpen a knife. Wynona fixed Tom with her eyes holding steady as if to say, "It's alright, he understands."

Tom mouthed, "I will come back." He looked over at the old man who kept his eyes fixed on his hands. Tom turned, opened the flap and left.

He arrived at the farm in late afternoon and told Rob what he undertaken to do. They decided to go to Brandon together. With Tom intent on remaining on the farm for the winter, Rob had made up a list of additional required provisions.

They set off before dawn the following day. With less than eight hours of light on a January day in Manitoba, they knew it would be dark before they reached Brandon. If the wind remained light, they would be warm under heavy buffalo robes. But Pete and Old Harry could suffer in the sub-zero temperature. Rob had devised a pair of heavy wool blankets to attach to the oxen's harness. The wool absorbed the beasts' sweat and retained their warmth.

The following morning, after a breakfast fit to hold the frigid temperature at bay, the brothers made their way to the Northwest Mounted Police office. They were told that there was little the local police could do and that the best approach would be to send a formal deposition to police headquarters in Winnipeg. Tom and Rob spent the better part of the morning drafting their statement.

The morning after their return to the farm, Tom told Rob he wanted to spend some time on his own and that he would head out to Old John's camp to inform them of the action they had taken. Rob said he would come along. Tom was visibly upset. "No," he said, "I would rather travel alone."

Rob had noted a significant change in Tom since his return to the farm. He was not nearly as talkative as was his wont and seemed quick to challenge Rob's suggestions when they involved him. Rob put it down to the recent experience of battle and capture and thought that in time their former relationship would be re-established. But Tom's insistence on traveling alone once more to the Lakota camp irked him. Was something else afoot? Was there more to Tom's undertaking to the Sioux than he had let on? Rob decided it was not the time to question him.

Tom reached the encampment mid-morning and went to find Ohista. When he heard the news, he informed the elders they should gather at Old John's tepee. Tom was careful not to suggest that his action would necessarily have the result the elders wanted, but he still urged them to wait to see if the police in Fort Walsh would release the young men. Ohista translated his words. There was a long silence around the circle. Then various elders spoke in short, guttural tones, the conversation moving slowly around the circle, broken by long pauses. In time, agreement seemed to emerge. Ohista told Tom that they agreed no one should return west at the moment. They would await the outcome of Tom's intervention.

Tom felt relief along with the lingering guilt. Still, this decision allowed him precious time to pursue his relationship with Wynona. He excused himself from the circle and went immediately to find her.

She was at the family tepee with her mother and had clearly known that he was in the camp. Her face alight with pleasure, she beckoned him in and her mother quickly placed food that had been cooking on the fire before him. It was as though her mother had been expecting him, had already welcomed him into the circle of the family.

Tom proposed that they spend the afternoon walking together.

He was in no hurry to return to the farm. The sky was clear and a near full moon would provide plenty of light for the return journey after dark.

Once in the shelter of some trees, he pulled her closely to him. She lifted her face to his without hesitation. Again, the heavy clothes of winter awkwardly impeded access. By now, the long months of restraint and imagination propelled him much faster than he had planned. He climaxed with embarrassing speed, trying to hide the fact. She held his head hungrily, searching its contours with her eyes. They were now on the ground, the snow imprinted with their passion.

They lay quietly, side by side, her long, black hair falling across his face. Through the bare branches stretched the luminous blue of a Manitoba winter sky, the brilliant sun reflecting the radiance he felt within. There was no need to move. He felt he could lie there forever.

He came back to awareness with a start. She was sitting beside him looking down tenderly. He rose on his elbow, pulled her to him and kissed her slowly. They heard the chatter of women approaching through the wood and lay quite still smiling at each other. The women passed a few yards away either without seeing them or choosing not to notice. They got up quietly and walked back towards the camp.

It was late afternoon. Tom asked, "Your mother and father, do they know about us, do they know what you feel for me?" Wynona nodded. "Yes, when you sent fox pelt, they asked. I told them you were man I want children with. They understand. They happy if I happy."

They walked on. Wynona said, "You stay here tonight, you stay some days, yes?" "Yes," Tom replied.

When they arrived at the tepee, Wynona led the way in. Her father was talking with another man while her mother tended the fire and prepared the evening meal. Wynona spoke with her in Lakota. She smiled and looked at Tom. She handed him food and they ate in silence in the light of the shimmering fire. Tom noticed that buffalo robes had been laid out in a sleeping pattern on the other side of the tent from what appeared to be the family's sleeping quarters. After eating, the old man left the tent. The women busied themselves with end of day activity, stoking the fire, storing the food.

Tom sat silently watching the young woman. He thought he should somehow feel awkward in this undefined role but he did not. He found he was deeply content to watch the women as the light from the fire danced on the tepee walls. He thought of that fearful aloneness he experienced the first night he spent in another tepee, the night of his capture after the Cutknife Creek battle. The contrast with his present mood could not be starker.

He must have dozed off. He awoke to Wynona's hands on his shoulders. She smiled and beckoned him to the newly laid-out buffalo robes. He saw that her parents were settling into their sleeping robes. He rose and she accompanied him. He lifted the top robe, removed his shoes and lay down. She removed her outer garment and lay down beside him, showing no shyness or concern that her parents would see. He drew her closely to him and fell asleep.

It must have been some hours later. He awoke and at first did not know where he was. Then he felt her breathing body next to his. The tepee was pitch dark. All was silent save for the occasional snort of sleeping horses in the fields beyond. There again was the lovely scent of her body that he had remembered from months past, a mix of smoke, sweat and deer hide. He was still fully clothed. Slowly he released his buckle and worked his pants down off his ankles. Then he slid his hand across her body and found a parting in her garment. She stirred slightly. He found the warmth between her legs. She moved her legs to engage his. All remained silent save for the rustling of the buffalo robes and her short, sharp breaths as she rose to his ardour. It was over quickly. They settled back into the humid warmth of their shared space. No words were needed. Just the gentle stroke of her hands around his face.

Chapter

27

Tom had been gone two days and Rob was beginning to worry. The days were moderately warm for January and there had been no snow to speak of so the weather would not have been a cause for his delayed return. Rob continued the work they had been doing, felling the aspen along the Pipestone to supply the wood for Tom's house. He was beginning to wonder if a trip into Brandon in six or eight weeks to sell the balance of his grain would require the building of a sled. If the snows were as they had been over the previous winter, the wagon would not be able to make the trip in February.

He decided to give his brother another day. If he was not back by then, Rob determined he would ride to Old John's camp.

The next day dawned clear and cold. Rob saddled up and was in sight of the camp in just over an hour. He found Ohista and with him made his way to Old John's tepee. The old chief was very pleased to see him and bade him sit alongside him by the fire. He thanked him warmly for the messages he and Tom had delivered to the police and said that he hoped this would restore the good relations with the authorities at Fort Walsh.

Rob asked when he had last seen Tom and whether he knew where his brother was. Old John showed some surprise and indicated he had been staying here in the camp with his relations. Rob continued sitting with the chief for some time as custom required but finally bid farewell after receiving directions to the family's tepee.

As he approached he saw Tom walking towards the tethered horses, a young Lakota woman at his side. They were laughing and bantering in a manner that was highly unusual between a white man and an Indian woman on her own. He walked over to them.

Tom turned at his approach and looked startled. "What has delayed you so long?" Rob asked, his voice more demanding than he had intended. Wynona stepped back from the encounter. Tom stumbled for words. "I'll tell you later," he managed to say. He turned away and then abruptly faced Rob again. Trying to control his voice, with colour rising in his face he gestured, "I want you to meet Wynona. She is the reason I have stayed on here."

Rob was thunderstruck. He looked at the young woman who kept her eyes to the ground. He could not extend his hand and did not know what to say. He stepped back and looked at Tom. "When do you expect to return to the farm?" he asked. "When I am ready," Tom said defiantly.

Rob was shocked and bewildered. He turned and walked back to the chief's tepee where his horse was tethered. So this was what had been going on. Now he understood the urgency behind Tom's insistence that he travel alone to Old John's camp. There was much more that had to be explained but for the moment Rob saw no alternative but to ride back to the farm alone. He knew Tom was his own man and his role as older brother no longer gave him any authority.

Tom returned to the farm the next day. Rob was working along the river when he joined him. After a somewhat stiff greeting, both men returned to the work of felling and limbing trees. Neither mentioned their exchange of the day before and their conversation was sparse. The issue hung heavily and unspoken in the air between them until Rob at last asked. "Do you intend to make the Lakota woman your wife?"

"The Lakota woman has a name," Tom replied belligerently, "it is Wynona and yes, I intend to spend my life with her."

"But she is not of our culture, of our faith. Mother will never understand."

"I love her. I have since we first met during my captivity. She loves me. Everything else flows from that," Tom replied.

"Tom, you know I respect these people. They are my friends.

But God did not intend us to marry into their ranks. They do not know our ways. A child born of your union will face great barriers. We are both lonely in this wilderness. In time, you will find the right woman."

"This is the right woman," Tom shot back, turning on Rob angrily. "I do not need your approval or my family's blessing. If we are to work together, then respect my judgment and keep your opinions on this to yourself."

Tom strode a few steps off towards the farm, paused and turned to his brother again. "I am returning to her camp for the night. I shall be spending most of my nights there and will come here in the morning to continue this work."

Rob stood in the cold trying to come to terms with this new knowledge. On his own, he could not load more logs onto the wagon. He climbed up, slapped the reins on the oxen's rumps and drove them along the track towards the copse where Tom's house would be built. He could see Tom on horseback heading off to the camp. He left the wagon unloaded and led the oxen back to the barn.

The following days fell into a pattern. Tom would arrive an hour or so after sunrise. They worked steadily, stripping, cutting and notching the logs. The focus of their conversation was always the work at hand. Rob made a point of saying nothing more about the Lakota.

Sometimes Tom would spend the night at the farm but he never volunteered anything about his life at the camp. Other times he did not turn up for two or three days. Rob had asked him to let him know if he was planning to stay away but it made no difference. He found himself increasingly in the company of the young McIvors as a means of passing the long dark evenings.

The winter months passed slowly. In early March, the brothers travelled to Brandon to sell the remainder of their grain harvest. They had devised a means of attaching sled rails to the farm wagon so that Pete and Old Harry could traverse the deeper snow the winter had delivered. The visit was also an opportunity to send letters to the family and receive the first news from them in months.

The news was terrible – their sister Elspeth had died. She had caught pneumonia following a winter outing with friends and had succumbed quickly. Both were hit hard. For the rest of the day, they continued in the pattern they had adopted in recent weeks, but that night in their shared room, Tom broke down. He had been close to this younger sister. What made it particularly painful was that she had died just before Christmas and they had only heard two months later. Their father had taken the news very hard and was himself in frail health.

Tom sat on the edge of his bed, his head in his hands, weeping. Rob sat quietly. "Oh, we have paid such a price for this venture," Tom said brokenly. "She was such a special lass, such a bright spirit. To think we shall never see her again."

Rob crossed over and sat beside him on the bed. 'We are blood, Tom. We share so much and we now share this sorrow." He put his hand on his brother's shoulder. "We will see this through together and one day, we will all be reunited. You remember how excited Elspeth was at the prospect of eventually coming here to join us. We opened a window for her."

The next morning they unloaded their grain at John Holmes' warehouse. Prices were much better than they had been in the fall. They finished buying needed provisions by early afternoon and took the rest of the day to write the family. Tom wrote separately to Hermione who would particularly feel her sister's loss. Rob wrote to his mother. Neither mentioned the state of their relationship nor the cause of its dissension.

Spring came early. By mid-April most of the snow was gone and the winter wheat was well above ground. Within a couple of weeks, the ground was dry enough to take the plough. The walls on Tom's house were up and the men took a break on construction to get the spring planting done. Hoping that by the fall Agnes would have joined them, Rob put in an extra-large garden. Any surplus vegetables could be sold in town or to other settlers passing by.

Tom was still spending a couple of nights a week at the Lakota camp. But it was becoming apparent to him that he had to take some action to formalize his relationship with Wynona. He had noticed that none of the other unmarried women in the camp ever allowed themselves to be alone with a man who was not a relative. Perhaps he had been allowed access to Wynona and her family because he was a white man or because they themselves were not from this camp. Whatever the reason, he had been aware that the earlier ease of his presence in the camp was changing. Her parents remained open and warm but others were showing indications of hostility.

One morning, he asked Wynona to walk with him. "I want to be the father of your children," he told her. "I think I should ask your father if I can marry you."

She nodded. "My father must agree if I marry you. He want it done Lakota way," she replied. "In our way you give gifts to my father. If he accepts, we can marry."

"What kind of gifts?" Tom asked. "Horses good," Wynona said. "Buffalo robes. Guns. You give to him. If he agrees, he keeps. If not, he gives back and we cannot marry."

"But if he does keep them, what happens then?" Tom asked.

"We then marry in Lakota way. You will see."

Tom had none of the suggested gifts but he did have the money to procure them.

The next day he returned to the farm. He told Rob that he intended now to marry Wynona in the Lakota tradition and that he would be going to Brandon to buy the necessary gifts to offer her father.

Rob was clearly distressed. "You know I do not agree that this is right. You are once again acting without forethought. You have a whole life to live and it is best done with a woman from your own culture. With more and more settlers coming, you will find a woman to love."

"I have found a woman to love. I have known this woman now for many months and in different situations. I want to spend my life with her and none other," Tom replied glaring at his brother.

"Well, it's your life and your choice," Rob said reluctantly. "If you are determined to marry her, then at least seek a Christian marriage. There are others who have married into these tribes and done so in the church."

"No, that would have no meaning for Wynona and her family. I am taking their daughter away from them and I want to do this in a way that is most acceptable to them."

"But you will not be married in the sight of God," Rob pleaded.

"My God is God of the Sioux as well as the Scot. Their tradition is at least as honourable as ours. I will marry in their tradition. And I hope you will be present at the ceremony."

Rob turned away without answering.

A few days later Tom visited the three livery stables in Brandon and bought two fine saddle horses, a roan and a palomino. He then purchased a Centennial model Winchester rifle, a set of steel cooking vessels, two heavy woollen Hudson Bay blankets and a bolt of fine tweed. These purchases made a considerable dent in his savings but he in no way begrudged the expenditure. Satisfied that what he had secured would show to her parents the worth of their daughter in his eyes, he roped the animals to his saddle and headed back to the farm.

Two days later he left well before sunrise for the Lakota camp arriving as the dawn was lifting the eastern horizon. As he approached the family tepee he saw from the shadows on its walls that the fire was already burning brightly. The family would be awake and at the morning chores. He dismounted before the entrance. They had heard the horses' hooves and Wynona opened the flap slightly. Her face broke into a wide smile.

"I wish to speak with your father," Tom said, his face solemn, his heart racing. Moments later the old man appeared. Tom held the reins of the two horses high in one hand, the rifle in the other, and the remaining gifts at his feet. "I wish to have Wynona as wife," he said. The old man looked up, his eyes reflecting surprise for an instant. Then he nodded, looked Tom in the eye and took the reins and the rifle. He called out and Wynona's mother appeared. Her eyes shone, a smile tempting the corners of her mouth. She bent to pick up the blankets, cloth and cooking vessels. The family re-entered the tent leaving Tom standing in the early morning chill. They had not invited him to follow.

Tom stood quietly for many minutes. People from neighbouring tepees had stopped their activity and were watching. Then Wynona reappeared. "My father say yes," she whispered. "You now go. Come back three days for ceremony." Seeing the watching neighbours, she smiled slightly, lowering her head. Tom stood for a few moments, his eyes closed and then turned, remounted and headed out of the camp. Once past earshot, he let out a whoop, spurred the horse and galloped across the plain shouting his jubilation. That night he told Rob that the marriage ceremony would begin in three days. Rob said nothing.

Over the next two days, Tom worked feverishly as he still had to finish the roof on his house. Rob was breaking the soil to prepare for spring seeding. They said little to each other.

Rob was in deep conflict. He had a high regard for Old John's people but to marry into their ranks diminished both them and his brother. The marriage could not last. The chasm between their worlds was too wide. It would surely result in another tragedy for Tom and inflict grief on yet another family.

He had seen native women in Brandon and Winnipeg who had been enticed into a relationship with white men, who had then lost their place among their own people and ended up either abandoned or in servitude to the white man. But what could he do? Tom had made it abundantly clear be would brook no interference. Rob loved his brother despite their differences and feared he was once again headed into a dead-end relationship. He went to bed the following nights with a heavy heart.

28

Two days later Tom rode alone into the Lakota camp an hour after dawn. As he approached he heard drumming and the sound of women's voices singing. In the middle of the camp women had gathered in a large circle, at the centre of which five men pounded their drums and a number of women and children danced. Beyond the circle, other women were tending fires cooking meat and bread. Wynona and her mother disengaged from the circle, beckoned Tom to come to their tent and then left him alone. Moments later Wynona returned with Ohista.

The latter was smiling broadly. "You will be married today," he said to Tom. "You must stay here in tent. We come to get you this afternoon. Then you go to see new tepee and then medicine man makes you married. Understand?" Tom nodded. While they were talking, Wynona's mother had piled buffalo robes by the fire and brought in roasted meat and bread. She beckoned Tom and Ohista to sit. She and Wynona then left to rejoin the women's circle.

The sound of drumming and singing rose and fell. The rising sun creeping up the walls of the tepee warmed the air. Ohista left Tom alone. It had been an early start following three days of hard, physical work and Tom began to doze. It seemed that hours had passed when Ohista returned. "Chief wish to see you."

They walked past the circle of dancing women and children. Many eyes followed them. Ohista pulled aside the flap on Old John's tepee. Inside the chief and his wife sat beside a low fire. "Oh my friend. You are welcome," Old John said. "So you now become family as well as friend. You marry daughter of my wife's sister." Then he switched to Lakota and spoke for several minutes.

Ohista translated. "Chief says he very happy you take wife by traditions of Sioux people. He ask if your mother and father will come to ceremony and if they are happy about your marriage."

Tom looked down awkwardly. He realized he should have also brought a suitable gift for the chief whom he remembered too late was Wynona's uncle by marriage. "No," he answered. "My parents are many miles away across the great ocean in Scotland. They do not know Wynona and they have not heard that I am to be married. But when they know her, they will love her as I do. Perhaps they will come by the time of next year's planting."

The chief spoke again in Lakota. Ohista translated, "In our ways, a woman cannot marry unless her father agrees. For young men also it is better that father agrees but men who have tasted battle, they can marry without father and mother. I think you have tasted battle."

Tom reddened. He saw again the bare, brown back of the Cree warrior, his life blood pouring from the bayonet wound, smearing his chest and hand as he struggled to hold the Indian's fist-clenched knife away from his own body. His face darkened with the awakened emotion. He felt disoriented. "Yes, I have," he mumbled.

"A man who has tasted blood knows how to protect his woman," the chief continued through Ohista. "That is good. My wife's sister will be happy. Today you will be welcomed by all my people."

They then sat in silence for many minutes. Tom was accustomed by now to these long, quiet interludes and no longer felt the need to fill the space with conversation. John's wife rose, left the tent and returned minutes later with Wynona's mother and another woman bearing meat and bread. She first served Old John and then Tom. Then the two older women sat either side of the chief and began to banter back and forth, prodding the chief and laughing mischievously.

Rob asked Ohista what was happening. He blushed, smiling wryly. "Chief's wife is telling sister about first night after marriage.

She says chief pushed all other people out of tepee and when he came to her, his stick very big. They did not sleep that night."

Now it was Tom's turn to blush as Wynona's mother looked at him, laughing. "I like these people," he thought to himself. "They embrace life without pretense." He leaned back on the buffalo robes and stretched his feet. He felt the same relaxation take over his body he would have felt after a shot of strong whisky. His anticipation of the day ahead and the night that would follow mounted.

People came and went as the day progressed. Old John had drifted off to sleep leaning on his wife. The singing and drumming continued in the distance. Voices rose and fell and the hours passed. Judging by the sun on the tepee walls, it was late afternoon.

Then Wynona entered the tent along with her sister and several other young women. Ohista told Tom is was now time to go out and inspect their new tepee. Tom rose, followed by Wynona's mother and Old John's wife. The party moved to the new tepee across from Wynona's parents'. Its walls were light and clean, no fire had blackened its smoke hole. Buffalo robes marked the sleeping area. Stones in the centre formed the cooking fire which had been laid but not lit. Several leather sacks stood along the walls. And the luxuriant bronze fox pelt shone on the tepee wall. All seemed ready for their occupation.

They were only in the tent for minutes when the flap was thrust back and the medicine man entered, his head adorned with paint and feathers, a long green aspen wand in his hand. The hour of the ceremony had arrived and they were all ushered out of the tent. Four men stood holding a large blanket by its corners high above their heads. In their other hands they held spears.

The medicine man placed the wedding couple under the blanket and with a long shouted proclamation, led a slow walk all around the camp with the rest of the party joining the procession. Drums started beating a ceremonial rhythm. They halted before each tepee as its occupants came out with smiles and shouts of encouragement before joining the winding queue, often adding their drums to the beat. All danced and swayed to the tempo, the children shouting and running in and out around their dancing parents. When all the tepees had been visited, the noisy procession wound through the village until the sun began to set in the west. Then the medicine man lifted his green staff high and in a loud voice dismissed the crowd.

Ohista came forward and told Tom to follow him. Wynona was led off in another direction by the young women. Tom was taken back to the new tepee and told to light the fire and keep the flap of the tepee open. As darkness began to fall he could hear singing and a group of women appeared bearing torches. In their midst, six women carried the same blanket they had earlier processed under, and on that blanket sat Wynona, her eyes shining and her head thrust back in laughter. They entered the tepee and placed their happy burden at Tom's feet. Having been instructed by Ohista, Tom took the Winchester rifle which he had earlier given Wynona's father and playfully pretended to strike her exclaiming, "You are mine!"

At this, all laughed and seated themselves around the tent. Wynona stood and, helped by her sister, began preparing a meal for her new husband and their guests. The eating of the meal marked the end of the wedding ceremony but no one made a move to leave. The guests, including Wynona's mother, appeared to be settling in for the night. Finally, Wynona whispered to Tom. "For us to be alone, you must push them out." Tom looked puzzled. "How?" he asked. "You kick," came her reply.

Tom rose smiling, looking somewhat sheepish. He approached Wynona's sister, pulled back his foot and pretended to deliver a crippling blow. She screamed, laughing, and scrambled to her feet. Tom then proceeded around the room threatening each with a playful kick. Hoots of laughter filled the tepee as the women scurried out the door, playfully jostling each other and shouting teasing warnings to Wynona. Now Wynona was blushing but she quickly tied the throngs securing the flap and returning them finally to privacy. She turned to face Tom but he was right behind her and took her greedily in his arms.

Chapter
29

IT HAD BEEN THREE DAYS SINCE THE WEDDING CEREMONY AND ROB KNEW Tom would remain in the Lakota camp for several more. The ploughing and sowing could be delayed no longer. The river was still high with the spring run-off but the land was sufficiently dry to take the plough without compacting the soil.

Rob finished his early meal and went out to round up the oxen. They were usually near the barn in the early morning anxious for their ration of oats but he could not see them. As he turned the corner he heard a distant bellowing from the direction of the river. Alarmed, he followed the noise. Pete was standing on the bank, his head raised, bawling distress. Reaching his side, Rob looked down into the river bed and to his horror saw the body of Old Harry lying in the shallow water, his head submerged.

He scrambled down the bank. The mud was churned up where a struggle had taken place. Perhaps he had been killed by the wolf pack Rob had occasionally heard or a wandering grizzly very far from its normal haunts in the Black Hills south of the border. He crouched beside the body but there was no sign of predators. Then he noticed that Harry's front legs were sunk in the mud up to his shoulders, pinning his head below the water and what had happened became clear.

Old Harry had gone to the river to drink, likely during the night. The run-off had turned the low bank into a mud hole. Harry's feet had sunk and in his effort to free himself, the movements had sucked him in deeper. He had obviously thrashed about, but his efforts only condemned him. Finally his head had been pulled

under the water and he had drowned. He was certain to have bel-
lowed out his distress, but the river banks would have muffled the
sound and Rob slept so deeply he would not have heard him.

Rob climbed to dry ground, sat on his haunches and wept. Old
Harry had served them mightily. He was so steady, so strong, so
dependable. Rob had felt a special kinship with the huge animal,
for Harry and Pete were so similar in temperament to Tom and
himself. And Harry mirrored his personality. This would be a major
blow to their work schedule, already delayed by the wedding. But
the grief he felt was not for their misfortune, but sorrow at parting
from such a friend.

He remembered the long days when he had been alone on the
farm and Pete and Old Harry were his only companions, the times
he had chosen to sleep in the barn so their heavy breathing and
clomping movements provided the comfort of other living beings.

He was alone on the riverbank and allowed full rein to his emotions. He was surprised at the intensity of his feelings. But it was
not Harry's death alone that shook his body. Tom's marriage, going
so against the traditions of his family, his own drawn out separation from Agnes, the death of Elspeth, the long absence of all his
dear ones. He had carried these burdens stoically because there
were so many challenges that needed his attention. But the dam
broke with Harry's wretched dying and the accumulated sorrow
overwhelmed him. He wailed, his shouts accompanying Pete's continuing bellows. Minutes passed and he found relief in the release
of emotion. As calm returned, he smiled wryly through the tears,
"What a pair the two of us are," he said to Pete. "Fellow mourners,
much closer to each other in nature than I had ever thought."

He rose and went to Pete's side, put his arm around his neck
and scratched the curly forehead. "We'll just have to soldier on, old
man. Perhaps we can find you a new partner. What about a nice
young female?" He smiled again, took Pete by the halter and led
him up to the barn. He would have to go to the camp and talk to
Tom. One of them would need to go to Brandon as soon as possible
to get another ox. He would need Tom's help to dispose of the body.

He was at the camp within the hour, feeling suddenly awkward at this first encounter with his married brother. Tom looked up from his seat before the tepee, his eyes expressing his surprise. Rob dismounted, his speech halting, and related the reason for his return. Tom was clearly dismayed but quickly focused on the needed action. Wynona emerged from the tent. Tom would ride to Brandon to buy another animal while Rob continued seeding. They could not plough without a replacement for Old Harry. Wynona would remain at the camp.

Her father had come out of his tepee across the path. When he heard what had happened he asked what the brothers planned to do with the carcass. He suggested it could feed several families in the camp for several days and asked whether a party of young men could cut it up and bring it back. The brothers readily agreed.

Tom returned to the farm three days later leading a strong, young female ox. They called her Harriet. Pete showed as much excitement as an ox was capable of, nuzzling her and gently mooing. She had had some experience pulling the plough and with Pete's direction soon settled into the routine.

The intervening days had been clear and dry and the soil took the plough with ease. By the end of the next week they had broken a further ten acres and seeded all the rest. Tom's absence the previous autumn had meant that Rob had only been able to seed some five acres to winter wheat. With the bulk of their grain crop sown in the early spring, they would be at the mercy of the weather in the autumn – a hard, early frost, could cause the loss of much of what they had just sown.

Tom returned to the camp most evenings. Work on the land delayed his efforts to complete his house, but once the crops were sown he resumed this task. But the trips to the camp cut into the day's work and Tom told Rob one morning that he intended to bring Wynona to live on the farm and bring the tepee until the house could be occupied.

Her arrival two days later brought home to Rob that his relationship with his brother was forever altered. He had sought change from the day he and Tom had quarreled bitterly. But he did not envisage it would be so drastic. Tom had struck out on his own. Rob was grieved by his defiance and fearful of its outcome.

He did not condemn or judge Wynona. He could not reject her as an individual but neither could he accept her as his brother's wife. She, too, was not at ease in his company and kept to Tom's tepee. From a distance, Rob noticed her grace and beauty. She appeared strong and accomplished.

He focused on preparations for the return to Scotland. He had written Agnes that the way was now clear for his departure. He would make his way to Montreal and take the first boat bound for Scotland or England. There would be no way to contact her again before his arrival but she could expect him sometime in early July. They could plan an August wedding and set sail before the end of that month to return to the farm by the middle or end of September, in time for the harvest.

He could feel his excitement rising. Nothing now stood in the way of the planned departure. The summer's work would not be strenuous and the McIvors were close at hand should any emergency arise. Four other families had arrived that spring and had taken land to the west and south of them. Two were from Ontario with previous homesteading experience and one each from Scotland and Ireland.

The railway had passed through Brandon and had now reached the settlement of Virden some twenty miles north of the farm. It was likely that Virden would become the place to buy and sell, making unnecessary the long journey to Brandon.

The day came in mid-May when it was time for Rob to go. Tom had still not written his parents about his marriage or his adventures in the Northwest Territory. With Rob's departure, he knew he must now let them know what he had done and why – he could not leave it to Rob. "You will be surprised to know that I have taken a wife. This will come as a shock but she is a young woman I met staying with the Sioux and she is the finest young woman I have ever known. Her name is Wynona. We were married in the Sioux tradition. She is a graceful, beautiful woman and she deeply loves me. You must know that I have never been happier. I know that you will come to love her."

The brothers set off for Virden where Rob would board a train to Winnipeg and then on to Montreal. Tom had wanted Wynona to come but she was reluctant to go into the white man's town. Tom was eager to confront any hostility face on and establish for all to see that he and Wynona were man and wife but he knew he could not impose this on her.

As the train pulled in, Tom took his brother by the elbow and with the first sign of genuine affection in weeks, looked at him and said, "Travel safely, Rob, and have a splendid celebration as you finally marry that lovely woman." Rob had tears in his eyes as the train departed.

Chapter
30

THE TRAIN TOOK FOUR LONG DAYS AND NIGHTS TO REACH MONTREAL, STOP-
ping often to pick up passengers and goods, even in places
where there was seemingly no habitation and people by the tracks
waved it to a stop. Pulling into Toronto, Rob was startled at the size
of the city, as he was again on reaching Montreal. After almost two
years living on the open prairie, he had forgotten how crowded and
dirty great cities were. He could never live in such surroundings.

Once off the train, he made his way directly to the harbour and
stopped at the first shipping agent's sign he saw. He was in luck.
A vessel was due to depart the next day for Bristol in southwest
England. He booked passage and this time decided to travel second
class. He had earned the comfort and was anxious to arrive well
rested and ready for the intensity of his homecoming.

By the seventh morning out, they were steaming into Avon-
mouth harbour, the hills of Somerset rising gently down the coast.
It had been a smooth and uneventful passage, such a contrast to
their original journey. A short carriage ride from the docks into
Bristol took him to the rail station and an afternoon train to London
for an overnight passage to Edinburgh.

He arrived in the great, grey Scottish city in the early morning,
its spires reaching into the low clouds and its ancient castle high
on the hill almost obscured by them. He no longer noticed the
crowds and the dirt, so comforting it was to be back in familiar
streets. He even forgave the acrid smell of coal smoke from the
early household fires. All around were the accents of his youth,

turns of phrase that signaled he was home. He sensed his energy as boundless as his anticipation of seeing Agnes and his family.

He took a carriage to the staging inn on the southeast corner of the city where coaches regularly plied the roads leading along the North Sea to Eyemouth and beyond. By noon he was in the village of Coldingham, a little over a mile from Abbeylane Farm. Leaving his cases at the crossroad's public house, he strode up the Reston road. It was as though he had never left. He knew every field, every tree. Those he passed on the road stopped him with excited greetings, wanting to hear about his adventures. His courtesy was taxed in the extreme as he tried to break free as swiftly as possible to continue towards the farm's entrance.

Finally he turned left into the lane, seeing the top of the stone house behind a gentle rise. He broke into a run, shouting to any who could hear. His mother stood from the garden, looked in his direction and ran into the lane. His father emerged from the barn walking toward him, supported by a cane. Hermione saw him from an upstairs window and ran down to join the tumult. Isobel reached him first and flung her arms around his neck, weeping and laughing in her joy. Hermione arrived next to join the crush. Scottish reserve had no place in this homecoming. The three of them moved towards Thomas who was making his way slowly towards them. Rob approached his father alone, the women behind him. He gently enveloped the old man whose rheumy eyes were filled with tears. "Father, it is so wonderful to see you." Rob held the man in a long embrace; Thomas so overcome he could not speak.

The four walked towards the house, Rob offering his arm to his father, Isobel and Hermione laughing like school girls. "Where are Peter and the younger boys?" Rob asked. Peter was in Eyemouth purchasing supplies for the farm. The boys were, of course, at school. They walked through the back door into the kitchen, redolent with its smells and memories. Isobel immediately put water on for tea.

"Oh, there is so much we want to know," Isobel began. "Above all, how is Tom?"

"Mother, he is very well. There is much I want to tell you about Tom, but that will wait until later."

They peppered him with questions about the voyage, the farm, the house he had built, the views in all directions. He hardly had a chance to get in the one question foremost on his mind. "And how is Agnes?" "Oh, she blossoms," said Isobel. "She was often here when she was back from Edinburgh. But she has now completed her studies and waits for you at Norfield Farm. We must let you go so you can see her. Why not go now and bring her back here with you for supper? We shall have a celebration feast."

Rob smiled broadly at his mother. She was always the one to recognize the heart's priorities. "I'll do that, Mother. Is there a horse in the barn I can take?"

"Oh, I completely forgot to tell you," Isobel said, her face darkening. "William Runciman died last week – they say it was a heart attack. He was out working in the barn and one of the children found him. The funeral was only three days ago; we were all there. Perhaps you should stay overnight at the Runcimans' in the circumstances."

"Oh, that's terrible news. Poor Norah. Was Agnes home when it happened?"

"Yes, she had been back from Edinburgh some three weeks," Isobel replied. "But you should go right away. You will have a better sense of what to do when you get there. And do stay overnight if you think that is best."

"Before I go, I must get you a letter I have brought from Tom," said Rob. "I am sure it will tell you about all that has happened to him in the last months."

Hermione left with Rob to help saddle the horse. "Mione, it is so good to see you," Rob said, putting his arm around her waist. "We so missed you and Elspeth. Perhaps very soon you could take me to her resting place." Hermione's eyes filled with tears. She nodded wordlessly.

He was back on the Reston road in minutes and two hours later turned into the long, treed drive leading to Norfield Farm. No one was about in the mid afternoon. He tied the horse and knocked at the front door. Moments later Norah Runciman, her face drawn and lined, opened it and, with a startled expression, shouted, "Oh Agnes, he's here." Immediate sounds of running and excited children's voices came from the upper floor. The kitchen door flew open and Agnes ran down the hall flinging herself into Rob's arms.

"Oh my love. You're here at last." Her face wet with tears, she clung to him. "I have so often prayed for this day." He held her strongly, deep emotion and relief coursing through his body. It was as though the burden of two years of challenge and turmoil flowed out of his being.

They slowly unwound, Rob keeping his arm around her waist. He turned and gently embraced Norah. "I am so sorry to miss William. I am so sorry for your loss. God rest his soul. I did love to be in his company." Norah smiled weakly and lowered her eyes. The other children were now standing around expectantly. Rob embraced each one in turn. "Come," said Agnes, "let's sit in the parlour. I will go and make some tea."

"No, you stay with Rob," her mother answered. "The children and I will prepare the necessary."

Rob turned to Agnes to ask about the circumstances of her father's death. "Sadly, he was alone. He had been cleaning stalls and did not come in at the appointed time for tea. Catherine found him. Mother says he had been feeling pain in his chest for a number of days. She urged him to see the doctor. But Father was not a man to be concerned about his health. He had always been so strong and robust. These were clearly warning signs but they were not heeded."

Norah returned with tea and scones. The children were subdued but clearly eager to engage Rob in conversation. Agnes sought to change the mood and began asking questions about the voyage. It did not take long for the children's questions to tumble forth. "Did you see any pirates...What are the red Indians like...How much snow do you get...Were you in the war with the Indians?" Their faces were so attentive as Rob answered each one.

"Now, children, off you go and play. Agnes deserves to have some time with Rob alone," Norah said.

They walked together under the familiar trees of the orchard. For a time they were silent, the conflicting emotions of sadness and joy merging. And then Rob began to talk.

He described all the details of the farm, the river with its border of aspen and cottonwood flowing some two hundred yards north of the house, the prairie reaching east and south unbroken to the horizon, the gravel hills to the west; the lay-out of the house and its root cellar; its garden front and back. Agnes seemed to have a hundred questions. He then turned to talk of Tom and told her the whole story of his escapade, their subsequent quarrel, the surprise of his relationship with Wynona and the marriage that followed. Agnes was wide-eyed and silent.

"Do your parents know? Is Tom truly happy?" He explained how difficult it had been to go through the rupture with Tom and then to come to terms with the course his life had taken. "Our relationship has changed. Tom is his own man. His anger and restlessness have subsided. But life will not be easy for them. Most people deplore marriage between our people and the natives."

He grew quiet as he sought to frame his thoughts about his relations with his brother and Wynona. "Tom has turned against the tenets of our tradition and faith. He has contracted a marriage with one to whom these things are completely foreign. I fear he has set himself up for another fall, given his disposition, his past instability.

"Tom is always impetuous," Rob said with a slow shake of his head. "When he finds out how difficult it will be for people to accept Wynona as one of them, his anger will return and he will retreat into isolation. I do not blame or judge Wynona, but I cannot pretend to be happy about what has happened."

Agnes took his arm and held it firmly. She was silent for several minutes before she spoke. "Rob, you can do nothing about this now except help your parents come to terms with it as best they can."

Rob was conscious that this preoccupation with Tom had clouded their coming together.

He had been silent too long. "Will you come back with me to Abbeylane for a few days or should I stay here with you and the family?" he asked. "I am ready to do either but I do not want to be parted from you."

"Perhaps we could do both," she said. "I will come back with you tonight so that you can see more of your family and then the two of us can return here in a day or two."

They arrived back at Abbeylane in the late dusk to find dinner waiting. It was not until the next day that Isobel broached the subject of Tom. The other children were out of the house, at school or at farm chores. Isobel and Thomas by now had read Tom's letter and they gently began to ask questions about their third son. Rob's face clouded. "Tom has contracted a marriage, not with our own kind but with a woman from the Sioux tribe." His parents' faces were wide-eyed and solemn. Isobel broke her silence. "Rob, is this an actual marriage?"

"According to Sioux tradition it is. Of course it is not recognized in our society. But Tom and Wynona are now living as man and wife."

"Is he happy?" Isobel asked.

"Tom seems happy, but they face a hard future. I fear for them and for any children they may have. I do not know her well," he continued. "She has kept away from me for the most part. But I understand why Tom is attracted to her. She is striking in her beauty. She is composed and dignified. And she works hard."

Thomas said nothing, his shoulders slumped, his face ashen. He had feared that even a move to Canada would not change what he considered his son's wayward ways. And now this confirmed his fears.

"We need time to consider this," Isobel said. "I do not care what other people, what society thinks. All I want is for Tom to be happy and fulfilled. Rob, you know that your brother is cut from different cloth. He always has been. If he loves this woman, and she loves him, then they will find a way together. And Rob, you must help them. That's what blood is all about. Let the world turn its head away," she said firmly. "We cannot as a family."

Rob was keen to start work on the farm with Peter and his father. The sixteen-year-old lad he had left two years before had added inches to both his height and the breadth of his shoulders. He was now a young man in whom confidence and doubt struggled. In so many ways Peter reminded him of himself at that age, able to do far more than he gave himself credit for. Rob smiled, glad that the years had shed most of his own self-doubt and sure that the same would happen to Peter. He complimented him warmly on the state of the crops and the health of the cattle.

That night, Rob occupied the room he had shared with Tom, full of bitter-sweet nostalgia for all that had been. With the sun in this northern clime reluctant to sink behind the horizon, he lay on his bed running through the extraordinary events of the last two years: a tapestry of hope and travail. Despite the joy and comfort of the old surroundings, he was deeply content that he had ventured forth. He had become his own man and now it was time to claim his full manhood in the arms of a wife.

For the first time in many months he became aware of his full sexuality rising impatiently. She was his and he would claim her fully. She was down the hall, sharing Hermione's room. His principles decreed he wait but the months of repressed passion riled against patience – it was only Hermione's presence that excluded immediate action. He turned to the wall and allowed relief to take its course.

The next morning he was back in the familiar fields of Abbey-lane. The contrast with his land along the Pipestone could not have been greater. There the land met sky, often becoming one when storm clouds rolled out of the west. Here, the fields tipped gently to the east where ridges topped by great wind-sculpted pines arrested the view. Beyond the ridges, cliffs plunged to the North Sea.

Most days you could hear the waves beating on the coast, their sound carried inland by the ever-present wind. And on that wind, the sharp tang of salt reached to the sternum telling those raised by the sea they had come home.

The wind blew incessantly on the prairie as well but the sounds and scents it carried depended on the season. In high summer the rustle of long grass accompanied the slight fragrance of prairie blooms. In winter, the wind howled alone in the bleak landscape and the bitter cold erased any scent. Come spring, wind carried the pungent odours of soil waking from its frozen state mixed at times with a whiff of smoke from distant prairie fires.

Here, the soil was heavy with clay, embedded with a multitude of small stones. A miracle, indeed, thought Rob, that such yielded crops year after year even aided by the bowels of the farm's many animals. On the prairie the loam was dark and rich – no fertilizing needed there, at least not for many years.

It was a strange feeling to be so deeply attached to two such distant places but he did not feel divided by those loyalties, felt no tension between them. In fact he felt gratitude that he was grounded both in the landscape that had made him what he was and the soil that held all his hopes for the future.

The hours passed as the serried ranks of ploughed soil transformed the mottled green of the weed-strewn field into a uniform grey-brown. His spirit satiated with the sights, sounds and smells of that summer field, he let his mind turn to the events of the coming weeks. Even with the recent death of Agnes' father, they were going to have to plan a wedding soon. It was only four weeks before they would have to be on a boat so as to arrive in Manitoba by early September. He needed to gather his parents, along with Agnes and her mother to decide the details of the ceremony.

Two days later they all met in the Runcimans' parlour. Norah had asked their Methodist minister to officiate. His chapel in Reston was clearly not going to be large enough to accommodate all those who would wish to attend so he undertook to ask if the ancient abbey church in Coldingham could be used for the occasion. A date was set for the third Saturday in July. The celebration dinner would be held at Abbeylane as it was much closer to Cold-ingham than the Runcimans' farm.

Rob and Agnes had wanted a small ceremony with only imme-diate family. With the return trip to Canada hanging over their heads, they wanted to avoid the hassle of a community event but no one else would agree. This would be the first marriage for either family and Isobel was determined that it be a memory that would help compensate for the loss they would endure with Rob and Agnes' departure.

Chapter

31

THE DAYS FOLLOWED AT A FEVER PITCH. THE ANCIENT ABBEY WITH ITS immense stone walls and windows high above the ground, remnant of the days when it protected the monks from sea-borne invaders, had to be made colourful and welcoming. Great tables of food had to be prepared so that all who came could be heartily fed. Isobel assigned tasks to all save her husband, Thomas, and next eldest son, George, who sat by the fire in the kitchen watching the endless swirl of activity around them. Thomas could not keep up with the pace and happily allowed Isobel full rein.

Only when George was seated quietly in the kitchen, did Rob realize that in the tide of emotion and activity that had swept over him since returning, he had barely spent a moment with George. His younger brother had faded greatly since he had last seen him. He was losing muscular control and was uncommunicative most of the time. It was strange how familiarity led to detachment. No one would ever allow George to be without food or physical support when he needed it. But he was always there, on the periphery, and as the life of the family ebbed and flowed around him, Rob saw with fresh eyes how little it involved him. Perhaps that was one reason why he was fading

Rob looked at him intently and said, "George, I want to ask you a favour. I am going to be married soon to Agnes. Will you be my best man? That means, will you stand up at the front of the church beside Agnes and me when we are getting married? And will you hold the ring that I will give to Agnes and then hand it to me to put on her finger? It would mean a very great deal to me if you would do that."

Rob saw George trying to process what he had just been asked. He looked somewhat frightened. "No need to worry. I will show you what to do. Just stand up beside me while I wait for Agnes to come up the aisle and then be with me while the minister marries us. It will not be difficult but it would make me very happy."

George looked at his brother and then nodded his whole upper body. His mouth was gaping as he attempted to speak but his eyes smiled in assent. Rob took him in his arms and held him a long time.

The day of the wedding Rob was up well before dawn. He had planned with his sister, Hermione – with the agreement of the neighbours – to raid their gardens to select the flowers for Agnes' bouquet and to bedeck the church. Rob entered Hermione's room and gently shook her. "Time to harvest blossoms, Mione."

The contours of the pines atop the ridge to the east emerged as the sky shed its darkness. Rob put on tea. His sister came down, the spell of sleep still roughing her features. Rob stood and embraced her. "I didn't sleep much last night," he said. "I can't believe that the day has finally arrived. I hope Agnes slept more soundly than I."

"That just shows how little you know women. Agnes will have been awake all night. But we are better suited to enduring sleeplessness than you men. After all, our sleep is broken for most of our lives taking care of you lot," she responded with a grin.

Rob smiled. They drank their tea in silence, allowing the heaviness of sleep to ebb away. Hermione had a gift for colour and had already designed the flower arrangements. They featured daisies and asters, the sharp, white faces of the former set off by the striking blooms of multi-coloured asters. In the church she wanted these flowers backed by banks of deep red phlox. Daisies grew in rich clusters in their garden and the neighbours had bountiful beds of phlox and aster.

By the time the family began to assemble for breakfast Rob and Hermione had finished their work and stored the flowers in the coolness of the barn. The wedding was to be at three in the afternoon but there was still much to be done before. The Runcimans would arrive shortly, save for Agnes who was to spend the morning quietly with a friend at the neighbours.

Isobel and Norah had tasks allocated for all the young people. Some were to set up tables in the rented canopies on the front lawn under Rob's overall direction. Others were assigned to visit the neighbours who had prepared food for the evening reception. Energy and excitement suffused the air.

When Rob had finished his supervisory duties he told his mother he would be off alone for a couple of hours. She smiled in understanding. She knew he needed solitude from time to time especially on the cusp of this much anticipated event.

He headed for the sentinel pines edging the North Sea. Breasting the slope in record time, he scanned the promontories, the quiet coves and the grey sea beyond. He found his customary path down the slope to the water's edge. Observing the position of the sun in order to gauge the time he had left before he would have to be back, he set off down the beach heading for the point from whose tip he could see the fishing village of Eyemouth.

The sea, quietly advancing with the incoming tide appeared gentle and benign. He found a rock against which he could lean and began to ponder the coming events of this day and the weeks ahead. He remembered the uncertainty that dogged him as he first found himself drawn to Agnes, so sure that he would never be able to win her affection. He laughed quietly to himself, mocking the insecurity that had plagued him as it did many young men behind their brash exterior.

He breathed deeply of the salt-scented air, the wash of the waves and the gulls' cries lulling him to sleep.

He started awake in a panic. He looked immediately for the sun to get a sense of the passage of time but the clouds had thickened obscuring its location. Scrambling up the slope, he grasped a bush to lever his ascent but its roots, set only in the cranny's shallow soil, gave way. He fell back and tumbled some fifteen feet before managing to arrest his fall against a rocky outcropping.

Panting heavily, he lay still assessing his situation. His face stung and he was aware it was bleeding when he touched it. His left ankle throbbed painfully. He sat up and tried to climb again but the pain was excruciating. His ankle could hold no weight. His only option was to crawl on his knees and hope that at the top he would find something that could help bear his weight while he tried to walk home.

He breached the top of the cliff, sweat from the pain and exertion mingling with the blood on his face. Then he heard shouts. It was Peter two fields away. He had seen him and was running towards him. He struggled to the nearest tree to take his weight and waited.

"Oh, my Lord, what has happened to you?" Peter was upon him, taking his left arm over his shoulder. "Don't try to talk," he said. "Wait a minute while I look at you. You're in bad shape, brother. Stay here while I run for help."

Rob grunted his assent and almost passed out with a mix of pain and relief. "I am going to make it to the church. Tell them to wait for me. Whatever state I am in, I am going to be there." Peter was off. Rob slid his back down the tree and waited.

It seemed half the day had passed before he again heard voices. Peter was back with several of the neighbours. Peter placed Rob's arms over his shoulder and that of another man and together they managed a decent pace. Once back at the house, Isobel took charge of assessing the damage. Rob insisted that the wedding go forward and Hermione was dispatched to the abbey to inform the minister and arriving guests of the reason for the hour's delay.

One of the neighbours turned up with crutches. George was there, dressed for the occasion but looking very worried. "Nothing to worry about, old man," his brother said. "But now I am really going to need your help." Isobel bandaged the gash on his forehead, wrapped his ankle tightly and helped him dress for the ceremony. She slipped him some brandy to help with the pain. "I'll be arriving at my own wedding looking and smelling like a ruffian," he protested.

"Your bride will not mind in the slightest as long as she has you there, mind and body somewhat intact," his mother retorted.

A carriage was at the door. Rob had planned to arrive at the abbey on horseback. It was his idea of a symbolic Canadian entrance. Now he had to travel sedately with his parents and George but if he was disappointed, he did not show it. They pulled up at the side door of the abbey and quietly entered, Rob trying to walk as upright as he could on the crutches. George followed closely behind. The murmurs of the crowd turned to applause as they saw him. Rob beamed back and noticed Agnes standing surrounded by her mother and siblings at the back of the church. She looked alarmed. Rob looked directly at her and smiled broadly. Her face relaxed.

The ancient organ began to play: "Praise my soul the King of Heaven" and the crowd belted out the majestic hymn. Agnes moved slowly down the aisle, her mother behind, followed by the children. She came abreast of him. Rob handed George his crutches while she took his elbow, providing the support he needed. Together they turned to face the minister and the rest of their lives.

By the time they arrived back at Abbeylane, tables were burdened with food, children were running in excited circles and guests were pouring across the lawns. Rob and Agnes detoured into the house and sat resting in the parlour. Rob's ankle had to be bandaged again to compensate for the swelling. "I wouldn't mind another shot of that brandy," he told his mother.

Out on the lawns the women's dresses matched the colours of that summer afternoon, their hats showing off the glories of Scottish millinery while the somber garb of the men, true to rural tradition, belied the gaiety of the occasion. Rob and Agnes moved through smiling people, taking their places atop a small incline.

The milling crowd began to form a line, the children jostling for first place.

Small hands and shy smiles greeted Agnes as the line began to move. So many memories crowded Rob's mind as friends, relatives and neighbours passed by: men he had wrestled as schoolboys, old Sunday school teachers, farmers with whom he had broken solitude, townsfolk who had shared pews. His life flowed past, alive with the warmth of community and shared experience. What a contrast to the life they were embarking on where neighbours could be counted on the fingers of one hand and shared experience was defined by endless sky and yawning horizons.

Rob remained upright on his crutches until the line ended and was relieved to take a chair at a nearby table with Agnes on his left and her mother, Norah, on his right. The guests had made their way to other tables spread across the lawns. Isobel was directing a small army of young people bringing in the food. Rob wished he had more of that brandy but he did his best to focus on his mother-in-law.

Norah was looking solemn. With the marriage achieved, it was evident from her conversation that she was already feeling the pending absence of her eldest daughter. Rob tried to assuage her anxiety by suggesting that she and some of the children plan to journey to visit them in a year or two. "By then, of course, you will likely have a grandchild to meet," he said cheerfully, quickly realizing by her startled reaction that he had crossed the bounds of accepted conversation for a wedding day. He swiftly changed topics.

His brother Peter had readily accepted to manage the festivities. In due course he rose and with a voice that belied his youth, called for all to listen. It was the custom that the groom's father led the tributes on such occasions and he introduced Thomas.

Thomas rose slowly and turned smiling to his son. "Robert, your long wait is over. You have been an unending source of comfort and joy for your Mother and me ever since you were a wee bairn.

"Your reward sits by your side, the only woman I have come across who can hold a candle to your Mother, with apologies to all the other fine ladies present. You deserve each other." Thomas had to pause as his voice began to break. "God bless you both and the life you have chosen," he concluded, sitting down abruptly, his face flushed.

After what he assumed would be an emotional opening, Peter had lined up several of Rob's friends to lighten the tone. One said that at any cattle show, Rob could be relied upon to scrutinize the beasts with great care. "However, whenever Agnes appeared on the scene, the animals got short shrift. I could readily have persuaded him that an aged beast was a prime young heifer worthy of parting him from his money."

The jocularity continued and the crowd loved it. Rob noticed that he had been smiling so much that his face began to ache.

Finally, Peter turned to the couple and indicated it was their turn. Agnes rose slowly, her gaze sweeping the crowd. "I see the whole of my life spread before me. People have asked me how I could trade all that I have known and loved for a land and a life that is completely unknown. The answer sits beside me."

She turned, looking down at Rob. "I am happier than I have ever been in my life. I feel complete and you have made me so. Whatever the future holds, I know that you and I have made the right choice." She sat and the crowd, silent for several seconds, then began to applaud vigorously.

It was Rob's turn. He had thought carefully about what he would say. He began by recounting what life had been like several years before. "While I loved my life on the farm and was always grateful to be in the midst of such a loving family, inside I was restless and insecure. As many young men do, I was always comparing myself to others and coming up short. I had little confidence.

"And then one day I saw this lady and hope rose in my heart. I hardly dared take notice of it, but that warmth persisted and any time I found myself in her presence, hope was confirmed. And so began a wonderful journey of exploration, patience, forbearance and affirmation. And today we are here.

"I have seen the awesome hand of God spread across an ocean

of ice. I have felt intense excitement as, plough in hand, I broke for the first time the prairie soil. But that awe and anticipation pale before the prospect of taking you, my dear, as my wife. Thank you. Thank you from the bottom of my heart."

The crowd erupted, young men cheering, older folk turning to smile at each other, to comment on the ability of an occasion to turn a ploughman's son into a poet.

Peter allowed the happy clamour to subside. "Ladies and gentlemen, please fill your glasses and we will toast the bride and my lucky brother."

The long afternoon had stretched into the early hours of evening before Rob and Agnes took their leave. Abbeylane housed too many to be a suitable place for their first night together. Isobel had rented a cottage along the sea front and Peter completed his tasks by driving them there in the carriage that had delivered Rob to the abbey that afternoon.

The rooms were filled with flowers from the abbey. Scones and jam and cheese graced the table and someone had put on a kettle that boiled quietly on the stove. Peter awkwardly ushered them in, putting their small bags in the bedroom. He smiled, shook their hands warmly and left.

Neither of them wanted to eat. Agnes turned off the stove. Rob came up behind her, took her by the waist and led her out onto a balcony overlooking the circular bay that lay below the cliffs. Gulls were wheeling inland from the sea for their night's rest. The sky shaded into a pastel array which the sea mirrored. They breathed deeply, letting the silence, broken only by the gentle wash of the waves on the gravel below, shed the intensity of the day's events.

So this was the culmination of his awakening, the climax of a passage marked by longing and forbearance, aching loneliness and intense expectation. He almost did not want the anticipation to end, to be replaced by resolution. But the tide of emotion was running and brooked no stemming. Rob turned and embraced her. Agnes took his head in her hands and covered his lips with hers. Rob could feel his whole body tighten around his sternum. He gently placed his arms around her back, lifted her and walked into the bedroom.

Placing her on the bed, he slowly undid the front of her long dress. The muscles in his body contracted again and his breath came much faster. Agnes started to unbutton his shirt but now that their coming together was sanctioned, Rob's impatience drove him to hasten the pace. He wrestled his trousers off, lifted her to remove her dress and lay beside her, their bodies charged with delayed longing.

Rob knew he was coming quickly, the anticipation accelerating his arousal. He moved onto her, found the site of his passion and entered her just as his body erupted. Agnes cried out softly and then relaxed holding his head tightly to her face. They lay breathing heavily, Agnes covering his face with slow kisses. Rob slid his arms around her and held her. He had never felt so complete, so fulfilled. She was weeping silently. "Oh my dear, did I hurt you?" Rob asked alarmed. "No, these are tears of joy," Agnes replied.

Only then did he notice the burning in his ankle. "This is better than brandy anytime," he laughed. She smiled and they lay quietly, passion accomplished.

Rob finally rose, found a change of clothes and began to dress. Agnes lay still, watching. Rob went into the kitchen. She could hear the kettle boiling again and minutes later, he returned with tea. She got up, hung her crumpled wedding dress, selected a bright housecoat and they took their tea back to the balcony. By now the sky and sea had turned grey and it was soon apparent the evening had turned chilly. They returned to the kitchen. Someone had laid a fire in the grate and Rob soon had a warm blaze burning. "And so begins our life together," he smiled, pulling her down beside him on the settee.

Chapter
32

T HEY HAD ARRIVED IN THE LATE AFTERNOON AFTER AN ARDUOUS FIVE DAY train ride from Montreal. Tom met them in Virden – alone – Wynona still reluctant to travel to town.

Agnes descended to the platform first and saw Tom a carriage away. She had thought a good deal about the nature of her relationship with her brother-in-law and had decided she would do all she could to sustain the bonds within the family, including Wynona. She walked swiftly towards him and embraced him warmly. Tom was somewhat taken aback but quickly responded in similar fashion. Rob followed shortly, his arms burdened with cases

"Welcome home." Tom smiled. "You both look grand despite two weeks on the sea and the rails. You will be glad to get your feet firmly planted on the ground. But we have a couple of hours yet in the oxcart before things stop moving."

They went into the station to await the rest of their baggage. Agnes was fascinated by the mix of the crowd around them and the number of languages being spoken. It had been this way ever since they arrived in Montreal but the diversity had multiplied the more they headed west. She was clearly animated. "I can't believe the energy I feel out here, the excitement of opening a new country. Is there still land available for people?"

"Despite its vast size, it is filling up quite quickly," Tom explained. "Most people now have to travel further west and north to get free land. We have seen at least a dozen new families move in to the west and south of us so far this summer."

Tom brought the cart to the back of the station and Rob

immediately went to rub the muzzles of his friend Pete and the new ox, Harriet. "You remember me, old boy, don't you? Now I have a new partner as well," he said as he guided Agnes over to them. "Pete, here, shared all our travails and adventures almost since the day we arrived on these plains. I wish you could have met Old Harry. He was such a strong and reliable friend."

They loaded the five cases and tied them down. "You'd be thinking to set up a fine salon with all these belongings," said Tom. "Well, now that we have a lady in the house, it is time we had a few of the finer things of life around," Rob replied. A shadow fell across Tom's face. Rob instantly saw his mistake, as did Agnes.

"I'm sure Wynona has made your life very comfortable," she said. "Your brother has some catching up to do." Tom's face was set.

They were outside the small town quickly and on to the unbroken expanse that pushed to the horizon. Only a sliver of sun remained in the west, a palette of colour burgeoning across the sky. Rob could see that even in the few months since he travelled this way, new houses and barns interrupted empty spaces and more people seemed to be on the road.

Agnes sat entranced. It was one thing to view this land behind the windows of a train, another to be in its midst, open to the wind, the scents, sights and sounds. She nestled close to Rob, holding his arm in anticipation.

The last hour of the journey was in the dark, the oxen sure in their knowledge of the road. They entered Rob's house by lantern light. Agnes was delighted with the beauty of its simple furnishings. Tom, or more likely Wynona, had laid bread, cheese and apples on the kitchen table. Wynona was nowhere to be seen. Tom helped Rob unload the cart, excused himself and led the animals to the stable before walking to his house a half-mile away.

They unpacked their small bags. This bed that had welcomed his weary limbs so many nights and allowed him to rise restored by morning, was now going to be shared for the first time. Rob felt a deep warmth rise within him. It wasn't sexual excitement so much as relief and delight no longer to be alone. They undressed and Rob gently led her to the near side of the wood frame. He had bought a cotton stuffed mattress and linen sheets to replace the straw-filled bedding on his last trip to Brandon. There was no way he was going to subject her to that rough, malodorous resting place. They lay quietly together and Rob quickly fell asleep.

Agnes was too animated to sleep. She stretched fully, exulting in the newness of her surroundings. Through the adjacent window the partial moon revealed a silvered but featureless landscape, save for a band of trees towards the river. Rob's breathing rose and fell. Coyotes talked in the distance. She could hear the animals stomping occasionally in the barn. All was peaceful. At last, she too slept.

She awoke early, the first morning in her prairie home, rose quietly, pulled on a sweater and walked into the early morning. She first noticed that unlike in Scotland, there was very little dew on the grass. A mist hung over the path the Pipestone cut into the prairie. She walked around the garden behind the house, delighting in the array of vegetables growing in the black earth. Then down to the pond that separated the house from the barnyard. Ducks swam swiftly to the other side.

Light was growing and then the sun broke the eastern horizon. She watched its semi-circular rise across the prairie, unimpeded, until it became too bright to look at. To the north, the band of cottonwoods and aspen traced the sides of the Pipestone. To the south, the prairie was treeless save for a copse which she could now see surrounded another house. That was likely Tom's, she thought.

She crossed into the barn, to the warm, furry scent of the animals. Small, munching noises came from the stalls. She leaned over to scratch the back of one of the oxen; she could not remember which it was. Then she saw the horse in the back stall. A cow was standing in an open enclosure off another stall. Everything about the barn was orderly. She smiled thinking of her husband's thorough manner. In the distance she heard Rob calling.

"I'm in here making some new acquaintances," she called. In a moment he was at the door smiling. "Why, you're just in time to milk," he said. "Might as well get right into it." He carried a pail with warm water and a cloth in one hand and an empty pail in another. Handing them to her he went through the stall to bring the cow into the aisle, tethered her and washed her teats. "Here," he said smiling, pulling up a stool. "This will be the first of your assigned tasks."

Agnes laughed, sat on the stool, her shoulder to the animal's flank, with the milk soon pinging into the empty pail. "I knew you would be good at that," Rob said. "That's why I married you." She kicked him playfully.

The warm milk half-filled the pail and they walked back to the kitchen for their first meal.

"What would you like to do first," Rob asked, "unpack the cases?"

"No, the first thing I want to do is to go and meet Wynona," she replied.

"Shouldn't we talk about that first?" Rob asked.

"What's there to talk about? She is my sister-in-law and I intend to be her friend."

Rob looked pained. "But she is not married to my brother. We have no reason to believe this relationship will last. I have told you that much as I admire her, I cannot see her as family until she decides to share our culture and our faith. I do not want to encourage Tom down a path I am sure will lead to distress."

"Rob, dearest, I know you find this difficult. But we can't ignore her. Trust me as a woman in this circumstance. Your principles are important but my instinct is to extend a hand to Wynona. She is what she is but who knows what she may become if we keep open to her. I think it is important that you come with me."

They walked along the fields already full with ripening grain. Wynona was in her small garden beside the house watching as they approached, her face displaying no emotion. Agnes led the way. "I am very pleased to meet you, Wynona. My name is Agnes and we will now be neighbours and I hope good friends." She extended both her hands. Wynona took one of them shyly.

"Happy to meet you, also," she said casting a glance in Rob's direction.

"I hope you are well," Rob said awkwardly.

"Thank you, yes," she replied.

"You have a lovely garden. Will you show it to me? I need to understand what grows best in this climate. It is so different from Scotland."

The two women walked toward the garden. Rob heard his brother close the door of the back shed and went looking for him.

"We will have much in common," Agnes said, "married as we are to two brothers. I will need to learn much from you. Everything is so new and different." She noted Wynona's beauty, her long, black hair falling almost to her waist. She wore a beaded deerskin jacket tied loosely around her waist. Her eyes were clear and looked straight into Agnes'. Below the jacket her abdomen bulged slightly, and Agnes wondered if perhaps she was pregnant.

Rob and Tom sat on the back porch. There was much to catch up on. Rob had given his brother letters from the family when they had met at the station but Tom wanted to know greater detail about his father, about George, about the state of the farm and whether his parents believed they could continue there into the future.

Then there was the state of the crops on their own land, the prospect of prices for produce in the fall, news of the neighbours. When they had exhausted the easy topics Rob asked awkwardly, "Have you been to church at all, Tom? Did you take Wynona?"

Tom turned his head sharply. "I won't subject her to the hostile stares of those so-called Christians. I can't walk down the street without being aware of the mutterings accompanying me. I was used to such behaviour in Scotland when my actions had led to tragedy. Here, I thought things would be different. They are not, still the same small-mindedness."

"But, Tom, things would change if Wynona became a Christian and you married her in church. These people see you living with someone you are not married to. It would be the same if you took up with a white girl to whom you were not married."

"You're wrong. These are bigots. I like most of them but can't stand their rigid views. And they're so sure of their righteousness. It seems that crossing the waters brings out all the worst characteristics of our narrow society. Don't expect me to darken the door of a church any time soon."

"But Tom, you can't cut yourself off from your own people. This is exactly what I feared would happen when you took up with Wynona."

"I did not take up with Wynona," Tom said, almost shouting. "I married her and I will not have you regard her as anything less than my wife." Slamming his fist on the floor, he rose and walked around the corner of the house towards the barn. The women heard his raised voice and looked with concern in their direction. Rob sat quietly for a few minutes, picked up his hat and walked towards his house.

Agnes did not return for another hour. Rob was in the barn reacquainting himself with the animals after three months away. It was peaceful to be around them after the sharp emotion the exchange had produced. He did not know what to do. He did not want to see the ties with his brother broken again but it was more than he could do to pretend Tom and Wynona's relationship did not exist. He heard Agnes calling but for the moment he needed time alone.

He did a quick inventory in the store-room of the available feed. They had barely enough grain to last until the next harvest. He would have to restrict its use to the cow. She would need the protein for her milk production. Pete, Harriet and the horse could get by on the summer's grass. He noted much about the barn that needed repair already. It was a mixed blessing to see things with fresh eyes. Most could wait until the harvest was over, but doors coming loose on their hinges needed immediate attention.

He heard Agnes come into the barn. "Oh, there you are. I was worried."

"No need to be. Just catching up on chores." He tried to sound casual. "Did you have a good time with Wynona?"

"She is a fine woman, Rob. She will make Tom an excellent

partner. I noticed the two of you in some sort of altercation. What was that about?"

"Oh, only a brotherly disagreement," he said evasively.

"It seemed quite sharp," she observed watching his face closely.

Rob stiffened. "Look, Agnes. My relationship with my brother is complicated. I need to sort it out myself. I would prefer if you would let me do that."

"Of course," she replied, "But you should know Wynona is pregnant. The child is due in about four months."

Rob looked startled. He paused, and then spoke. "That settles it I guess. There is no going back."

The next day Rob knew he had to speak with Tom. He did not want to return to the issues that had caused the flare-up but they had to start planning how they would go about the harvest. The acreage they had ploughed last autumn and then sown, both at that time in winter wheat, and in the spring to oats and barley, was now too extensive to be cut by hand. They had talked before he left of new machinery they would need to buy but had postponed the purchase until his return.

Later that day he headed over to Tom's barn. Tom was under a wagon working on a split axle.

"G'day," Rob began. "Look, I am sorry if you thought I was being disrespectful of Wynona yesterday." Tom grunted. "I did not intend to be. It just takes me a while to come to terms with the situation."

"Well, you better get on with it," Tom said indistinctly from under the wagon.

"I came to talk about buying machinery. Have you had a chance to price sickle mowers and hay rakes?"

Tom pulled himself out from under the cart. "Yes, when I was waiting for the train in Virden I took a look at what was available there – pretty pricey. I think we could get a better deal in Brandon and while we are at it, we could see what the forecast is for grain prices this fall. Do you want to go or should I?"

"Well, if you don't mind going. I'm reluctant to leave Agnes until she gets a better feel for the place. Give me a day or two to come up with a list of supplies. Agnes is beginning to discover things she needs and we have to stock up on the staples I used up before I left."

Rob wondered if he should congratulate Tom on the prospect of having a child but quickly dismissed the thought and walked back to his homestead. It was good to feel the rich, black earth beneath his feet, knowing that no landlord could ever take that away from him. He realized that much as he loved Scotland, its hills and valleys, his family and friends there, it had not taken twenty-four hours before he felt firmly rooted again on this wide and verdant plain.

He suspected it would take Agnes longer. She will go through a period of mourning what she had left behind as he had. He must be attentive to her. He had been too defensive yesterday when she tried to influence his approach to Tom. She might be able to help rebuild that relationship in ways he never could. He must give her space to do that.

She was bent over in the garden when he returned. Clearly Tom, or more likely Wynona, had attempted to keep the weeds in check while he was absent, but with everything they had to do on their own property, not much progress had been made.

He came up quietly behind her and wrapped his arms around her waist. She stood and turned round. "You're so beautiful," he said, brushing her lips. "I am so glad you are finally here."

"You have done so much in the last two years, far more than I had expected."

"Well, there is much more to be done. But it can wait. I want to walk you around the boundary of our property, to see its hidden qualities. Tom and I may not have been here long but there are many stories the land will reveal as we walk it. And as you hear them, you may become as attached to this lonely space as I have."

He took her hand and walked down to the river close to the spot where Old Harry had drowned. Out came the stories: of the night in the frigid desert when the brothers survived by standing between the oxen, of the many mornings when the oxen had pulled piles of logs to the river to await the spring thaw, of their long solitary rides together across the plains.

West along the river lay small hummocks of gravel, perhaps the leavings of retreating glaciers. These would be valuable once road-building caught up with settlement. They turned south where the prairie ran endlessly to the American border. Over to the left was the copse of trees that marked the start of Tom's land. They could see his house. Rob spoke of the strange mirage amidst a blizzard's swirl that he had taken for a burning house, its smoke billowing above the trees and the unease that had invaded his soul. Agnes held his arm tighter.

He showed her land they had not yet broken its grasses home to delicate prairie blossoms. On the other side was the McIvor homestead and he talked of the first harvest when Tom had not returned and the McIvor brothers had come to his aid to work with nothing but scythes, an oxcart and sweat to bring in the precious grain.

They returned to the garden together. Rob described his early contacts with his Lakota neighbours and his friendship with Old John. "I used to defend their right to the land and the way they lived on it and felt deeply the injustice of our occupation of so much of it. And Tom would argue that our ways represented progress and that the only justification needed was that we were far more productive. Now our positions seem to have been reversed. Tom identifies with them far more than I think I ever could."

Three days later, a Sunday, Rob and Agnes hitched the horse and rode the five miles to Reston, a village that at present consisted of little more than a crossroads where four of the settlers had decided to build their homes in close proximity to each other. Rob had heard there was to be a church service, an event that was still a rarity. The sight of carriages lined up outside one of the barns identified the location of the service. Tethering their animal in the barn's shade, they entered a cleared area where some thirty people were sitting on benches and straw bales or standing in the aisles talking. A handful of children played noisily in the background.

He steered Agnes over to two family groups who had been at earlier services and introduced her. There was nothing hesitant about the conversations that ensued. Everyone had shared experiences to talk about and new perspectives as life was changing so fast around them.

A young man entered the barn with a clerical stole around his shoulders and people moved to take their seats. He greeted them in a pronounced Highland brogue. His preaching skills were as yet unknown, but he sang with a strong tenor as he led the opening hymn, "Guide me, Oh Thou great Jehovah". Printed words and music were not available but enough of the crowd had sung this since their youth that they were able to stumble along. Those who did not know the words sang the tune to whatever syllables came to mind. By the third verse, the volume had become vigorous.

The service followed a familiar format. The preaching was rather vapid but mercifully brief. Rob concluded the young man was short of life experience to be fulfilling such a role but at least his presence had caused them all to come together.

As was becoming the custom on these occasions, everyone brought food for all to share. Boards had been set up on stacked straw bales under trees in the yard and it was soon evident that food was not in short supply in this isolated place.

Rob joined a group of men who were standing back while the women set food on the buffet table. Conversation quickly turned to darker topics. There was a rumour that settlers living close to Turtle Mountain southeast of them had been raided and had lost some fifteen head of cattle. Even worse, it appeared that a prairie fire had been deliberately started by the raiders and had it not been for an early alarm being sounded, several of the settlers' homes and barns could well have been consumed.

The speculation was that it was the Indians living further up on the mountain, Old John's people, who were responsible. Rob had heard for some time of increasing tensions, but with his trip to Scotland and all that preceded it, it had been months since he had seen Old John or his people.

274

He wanted to know further details: had anyone been hurt, had the police taken action? There was talk among certain quarters of forming a posse and going up to confront the Indians. Rob urged caution until they could determine what the police were going to do. "Why should we listen to you?" a large red-bearded stranger at the edge of the crowd asked belligerently. "We all know that your brother has taken one of their squaws to his bed."

Rob bristled but another answered for him. "No, Rob is right. We want the rule of law in our communities. We should go up and see if we can help our brothers but leave punishment to the police." Nodded assents rippled through the crowd and people moved off towards the make-shift tables. The red-bearded man crossed Rob's path and growled, "You warn your brother he's in for trouble unless he ditches that squaw. We don't want no mixed-bloods around here."

Rob gave in to his anger. "If you lift a finger against either of them, you will taste the sharp sting of frontier justice. The police know how to deal with the likes of you." The other man snorted.

On the ride home, Rob's silence betrayed his concern. Agnes broke into his thoughts to ask why Old John's people would have raided the settlers. "Most of the Sioux on this side of the border have been granted land by Ottawa where they can permanently live and farm. Some have even had larger areas marked out for hunting and gathering until such time as the expanding settler pop-ulation needs that land," he explained.

"But, so far, those living on Turtle Mountain have been refused all such requests. It appears the government thinks they are too close to the American border and that might lead to raiding forays south. This could provoke the American cavalry to attack across the border into Canada. There are still powerful voices in the United States pushing for their government to find reasons to move sol-diers into Canada and annex large parts of our under-populated northwest. Ottawa wants to give them no excuse."

"What's the alternative?" Agnes asked. Rob explained that the government wanted them to disperse and join other Sioux communities. "They regard them as refugees and therefore they say they have no right to a treaty or any of the benefits or support that might come with a treaty. I think Tom and I had better go up there as soon as possible and find out for ourselves what is going on."

They arrived home in the early afternoon and, with only the essential chores to perform, Rob decided to find Tom to pass on the news about Turtle Mountain and see if they could ride there that afternoon. Tom agreed and within the hour, having bid farewell to Wynona, they were on horseback bringing what they needed to spend the night as they knew that talks with Old John and his elders always consumed several hours.

On arrival they found the camp in turmoil. Despite what Rob had taken as a consensus that morning that no action be taken against the Lakota until the police had been consulted, a party of settlers had ridden in demanding the return of their cattle. There had been a stand-off with violence averted only by Old John placing himself between the guns of the settlers and his armed young men. The settlers left vowing to return with others. John was back in his tepee with some of the elders while others were in heated discussion across the encampment. As Rob and Tom approached, some of the young men made to grab their rifles again until they recognized the brothers.

Rob and Tom went directly to Old John's tepee. The gathering inside was subdued, their presence recognized only by a few grunts. By now, Tom knew enough Lakota to roughly follow the conversation and he kept Rob abreast. Old John admitted he was having trouble with his young men. Some had recently crossed into the United States and had returned determined to resist any further settler encroachment. He could not say whether it had been these who had raided the neighbouring farms but was certain they would not have set a prairie fire.

"Why do not White Mother's officials accept our right to be here? We have documents and medals from her grandfather's officials showing we were in this land long before settlers came. They have made terms with our brothers to the west and north but refuse our claim to land. They say we must leave this mountain and live with our brothers. But they do not give enough land for our brothers to survive – if we move to where they are more of our people will starve."

Others raised their voices. Some said Canadians were no different than Americans; they would talk peace but use their soldiers to take the land. Rob kept his counsel. He knew that it was important to allow all to speak their mind. When they wanted to hear his views they would ask him. Finally they were ready. "What do our good white brothers think?" Old John asked. Rob looked at Tom but his brother remained silent. Rob spoke.

"You are right to be concerned. You must insist that the mountain is your land. The government must recognize your right to have enough land to feed your people and your people's children. If you wish it, my brother and I will go with you to meet the White Mother's officials in Winnipeg. You must take your papers and your medals. I believe that justice can be done. We will do what we can to get an agreement."

He paused and looked at Tom but the latter's face showed no emotion. "Are you with me on this?" he asked. "It is the least we can do. But we cannot go until the harvest is in. The discussions in Winnipeg could take several weeks. We could lose the crop if we went immediately." Tom nodded. They returned to the farm as the sun was rising the next morning having assured Old John they would be ready to travel with him to Winnipeg by mid-October. During the night the wind had shifted from the north and heavy grey skies in the west threatened snow. Rob knew that the grain was barely ready for harvest, still retaining a high degree of moisture. But if the cold became deeper, they could lose much of it to frost.

Agnes had expected them and a robust meal of oatmeal and salted pork gave them a chance to confer about the choices ahead. The brothers concurred that it was better to bring the grain in now rather than wait for it to mature further and risk heavy losses due to the weather.

They worked long into the evening. It had remained cold but

dry. The waves of grain had been cut into a labyrinth of flattened stalks circling the fields. The sun had not managed to break through the grey ceiling. But fortunately the night dew had been very light in recent days and Rob planned to wait until the next day to gather the grain into sheaves.

But the night turned penetratingly cold. Rob woke with a premonition in the early hours and went outside. The light of a clear moon seemed almost malevolent and he could tell that the grain would be severely stressed. If they did not lose it, its quality might be so poor as to reduce it to animal feed. Sleep eluded him the rest of the night.

A grim-faced Tom arrived with Wynona just as he and Agnes were finishing their meal. Seeing the frost painted on the rows of flattened grain, they realized had they used their time yesterday to bundle the grain into sheaves and keep the precious kernels above the ground, the damage might have been less. The task ahead was straight-forward but back-breaking, making sheaves and stacking these into stooks.

The four of them set out together, working parallel rows, binding the grain and stacking four sheaves to a stook. It took them the whole day to gather all the grain that had been cut the day before. The next night continued cold and when Rob went out to begin mowing again he saw that even the standing grain was faltering. Rob mowed for half the day and then joined the others tying sheaves.

At the end of each day's work, they were numb with fatigue and badly chilled. Agnes would set a large pot of water to boil and they bathed in the galvanized tub before eating and collapsing into bed. The pace was relentless in their race with the cold. Agnes and Wynona kept pace with the men, only breaking early to prepare food and heat water.

But Sundays were sacrosanct. Regardless of what it might cost in spoiled grain, neither brother strayed from their Sabbath tradition. No church service was available, but Rob and Agnes sought rest for their bodies and succour for their souls in quiet reading.

Tom and Wynona kept to themselves. No one contemplated visiting. Energy was hoarded for the coming six days of labour.

Three and a half weeks later, their work was done. The grain had been dried, threshed and winnowed, and sat in multi-tiered rows of bags in the barn. They had separated out the grain that had relatively high water content – it would have a limited shelf-life and would need to be sold first. But the market would be flooded with this quality of grain as everyone else had been forced to harvest under the same conditions. The brothers considered buying additional livestock – pigs and cattle – and feeding them up over the winter as a means of obtaining better value than they were likely to get by selling all the grain.

The women turned now to harvesting and storing the root vegetables that had survived the frosts. All the other vegetables – tomatoes, beans, broccoli – had been lost to the cold. Tom and Rob headed to Virden in search of livestock with the oxcart full of sacks of grain.

Rob had watched Wynona over the harvest weeks and had been struck by her resilience and the way she bantered with Tom, sensitive to his moods and bolstering his spirits. Rather than being so aware of her "otherness", he had started seeing her as a woman, with a personality that surmounted the racial difference. In the perspective of the challenges they faced together, how she became part of the family seemed less and less important. She was a fortunate addition to their venture. He wanted to express this to Tom without appearing to be condescending.

"I was mightily impressed with Wynona in the last weeks," he told Tom as they rode the road north. "She does you proud as a wife."

"I don't need your approval of her as my wife any more than you need my approval of Agnes," Tom shot back.

"I know, brother. But I just want you to know that I was wrong to criticize you for marrying her." Tom said nothing further until they reached the town.

Virden was very quiet. The few people on the streets seemed to reflect the grim future the early frost would impose on everyone.

They made their way to Ian McAllister, the local grain merchant, and found him in a dour mood. Clearly he expected a much reduced flow of premium quality grains and therefore a slump in his business. Three others were at the depot before them and from the snatched conversations; all were trying to sell grain that could only be used to feed animals.

When their turn came and they opened the first sack of barley, McAllister's face lightened. "T'is the first decent grain I have seen in two days," he said dipping his arm deep into the sack. "There's going to be a pile of hardship the coming winter." He checked the rest of the sacks. "You'll get a decent price for this as there is so little worth shipping coming in. Do you have any more available?"

"Most of our wheat is frost damaged," Rob replied. "We planted the barley on higher ground which spared it the worst of the frost. We have about forty more sacks of decent grain which we will bring on another trip. But we want to buy cattle and hogs. Do you know who might have some for sale?"

"You'll be hard pressed to find any at a decent price. But if you move fast, you might get some before most others realize that their grain is only good for hog feed. Old man Boychuk on the road to Lenore has a pig operation. He might be open to sell some young stock."

The transactions competed, the brothers left with two-hundred and twenty dollars in their pockets and considerably lighter spirits. There would not be sufficient time to travel north, secure the hogs and get back to the farm before the cold night descended so they decided to stay in Virden and use the time to scout out sources of cattle. They could haul a dozen or fifteen young pigs in the cart, but the cattle would have to be driven and that argued for them to be sourced as close to Pipestone as possible.

They staked the oxen in the lee of a barn behind the Alexandra Hotel and took a room. The late afternoon's light was rapidly failing and the increasing chill made an early supper highly desirable. The local tavern with the unusual name of The Elegant Moose proved inviting. Tom promptly ordered a pint of stout but Rob chose tea.

Following Tom's retort to Rob's comment about Wynona, their

conversation had restricted itself to matters of business. Tom broke the pattern. Raising his glass to Rob he said, "I really appreciate the way Agnes has gone out of her way to make Wynona feel comfortable. She is one Scot who does not let her principles get in the way of her heart."

"Meaning I am not?" replied Rob with a wry smile.

"Well, brother, marriage is improving you," Tom answered. "It took me a long time to figure out how you could be such a friend to Old John and his people, so much at ease in their company, and yet so opposed to my relationship with Wynona. But then I realized that as a true Scot, your heart could be warm but your soul cold. We have a national habit of putting principles before people but I can see that is changing and you are a much better person for it."

"Tom, my boy, I will drink to that." Rob said with a grin. "Kindly order me a pint of that stout you have."

Chapter
33

A FEW DAYS AFTER RETURNING TO THE FARM, ROB HEARD THAT SOME OF THE settlers around Turtle Mountain were doubtful about carrying all their cattle through the winter months. He and Tom decided to see if they could arrange a purchase and combine that with a visit to Old John to discuss the journey to Winnipeg they had proposed earlier. The days were getting decidedly colder and they hoped to make that trip before the worst of the winter storms set in.

They left before dawn as it could be a long day, leaving the women to continue their work of preserving food. Visiting the settlers meant a detour of a couple of hours but they decided to scout out the cattle prospects first and, if successful, return another day to herd the animals back to the farm.

By mid-morning the first of the farms was visible, smoke rising from its cabin. The welcome they received was decidedly strained. The farmer was not interested in selling and doubted that others would be prepared to either. Rob wondered whether he had been misinformed. There was one settler family at the end of the valley whom Rob knew from several conversations at church services. Perhaps they would level with the brothers. They found George McManus behind his barn working his way through a large pile of fire wood.

"We are hoping to buy a few head of cattle and had heard that folks up this way were interested in off-loading some," Rob said after their initial greeting. "Would you have any for sale or would you know others who might?"

"Well, that was before the police came up and arrested those thieving Indians", said George leaning on his splitting maul. "People were afraid they would lose more to those red rustlers and so they were looking to sell. But now that they have been put in their place, the pressure is off."

Rob and Tom knew nothing of this. Further conversation with George revealed that, a couple of days previously, police had arrived at Old John's encampment and demanded that the men who had raided the farms be handed over. No one would identify them. In retaliation, the police rounded up eight young men who happened to be in the vicinity, hand-cuffed them and threatened to take them to jail in Brandon unless those who had conducted the raid were identified. No names were volunteered and in the end the police left with their prisoners.

The brothers were shocked. McManus was clearly unhappy about the situation and predicted that relations between the two groups would only get worse. Clearly their intended visit to Old John was overdue. Tom was visibly angry with the news but Rob did not want to forgo the other aim of their journey – that of trying to buy some cattle.

McManus had several heifers he would be prepared to part with for the right price and they went into the barn to take a look. They were a mixed breed but several had distinctive short-horn features which meant they would be reasonable meat animals. Rob concluded a deal for five and said they would be back in a few days to drive them to the farm. Tom had withdrawn into silence.

Back on their horses, Tom continued to brood. Rob was equally upset. This action, if it in fact was as described by McManus, contravened the code of behaviour that had marked police action across the West and had enabled peace to prevail generally between the Indians and the advancing settler population since the end of the last Riel rebellion. Whether it marked a change in policy or was the action of rogue elements within the police, they had to intervene. The journey to Winnipeg took on a more urgent necessity.

They arrived that the encampment in the early afternoon and made their way directly to Old John's tepee. The atmosphere was grim and the greetings perfunctory. Rob began by explaining what they had heard about the police raid. Old John confirmed the story and then added that two of the young men taken had been his sons. They believed that they had been taken to Brandon but they had heard nothing since the police left some ten days earlier.

Rob looked at Old John. "I do not agree with what the police did. Their action to arrest those men without sufficient evidence broke the law. But you know that if any of your people engage in stealing or violent activity, the government could expel you across the Medicine Line back into the United States.

"I am not happy to say this, but I think you must identify the men who took part in the raid if we are to free those who are innocent and if we are to negotiate a settlement. Are you prepared to do this?"

There was silence after Ohista had translated Rob's remarks. One by one the elders began to speak. As the discussion progressed, the tone of their voices signaled much disagreement. Finally Rob felt they should leave and go to Wynona's parents' tepee where her mother's welcome was fulsome.

Some hours later Ohista informed them the elders were ready to talk. Old John looked haggard and worn. "We not leave Turtle Mountain. We not give any more young men to police. You tell police give back young men. I promise no more raids. Any who do not obey chief, get sent back across Medicine Line. Please come with us to Brandon to get young men."

"Yes, we will go to Brandon with you, but then we must go on to Winnipeg to see White Mother's officials. You must come with many elders and with all your documents and medals from White Mother's grandfather. When would you be ready?" asked Rob.

More discussion. "We go after three nights," Old John replied.

"Good. You must be prepared to be away for one month – these discussions take time."

Leaving the tent Rob suggested they spend the night at the encampment and return via McManus' to drive the cattle back to the farm in the morning as they had no idea when they would be back from the trip with the Lakota. Tom agreed and went to arrange matters with Wynona's mother.

Agnes and Wynona were taken aback at the prospect of their husbands being away for up to a month. Rob informed the McIvors of their plan and was assured that the brothers were ready to help whenever needed. They offered an extra horse to carry the baggage needed for a month away. The women decided to move in together for company.

Three mornings later as they were saddling the horses, they spotted a substantial number of riders approaching from the south. Old John had seven elders with him as well as half a dozen young men and several women to help set up camp and care for the older men on the journey. The elders wore their ceremonial finery and the young men were painted as though on the war path.

That evening, Old John's party set up camp on the edge of the coulee above Brandon while the brothers sought a room in their favourite boarding house. They arranged to meet the next morning at the police barracks.

Rob and Tom arrived at the police station just as the party of Indians turned onto the main street. Old John and the elders were accompanied by the young men dressed for the confrontation. Rob proposed that Old John, Ohista, Tom and he go in first to arrange a gathering where all the elders could participate. The young officer at the desk was clearly uneasy. He disappeared into an inner office and emerged minutes later with a grim-faced senior officer. On hearing the purpose of the visit, the officer flatly refused to meet with the larger party.

"There's nothing to accomplish. The future of the Indians in custody is in the hands of headquarters in Winnipeg. I see no point meeting with your group when I have no power to meet any of their requests," he said.

"But you must know that peace with the Indians depends on keeping the dialogue going. Even if you can do nothing, they must know that they can be heard," Rob urged.

"These young men are charged with serious offences. Stealing cattle and setting prairie fires with the purpose of driving out those who have legally acquired their land, are heinous acts," he replied heatedly. "Her Majesty's government is not prepared to negotiate with those who break the law."

"I recognize that, but these elders have authority over their young men. If you are not prepared to hear them out, then you risk turning those who have been peaceful and cooperative against the government. Even if you cannot meet their demands, you must hear them out."

The exchange had been rapid and heated and it was doubtful that Old John could have followed it. The officer stared sternly at Rob who returned the gaze. "You do yourself no good by mixing with this affair. We do not take kindly to settlers siding with the Indians."

"The rule of law for all citizens is what holds this new country together. There is not one law for the Indian and another for the settler. You are the one who will regret not upholding it or not being seen to uphold it fairly for all." Rob replied.

The officer looked out the window, a scowl on his face. "Come with your party at one o'clock this afternoon. We will meet in the parade ground behind the barracks," he said and turned away.

When the brothers with Old John and his people arrived that afternoon, they were met by a large crowd of locals. The senior officer sat on a raised dais flanked by six other police, all dressed in formal uniform. The citizens of Brandon formed a semi-circle either side of the platform. Rob and his party were directed to blankets set out before the platform. No chairs were provided.

The elders sat, the young men surrounding them. Rob and Tom refused to sit. They smelled the intimidation that was intended and refused to accommodate

Rob addressed the police. "I want you to listen to the voice of Old John, chief of the Sioux people living on Turtle Mountain. Old John came with his people to escape the atrocities of the American cavalry but before that, his people lived on this land and were regarded as friends and allies by the grandfather of our present Queen."

The crowd became quiet. Old John gathering his robes around him, slowly rose and stepped forward. "We thank the Great White Mother for welcome back to land of our ancestors. I have medals and documents from her grandfather telling us we are friends.

"We wish live in peace on our traditional land but we need land for our people. We need treaty like one Great Mother made with other Sioux brothers. But her officials deaf. Do not talk. Many times we ask talk. No reply. Our wives and children hungry. Settlers move to land where we hunt. Now some young men angry. I tell them wait. White Mother will do right thing.

"Now it is said my young men raid, steal cattle. Yes, they did. Elders angry with them. Also said they set fires to scare settlers. That not true. No Sioux under me does coward act. You police come to my camp with many guns. You take away young men who steal and do not steal and keep them here long time. We want them back. I know who steal and not steal. We already return cattle and we punish thieves."

Old John sat down and the elders nodded. There was murmuring in the crowd.

Rob stood up. "We are proud in this country that the rule of law under the generous guidance of our Great Mother, Her Majesty the Queen, applies to all whether settler or Indian. This has given us, for the most part, peace as we have opened up and shared this country unlike the warfare and bloodshed to the south.

"But the rule of law must be applied consistently if it is to be respected. Some young men from John's camp broke that law. Chief John admits it. But the police, instead of coming to the camp to talk with the elders and get their cooperation, arrived and quickly rounded up whatever young men they saw, arrested them and brought them in handcuffs here. This is not the rule of law. They would not treat the sons of settlers this way. We ask only that you negotiate with the elders so the guilty are punished and those not guilty set free."

The senior officer began consulting with his comrades. Then he summoned several men from the crowd, one of whom Rob recognized as a lawyer. Finally the officer rose.

"We thank the chief and his elders for coming. We want to live in peace with his people. But that peace has been broken. That cannot happen again. The Great Mother's police must ensure the law is never broken. So until her courts have examined what happened and decided on punishment, we cannot allow any of these men to return to their camp."

With this, he beckoned for his fellow officers to follow him and they left the parade ground without any further gesture to the Indian party. The crowd slowly began to break up but Rob noticed the lawyer moving towards him.

"Mr Dunbar, I'm McGrath, a lawyer in town. I respect what you are trying to do but I recommend you take your concerns to police headquarters in Winnipeg and to the local representative of the Ministry of Justice there. I do not think that proper procedure was followed here, but you are unlikely to get the police here to acknowledge that. Go to Winnipeg and take the Indian elders with you and good luck."

Old John looked up, but remained seated, his face passive. There was silence among the elders. Tom noticed some among the crowd snickering. Children stared at the elders unabashedly. The young men were restless, their faces scowling.

"Let us go back to your camp. We will consider there what to do next," Rob suggested. Old John grunted his assent.

It took them two days to reach Winnipeg where they camped north of the city by the trading post known as Fort Gary. This was a large post, still busy in the waning days of autumn, its stockade walls harbouring a garrison as well as large fur warehouses. Several encampments of Sioux, Ojibwa and Salteaux shadowed the walls. It was decided that Old John and another elder, Rising Sun, would accompany Rob and Tom along with Ohista into the city to arrange meetings the next day.

Rob led them first to the office of the Indian Commissioner

for the Northwest. It took a wait of three hours before they were finally ushered into his office. Rob informed him of the police raid and the unwarranted arrest of innocent men but added that the deeper cause of the unrest was the lack of response to requests for discussions to provide a permanent reserve on Turtle Mountain. He requested that the Commissioner call a meeting with the senior police officer and the head of the justice department in the territory.

The Commissioner's response was abrupt. "We only discuss these matters with the concerned natives. We are not prepared to allow settlers to participate. If the chief wishes a meeting, it must be with himself and his elders alone."

"But these are my neighbours and my friends. A grievous injustice has been done to them by the police in Brandon. And their situation on Turtle Mountain has become untenable. Our settlers have taken most of the lands they use for hunting and their people are hungry and despairing," Rob replied.

"Then they can return from whence they came. No one is stopping them," was the response.

"I cannot believe what you are saying," said Tom entering the exchange, his anger visible. "Our government promised the Sioux that they would be treated honourably as long as they lived in peace, did not raid across the border or quarrel with the other tribes in Canada. But you have turned a blind eye and a deaf ear to the plight of the people on Turtle Mountain. For no fault of their own they have been excluded from the treaty arrangements you have made with the other Sioux settlements. I have no faith you will behave differently unless those of us in the settler community take up their cause."

"You are free to do what you wish, but if the chief and his elders want a meeting here to discuss these matters with the government, it will not take place if you are present."

"That is outrageous," Tom shouted back. "Why would you deprive them of the support they need?"

"That is the policy that comes from Ottawa. In fact, there is a law being considered in Parliament that will make it a criminal offence for non-Indians to provide advice or to raise money to pay for legal assistance to Indians in any dispute with the government. I would advise you that if you have their best interests at heart, you desist from your involvement."

The brothers were stunned. Ohista was quietly translating for the Indians. Rob did not know what to do next. The tone and deportment of the Commissioner gave him no confidence that he would alter his position.

"I am not prepared to accept what you say," Rob said firmly, "but I see there is no point in arguing further with you. As a citizen of this country, I wish to make two points before we leave. I ask that you meet immediately with the chief to hear his concerns and I assure you that we will be contacting those members of Parliament we know to ask that they challenge this unjust policy."

The superintendent turned to Old John. "Do you wish to meet with government officials on your own without the Dunbars?"

The chief looked confused. He murmured something to Rising Sun who nodded. "I not understand why friends not participate," Ohista translated. "But we come so far. We must tell our people something. I will meet."

"You come back here in two days. We will talk," the superintendent replied. As the party rose to leave, the official beckoned to Rob. "Please remain behind on your own a few moments."

Rob told Ohista he would join them shortly. Tom lingered, clearly wishing to stay but Rob put his hand on his shoulder. "Trust me. We need all the information we can get. I'll join you in a minute."

He turned to face the Commissioner who was still sitting behind his over-sized desk. He gestured for Rob to sit again. "Mr Dunbar, if I may speak in confidence. You must understand, the government cannot agree to a reserve on Turtle Mountain. It is too close to the American border. The danger of raids either way is too great. There are those in Washington who seek an excuse for the American cavalry to bring their war against the Sioux into Canada and to make that part of a strategy to seize our under-populated territory. That is of far greater importance than agreeing to the demands of a small group of Indians.

"The government views these Sioux as refugees without a claim for land and treaty rights in Canada. We will be prepared to offer Old John's people assistance to move into the territory of the other Lakota Sioux. But we will not cede any more territory to them."

"But Chief John has documentation and medals awarded his ancestors by King George III, attesting to their presence on this territory and the fact that they were regarded as allies," Rob replied.

"That may be. But you know as I do that these people have been nomadic for generations. One year they are here. Another, they are hundreds of miles away."

"From their perspective, we are just as nomadic. We were not here a hundred years ago and now we suddenly claim this land as belonging to Her Majesty. Is that not just as nomadic?" Rob replied.

"Mr Dunbar, be reasonable. We are here to stay and you know this land was under-utilized. We will offer them assistance to move but we will never agree to a treaty and a reserve on Turtle Mountain. Please try to convince them of that."

"But what of the young men who were arbitrarily taken from their encampment without evidence they were responsible for the cattle raid?"

"If you can get the elders to agree to move from Turtle Mountain, I will try to persuade the police to hand over all their captives in return for an assurance that the elders will constrain any more hot-headed activity."

"And why can we not be present at your next meeting with the chief and elders?"

"My hands are tied. I will overlook any advice you give them from behind as long as they agree to move."

Rob rose and left. He joined the others on the street. It was late afternoon and dusk was fast descending. A chill wind blew. The wide, rutted street was full of carts and drays speeding towards homes and stables. Tom eyed Rob nervously but Rob said nothing. They headed back to the Fort Gary encampment.

Chapter
34

In the days following their return from Winnipeg, they had to assess their situation in the light of the severely damaged crops. They had sufficient root vegetables to last the season but their supply of other staples was low and it was clear they had insufficient money to take them into the spring. They would need to find a source of funds to get them into the summer.

By this time it was evident that Wynona was pregnant. On that account, Rob and Agnes decided that they should spend the winter away in paid employment. But Tom was restless. Ever since the meetings in Brandon and Winnipeg, he had withdrawn further. He and Wynona made several trips to the encampment on Turtle Mountain and every time he returned, his anger had increased.

Despite the superintendent's assurances of assistance, Old John had been told that he and his people had to join the other Lakota Sioux reserves but could carry with them no increased land or support. Old John would not agree and so he remained isolated and increasingly desperate. Some of his people had quietly slipped across the border to an uncertain future. A few others had gone to visit relatives in the other Sioux reserves and not returned.

One evening, Rob went to Tom's house. Wynona was not there and Tom had been heavily into drink. Rob had noted on several previous occasions the smell of alcohol on his brother but had not connected it to his increasing anger. He was taken aback by the degree of Tom's drunkenness.

"Tom, Wynona needs a settled place over the winter. Agnes and I feel that the two of you should stay here. We will head up to

Elphinstone to get work. We could take the oxen and hire them out as well. I am sure that Agnes could get employment in the school. Between us, we could probably return with several hundred dollars by the end of the cold season."

Tom stared at his brother for several moments without replying. Then he rose unsteadily and paced the floor. "I am not going to spend a whole winter in this God-forsaken place where every time we venture out we face the stares and whispers of bigoted neighbours. I would move to live with Old John's people but there is not enough there to give us sustenance.

"No, we will move north to Elphinstone and I will find work," he continued. "There is enough going on up there between the red men and the white that few look askance at a marriage between the two. And the mixed-blood, the Metis, are part of every-day life. Whether we come back to the farm after the winter or choose to stay there will depend on what we find.

"I will not subject Wynona to the condescension she faces daily here," he said, his voice rising. "Her only solace is her friendship with Agnes, but if you leave, there is nothing for her here but the long, silent winter. No, you stay, we will go."

The daylight saw Tom, haggard but sober, as determined as the night before. Wynona gave silent consent. Rob understood the reason for his decision but still thought it unwise given Wynona's pregnancy but Wynona's people would certainly have undertaken such arduous journeys with their women close to birth. Perhaps he underestimated her resilience.

Tom and Wynona were determined to leave the next day and the women set about preparing for the journey, packing what was needed for life in Elphinstone. The oxen, Pete and Harriet, were in good shape and would have no difficulty pulling the laden cart provided snow did not descend in blowing drifts.

Rob knew how keenly his brother felt the coolness that characterized his neighbours' attitudes to Wynona. It had also spread to include Agnes. She had been invited to social gatherings with the women and had tried to persuade Wynona to join her. On the one occasion when Wynona had agreed to come, the disdain she met was so thinly disguised as to cause Agnes to depart early. Now she turned down most invitations. She and Rob had discussed what they could do to alter the situation but saw no early solution.

The morning of their departure broke clear and cold. Buffalo robes would protect them from the wind. The cart stood piled high with basic furniture and provisions. Agnes had prepared a large breakfast of oatmeal porridge, eggs and thick slabs of pork and the four ate together in silence, the uncertainty of the future and the long, icy months of the coming winter hanging over their spirits.

Determined to break the shadows, Rob spoke of the trials they had overcome and the life they had built free from debt and landlords, beholden to no man or outmoded custom. Here he checked himself. "Yes, there is one residue of the old society that survived the oceans and that is the attitude of our people to those of a different colour or creed. But we will upend that, given time," he said.

Rob ruffled the oxen's heads. The cart was mounted, robes wrapped and they headed north. Rob and Agnes stood watching until the cart disappeared into the gully along the Pipestone.

Towards the end of the third day, the valley of the Little Saskatchewan River unfolded before them. They had been fortunate – the days were bone chilling, particularly sitting atop the cart and they had frequently walked beside the oxen to keep the blood circulating but the snow had held off. There was a mere dusting on the road.

The village of Elphinstone had almost doubled in size in the few years since Tom had left to go west with Boulton's Scouts. They headed to George and Martha McIntyre's general store.

"Why it's Tom Dunbar. You're a sight for sore eyes!" Martha, broad and warm as ever greeted Tom as he knew she would. But he watched her closely as her gaze fell on Wynona. A slight widening of her eyes as her mouth opened a crack. "I want you to meet my wife, Wynona," he said with a certain defiance in his voice.

"Why, Tom, what a lucky man you are," she said, her voice only slightly forced. "Come in, both of you, and warm your insides with some hot tea. And you will just have to stop for supper." Tom tied the oxen while she hustled Wynona into the store.

"And what brings you back to these parts?" she asked when Tom had joined them in the store. He told her the reason for their journey and his intent to work the winter in the woods. "Well, spend the night here if you don't mind making do in the attic where you and Rob stayed the last time. Elphinstone's a mite crowded these days so you may find getting space harder than last time. But you can start to look in the morning."

Wynona remained with Martha the next morning while Tom headed out to search for work. Martha's husband, George, had died the year before and she was struggling to keep the store going. She had a winter shipment of food stocks to unpack that had arrived a few days before by oxcart and Wynona offered to assist. Warm and inquisitive, it did not take Martha long to begin questioning the young woman about her family and tribal heritage.

Wynona was cautious at first but the older woman's open manner encouraged her. "My people are Lakota. They live more west. They rescued Tom when he was prisoner of Cree after battle at Cutknife Creek. We meet in my father's tepee and we marry many months later when we meet again near Pipestone farm."

"You're married? That is good – the ceremony must have been in a church then?" Martha asked.

"No. We marry by Lakota custom. I not go to Christian church."

"You are not Christian?" Martha's brow furrowed. "It must be difficult living in a settlement with Tom's people if you have not accepted the faith."

"Yes. White people cold – they not understand my culture." Wynona paused and then asked, "Why are they afraid?"

Martha was silent for a moment. "Perhaps they are far away from home. They are not yet comfortable in this land. Perhaps they hold too tightly to what was familiar from the old country. They come from a country where everyone has the same culture, the same history, the same religion. And they believe their ways are better than those of other people. Sadly, it will take a long time before that changes."

The women were silent for many minutes, the only sound the scrape of boxes being stacked on the rough wooden shelves.

"Tom is good to you?" Martha asked.

"Yes, he is good man but he has become angry man because neighbours do not accept me. I think he finds living with my people better."

"But you will soon have a little one. Perhaps things will change with the people of Pipestone when the baby is with you." Wynona looked wistful but said nothing.

By the end of the day, Tom had found no work in the village. Martha had clearly taken to Wynona, welcoming her help and suggested that they stay on in the attic until they could find a more permanent arrangement. With that assurance, Tom determined to head out to see Glen Lyon to scout out work there.

Martha had a neighbour with a horse and the next morning she arranged for Tom to borrow the animal. Tom left before noon up the bush road he and Rob had travelled two years before.

A dusting of snow showed that none had travelled it in several days. The towering aspen, bare of leaves, seemed like a walled stockade accompanying his journey. The failing sun lit the interior of the forest opening its secret depths to his gaze. He loved being surrounded by trees again, realizing afresh how much he missed their company on the bald prairie. The leafless branches formed intertwining silhouettes, never thick enough to block the view into the forest's depths but creating an enchanting domain that sustained a life different from that found on the forest floor.

Time passed quickly and with the sun close to the western horizon, he approached the gate to Glen Lyon Campbell's land, the faded Hudson Bay flag, its insignia now almost invisible, still hanging from its post. He had not seen his friend since the day of the battle at Cutknife Creek. He knew Glen Lyon had survived and was back on the property his father had cleared years before.

Tom hitched the horse to a rail and knocked firmly on the door stepping back in anticipation. Within moments the door opened revealing a startled Glen Lyon, momentarily taken aback, and then bounding forward to wrap Tom in his long arms. "Dunbar, I thought you lost to the Cree and God knows what kind of dastardly death. Where have you come from? Where have you been?"

He pulled Tom into the house, shook him by the shoulders, his face beaming his relief.

"It's a long story but I am mighty glad to see you, too," said Tom. "The last time I glimpsed you, you were trying to get that Gatling gun up the hill to halt the swarming Cree."

"I want to hear the whole story, but first, come in, sit down. You have been riding all day and will be in want of a good meal. But you must first meet Sheila, the woman I took to wife three months ago."

The noise of their greetings had already brought a young woman out of the back rooms of the house. "Sheila, this here is Tom Dunbar, a man who foolishly followed me into battle and whom I had thought had been lost in the conflict. Tom and his brother were here with me in the winter two years ago. And then we went west with Boulton's Scouts at the time of the Cree uprising. He'll be joining us for supper and I am sure for the night as well."

Sheila's greeting was warm and Tom noted her accent, dark hair and eyes spoke of Irish ancestry. Glen Lyon took Tom out to stable the horse. As his wife prepared the evening meal, he eagerly plied Tom with questions.

A hearty meal of venison stew set the stage for the two men to swap stories. Glen Lyon was intrigued with Tom's account of meeting Wynona following his capture by the Cree and then the coincidence of seeing her again the night his horse stumbled into Old John's encampment in the raging blizzard. There was no hint of concern or even surprise that she was Lakota and that the relationship had led to marriage. For Tom, this was unexpected and encouraged him to believe that this farm might be a haven for Wynona during her pregnancy.

Glen Lyon's queries about his future gave him the opportunity

to enquire about employment. There was always work for additional hands. Logging had to be done in the winter months when
the timber could be skidded to the river to await the spring breakup.
Tom asked about accommodation for Wynona and himself at the
farm over the winter. Would there be room in one of the outbuild-
ings for the two of them?

Glen Lyon said he would talk the matter over with Sheila but providing adequate warmth through the bitter winter months would be
a concern. They had sufficient provisions for themselves but would
need to bring in additional supplies to support two more people.

Could Tom find accommodation for Wynona in town while he
worked at the farm? Tom sensed he had overstepped his boundaries. They were not family and therefore owed him no obligation;
Glen Lyon was a friend but friendship could be soured if imposed
upon.

Sheila was guarded at the table the next morning and Glen
Lyon looked perturbed. It was clear to Tom that it was not going
to work. Tom assured them that he was certain he could find both
work and housing in the town and that he and Wynona would
come up for a visit as soon as they had established themselves.
Sheila immediately looked relieved but Glen Lyon was clearly saddened by his inability to help.

Tom left shortly after breakfast. As he was in the saddle, Glen
Lyon thrust a large parcel of food into his hands looking somewhat
shamefaced as though he had let his friend down. As he rode off,
Tom could not help but wonder whether Wynona's background
was at the root of their unwillingness to overcome the inconve-
nience of spending the winter with them.

The day was overcast and colder. Wind whirled the light snow,
chilled his face and sharpened the ache in his spirit. He wished he
had brought drink. It would be a long day.

On his return to the general store, Wynona immediately sensed
his disappointment but he shielded her from his thoughts – why
add to her sense of isolation? Martha was warm and encouraging.

"There is no rush. Things will sort out and until they do, you stay here. Wynona can be a great help to me."

A robust evening meal gave some comfort and Tom and Wynona went quickly to bed after the long, cold day on the road. Though he was tired, Tom's need for Wynona's succour was much greater. He buried his face in the back of her neck and drew her close. Slipping his hands under her garment he held the precious round expanse of her belly, finding himself quickly rising to the scent of her body. She turned to him, open and available, showing no apprehension. He knew he had to be careful with his urgency so as not to harm the burden she was carrying. She brought him to relief and he fell back and found himself quietly sobbing. Damn the world out there – as long as he had her, he did not care how the rest behaved. And he would do whatever it took to protect and sustain her.

The next afternoon Tom learned that Mr Iredale, owner of the saw mill, was planning an expansion and that work would be available starting in about two weeks. Tom agreed on the spot.

The one task now remaining was to find housing for the winter. The village's population had outgrown its buildings. Bachelors' quarters were easily found but a location where Wynona would be warm and comfortable was another question. Martha had several suggestions but he found that two of these landlords claimed they were already rented when they learned of Wynona.

At the third, Tom concealed the fact that he had a wife. It was the house of a Reverend Ian Fyfe, where an extra bedroom had been built off the summer kitchen and, yes, it could be rented but he would have to supply his own firewood. There was a shed behind that with some work could accommodate the oxen. He could take occupation immediately.

Tom and Wynona returned in the afternoon to clean the room and prepare to move their few belongings. Mrs Fyfe opened the door and immediately expressed surprise. "I thought you were living alone. My husband said nothing about another person." She hurried inside leaving the two standing at the door. Minutes passed and Tom quietly cursed himself for exposing Wynona to yet another possible rejection. He should have been upfront about his requirements.

The Reverend appeared looking uncomfortable. "Mr Dunbar, I thought I was renting this room for you alone. Who is this woman? Are you married to her? I cannot have a man living in my house with a woman to whom he is not lawfully married."

Tom bit down hard to control his anger. "Yes, she is my wife. We have been married for the best part of a year."

"Then you will have a marriage license you can show me," said the cleric.

"No, I cannot. We were married according to Lakota custom. That is sufficient for me and for my family. It should be sufficient for you," Tom replied, increasingly defiant.

"No, I am sorry, it is not. We are trying to encourage responsible behaviour in this community. There is too much informal fraternizing and too many illicit liaisons. We, above all, have to set a standard. Now, if you would wish to be married in my church, we could let you have the room after the ceremony."

"Damnation on your room and your church. I will have none of this bigotry," Tom was nearly shouting.

"In that case young man, you can remove yourself and this woman from our property."

"Gladly, and she is not this woman. She is my wife!" Tom spit his reply.

Martha was appalled when she heard the story. "I knew we had trouble at times between settlers and Indians, but that confounds my expectations. I have been thinking that the two of you could stay here for the winter. I could use the help and the company. If you would be prepared to share these quarters, I would like to have you stay. We can improve the accommodation in the attic and share the kitchen. And we could come to an agreement about the work you could do around the place instead of rent."

Wynona had been silent since the confrontation with Fyfe, her eyes downcast. Tom's anguish at the wounds inflicted on his wife kindled a fury that was hard to control. But Martha's offer, so clearly genuine and forthcoming, drained his emotion. He moved to Wynona and put his arm around her waist. "Oh, that is so kind. Are you sure? I don't want you to do this out of sympathy for us. Our baby will be due in a couple of months and that will be an additional burden."

"My dear man, it would bring much joy to an old woman to be here when a new life begins. There are many benefits to me to have you around over this winter. I have struggled to keep this store going since George died and I have seen in the last few days how diligent Wynona is. If she can help in the store until the baby arrives and you help take care of things in the barn and around the property, my life will be so much easier."

Wynona looked up and smiled for the first time. "Thank you, thank you," she murmured.

"Well, that's settled. Now we better get some supper going," said Martha and headed towards the kitchen.

The presence of Wynona behind the counter caused more than a few stares among the customers in the first weeks. Undoubtedly this was accompanied by gossip and comment around the community but Martha's reputation for being formidable as well as generous soon silenced the critics. An unexpected benefit of Wynona's presence was that, one by one, the more outgoing among the local Ojibwa men began to buy from the store.

Occasionally, a few of the older Ojibwa women would venture in. One aged grandmother, Miigwaans, or Little Feather, took a particular interest in Wynona and would always enquire about the state of her pregnancy. Wynona told Tom one day that she had visited Miigwaans on the reserve at the edge of town and had been treated as though she was part of an extended family. Though their languages were very different, Wynona knew a few Ojibwa expressions and Miigwaans had some English. Miigwaans' daughters had been very welcoming and had given Wynona a traditional back massage. The relaxation displayed on her face as she told Tom about the visit evidenced the pleasure being among native women gave her.

One day, as the time came closer for Wynona's delivery, she told Tom that she wanted the baby born by native custom and at Miigwaans' house on the reserve. In recent weeks she had frequently walked the mile and a half to spend time with that family. In the absence of her own mother and other female relatives who would have played a central role in her delivery, she wanted to be with Miigwaans and her daughters. Tom had never been to the dwelling and wanted to see it before agreeing that their child would be born there.

He was taken aback by how bare the house was. It was little more than a shack. He was used to the tepee Wynona's parents inhabited which, though it was simple, had its possessions arranged in an orderly fashion. Not so in the Ojibwa dwelling. Its contents were a jumble of discarded clothing and goods from the town alongside a few traditional items. Perhaps it was Miigwaans' age or the youth of her daughters that caused the domestic chaos. Or was it a symptom of the malaise that seemed pervasive on that reserve perhaps because of its proximity to Elphinstone? There did not seem to be men around.

He said nothing until they were back in their room that night. He told Wynona that he would agree to her desire provided space could be made in the house that was clean and free of debris. "Oh, but baby will not be born in house," Wynona explained. "Miigwaans and daughters build special shelter of wood and bark with fire for birth so no men can be there. Also not you. Furs and fire will keep us warm and hot water to wash. You must not worry. I have been with my cousins during birth and I know what to do. And Miigwaans is family mid-wife."

Until now, Tom had not given much thought as to whether or not he would be present at the birth, but now he suddenly found himself protesting. "Not possible. Not our custom," Wynona told him firmly. "You can be with me until I push and then you go outside. You see baby when all clean." The tone of her voice made it plain that was the way it was going to be. Tom quietly assented.

He had agreed to be married by Lakota custom and this was evidently more of the same.

One night in mid-February, Wynona wakened Tom saying the baby was coming. Tom had intended to use the neighbour's horse and sleigh to take Wynona to the reserve when the time came. But they had not been expecting the birth for a couple of weeks. Tom woke Martha and then hurried to the neighbour's house. He was gone for what seemed a long time returning with the news that the horse had been borrowed by someone else. The only way to get her to the reserve was to pull her on a toboggan himself. Martha begged him to have the birth at the store. She had attended many a birth and reasoned that the distance, the cold and the lack of preparation at the house on reserve could put both Wynona and the child in danger.

Wynona was insistent that she wanted the native women with her at the birth. Martha proposed she examine Wynona and that, if there was time, Tom should run to the reserve and return with Miigwaans and her daughters while she made preparations for the birth here. Wynona hesitantly agreed. The examination showed there was still time and Tom took off.

The night was black but the contrast between the snow and the trees was sufficient for Tom to find his way. He had only been once to Miigwaans' shack and was not sure which it was among the huddle of buildings at the end of the road. A dog barked, followed by a chorus of baying. No lights were on and none appeared despite the noise. He knocked loudly on the door of the house he thought was hers. No response. He tried another house. Silence. Panic bred confusion. He could not remember which was the house and had little time. He turned back into the lane and shouted, "Miigwaans! Miigwaans!" The barking rose to a pitch. "Miigwaans!"

The dim glow of a lantern appeared in a window. A door opened and a man shouted in Ojibwa. Tom hurried to the door. The man held a rifle. "Enabigis. Please, where Miigwaans? I need Miigwaans," Tom stammered. The man's eyes were suspicious and uncomprehending. A younger man appeared over his shoulder.

Hoping the second understood some English, Tom continued, "My wife having baby. Needs Miigwaans' help."

The younger man pointed to the house opposite. "Mee-gwetch – thank you." Tom said and strode across the lane. He could hear movement inside and the door opened. It was one of her daughters, holding a lamp. Tom slowly explained what had happened and how much Wynona wanted Miigwaans with her. The girl beckoned Tom in and withdrew to a back room. Minutes later the old woman appeared, wrapped in a blanket. "I come," she said and withdrew again.

The minutes for Tom seemed interminable. What could be keeping them? Another daughter emerged, went to the other side of the room, took items from an old suitcase and returned to the bedroom. Finally, Miigwaans emerged, dressed in deerskin with a large fur wrapped over her shoulders. Her two daughters accompanied her carrying items wrapped in blankets. "We go," said the old woman.

It took much longer for this party of four to reach the store. Its lights were on and smoke was rising from the chimney. Tom ushered the women in, past a large cauldron of water heating on the wood stove and up to the attic. Wynona was on the bed with Martha beside her, arranging a pile of towels. At the sight of Tom and his companions, Wynona's head fell back on the pillow moaning relief. Tom moved beside her and kissed her forehead. "Now you go. I have help. I be alright," Wynona whispered.

It was the hardest thing he could do; pulling himself away from that bed, but that is what Wynona wanted. As he left the room, the native women began intoning a deep, rhythmic song. He watched them raise Wynona from the bed and help her to squat on the floor, all the while rubbing her back. Martha was standing aside watching. Tom went down stairs.

He slumped in a chair, his heart still pounding from the exertion of the last two hours and now perhaps from anticipation. The droning continued upstairs interspersed with loud moans from Wynona. He sat there for perhaps twenty minutes when loud cries from Wynona sent him rushing up the stairs. He opened the door. She was facing him, still on her haunches supported by the grand-daughters, her face wracked with pain, her long black hair heavy with sweat. Miigwaans saw him and shouted, "No – no!"

Tom had to leave but he could not stay downstairs being forced to listen to the struggle unfolding above. He grabbed his coat and went into the cold. The first shading of the morn lit the edge of the eastern sky. The cold was even more intense as it always is at dawning. He had to walk. The snow squeaked beneath his foot-steps, sounding like the mewing of a kitten or perhaps the first sounds of his new-born. He dare not go far, setting the top of the next hill as the point when he would turn back. But he reached it far too fast and kept going. Birthing was not the place for men in Wynona's world, nor in his. They were only in the way. They had made their contribution, and now the rest was up to the women-folk until the day, if it was a son, he would take him under his wing and teach him the ways of men.

The cold on his face relieved his spirit. There was something elemental about being out in this chill dawn while the offshoot of his own body was battling its way into the world. He did not know the outcome, but he found he was at peace and had to wilfully break the spell and turn around to meet whatever was unfolding back in the attic. But it was not long before his stride broke into a run with the eagerness to find out.

He opened the door, and there in the chair he had been resting on half an hour before, sat Martha, a wide grin on her face, holding a bundle in white linen. "Come, meet your son, Thomas." A torrent of emotion broke. He reached down and through vision blurred, saw the little red, wrinkled face that was of his blood and bone. He cradled the babe and with difficulty, mounted the stairs. He opened the door. Miigwaans and her daughters were rubbing Wyn-ona's abdomen and pelvic regions with herbs. Miigwaans again said no but this time, Tom disregarded the old woman and with shining eyes, approached Wynona. "Our son. We have a son!" he said jubilantly. She smiled weakly, raised her hand and placed it around the back of his neck. "We have a beautiful son."

Chapter

35

THERE WAS STILL MUCH WORK TO DO IN THE DAYS FOLLOWING TOM AND WYN-ona's departure. Although the fields had already been ploughed and the winter wheat sown on eight acres, the root vegetables had to be dug and stored under the house. He spent several days repairing the barn and sheds to withstand the gales of winter. And though he thought he had sufficient wood for the winter stoves, he could make use of the days before the snow to cut down the larger aspen in the hollows, buck them up and stack them behind the barn. The brisk sunny days of autumn lent themselves to such work.

They had been talking about what they might do to enrich their lives and speed the passage of the dark days. Agnes thought that with Wynona absent, it would be a good time to strengthen her relationships with the other families along the river and perhaps succeed in altering their attitudes towards her sister-in-law.

Agnes suggested that they make one final foray into Brandon to see acquaintances and stock up on supplies for mind and body. Reading would be an increasingly important part of their days when the cold and snow kept them virtual prisoners and they discovered their supply of books to be woefully inadequate. The trip would enable them to collect their mail rather than wait for the delivery that happened once a month when a post-rider visited communities west of Brandon. If they were fortunate, they could be there and back before the first snow.

Rob decided to check with the McIvor brothers to see if he could bring anything back for them. They had been planning their own foray to town, so the families decided to combine the journeys, making a pre-dawn start in two days.

The brothers rode on horseback, leading a third horse to carry needed supplies. A light dusting of snow had fallen the night before, and the dawn emerged grey and cold. It was the time of year when the prairie stretched out almost colourless – muted tones of brown and grey with only a few bushes retaining withered leaves. The McIvors led the way, their higher position on horseback giving them a better view of the road ahead, hidden from time to time by the snow.

Agnes nestled close to Rob, grateful for the bulk and softness of the buffalo robes. She placed her arm around his waist and beamed as he turned to look at her. She felt deep contentment at his side, under his protection. It had been a somewhat frantic summer, particularly with his extended visit to Brandon and Winnipeg with Tom, Old John and his people. The prospect of the quiet, isolated months of winter ahead during which she and Rob would spend extended, relaxed time in each other's company gave her great comfort. She realized that she was happiest when he was able to spend uninterrupted time with her.

Over the past several days, she had felt changes in her body, a little nausea in the early morning. Could it mean that she was pregnant? She had said nothing to Rob – better to wait until she was more certain. But they had decided some weeks before that it was time to have a child and had abandoned any precautions. It had made their coming together more spontaneous and exhilarating. Now, this journey to less familiar places added to her anticipation. Perhaps she would know while they were away if she passed nothing at her time of the month. Then she could tell Rob. She nestled closer to him.

Next morning, the McIvors went about their business and Rob and Agnes headed to the post office to get their mail. That was always an exciting if apprehensive event. They quickly thumbed through the letters extracting several from the family. Isobel's writing was immediately recognizable and there was a letter from Agnes' mother, but they delayed opening any of the letters until they had returned to their room. Family news, of whatever nature, was not to be learned standing on a street corner.

Rob sat on the bed and opened the letter from his mother. "Oh, dear Lord, he's gone," Rob cried out suddenly. "It's my father, he's died," he looked up at her. "It seems he caught pneumonia at the onset of cold weather. The funeral was at the end of September. Dear man, I feared I would never see you again." Rob lowered his head in his hands. Agnes moved beside him, holding him in silence for many minutes

"Rob, your Father was very proud of you. Your courage to set out for the unknown here gave him much satisfaction. I know. He frequently told me when I was waiting there for you. Even though he knew he could never come, the fact that you went gave him a new dimension in his life. How is your Mother?" Agnes asked.

"She seems to be coping. It was not unexpected. She says she has made no decisions about the future, yet. Tom will not know – I must get word to him. He will be cruelly cut up. He and father became very close when Tom was blamed for Kate's death."

There was other mail, but they put it aside unopened, and went down to the river, walking among the great Cottonwoods that presided with serenity along its banks. Rob took Agnes' arm. He remembered other occasions when he had opened letters, including hers, while seated along these banks. The place resonated with intimate memories.

They walked in silence and then Rob began to recount memories of his father when he was a young and vigorous man. He laboured long and hard to make the farm sustainable but was never too tired for his children. In fact, they seemed to give him strength. He would come in at the end of the day looking drawn and haggard, but as the little ones scrambled to sit beside him at the table, the burdens of the day seemed to fall away. It was only as the years took their toll and he appeared to have suffered from a stroke that he could no longer engage in the rough and tumble of their young lives.

"How will I get the news to Tom?" Rob wondered. "I will write him immediately, but have no way of knowing how long a letter would take to reach Elphinstone, if indeed he is there. What would you think if I took the horse and went to find him once we return home?"

"Let's talk about that," Agnes replied. "In the meantime, I

think this is the time to give you some other news." She paused, "I believe I am pregnant with our child."

Rob stared at her, open-mouthed. He took her hands. "What a mix of grief and joy. One generation departs, another arrives. Father would be so happy, his first – no, possibly his second grandchild."

Agnes smiled. "I think we should return to the room, see what's in the rest of the mail and then get something to eat. I am beginning to be exceptionally hungry." Rob smiled knowingly, and they set off.

A day later, they had completed all their purchases and Rob had written to his brother, care of the Hudson Bay post in Elphinstone. The skies to the west were ominously leaden as they set out in the early dawn. They were underway four hours when a heavy snow began to fall. It swiftly erased all trace of the road. The road was familiar enough that they were able to navigate by the lay of the land as long as the snow did not obstruct their larger view. But as dusk fell, this became increasingly difficult. The heavy clouds blotted the night sky offering them no light. It became impossible to proceed with the real danger that they would wander far off the trail.

Rob consulted Seumas and Dewar. They decided to find what shelter they could in the next coulee and wait for the dawn. They tethered the horses upwind from the buggy and Rob offered the brothers one of the buffalo robes. They refused, so they spread the robe on the ground beside the buggy so that all four could sit off the snow. Rob wrapped the other around Agnes and joined the other two men sitting with their knees up to their chins to preserve their body warmth. Agnes lifted the robe and put it round Rob's shoulders. He nodded off.

Some hours later he awoke with the cold. The men were huddled close together – their bodies now covered in snow, the only movement the rise and fall of their breathing. There was no wind. The snow drifted down like tiny ghosts in the blackness. The world around was deathly still, the only sound the occasional shifting or snuffling of the horses. He could see no sign of light on the eastern horizon. Agnes slept, her head on his shoulder.

36

THE LONG MONTHS OF WINTER PASSED REMARKABLY SWIFTLY. WITH THE anticipation of the new child there was something to look forward to and every day was energized by the promise of new life. Agnes had followed through with her intent to see more of the neighbours' wives and the pregnancy gave her an immediate bond with them. Several neighbours had building projects under way and Rob took the opportunity to help.

The onset of early snow had ruled out any journey by Rob to Elphinstone. They had a letter from Tom six weeks after their return from Brandon, telling them of the arrival of their son. He had not yet received the news of his father's death, but the arrival of Tom's letter assured them that at least the mail was getting through.

April began remarkably mild. The snow retreated rapidly and the winter wheat stood at least two inches green. Rob trusted Tom would soon return as no preparation of the land could be begun without the oxen. Warm, dry winds continued to blow from the Dakotas to the south shading the land from white to brown and then to tufts of green. Agnes decided it was time to prepare Tom and Wynona's home for their arrival.

With the snow's rapid melt, the Pipestone was close to bursting its banks. Red-wing blackbirds had returned, their calls shrill among the bull-rushes and the western magpies in their formal black and white attire would soon follow. The ground smelled with the rank odour of wet soil and rotting vegetation that always heralded the start of new growth. The land would soon be dry enough to plough. Where was Tom? Rob could not help but be concerned given his brother's proclivity for unpredictable behaviour.

The days went by. Agnes was now six months pregnant and Rob tried to keep his impatience under control by fashioning a crib from aspen he had cut and sawn into planks the previous fall. He suspended the crib from the frame by leather straps so that it could be rocked rhythmically. Then he constructed a changing table, fitting an enamel basin into it for a bath, carefully sanding both pieces of furniture. Agnes was delighted with his handiwork but when it was done, and there was still no sign of Tom, nothing could assuage his impatience. He decided one day to saddle the horse and ride to Virden. If he didn't find them, he at least could enquire from other travelers about the state of the northern roads.

He had the horse saddled and was bidding good-bye to Agnes when down the road along the river came the unmistakable profile of Pete and Harriet pulling the cart with Tom, Wynona and the child. Rob leapt on the horse and rode out to greet them. "What a fine sight you are! And you are arriving just when we need you most." He rode alongside them as the cart rolled into the yard where Agnes was waiting.

"Oh, such a sweet boy," Agnes said as she reached up for the child to help Wynona descend. "You all look grand. Have you had a naming ceremony?" Wynona smiled as Tom jumped down and embraced his brother and sister-in-law. "No ceremony but his name is Chayton, the Lakota name for Falcon," Tom replied. "He will soar high and see far."

The oxen needed a day's rest before the spring ploughing could begin. The first task was to plough a fireguard around all the build-ings. Prairie fires were always a threat, but particularly so in the spring as the warm winds dried the dead grass from the previous winter and the new growth, not being sufficiently advanced, left the fields exposed and vulnerable.

Rob and Tom conferred on the work ahead. When they had passed through Virden, Tom detoured to meet Ian McAllister, the grain merchant, to see if he had views about the nature of prices for the coming season. The early, severe frost the previous autumn had been widespread and led to high prices for the limited supply of quality grain. McAllister thought that wheat prices would stay high because stocks had been so low whereas the price for oats and barley, used principally for animal feed, would remain low.

The brothers decided to plant most of their land to wheat. The land that had been cropped the previous year had been ploughed in the autumn and it only required a disk to break the clumps of soil. Rob drove the oxen with the disk at a right angle to the ploughed rows to maximize break up. Tom then followed with a sling around his shoulders, hand-broadcasting the seeds with careful long sweeps of his arm.

This demanded constant attention to distribute the seeds evenly. They switched tasks to relieve the boredom and rest their limbs. Agnes and Wynona joined them at times to broadcast the seeds, Wynona with the infant in a pouch on her back. All that then remained was to hitch the oxen to the wide metal rake passing over the sown fields to give the seed good soil contact.

The task of seeding took the best part of two weeks and all during that time the warm southern winds continued to blow. Several times over the course of their seeding they saw smoke rising far to the west in sufficient quantity to indicate prairie fires but the prevailing winds were such as to pose no danger to them. They now needed rain – both to diminish the threat of fire and to restore adequate moisture to germinate the seeds and prevent the soil from blowing away. Just as they had been at the mercy of the weather the previous autumn when the crop took the brunt of severe frost, so all their work was once again held hostage. All they could do was pray.

Several days later, Rob was wakened in the night by the sounds of a severe electric storm, the sky illuminated by jagged fork lightning. An answer to prayer, he thought, expecting the skies to erupt with a deluge of rain. He listened for the familiar sound on the roof. But all was quiet save for the crack of the lightning.

And then he smelled the smoke. Leaping from bed, he raced

outside only to see the glow of fire low on the western horizon. There must have been a lightning strike on the prairie. This time, the wind was blowing from the west and he instantly sensed the danger. He roused Agnes, dressed, rushed to the barn and mounted the horse bare-back to waken Tom and Wynona who returned with him to join Agnes. While the women packed belongings in case they had to flee, Rob hitched the oxen to the cart and began loading it with what they could take with them. Tom climbed to the roof of the barn to better observe the advancing path of the fire.

The fire was on the other side of the river and was following its course from the west. Tom's homestead, lying further to the south, had a better chance of escaping the blaze but Rob's farm was clearly threatened if it leapt the water. The ploughed fireguard to the north and west of the house and barn was about twenty feet across and skirted the pond on the northern edge of the farmyard. Once the ox cart had been loaded, they gathered buckets and filled them from the pond. Tom climbed a ladder to the roof of the house. The others passed the buckets up and Tom emptied them across the sod to prevent sparks from igniting the roof. When the house was protected they turned their attention to the barn.

And then they waited thinking of their friends and neighbours in the path of the fire, hoping they had the foresight to make the same preparations. By now the western horizon was a steady blaze. The fire passed over the open prairie burning briefly and intensely on the dried grasses consuming them swiftly and moving on. Only where it came upon a building did it linger.

Now they could hear the fire, like the distant roar of a great wind. They debated sending the women and the child south and east on the ox-cart while the men stayed to try to protect the structures. But the fire's path was completely unpredictable and they could easily be caught in the open and surrounded. It was better to stay together. In the extreme, they could immerse themselves in the pond and pray they would survive as the intense heat of the fire sucked oxygen from the air.

And then the blaze approached the fireguard. The land they

had seeded lay to the south and east and would provide an additional barrier to the flames. The women manned buckets by the buildings while the men grappled with the oxen and the horse attempting to pull them into the pond. Panic stricken, their eyes wide and rolling up into their skulls, they resisted going towards the fire into the water. It took all the strength and persuasiveness the men had to control them but once in the water, they sensed relief and quietened down. Tom was able to cross the pond and tie the animals by long ropes to a tree standing to its west.

The heat was now intense. Rob yelled to Agnes and Wynona to enter the water. He and Tom took over the task of extinguishing the sparks that crossed the pond. The fire now surrounded the homestead on the other side of the fireguard. The roar was deafening, smoke and sparks engulfing the area, an inferno of hellish proportions. Sparks were landing, igniting their clothing. Tom and Rob dove into the pond, joining the women and crouching so that only their heads and that of the babe, who howled his terror, were above water. The passing of minutes seemed interminable but gradually the sound died and the fire passed leaving a charred and smoking landscape. They could see smoke rising from the roof of both the house and the barn. Rob told the women to stay where they were while he and Tom filled the buckets and raced to the smoldering spots on the roofs. By this time the fire was several hundred feet to the south and grey sky was emerging.

The women made their way to dry land and collapsed on the steps of the back porch, their clothes streaming water, their faces smudged with soot. Rob and Tom joined them, faces drawn by the fear and struggle. Rob sat behind Agnes and held her trembling body and whispered, "Father, God, you got us through the fires of hell. Please do the same for all those in the path of this inferno."

Tom took the baby and put his arm around Wynona and they sat for a long time breathing deeply. Then he climbed on the roof to see what damage the fire had done to his house and buildings but the land they had ploughed and seeded between the farms seemed to have deprived the fire of its fuel and it had skirted his property.

It was early morning, the sun just breaking through the smoke above the eastern horizon. While the women went in to prepare food, Tom and Rob took shovels and walked the charred land, digging at points where smoke continued to rise, covering smoldering vegetation with earth. They broke for food but then continued across their fields. The land that had been sown showed minimal charring but the wheat shoots had wilted in the heat. The entire unbroken prairie was a blackened wasteland. Fortunately, few of the trees in the valley along the river had burned. The natural dampness of those shaded areas and the shelter the valley provided had spared them the worst of the flames.

But what had become of their neighbours? Considerable smoke was still rising from several of the homesteads. Rob saddled up and rode over to the McIvors. Once he cleared the bend in the river he was horrified to see their house and buildings a smoking ruin. He spurred the horse to a gallop and came across a desolate scene. Fire was still licking at beams that were askew; the roof of the house had collapsed. The sheds were piles of smoking debris. There was no sign of the brothers or their animals.

"Seumas, Dewar," Rob yelled in mounting panic. He climbed over the fallen beams into the ruins of the house but could see no sign of bodies and the ruins of the sheds revealed no clue save the charred bodies of poultry. Where could they be? Could they have safely fled the inferno? But where could they go to escape the path of the fire? There was nothing further to do here, so he rode on to other neighbours.

Most had fared better than the McIvors. Some had lost out-buildings and others had asphyxiated animals but no one had died. There was no news of the McIvors.

Rob returned to the demolished, still-smoking McIvor homestead. He found a pitch-fork in the ruins of a shed and began levering the fallen beams and probing the smoking debris, horrified that he might feel the spongy resistance of a body. Nothing. The wind died, smoke rose straight in the air. Rob mounted the horse and was turning to go, when across the blackened fields he saw two men driving animals towards him. He raced towards them and leapt from the horse, embracing first Seumas and then Dewar.

They had not sensed the fire in the night until it was almost upon them leaving no time to fight it. They had opened the barn, mounted the horses bareback and tried to herd the rest of the animals to the river valley. Some in their panic had scattered and were lost but most made it to the water. The river was not deep enough to submerse the oxen and cattle and they knew that if the trees caught fire, they would likely die. But that had not happened. They had chosen to stay in the cool of the valley until all danger was past.

It was a disconsolate party that approached the Dunbar farm. Agnes was on the porch as they approached and once they had tethered their animals, she quickly shepherded them into the house, her face reflecting the tragedy of their news. Tom and his family had returned to their farm. Neither of the McIvors felt much like eating. They drank their tea and poked at the fried pork and bread Agnes spread out for them.

"Do we start again or throw in the towel and go home to Scotland?" Dewar asked mournfully. "You will stay here with us until you decide what to do," Agnes replied firmly. "And if it is to rebuild your farm, you will stay until you have your house rebuilt."

"Och, we could'na impose on you like that," Seumas said.

"It's no imposition. It is what neighbours do for neighbours," Rob replied. "We have enough food on hand and feed for your animals as well as ours. With your help we can fashion living quarters in the attic of the barn and with the warm weather coming, you should be right comfortable there."

"You're more than kind. Thank you," Dewar whispered.

The next day Rob decided to propose a community meeting to assess everyone's situation and decide where help was needed most. It was agreed to meet in Reston church the following Sunday. Reston had been spared the path of the fire and its families were keen to help those less fortunate.

Since their return from Elphinstone, the seeding and now the fire had fully preoccupied Tom and Wynona. The meeting in Reston would be their first chance to interact with the community. Agnes felt confident that her friendship with many of the wives and the fact that Wynona now had a child would overcome any hostility.

She was about to be disappointed. Rob and Agnes arrived first and after mingling for a while, Rob stood at the front and saw Tom and Wynona quietly take seats at the back of the barn as he suggested the meeting begin. "Let's come together now and start by making a list of people who need help and those who can volunteer their services."

Rob watched Tom and Wynona make their way to talk to a cluster of people at the side of the barn. As they approached, two of the women turned their backs on Wynona. Was it deliberate or simply a coincidence? Wynona moved closer to Tom but Rob could see that even the men in the group looked uncomfortable. Then one of the men said something to Tom, his face twisted in a sneer. Tom whirled and struck him on the jaw, sending the man reeling, then continued pummeling him as he struggled to regain his balance. A second man was on Tom's back, his arm around his neck. The others stood in a circle, some shocked by the eruption of anger, others smirking. Rob tore across the room, thrusting himself between Tom and the other man and grabbing Tom's shoulders, subduing him.

The barn had gone quiet. Wynona, with the child, had taken refuge behind a stack of hay bales and Agnes was at their side. People were staring, too shocked to resume their conversations. The man whose comment had started the confrontation left the barn, his face bleeding. Rob was trembling in his anger. He pressed Tom's shoulders forcing him to sit on a bench. Then he turned to the crowd.

"We don't want no squaws breeding with our boys," a woman's voice shrilled from the floor of the barn.

"Hush, you ignorant woman," another shouted. Argument erupted across the crowd. Tom took Wynona by the arm. "We're leaving. I don't want any part of this crowd," Tom snarled and stormed out of the building.

Somehow Rob had to get the meeting back on track. Too many people were desperate for help to allow it to end in failure. The crowd settled down again and he noticed several of the most vocal dissenters had left. Lists were made and an action plan was agreed to. Many had already finished spring seeding and would be available to rebuild barns and houses for the next month or so.

The McIvors had suffered the greatest loss and within a week a party of five men had joined Rob and the brothers working to clear the rubble from the homestead. Others arrived with cart loads of hay and feed for their animals. Still others were down in the valley along the Pipestone cutting and trimming the aspen to make beams for the new house and barn. Wives turned up with meals for the working men. The camaraderie of collective work helped dissipate the clouds of dissension and Rob's faith in the community was somewhat restored.

When the work was well underway, he urged Tom to join them, but Tom would have none of it. He and Wynona withdrew increasingly into the confines of their own farm. Agnes spent what spare time she had helping Wynona with the child and her household chores but could not erase the sadness from the face of her sister-in-law. She told Rob that Tom seemed to be drinking again.

They had hoped that Tom's winter work would have generated enough money to enable the brothers to buy a thresher in time for that summer's harvest but when Rob raised the matter one day with Tom, the latter showed little interest. "Let's see what the summer brings," was his only comment.

37

TWO WEEKS AFTER THE MEETING IN THE BARN, THE WEATHER BROKE AND THE scorched land was drenched with rain. The Pipestone swelled with black, muddy water. The loss of the prairie grasses exposed the soil to much greater erosion than normal but shortly thereafter, green emerged across the landscape. Most of the winter wheat had survived the fire and the newly planted spring wheat had been untouched.

Tom came to his brother and said that he wanted to buy another horse and take his family west to spend time with Wynona's parents. He could be back in about a month but would leave Wynona and Chayton there until after the harvest.

Rob was immediately concerned. Was this further evidence of his disaffection from the community? Yet, how could he be blamed? When they discussed the matter that evening, Agnes said that they must use the time when Wynona was away to speak bluntly to their friends and neighbours. "I do not want to be part of a community that excludes Wynona and Tom," she said. "I do not know what it will take to change attitudes but if our remaining here along the Pipestone becomes conditional on that happening, so be it."

Rob was taken aback. Of course, she was right, but would it come to that? Would they have to abandon all they had built? It was not just the outspoken bigots – you would not find a community anywhere in the West that did not have its share of those. Far more disheartening were the narrow-minded attitudes of the majority who kept their distance from anyone who differed in culture or race. He saw the body language and he heard the talk – not just about Wynona or her people, but also about the settlers from Eastern Europe with their strange garb and bewildering languages. Even in this vast and open land of new beginnings, the 'us' and 'them' outlook of the old world persisted.

"I will help Wynona prepare for the journey," Agnes said sadly. "She knows we love and accept her. Perhaps our relationship will be the assurance she needs that she has something to come back to. But if she doesn't, we will lose both her and Tom."

Tom was happy to be back with Wynona's people but his feelings of well-being did not last long. Although they had gained their own land in what was called a "reserve," they were virtual prisoners on it. They were not allowed outside its boundaries without a written permit issued by a government official called an Indian agent. Some had developed their plots and were raising both crops and cattle but they were not permitted to sell what they grew to anyone off the reserve. Attached to the reserve was land set aside for hunting and gathering. They had been told that this was for their exclusive use but already settlers had encroached on the land and the authorities turned a blind eye.

It took some days before Tom discovered the extent of this mistreatment. He only learned through hearing the talk of the young men. Tom could not stay on the side lines. After talking with Wynona's father and other elders, he stormed into the office of the agent and he demanded to know by what authority he had imposed these constraints. He was astonished to discover they had all been set out in legislation passed by the parliament in Ottawa. The agent was only doing his job.

The agent did not take kindly to the presence of a citizen of British origin staying on the reserve questioning his authority. He told Tom to back off or he would have the police remove him from the reserve. The fact that he was married to the daughter of a resident made no difference. Tom only contained his fury out of consideration for Wynona's family but told the agent that he had not heard the last of this.

The agent appeared to believe him for in the evening as the family were eating, they heard horses stop outside the tepee, the flap was pulled open and two police officers entered. They pointed to Tom and told him he had to go with them. Tom was astounded. Wynona's father stood and protested. The police were exceedingly nervous but insistent. Suddenly Tom recognized one of them. He had been with him in the small group isolated at Cutknife Creek, captured and held captive in the Cree tent.

"James, it's me – Tom Dunbar. We were together at Cutknife Creek."

"Tom – good God! What're you do'in here? Come outside with me. I have my orders." He looked nervously at his fellow officer. Tom followed him outside.

"Tom, look, I have been told to arrest you as a trouble-maker and remove you from this reserve." He looked again at the other officer. "I am prepared to say that we could not find you – but you will have to get out of here right away. I don't like it, but these agents have authority over people on the reserve that we would never stand for in our communities. Indians have no rights as you and I understand them."

"How much time do I have?"

"You need to be out of here by tomorrow night or a larger posse will be in here to find you."

"Let me think about it," Tom replied.

"I'm telling you, you have to go. They could arrest you and charge you for agitation and that carries a big fine or time in prison. You've got less than twenty-four hours."

Tom looked askance at the officer and returned to the tent. He told Wynona what had transpired. "I can't believe this. There's one law for the white man and one for the Indian." Wynona's eyes were downcast in resignation. "I don't want to take you and Chayton away from your family. We've just arrived. But it looks like I will have to go. And we left Scotland to find freedom! This is worse than anything the landlords and their political cronies imposed on us! It's even worse than what they do in Ireland," Tom seethed.

It took him a long time to sleep that night. Lying on the buffalo

321

robes with Wynona, the baby tucked between them, the fire still glowing, he could follow the path of the moon, its faint image showing through the tepee walls. He was glad to be in that space, glad to no longer feel part of a hypocritical society. He remembered his ignorance and intolerance when they first arrived in Canada, his arguments with Rob about the inferiority of the Indian and the rightness of the settlers' grab for the land. He was a wiser, yes, and perhaps a better man today, thanks to Wynona and her people. He wanted Chayton to grow up with his mother's perspective, with an intimate knowledge of her people's ways.

But how could that happen if he remained farming in the heart of a settler community? Was he approaching a parting of the ways with his brother and the dream they had shared when they had come to this country?

He slept just as the moon reached the peak of the tepee.

He woke to the gentle sound of Wynona suckling his son beside him. He wished the warmth and intimacy of this moment could last forever. He bridled at its contrast to the harsh world the boy was born into, the hurts and anger that inevitably would be his in the years to come. He had to raise this boy in such a way that his spirit would not be crushed.

He lay there until the nursing had finished. Then he reached over, picked Chayton up and laid him on the outside of the bed and took Wynona in his arms. Grief at having to leave wrestled with the desire he always felt when he held her close. He abandoned himself to the desire, feeling her body rise to him. The grief, the uncertainty of their life made his urging all the more desperate. He wanted above all else to hold on to her. The intensity of their love-making filled the tent but if her parents were awake, they showed no sign. This acceptance was one of the things he loved most about his life with her people. Life was taken as it came and to the full. There were no hidden corners, no pretenses. The storm passed and they lay still. Chayton was making gurgling noises beside them. Tom sat up beaming at him.

He delayed his departure until the early afternoon. He would take both horses with him and then return in time to have his family back on the farm before harvest. As he was preparing to leave, a young boy burst into the tepee to say that a posse of police had been spotted at the top of the coulee headed in their direction. Tom hastily bid farewell to Wynona's parents, embraced her and the baby. Fortunately, both horses were already tethered outside the tent. He threw the saddle on one, cinched it, grabbed the reins of the other and galloped through the encampment, scrambling up the other side of the coulee.

He had been spotted and the police gave chase but as they entered the encampment four or five young Indian men appeared from nowhere on horseback and charged directly into the police formation, scattering their horses in a confusion of shouts, dust and hooves. The melee lasted only minutes but was sufficient to give Tom the head start he needed. The police resumed their chase but as the distance between them and their target lengthened, they gave up.

Rob was helping erect the McIvor's house when Tom arrived. As soon as he got back in the evening, he went to ask Tom to join them for supper. Tom was asleep in the rocker of his porch. "Hey, brother, come and join us for some food," Rob said gently starting the rocker back and forth. Tom's eyes opened slightly, his speech slurred. "I'm too tired. See you in the morning."

"Come on, then. I'll help you get to bed. I'll bring some food up later if you wake up hungry."

"No, no, leave me alone. I'm a'right. See ya later."

Rob returned. He could smell the liquor on Tom's breath

Tom did not appear in the morning. Rob was needed at the McIvor house and did not see him so Agnes decided to go up to his homestead late in the morning. She had always been very fond of Tom, admiring his independent and impulsive spirit. He sensed that and would talk with her even when relations with his brother were strained. He had clearly been disturbed when he arrived back the evening before.

She found him half-dressed sitting on the porch, a meal partially eaten. He smiled as she approached and beckoned her to a seat. "Tell me about you journey and your visit. You made it home in record time," she said. Tom had been as good as his word – he returned in just over five weeks. Wynona and the boy were fine, her parents were welcoming but the conditions they and their people lived under were feudal.

"Not my choosing," he replied. If he had been an angry man when he left, his face was even more shut down now as he told Agnes of the injustices he had encountered. She was aghast when she heard. "How can behaviour like that be justified in this country? The government treats these people as though they were prisoners of war. We must find a way to bring this injustice to an end," she protested.

"I don't know if I can reconcile myself to living in this society," Tom replied. "I fear for my son. How will he be treated by the authorities? Will they imprison him too because he has Indian blood? It might be best if I took Wynona and Chayton and moved to the far west where these laws carry no weight." He looked broken.

Agnes was silent for several minutes. 'Whatever you and Wynona decide to do, you know you will always have our love and support. We will do whatever we can to bring an end to these cruel laws. We did not leave so much behind in Scotland to live with this kind of injustice here. Don't give up, Tom. We can make a difference."

Tom eyed her, his face full of doubt. "We'll see."

38

THE LATE SUMMER DAYS DAWNED CLEAR AND WARM. SUFFICIENT RAIN HAD
fallen so the crops were thrusting towards the sky. The prairie
mantle had shed its ashes and assumed a brilliant green. It was
as though the land had rebounded from its trauma, determined to
defy what it could not control. The wild creatures were back in
abundance – the prairie dogs would have found refuge from the
blaze deep in their burrows – the deer, foxes, coyotes, and skunks –
finding shelter in the narrow valley along the river. The winter
wheat would soon be ready for harvest.

Agnes was more and more aware of the new life within her.
She proudly showed Rob the swelling of her abdomen as they lay
on their bed an early Sunday morning. Rob was generally up with
the dawn, which broke ever earlier in this northern clime making
for a long and productive day. But Sundays were different. They
had always kept the Sabbath when he was a boy, only completing
the most necessary of farm chores. He tried to do the same now
unless some crisis interfered. This particular morning was languid.
The sun had been up for a couple of hours and the breeze it had
warmed ruffled the curtains as they lay marveling at this new presence in their midst.

Rob stroked her abdomen, Agnes guiding his fingers to feel the
head moving slightly, distending her skin. "Which do you hope
we have?" Agnes queried. "A boy would be a great companion on
the farm," Rob said, "but a girl would do much more to spoil her
father," Rob said with a laugh. "What about you?"

"Whatever God gives will be a wonderful gift," she replied. "And, of course, if we have one, we will have to have more. No child of mine is going to live in a household without brothers and sisters."

"In that case, I had better be up and get at it. We'll need to buy an extra quarter section to feed the tribe you seem to want," he said with a wide smile. "I'm going up to get Tom to join us for a big breakfast. Can we have fried ham and griddle cakes? Perhaps this will be a good time to talk to Tom again about buying the thresher."

Tom had pulled himself out of his black mood and had even joined Rob for a couple of days working on the McIvor brothers' new barn. He was fond of those brothers and while he avoided participating in any larger gatherings, he was not about to deny assistance to those who had been decent to Wynona. He had said nothing to Rob about leaving the community and his brother hoped that that had been a passing notion.

On the matter of the thresher, he seemed positive. They didn't have the cash to buy it outright and would have to apply for a loan from the bank in Brandon. But as Rob pointed out, the machine would probably pay for itself in a couple of years as they could hire it out to neighbours once their own crops were processed. To date, no one from here to Reston had such equipment.

The question they faced was how to get the machine from Brandon to the farm. The ox cart alone could not carry it, even if it could be broken down. It might take two trips or they could take the horses with them in case part of the machine could be pulled while the rest travelled on the ox-cart. The journey would likely take three days to give them enough time to arrange a loan with the bank, negotiate the purchase, arrange for transportation and haul the equipment home. They agreed to go early the following week.

The machine was as odd-looking as it was ingenious. Set on a wagon base with four wheels, its upper carriage stood some eight feet high and extended well beyond the base. The grain was first shaken to separate it from the stalks and then fed between rollers to shed the husks. The hulled kernels fell and were channeled into sacks below while the straw was shuttled forward into a wagon. Below was an elaborate gear system powered by oxen or horses.

The animals were strapped to giant cross-pieces and trod a circle under the upper carriage – hence the need for the upper carriage to be so high.

Rob and Tom watched in amazement as the dealer ran it through its paces. The only significant labour involved was forking the bundles of grain up to the upper carriage from the wagon that had collected the stooks in the field. After that, all that was required was to haul away the hulled grain and the straw.

They were convinced and the purchase was concluded. The height of the thresher made it top-heavy for long distance travel but it had been designed so that the upper carriage could be released from the base to be transported separately. They dismantled the machine, levered the four corners of the carriage slightly higher than the base, hitched the horses to the base and drove it out from under. Then they lowered the carriage onto the ox cart. The horses were able to pull the base without difficulty and with the oxen hauling the cart, they were set to go.

They arrived home just after sunset and decided to wait until the next day to move the carriage back on the base. In the morning, Rob could not wait to show the neighbours his acquisition and the McIvors eagerly accompanied him to see this wonder of technology.

Pete and Harriet were initially confused about what was required of them. The brothers had to lead them in the first circles but they soon caught on. Rob found a couple of bundles of straw from last summer's harvest.- most of the kernels had been flailed out but he fed it through the mechanism and out of the spout flowed a couple of handfuls of hulled grain. There were appreciative "oohs" and "aahs" from the crowd.

Rob had picked up mail while he was in Brandon and it included a letter from Abbeylane Farm. Isobel wanted to come the next spring for some months and would bring Hermione with her. Perhaps one of Agnes' sisters would come as well. Agnes was delighted. Having a couple of eager young women around to help with the baby and the summer chores would be a god-send. Rob was particularly pleased. He knew how close his mother and Tom were and of all people, she would have the best chance of helping his brother learn to manage the ignorance and prejudice that surrounded them. Her presence would only enrich their lives but would help Tom and Wynona put down roots in the valley of the Pipestone.

She couldn't come soon enough in Rob's opinion. Once the excitement of purchasing and assembling the thresher had subsided, he saw less and less of Tom. He was not doing well in the absence of his family.

One evening Rob decided to walk to his house for no particular reason other than to spend time with him. It had been a grey and rainy day. As the afternoon ended, the clouds lowered on the prairie forming a mist across the land. The wind started up. As he walked towards the cluster of trees around Tom's house, he suddenly thought the house was burning, with mist – or smoke – spirally up around it. The chill he felt at the base of his skull was the one he had experienced that winter evening, long before Tom had built his house, when it appeared a phantom building was being consumed by smoke in that same copse. There was the same ominous feel to the sight, the same sense of foreboding. Rob shook his head to dismiss the phantom and walked faster.

There was no answer to his knock on the door. Yet there was a lamp burning inside and a fire in the stove. He opened the door. Tom was slouched on a chair, half on the floor. He was asleep, clearly drunk, a bottle of corn whiskey half empty beside him. Dismay rent Rob. "Oh, Tom, brother, what's happening to you?" He knelt and placed his hand on the back of Tom's neck. Tom gurgled incomprehensibly. Rob began to be concerned that he might suffocate in his own vomit. He got up, linked his arms under Tom's shoulders and heaved him up and over on to the couch. He sat him up in the corner and raised his feet. Tom was barely conscious of what was taking place. He gently slapped Tom's face. "Wake up, Tom, wake up." No response. He slapped harder. Tom's eyes opened. "Wha'sha do'in?" he mumbled.

"You've got to wake up. I've got to get some food into you."

Tom heaved and vomited over his lower body. "Aw geez, lee me alone."

"No, I can't. Not in your condition." Rob got up – drew some cold water, sloshed it on Tom's face and began to strip off his soiled clothing. He threw a blanket around him. Tom was now conscious. "Stay there while I get some food."

There was precious little edible in the kitchen. Rob found some eggs which he scrambled and dried beef on which he poured boiling water to make a soup. When he returned, Tom was awake looking morose and guilty. "Here, get some of this into you," Rob said. He sat quietly while Tom ate. "What's the trouble, brother? Is there anything I can do?"

Tom was silent for a long while but when he spoke he was frank. "Oh, I miss my family. And I don't know about the future. I can't see Wynona ever being happy here."

"Give it some more time," Rob said. "I think we may be able to turn things around at least with some of the neighbours. Wait until Mother gets here with Mione. If Wynona is not content by the time she returns to Scotland, then I will help you sell your part of the farm so you have what it takes to get started elsewhere. I promise you."

Tom looked Rob in the eye. "Well, that may be the way to go," he said heavily.

"But in the meantime, brother, you've got to get a handle on the drink. You'll be no good to Wynona and the boy if you are drunk much of the time. Why don't you plan to come down to us for your meals until you go to get her? That might help with the loneliness."

Tom nodded his head in reluctant agreement

The waiting days of summer began – there were animals to feed, repairs to house and barn to undertake, the large vegetable garden to hoe and weed. But there was also time for other things. One day a young man on horseback came to call. He had recently been ordained as a Presbyterian minister and had been informed that the community along the Pipestone were looking for a preacher. Enquiries in the community had led him to the Dunbars' door.

Rodney McFarlane, tall of stature with a ready smile, had a gracious demeanour that spoke of a good upbringing. He had been born in Ontario of Scots ancestry. He was unmarried and seemed to have a keen mind. While a little over-eager, Rob put that down to his youthfulness. He had listened intently and was not prone to try to display his intelligence, a trait that would not have gone down well with future parishioners.

In the course of their discussion, Rob turned to the relationship between settlers and the Indians. "We are newcomers here but in a very short time we have gained the upper hand and displaced these people from their lands, their livelihood and, more importantly, often from their culture," Rob said. "We come from very different cultures and a great many of our people disdain cultures and practices that differ from their own.

"It does not take much reading of Scripture to know that such attitudes are not condoned," Rob continued. "We are called to see all peoples as God's children, 'whether man or woman, Jew or Gentile, slave or free'. So if you were to join us, I would want to know that you would encourage our people to respect and accept all, regardless of differences."

McFarlane looked Rob in the eye. "I must admit that being raised in Ontario, I am much less aware of this than perhaps I would have been living in the west. But what I see distresses me and I know that there are many in the church who believe that the sooner we can rid the red man of his pagan ways the better for his salvation. I tell you honestly, I am conflicted."

"My concern is not one of doctrine," Rob replied, "but the way my fellow Christians so often disdain the Indian as something less than human. It is that narrow-minded hostility and the grave injustices that are perpetrated by our laws that are the largest barriers to the Indian accepting our faith. Will you help us turn these around?"

"That is a tall order, Mr Dunbar," McFarlane said. "I can't speak with the same authority you can, but I know what Scripture requires of the human heart and I will do my best to proclaim that."

"That's all I can ask," Rob replied. "Thank you."

Later, Agnes was keen to hear of the conversation and of Rob's impressions. Rob welcomed his forthrightness and believed he was open to learn. It would be too much to expect him to champion justice for the Indians, but he believed he would address intolerance both from the pulpit and one-on-one when required. Rob liked him.

The long days of August began to diminish and the sunshine took on an ochre tone that was the mark of late summer. Nights began to be chilly. This was a deeply satisfying time of year. Much of the heavy work was done. Only the harvest remained though that would be grueling enough. But the onset of autumn was a time of drawing closer – to family, to neighbours. If the harvest was good and the stores of food laid up were plentiful, then it was a time to be grateful that once again you had managed to wrest a good living from the soil.

It would not be many days before harvest began and Tom left with the horses to collect Wynona and Chayton. The garden was yielding its bounty demanding many hours of work to store it for winter. Onions, potatoes and turnips were set in barrels of straw and carted to the root cellar under the house. Steam rose from the kitchen as Agnes bottled carrots, peas, tomatoes and beans. The sharp smell of spices often greeted Rob at the end of the day – that summer the stores in Brandon had begun stocking bottles and spices for preserving that would enable them to vary their winter diet beyond the dried and salted menus of the past.

The babe was increasingly making its presence known. Agnes was now large and the boost of energy that usually accompanied the last weeks of pregnancy was a welcome gift given the amount of work that had to be done to prepare for winter. Rob was solicitous, frequently sliding his arms around her, insisting she remain seated while he fetched and gathered. He awoke every morning with a keen sense of anticipation. He and Agnes had visited a woman in Reston who had been a midwife in Ontario and she promised assistance when the time came.

Some ten days after his departure Tom returned with Wynona and Chayton. The journey had gone without incident. He managed to slip into the encampment and leave again before the Indian agent or the police were aware he was there. They brought news that Wynona's parents would come in the late fall and spend the winter between Tom's farm and Old John's encampment on Turtle Mountain.

The days were sunny and cool. Rob walked the land frequently, gathering handfuls of grain, rubbing the chaff clear and testing the firmness of the kernels. The wheat on the slightly higher land towards to west end of the farm was now ready. The drier conditions there promoted faster ripening even if the kernels were somewhat smaller. They decided to start mowing the following Monday.

As Rob hitched the horses to the sickle mower and moved off on the field he recalled the endless, punishing hours they had spent wielding the hand scythes the first years on the farm. The click-click of the mower, laying down neat swaths of cut wheat, was a strong reminder of the progress they had made. The field, when mowed, looked like a golden labyrinth, mystical in its promise of the sacks of wheat it held. Given a few days to dry, the stalks still had to be bundled and tied by hand, and set in stooks. That remained back-breaking, dusty work which Rob, Tom and Wynona tackled together. Agnes was too far advanced in her pregnancy for all that bending and gathering. She cared for Chayton and ensured that those in the field were supplied with food and drink.

There was sufficient time to thresh the cut wheat before the rest of the crop was ready for mowing. This was the event they were all looking forward to. They gathered the first wagon load from the stooks. The oxen hauled the thresher to the upper fields and were then hitched to the cross-pieces. Rob started them in their circular path. The gears groaned and started turning, powering the flailing and hulling mechanisms in the upper carriage.

Tom mounted the wagon and began pitch-forking the bundles up to the carriage where Wynona directed them to the turning maws. Over the noise of the grinding they could hear the husked kernels raining down into the chute that directed them to the attached sack. As the process gained momentum, the grins on their faces widened and they gave vent to shouts of encouragement. The

ON THE WINGS OF THE MORNING

mechanism ground to halt as a new wagon load of wheat had to be gathered but by evening the job was done and they loaded sixty-two sacks of wheat on the wagon for storage in the barn.

Rob estimated it would be another four or five days before the balance of the grain was ready to mow. He would use the time to schedule those who had asked to rent the thresher. All told, he had six customers lined up between the farm and Reston. At ten dollars a day, that should bring in some $150 dollars, well over the annual cost of the interest they would be paying on their bank loan.

A couple of days before they were to begin mowing again, Agnes woke him in the night to say that her contractions had begun. They were not yet strong and continuous but Rob decided to ride to Reston anyway to get the midwife. He first went to Tom's to ask Wynona to stay with Agnes while he was away. The night was cold. He could hear the sharp sound of the hooves striking the frosted ground. A full moon illumined the landscape and the ride was a joyous one. Dawn edged the eastern horizon as he knocked on the woman's door.

They had to wait until the early afternoon before Rob, sitting in the kitchen, heard the opening wail of his new-born. Wynona came out, moments later, her face beaming. "You can come in now," she whispered. The midwife was bathing the child and wrapping it in a linen shawl. Agnes lay, propped up in the bed, her face pale and sweat streaked. The woman placed the bundle in her arms. "Rob, dearest," she said, beckoning him to come closer. "Meet Elspeth Norah Dunbar."

When he mounted the mower two days later, Rob seemed never to have known such happiness. Agnes had handled the birth as though she had been there often and was up and around by the next morning. The child seemed without flaw, with a halo of reddish fuzz above a delicate face. Tom and Wynona shared their happiness. Wynona took over the kitchen and fed them all for the first few days. Tom looked more content than he had seen him in months.

The noise of the mower spewing out paths of ordered stalks made Rob feel strangely close to Abbeylane Farm, until he felt he could almost taste the brisk salt-laden air that blew in from the North Sea. He could see the fields that rose up to the east, to the edge of the cliffs, crowned with their tall, wind-sculpted pines. It was all part of a continuum, those beloved green fields there and his own green and golden land here. Except that these he owned and was beholden to no one. Here a joyous continuity stretched into the future for his children and perhaps his children's children.

The rigourous days of harvest were coming to a close. The weather had held, dry and cool. They had never had such a bounteous crop and with wheat prices continuing high, they would be fine for the winter and could pay off a good portion of their debt to the bank. Neighbour women came by to see Agnes and Elspeth and Wynona was frequently at the farm when the visitors called. Agnes consciously drew Wynona into the conversations and was encouraged by a new openness in the other women. Wynona's level of comfort in their presence was increasing. Chayton was an asset in this process of creating new relationships. He was crawling vigourously, his pale complexion and long black hair competing with Elspeth as a focus of the women's attention.

The new minister moved into Reston shortly before the Thanksgiving festival. He boarded with a local family and his tall, good looks turned many a woman's head. Once the harvest was in, Rob and half a dozen others joined him in making the barn usable for services in the winter months.

Among the first services to be taken by McFarlane was the marriage of Dewar McIvor to Isobel Remphel, the daughter of one of the Reston families. Most in the community had concluded that the McIvor brothers were destined to die bachelors. Their shyness and rather unkempt ways seemed to make them less than attractive marriage prospects. Dewar had conducted his courting surreptitiously so that even Seumas was surprised when he announced his engagement.

A month later, shortly after the first light snow had fallen, Ohista turned up on horseback to say that Wynona's parents had arrived on Turtle Mountain and were staying with Old John. Tom and Wynona and the boy left with Ohista the next morning, taking sufficient provisions to spend a number of days at Old John's encampment. Rob had suggested that they take additional food in case supplies were scarce among his people. They borrowed another horse from the McIvors and left loaded with root vegetables and smoked hams.

Rob still had to transport much of their grain to the merchant in Virden. Tom helped him load the oxcart before his departure, and after bidding Tom and his family farewell, he set off for the day-long journey there and back. A slate-grey sky and dun-coloured prairie set a sombre mood. Little activity could be seen around the scattered homesteads – autumn work was over. Half way to town he passed the road to Oak Lake where an encampment of Lakota had been established a couple of years before. He determined he would stop by on his return. He knew that some of Old John's people had abandoned Turtle Mountain and moved there.

The pace of the oxen, hampered by the heavy load, was such that he only arrived in Virden in the late afternoon. Once business was completed with the grain merchant, he headed to the local boarding house, took a room, fed and watered the oxen and settled them for the night.

Rob was on the road early the next morning. He turned off at Oak Lake and drove the mile or so to the Lakota settlement. Sod houses, a few tepees and a gaggle of rough shacks spread along the road. There were occasional gardens and evidence that some fields had been sown to crops, the remnants of which did not appear very healthy – overall a dispiriting place.

He stopped at a sod house and knocked. An aged and wrinkled face appeared at the door. As soon as Rob greeted the woman in Lakota she disappeared but left the door open. Moments later a young woman came to the door. Rob asked in Lakota if she spoke English. She nodded and he explained that he was a friend of Old John and would like to meet any of those who had come from Turtle Mountain. The young woman disappeared and he could hear a discussion underway in the interior of the house. Minutes later she emerged and led him down the road to a tepee. "This people from Turtle Mountain," she said, opening the entrance flap.

Rob saw an old couple, a younger woman and three scrawny children. The tepee was virtually bare of belongings. The old man's face was deeply lined, like the bed of a pond, dried and cracked in the heat of a drought. His eyes swam in milky fluid. If as a young man his limbs had been strong, today they were lightly-fleshed sticks, skin hanging from elbow to shoulder. His wife was even more emaciated. Rob winced at the thought that their condition might reflect the state of all those in Old John's encampment.

"When did you leave Turtle Mountain?" he asked. "Less than a moon ago," came the translated reply. Further inquiries yielded answers that Rob had suspected – there was no food. The young woman said that they had been told that if they came to Oak Lake government officials would supply them with food and the means to build a shelter for the winter. They saw one agent a few days after they arrived but so far they had received nothing. "Our brothers here give what they can," she said, "but they also have too little food for winter." Her sad, empty eyes displayed diminished energy.

Rob was appalled. If this is what Tom and Wynona found when they reached Turtle Mountain, Tom would be in a towering rage. Rob felt the weight of the money he carried in his pocket from the sale of the grain. He had to do something immediately to help these people. He quickly counted out twenty dollars and gave it to the young woman. "Here, please take this. Perhaps someone can travel to Virden and buy some food for you and the other families. This is all I can do now but I will try to find the agent and get more help for you."

The young woman's face was completely passive, as though she did not know what to do with the money. She took it without acknowledgement. Rob turned to the old couple.

"I must go but I will get help for you." Hearing the translation, the old man nodded faintly.

Rob turned the oxen around and headed back to the main road, his spirit weighed down by the encounter. Why is the treatment of these people by the government so callous and so arbitrary? Are we so preoccupied with making a life out of the wilderness that we cast aside and trample those who were here first? Questions for which he had no answers. He girded himself to face the wrath of his brother.

That was not long in coming. Three days after Rob's return from Virden, Tom arrived back. He had left Wynona and the boy with her parents on the mountain. He was livid. He confirmed everything that Rob had feared. The young men who had been seized months ago by the police were still being held. It was evident that the government was trying to starve Old John and his people off the mountain. They had been denied any assistance and their ability to sustain themselves by hunting was severely eroded by the settlements that continued to grow around them. The harder life became, the more insistent was Old John and those loyal to him that they were within their rights to remain on Turtle Mountain.

39

ROB'S VISIT TO OAK LAKE HAD GALVANIZED HIM FOR ACTION. HE AND TOM had long discussions about the situation, regretfully agreeing that protests and petitions seemed to go nowhere and another course of action would have to be sought. Tom wanted to organize all the Lakota across the region to force the government back to the table. But no one in Old John's encampment had the energy to initiate such action and Tom knew he could not do it without their participation.

Rob proposed that they raise funds to hire lawyers to mount a court case to challenge the government's position. The argument that it had no obligations to the Lakota because they were refugees from across the border was untenable. The medals and documents that Old John possessed had convinced him that the Canadian government was disregarding previous agreements made by the British. The Lakota on Turtle Mountain had as much right to a treaty as any other group. Their efforts to persuade officials in Winnipeg had fallen on deaf ears and, other than violence, the only way to force their hand was through the courts.

Rob proposed that they ask Rod McFarlane to help organize a gathering at the church in Reston to raise the money they would need. Tom said he saw little evidence that the settlers would be prepared to dig into their limited resources to help the Indians. "They just want them out of the way and out of sight – until they need them for cheap labour," he observed grimly.

"That may be so, but among our neighbours are those whose Christian conscience can be roused if they are made aware of the suffering caused by the government's policies. That is why I want Rod McFarlane involved. Not everyone will rise to the occasion, but I am convinced that some will." Tom remained unconvinced but reluctantly agreed to participate.

The next day Rob rode over to see McFarlane. They agreed to hold the meeting right after the service the next Sunday. The minister said that he did not think it appropriate to participate directly but would certainly attend.

To Rob's surprise, Tom agreed to accompany Rob and Agnes to the service before the meeting. Wynona stayed home with the child. There were a few more in attendance at the service than normal. Not everyone stayed for the meeting but others not present for the service joined. Rob took the chair and began with a history of his friendship with Old John and his people from the earliest days along the Pipestone, how they had helped each other through good times and bad.

"Most of us know from first-hand the misery and injustice caused by governments that are indifferent to our pain," he continued. "We saw this country as a promised land where we could build a society fair to all. But we were mistaken. Injustice was here before we arrived. Do we just put our heads down and get on with making a life for ourselves or do we respond to our brothers' pain by taking action?

"The only way to force the government to make treaty with the Lakota is to challenge its position in court. But a court challenge will cost money the Lakota do not have."

There was a long silence. "They may be your brothers but they're not mine," a large man in the back row muttered, loud enough so that all could hear. Another joined in, "They're a dying breed. You just have to look at them to know they don't have it in them to survive. They make poor use of the land we have already given them. Why give them more?"

Then a woman stood and turned to the crowd. Rob could see her lip trembling. "We've seen what can happen to our own people in the slums of Glasgow. Starvation and exploitation turn sturdy

Highland folk into wretches as devoid of hope as these people. Yet we know they are our brothers as are these." She sat down.

Then Dewar McIvor stood up. His young wife watched him anxiously. "Most of you were not here at the beginning. Seumas and I were along with Rob and Tom. The Lakota were our neighbours. They could easily have forced us off the land or worse. But they treated us as friends and many a time came to our aid. We know them as brothers.

"I have no more time or money than the rest of you. But my conscience will not let me sit still and watch government officials do to them what the Highland lords did to my family."

Rob had never heard young Dewar say more than a sentence at a time. Others seemed to take courage from his forthrightness. Gradually the weight of opinion turned in Rob's favour.

The woman who had been the first to speak in favour rose to her feet again. "I agree with Rob's proposal that we try to raise the money needed to get legal help for the people on Turtle Mountain. My husband and I will put twenty dollars forward to get started."

At this point, the Reverend McFarlane joined the discussion. "I have stayed out of this debate. You are all here because you chose to help yourselves. You did not wait for someone to come along and offer you a way out.

"But some people are swept away by the forces of history, by odds that are too great for them. I think the Lakota are among those people and I, too, want to help. My twenty dollars is on the table."

Rob closed the meeting. By the time they left, they had one hundred and ten dollars in cash in hand and a further eighty-five dollars in pledges – enough, Rob felt, to warrant a trip to Brandon to scout for a lawyer.

Tom left a couple of hours before sunrise. He hoped to be back that night. They did not know any lawyer personally, so Tom decided to ask the manager of the general store whom he would recommend. Two names were forthcoming but the first, Clarence Smith, was away in Winnipeg. The second, Charles Braintree, had offices on the main street and was there when Tom walked in.

He immediately mistrusted the man. There was something condescending and devious about him. Tom at first hesitated to tell the man the purpose of his visit but decided to proceed. The man narrowed his eyes as Tom spoke.

"You realize, of course, that what you are proposing is against the law," Braintree said. "Federal legislation in the Indian Act forbids non-natives from raising moneys for the purpose of financing legal assistance to Indians in any dispute with the government."

Tom was stunned. "How can that be?" he asked intently. "This is a democracy founded on principles of justice. How can a whole section of its people be excluded from that?"

"Mr Dunbar, before you get too upset, you have to realize that Indian people are governed by their treaties with the Crown. They have rights and privileges that non-Indians do not have. But voting in elections and accessing the courts are not among these.

"As for these Lakota, I understand the government does not recognize them as British Indians. They are refugees from the United States and they need to go back from whence they came. If the government provided assistance, they would simply remain where they are not wanted."

Tom could see he could make no headway with Braintree. Torn between shock and anger he decided to look elsewhere for assistance but just as he was getting up, the lawyer said abruptly. "There may be something I can do for you. Please come back at three o'clock this afternoon. I may have a proposal to put to you."

Not knowing where else to turn, Tom went back to the general store to enquire about other possible lawyers and was told that the only others were in Portage La Prairie and, of course, Winnipeg where some might be prepared to challenge the restrictive legislation in court. "I should have warned you about Braintree," the store manager said. "He is a hard-nosed bastard and the local bagman for the Conservative government in Ottawa. He won't be risking his reputation by going against government policy."

"Well, it certainly would have helped to know this before I saw him," Tom retorted caustically. Still, he was curious about the proposal Braintree had in mind. He decided to stay the night in Brandon so that he could hear him out.

Shortly before three o'clock he returned to Braintree's office but was immediately alarmed. The lawyer sat behind his desk looking decidedly ill at ease. Standing beside the desk were two police officers from the local detachment.

"Mr Dunbar, it is evident that you have already engaged in illegal behaviour by raising funds for these Indians. I have no option but to turn you over to these gentlemen," Braintree said without meeting Tom's eyes.

"You are under arrest, Mr Dunbar. Come quietly, sir, or I shall have to place you in hand-cuffs," the older of the two officers said.

"This is outrageous," stormed Tom. "I came here with an innocent enquiry, to seek legal help for people who are friends and relatives. And you propose to put me in jail because of some unjust law of which I was completely ignorant."

"Ignorance is no defence before the law. Come with me," the officer replied gripping Tom's arm.

Tom shook himself free, his eyes blazing. "I am a free man, a subject of Her Majesty and a citizen of this country. You will not imprison me as you have the Lakota." He turned to go but the police seized his arms. A struggle ensued and Tom was thrown flat onto the lawyer's desk and handcuffed with his hands behind his back. The police, with the lawyer's help, frogmarched Tom out of the office, down the street to the detachment. Not a few on the street stopped to watch. Within minutes he was behind bars, the lock snapped shut behind him.

When Tom did not come back that night, no one was overly concerned. Travel was unpredictable. But when he did not appear the second day, Rob became worried. Agnes was considerably better and the babe did not seem to be infected, so he asked Wynona to move down with Chayton and left for Brandon.

He was relieved to find no trace of his brother on the road – that must mean he was still in Brandon. Rob enquired at the boarding house they always used and the owner's wife said Tom had made an arrangement to spend a night but never turned up. He went to the general store. The manager recounted his interactions with Tom and the latter's concern about the lawyer but had not seen him for two days. Rob's concern grew. Was it possible that some mishap had befallen his brother? He made his way to the police station.

There his search ended in astonishment. He learned that Tom was being held pending word from Winnipeg as to what they should do with him. Rob demanded to see Tom and the police reluctantly complied. Tom was dishevelled, dark bags under his eyes. The police told Rob that they could do nothing until they received instructions from headquarters in Winnipeg and these might be several weeks in coming. Rob was not prepared to leave without Tom. He now needed legal assistance and Braintree would clearly be of no help.

It turned out that Clarence Smith had returned the previous day from Winnipeg. Smith welcomed him and quickly grasped the nature of the situation. Though Rob had never met him, Smith seemed to be familiar with the Pipestone community and personally knew several of the Dunbars' neighbours. He told Rob that he would be prepared to try to obtain Tom's release if Rob would guarantee Tom's return to face any subsequent charges.

Smith went alone to see the police and returned an hour later with Tom. He told Rob that they would have to return in two weeks' time to learn if any charges were forthcoming. In the meantime, they were to refrain from any activity related to a court challenge on behalf of the Lakota. This was a condition for Tom's release. Tom had reluctantly agreed.

On their return home, it was clear to Rob that they had to reassess their course of action. Clarence Smith had confirmed that federal legislation forbade the raising of funds to assist Indian groups to challenge the government in court. While this was a grave injustice, overturning such legislation would be a long process. Old John and his people would be starved into submission long before this was accomplished.

A week later, Rob, Tom, Dewar McIvor and Rod McFarlane rode to Virden and caught the train to Winnipeg. After consulting those who had shown the greatest interest in helping Old John, they had decided that the only course of action open to them was to appeal directly to the Indian Commissioner.

They were told that the earliest the Commissioner could see them was the next Thursday. The brothers had not been in the city for many months and it had changed dramatically. They decided to use their time to explore and Dewar eagerly joined them.

The railroad company had built a large marshalling yard where the Red and Assiniboine Rivers met. There, scores of railcars stood awaiting transhipment. Warehouses occupied blocks around the yard and a fine hotel was rising, having already reached five stories. A massive new City Hall proclaimed the pride and ambition of this prairie city.

As they walked south from the city center along the banks of the Red, they marveled at the great houses that were being built, rivalling the mansions in Edinburgh or Montreal. Some were clearly acquiring great wealth from the sale of land, wheat and timber.

Weary from much walking, the men spotted a theatre in the midst of the warehouse district. Its front displayed a Greek elegance and a rail line ran directly behind it where boxcars full of sets, trunks of costumes and everything else needed to construct theatrical fantasy were being delivered directly to the backstage. They booked tickets at twenty cents apiece for the afternoon performance.

They seated themselves just in time to watch the voluminous velvet curtains rise to reveal a Venetian scene with at least a dozen jugglers dressed as clowns tossing all manner of objects into the air and catching each before it hit the ground. The audience stamped and whistled their delight.

Then in came a line of lithesome young women, prancing in time, their skirts lifted high revealing brilliant red bloomers. The whistles from the crowd of mostly young men grew to a crescendo and Tom participated with the best of them. Rob smiled broadly reveling in the enjoyment all around.

No sooner had the chorus line withdrawn, when three young men in tuxedos emerged from stage left and engaged in a comic routine, inspired by the retreating dancers, whose content was as bawdy as anything Rob had heard in an all-male saloon. Young Dewar looked quite dazed, whether by the lewd script or the noise and colour of the ever-changing scenarios.

When Thursday came, the Indian Commissioner had two other officials with him when they were ushered in to his office. The Commissioner began his remarks by stating that there could be no discussion about the government's willingness to enter treaty negotiations with the Turtle Mountain group. "This is a matter that is beyond my jurisdiction but I can tell you I see no willingness on the part of Ottawa to extend treaty rights. These are not British Indians. They are refugees from the United States and need to return from whence they came."

It was their turn and McFarlane made an impassioned plea to the Commissioner's conscience to take action to stem an impending tragedy. His entreaties had little impact.

"Reverend McFarlane, surely it is better to employ hardship as a means of persuading them to depart than to use force of arms to achieve the same end," the Commissioner said with diminishing patience.

"These are friends and some of them are relations by marriage," Rob forcefully interjected. "We have known them since we first broke the prairie years ago. They stood by us in those early days. There will be great anger among the settler community if by your inaction, people are starved to death in the coming winter. I assure you, Commissioner, Ottawa will hear about this and Mr MacDonald's government will be publicly shamed."

The Commissioner looked uncomfortable. After a considerable pause he said, "Gentlemen, please leave us. We wish to consult privately. You may wait in the anteroom."

"We may have them on the run," Rob said quietly once they

were outside the office. "If we get an agreement, we must be sure that it includes the dropping of all charges against Tom and the release of the young men seized unjustly on Turtle Mountain."

"We'll have to pay quite a price for such a package," McFarlane commented.

An hour later, they were summoned back. "We have a proposal to put to you," the Commissioner began. "There can be no question of a separate treaty for the Turtle Mountain group. But if you give us a solemn undertaking that you will desist from any further agitation for such a treaty, and if you secure the agreement of the chief and his people to leave Turtle Mountain and resettle at Oak Lake, then the government will undertake to provide them and the people of Oak Lake with sufficient supplies to carry them through the winter months until next year's harvest and with the horses, equipment and seeds they need to grow sufficient food for themselves."

Rob immediately felt Tom stiffen and quickly asked for an adjournment to consider the proposal. They agreed to meet again after lunch.

The four men walked to a café down the road in silence. "They are using the misery of Old John's people to blackmail us into complicity," Tom said. "I cannot be party to this injustice."

"It is an injustice," McFarlane replied. "And they cannot deprive us of our rights to act to try to change the law. But people's lives are at stake. There is not the time before winter sets in to change anything."

"I can't live with starvation on my conscience," Dewar interjected.

McFarlane nodded appreciatively at Dewar. "If we can secure a written guarantee of the Commissioner's offer of supplies, then I think we must try to convince Chief John and his people to move. But we cannot agree to give up our right to work for change."

They ate in silence, Rob's thoughts in a whirl. As they finished the last of their meal, he proposed, "Let's tell them we will use our best efforts to persuade Old John to move. In return, we want a written guarantee of the type and amount of supplies they will make available and an undertaking that any charges related to our fund-raising are dropped, the young men who were arrested during the raid on Turtle Mountain be freed, and the rights of any citizen to take peaceful action to achieve political change are respected and upheld."

McFarlane and Dewar nodded. Tom was silent but Rob took his silence as concurrence.

The Commissioner listened carefully to Rob's proposal. He looked at the other officials both of whom nodded imperceptibly. "We will prepare the document," he said, "but will only deliver the supplies and free the rest of the young men if you succeed in getting the Indians to abandon Turtle Mountain. If you do not, then the status quo remains."

The men were grim faced as they left the office. "I think it was the best we could do in the circumstances," McFarlane said. "But I do not envy you the task of turning Chief John's mind. The success of this plan rests on your shoulders," he said looking at the brothers.

Chapter

40

WYNONA INSISTED ON ACCOMPANYING TOM AND ROB TO OLD JOHN'S camp, taking Chayton with her. Neither she nor Tom was happy with the arrangement but she sensed the desperation of her family and the impossibility of getting what her uncle wanted. "I may be only one to persuade him," she said quietly to Tom.

Snow already had enrobed the hills around the encampment. Of the half-dozen or so tepees that still stood, smoke arose from only a few despite the frigid air. When Tom announced their arrival, it took some minutes for the flap on John's tepee to open. His wife, looking drawn and down-cast, beckoned them in. Old John was asleep under buffalo robes. Tom brought in several boxes that had been strapped to a pack-horse and gave them to the woman. "Food for you and the chief."

Wynona and Old John's wife carried on a whispered conversation. "She says chief very ill. Not eat for many days. Cannot talk now."

They went next to the tepee Wynona's parents occupied. Despite their delight at seeing their grandchild and his mother, it was evident that they too were low in spirit. More food was brought in. After sitting a while around the low fire, Rob said that they wanted to talk with the remaining elders at the camp. While Wynona and her mother prepared food, her father and the brothers went to the remaining tepees. Rob suggested that the meeting be held in the parents' tepee because of Old John's illness but Tom said that nothing could be decided without Old John's participation. It was agreed that they would meet in the chief's tepee in the early afternoon.

As the elders came in, Rob could see the toll hunger and cold were exacting on the lined faces. Eyes were devoid of energy, hands trembled. There was much coughing and shuffling. Old John had been propped up on his robes but did not seem aware of the others. He was breathing heavily. Young Ohista came in with the elders. Even he appeared wan and slow in his reactions.

With a conflicted conscience, Rob began to make the case. He felt he was betraying these brave and good people by being the instrument to put the government's proposals to them. He felt nauseous but knew he had no choice but to continue.

"I come with a heavy heart. My people and my government have been very unjust. We have taken much from you, promised you much and given you little. I wish I could change that. But what is done is done," he began. He then went on to tell them about the families raising money to help, about their trip to Winnipeg and their discussions with the Indian Commissioner. Ohista translated as he spoke.

"I have to tell you that the government will not make treaty with you. We asked them to do this but they have refused. They know that many will die this winter if you stay here on Turtle Mountain. They want you to move to Oak Lake. If you agree, they will give you the supplies you need to get through the winter until the summer harvest.

"I have here the letter that promises this and the list of supplies. I give you my word that these will be delivered to Oak Lake as soon as you move. I do not like what the Commissioner requires but I cannot change it. I have promised to tell you exactly what he told us. Also, if you move, all charges against your young men will be dropped and they will be free to come home. That is what I have to say."

Silence descended as Ohista finished translating. Rob did not know if Old John had understood. He continued to stare at the tepee wall. Finally, one of the elders spoke, "We must talk this. Please leave us," Ohista translated. Rob and Tom left but Wynona after exchanging glances with her father, remained.

The talk went into the evening hours. The brothers and Chayton settled in for the night at the parents' tent. It was hours after dark when Wynona and her father returned. "No decision yet," she told Tom. "Most want to go, but not Old John. Others will stay if he stays. We talk again in the morning."

Dawn had not yet etched the day when Rob was wakened with the wailing, a high keening matched by deep moans. It was coming from the next tent. Rob rose to investigate but Wynona cautioned him not to leave. Her father rose and left the tent and they heard his voice join the mourning. It was clear what had happened. Wynona and her mother left the tent.

Old John was dead. He would leave his bones, after all, on Turtle Mountain. Any consideration of a move would now wait until funeral rituals were observed and that would take several days. Rob needed to get back to Agnes and the baby but Tom and Wynona chose to stay to bid farewell to her uncle. They would not be able to resume the discussions about a move to Oak Lake for some days, though with Old John no longer there, arriving at a consensus might be easier.

Rob entered the tepee and squatted beside the old chief's body. In his wizened face he could see the passing forever of a valiant struggle and a noble and long-suffering way of life. He turned to John's wife and slowly bowed his head. Then, still on his knees, he backed out of the tent as he had been told to do.

Tom, Wynona and Chayton now entered the tent which quickly filled after them with mourners, the tent flap open to accommodate others at the entrance. The cries of many voices rent the morning air. The younger men brought in a drum, its slow, deep sounds grounding the mourning, giving it rhythm and structure. Then a group of men left the tent and walked with their axes across the clearing to the forest beyond. Soon the sound of axes joined the stridency of drum beats and wailing voices.

As the day progressed, the men returned with aspen poles and built a tall platform some one hundred feet from the encampment. Then the Sacred Pipe was unwrapped, its tobacco lit and passed around the encircling elders. When all had smoked, the men spread a buffalo robe and gently laid the body on it, wrapped and tied it firmly.

Followed by the mourners, the men carried the body through the darkening shadows, raised and placed it in the middle of the platform, tying it down carefully. The drums continued their slow beat. Old John's widow, her sister, her husband, Wynona, Tom and Chayton and a dozen others who had been close to the chief, remained seated around the platform through the night.

Two days later, Tom and Wynona bade farewell and made their way back to Pipestone. They agreed to come back later to continue what had been interrupted by John's passing.

Some days later Ohista turned up at the farm to say that the remaining members of the encampment had decided to move. Most would go to Oak Lake. A few would join families at other Lakota settlements. Rob immediately wrote the Indian Commissioner to ask that the promised supplies be on hand when people arrived at Oak Lake and to enquire when the young men would be released.

Autumn was now fully upon them. The trees in the hollows along the Pipestone shone golden against the gathering skies, brilliantly so when shafts of sun broke through the towering clouds. Wafts of snow foretold the season to come. The last produce from the gardens was being stored in root cellars or preserved in jars. Fires burned all day now, particularly as little Elspeth's presence required warmth through the house. Rob hoped their store of wood would last the winter, given the need for greater warmth.

The abundance of the last harvest meant there was no need to look for employment outside the farm this winter. Though the long, cold winter months stretched ahead of them, the season had its advantages. Spring, summer and fall afforded little chance to spend time with their growing community.

But when cold and snow blanketed the land, people sought any excuse to share the warmth of fire, food and conversation, to extend the few hours of daylight and drive back the darkness and loneliness that always hovered.

Hardly a week passed without some event that drew people

on horseback or in their sleighs to each other's' homes or to the church which had become a community centre. Ladies gathered more frequently – to sew, to bake or just to seek the comfort of other women. There were no pubs as in the old country but several men had built workshops heated by woodstoves and these, with the prospect of home-brewed beer, became their favoured gathering places.

Tom would, by his nature, have been an eager participant in these events had he not been embittered by the prejudice he and Wynona had encountered earlier. But attitudes were changing. Wynona was now a frequent participant in the women's gatherings thanks to Agnes' persistence. The first time Tom joined Rob at the McIvor's new workshop, a couple of the men who Tom had physically scuffled with previously were present. But the evening's ambience was such that it became impossible to sustain grudges, and even though Tom drank more than most, his sense of humour prevailed and enlivened the gathering.

Then there were talent teas held occasionally on Sunday afternoons at the church. These were among the women's favourite occasions and they competed in the provision of food and decorations. The men were mostly dragged along, persuaded more by the prospect of food than artistic expression. Poetry featured large, tending towards the florid and sentimental, nostalgic for memories of far-off shores. Occasionally, a man would rise and make an offering, but its masculine character or even, at times, ribald nature never seemed to win the ladies' whole-hearted approval.

Music was always on the program. Out came violins, flutes, even a battered trumpet. The long winter evenings encouraged competency on the part of many players. Some played exceptionally well and the beauty of the music wove an invisible but fierce web of belonging among these fragmented folk. The silence that followed these renderings spoke to the hunger for deeper nourishment.

And so the winter months passed. Wynona's parents returned west to their community following the completion of the funeral ceremonies for the old chief. Rob and Tom journeyed to Oak Lake in early November to visit those who had moved from Turtle Mountain. For once the government had kept its word. Six wagons had arrived some days before with flour, dried meat, bedding, and lumber and tools sufficient to build six or eight shelters. In all, twenty-seven people had moved to the settlement including Old John's widow.

Chapter

41

AND THEN IT WAS SPRING — PLOUGHING, SEEDING THE FIELDS AND VEGETABLE gardens, supplementing the winter diet of hay with oats to fatten up the cattle. As the days lengthened, so did the hours that everyone put in to get the tasks completed. There had been sufficient snowfall to provide early moisture and the winter wheat was soon showing green. Rob decided to break further land that spring. They had not expanded their ploughed acreage for a couple of years but now felt that they had a sufficient handle on the work to justify expansion. And with the growth of the cities in the east, the markets for their produce grew steadily. It appeared, finally, that their gamble was secure, that a sustainable living on this wide prairie could be wrested from the earth.

The children — Chayton and Elspeth — were a source of constant delight. Chayton had the dark hair and olive looks inherited from his mother but the gregarious nature of his father, and had picked up Tom's habit of singing whenever the spirit moved him. He adored his father and was rarely away from his side. His infant cousin, blonde as he was dark, fascinated him. Their ability to play together for hours at a time was a boon to both busy mothers when they took the children out into the barns or the fields to carry their share of the work.

The prospect of Isobel and Hermione visiting in the summer had sustained them over the long winter, so it was a harsh disappointment when a letter arrived saying the trip was off. Their brother, George, had begun having seizures and Isobel had to have him moved to an institution where he could receive constant care.

She felt she could not be away for an extended time until he had become accustomed to his new surroundings. She was certain that she and Hermione could come the following summer.

That arrival, however, kept being postponed. By the next summer, both Hermione and Peter had become engaged to be married and two summer weddings took precedence over a trans-Atlantic journey. And so the years passed. When Elspeth was four, little James arrived for Agnes and Rob. Anticipating his birth, had used the quieter months of mid-summer to extend the house, adding two bed-rooms and a wrap-around porch. There was no indication that Tom and Wynona intended to enlarge their family.

After two years of excellent crops, the pattern was broken by an exceedingly dry summer. This time virtually their entire crop of wheat, oats and barley failed to grow sufficiently to produce harvestable heads of grain. A few acres on lower land held sufficient moisture to produce some winter feed for the animals but no surplus to sell. The land was so dry that they did not dare risk ploughing under the residue of the failed crops for fear that the winds would sweep up the topsoil before there was sufficient snow cover. This also eliminated the opportunity of sowing any winter wheat.

They were not alone in their misfortune. Every other homestead across this stretch of prairie faced the same scarcity. The Dunbars had sufficient funds from the previous years' surpluses to tide them over these lean times but others were not so fortunate. For several families between Pipestone and Reston, the summer drought combined with other hardships was sufficient to cause them to abandon their struggle and return either to eastern Canada or to Scotland or England. Their farms were up for sale but at prices that were well below what land had been selling for before the drought.

When they heard that Dewar and his wife Isobel, along with his brother Seumas, were considering the same course of action, Rob and Agnes decided to intervene. The McIvor brothers had over-extended themselves, buying more machinery than they could pay cash for and the bank was threatening to seize the farm in lieu of missed payments. Rob consulted Tom and together they offered to buy some forty acres of the McIvors' land that was adjacent to theirs' at a price that reflected the land values of the years before the drought. This would be sufficient to pay off their accumulated interest to the bank, give them enough resources to get through the winter and purchase seed and other supplies for the spring.

Now, finally, it seemed nothing would stop Isobel from coming to see her grandchildren. A letter arrived late in the winter to say that she had booked passage in May and that Hermione and her husband, John Simpson, would be coming as well. Simpson was employed as the manager of the fishermen's cooperative in the port of Eyemouth some six miles from Abbeylane Farm. He was apparently intrigued by all he had heard of the brothers' lives on the prairies and wanted to explore the possibility of following suit.

So it was with heightened expectation that the days of spring passed with their endless round of tilling and planting. The snow cover had been sufficient to restore normal moisture levels in the soil, and though there was no winter wheat greening the fields, the spring crop emerged on time and consistently.

Wynona contributed what she could but over the winter she had spent considerable time at Oak Lake helping the people from Turtle Mountain make a new life. She seemed increasingly divided in her spirit. Though she was accepted and welcomed by most of the settler families, her allegiance to her own people made increasing demands on her time and attention. Tom frequently joined her on visits to Oak Lake that lasted several days.

Rob felt his absence. His share of the work often lagged and Rob sensed a waning interest in the decisions necessary to the farms' management. He saw this in fences and gates that remained broken, cattle that were not consistently fed. Perhaps the arrival of their mother and sister would reinvigorate his interest. In the meantime, the additional work fell to him.

Agnes learned that Wynona had been deeply troubled by her experiences at Oak Lake. The inability of her people to adjust to the life that had been forced on them, their lack of aptitude and skills to farm successfully, the restrictions they had to live under, combined to compound their despair. That led to drunkenness and violence. After a recent return from Oak Lake, Wynona had miscarried. Wynona had taken this mishap as a sign that her life in the settler community was cursed. Tom had started drinking again.

Rob was at a loss as to what he could do. Agnes resolved to see more of Wynona, but time was limited with the demands of children and the farm. Perhaps Isobel's arrival might make a difference.

Isobel and the Simpsons were due to sail on May seventh from Glasgow. That would put them into Montreal around the fifteenth of the month. Giving them about ten days to make their way to Winnipeg and then Virden by rail, they would arrive in the last week of May.

As travel was uncertain and communication by any means slow, Rob had no way of knowing the date of their arrival. There were three trains a week that came through Virden from Winnipeg. The best he could do was to estimate the earliest they could arrive and meet each train in Virden. He had to talk to Tom. Perhaps they should both go. It would give him some unhurried time with his brother, something he had not had for several years. Perhaps Wynona could move in with Agnes for the duration.

The brothers left early on a Monday morning. They were on the platform when the great steam engine hove into view. Rob was startled at the number of box-cars and coaches it pulled. Its destination was the town of Edmonton in the far north-west of the territory. Its length was testimony to the settlement in the last twelve years.

They watched as a wide assortment of people emerged. Most were folk who appeared to be well settled though there were a few dressed in the picturesque garb of far-away places and carrying large quantities of luggage, clearly bound for new homesteads. But no sign of their mother. The next train was not due until Wednesday. They headed to the Alexandra Hotel to get a room.

Tom was looking brighter. He had not seen Isobel since Scotland and the prospect of seeing her in the flesh was a matter of keen anticipation.

They decided to eat at the Elegant Moose, Virden's only tavern, in honour of the expected arrival. Their conversation over the meal was easy, but after they had taken the initial edge off their hunger, Tom put his fork down. "Rob, I just don't get as much satisfaction out of toiling on the land as you seem to. It gives me and my family a living and for that I am grateful. But that's all it does. Wynona greatly misses her people's way of life, their customs and rituals. For all its hardship, there was a peace and nobility to it that I can't find living the settler's life. I wish as a family we could spend part of the year living as they used to before being forced into a settlement."

"Well, what's to stop you?" Rob replied.

"The weather, perhaps," Tom reflected. "Mighty uncomfortable in a tepee in the dead of winter. That, and the end of the buffalo, the limits on where you can hunt and the fact that so many of her people are broken. It's not the same any more. She is pining for a life that is vanishing."

"But there are times in mid-summer and in the fall after the harvest when you and she and the boy could ride out and live on the land for some weeks, perhaps travel west closer to where her parents live. Maybe make camp in the Cypress Hills. That country is still wild and full of game. You could try to get the best of both worlds."

Tom was thoughtful. "Wynona and I appreciate what you and Agnes have done to encourage her relationships with other women in the neighbourhood. She doesn't feel at home with them, but she is happy to be in their company from time to time. But nothing takes the place of her life with her own people. I had no idea that she would live with this sense of loss because of her decision to come with me."

Rob was silent for a time. "Are you concerned about how she will feel with Mother arriving?"

"No, not at all. I know Mother will take to her immediately. It may help her feel closer to the family. But she will always feel apart, will always be looking over her shoulder at the life that is past. I wish I could fill that void. I've tried but I can't. Perhaps if we had another child she might be readier to live in the present."

Chapter

42

TWO DAYS LATER THE NEXT TRAIN CAME INTO VIEW. IT WAS AS LONG, IF NOT longer, than the first. Again a motley crowd disembarked and the brothers strained to identify familiar faces among the crowd. Just as they were about to give up, Rob spotted Hermione at the back of the crowd with a tall young man at her side. And there was his mother. They shouldered their way through the throng of people, luggage and boxes. Rob came upon Hermione first and folded her into his arms as her husband stood quietly aside.

He saw change in Hermione. The girl had given way to a gracious young woman with a confidence about her brought about most likely by her marriage to John. Tom had passed them and swept his mother off her feet. Isobel was weeping with joy. Tom held her aloft for several seconds. Then Rob embraced her. She then held him at arms' length and looked deeply into his eyes.

"You look so well," she said. "You both do. Life in this land suits you."

Rob turned to meet Hermione's husband, John. "Welcome to this prairie paradise. I am so glad you came."

Isobel took Tom's arm as he led them to the front of the train where their cases were being unloaded. "You haven't changed at all, Mother," said Tom. "I didn't know whether I would recognize you after all these years. There must be something in the North Sea air that preserves a woman's beauty."

"Nonsense," said Isobel. "I feel old and faded, but then we have been on the move for over three weeks. It will be good to plant one's feet on the ground and stay a while."

Rob noticed the large number of cases and boxes his sister and her husband had brought – it suggested that they might be seriously considering a move to join them. He proposed that John ride with him up at the front of the carriage so as to get to know his new brother-in-law.

Though Rob knew many in the town of Eyemouth, he had neither met nor heard of John Simpson. He liked him instantly. He had been born and bred in Eyemouth, the son of a fisherman who had died in a freak storm. His widowed mother would not let her only son go to sea, so he had found employment managing the cooperative that marketed the catch. Simpson was keenly interested in the life Rob had led and, after initial pleasantries, began plying him with questions.

They reached the farm in the late afternoon with the sun still high on the western horizon. Seeing it through his mother's eyes, Rob thought how well-ordered and green it looked, the fields garbed in a carpet of emerging grain. As he climbed down from the carriage, his mother descended, her eyes shining. "What a wonderful scene. I feel immediately at home. You and Tom have done a magnificent job."

Agnes came running from the house with James in her arms and Elspeth beside her. Wynona followed hesitantly behind, holding Chayton's hand. Isobel embraced Agnes and then bent to meet Elspeth. Hermione joined them leaving Isobel free to turn to Wynona.

"My dear, I am so pleased to meet you," Isobel said holding out her hands to Tom's wife. Wynona took both her hands. "I have wanted to meet you for so long. I am so happy that you are my Tom's beloved wife and that you are part of our family." She then turned to the young boy who stood shyly aside. Isobel bent down and shook his hand. "And I want to get to know you, Chayton. You are my first and eldest grandchild and therefore a very special person in my life."

They moved the cases into the two rooms Rob had built the previous summer. Then they all settled on the covered porch that looked west over the pond to the trees that traced the path of the Pipestone to the far prairie beyond. The sun was now in decline fashioning a multi-hued canvas on the wide sky. Hermione expressed wonder at the vastness of the canopy above and the uniformity of the prairie stretching out before them.

"I want to see your house, Tom, and I want you to take me around the land first thing in the morning," Isobel said. "Then I want to know how I can be useful. I did not come just to sit around and be served."

Rob had a meeting the next morning in Reston and took Hermione and John to introduce them to the wider community. Tom came down to pick up his mother and after visiting Wynona and the boy at the house, they set off arm in arm to walk the property. Isobel was full of questions, about the land, the quality of its soil, the dependability of the rains. Then the conversation turned to Tom's life.

"Was it the right choice to come here?" Isobel asked.

"Without a doubt – my life is richer," Tom said firmly. "I have Wynona and Chayton, but I have also come to know Wynona's people. They have stretched my spirit and in their company and their traditions I have found the first real peace I have experienced. I am proud of what Rob and I have been able to do on this land but I experience it differently than Rob. For him, winning a livelihood from the land, making it productive for this and future generations is what he loves most. He is a natural farmer.

"I'm afraid that I am a natural wanderer and Wynona is a kindred spirit," Tom continued. "We love the land but we would rather harvest it without transforming it, the way her people have. And that is no longer possible around here. There are times when I would like to sell the farm and move north and live a life that is less structured, less predictable, less confining."

Tom was quiet. Isobel resisted the urge to comment. Tom went on. "Life is much better for us now than it was a few years ago – then if you were married to an Indian woman you were shunned. But you are still expected to fit in and as you know, Mother, that has never been my way."

"And what does Wynona feel?" Isobel asked.

"Well, the truth is, she hungers for the life her people had when she was growing up. They would move with the seasons. They had their wintering quarters, their summer lands where they could hunt and gather and their journeys between when they would meet up with and celebrate their rituals with relations and neighbours. But that is no longer possible in their traditional territories. Only in the north could you today live a life that had some resemblance to these past ways. Wynona would be happy to move tomorrow."

"Have you talked to Rob about this?" she asked.

"Only recently. But I think he sees this as a passing fancy. It would be quite a blow to him if we up and left. I do love the house Wynona and I built. It is warm and comfortable but it too is part of the prison. If it went up in smoke tomorrow, that would give me the excuse to make the break that I think will come sooner or later."

"You've always followed your heart, Tom. That has brought you pain but also fulfilment. You will do so again and I won't try to stop you. But I am so glad you have had these years here with your brother. Whatever the future holds, you will look back on these years with gratitude."

"Perhaps," Tom said, "perhaps."

In the days following, the visitors settled in to a normal routine. Hermione willingly helped Agnes with her children and the labour involved in sustaining a household of seven. John embraced whatever tasks Rob or Tom required of him. After accompanying Rob for a while, he took over the reins of the oxen, ploughing the remaining McIvor land and then learned to operate the seed drill planting the land to rye.

Isobel spent considerable time with Wynona and Chayton, working with her to prepare and sow the vegetable garden, something she knew much about. The more time Isobel spent with Wynona, the more she came to admire the young woman and her courage to step into the white man's world for the love of a man. She noted her strength and endurance – the many hours in the swelling heat of the sun – turning the soil of the garden, gathering the wood by oxcart from the Pipestone valley and stacking it to dry in the summer winds. She respected the distance she kept from people, not out of hostility or fear but she suspected from the way a woman of her tradition would focus on the work at hand and keep her counsel.

As the days passed, Wynona relaxed somewhat around her, smiling occasionally and even initiating conversation at times. Isobel could not help admiring her beauty of form and character. She knew why Tom's attachment was so deep. Strength and grace were evident in her lithesome hands and arms. Her quiet but commanding presence resonated with the echoes of generations who had traversed this harsh, bountiful land. Wynona was heir to their feats and calamities.

When the mid-summer lull was upon them, Tom decided to take his family out on the land. They would head to Moose Mountain some sixty miles due west where the sloughs and small lakes had left much of the area free of settlement. He suggested his mother might wish to join them.

Isobel was delighted at the prospect. She and the Simpsons were scheduled to depart in early September in order to secure crossing well before the storms of the north Atlantic and she would easily be back before they were due to leave. Wynona, Isobel and the boy would drive the carriage while Tom rode on horseback. They could then leave the carriage at some point and travel a short distance cross-country with Tom walking and the women and Chayton on the horses. Tom still had the tepee he and Wynona had lived in while they were building their house.

The road went due west from Pipestone passing familiar sights and people for the first few hours. Then they were in territory Tom had not crossed since his trip back from captivity and Fort Walsh. To Isobel it was as though they were on a terrestrial sea, the wind tracing its passage across the young crops, the horizon flat and featureless, the sky a vast, blue arc above.

By late afternoon they had entered broken country of small lakes and bush. The land was undulating and pristine. Small bodies of water kept everything green save at the summit of the hills. Signs of wild life abounded. An hour into their off-road travel they came to a lake with a spit of land reaching into it that made a perfect camp site. Tom cut aspen to make poles for the tepee and within an hour they had a fire going and the evening meal in preparation.

That evening they sat warmed by fire, the sky a torrent of starlight, the call of wolves breaking the silence. Isobel could feel her senses taut and alive and understood the allure the unstructured wilderness had for Tom. If she had been a young woman, she knew she might well have chosen to move out beyond the settlements with their rough comfort and conformity, to this land where you were aware only of the power of nature and your own individuality. They sat many hours in that awed circle before sleep overtook them.

The day dawned clear and warm. Tom and Chayton had left by the time Isobel awoke. She could see them fishing from the end of the promontory. She walked out to join Tom and the boy but sat at some distance so as not to disturb their efforts. Standing together, the boy showed the same profile as Tom. She watched as Tom bent close to show him how to bait his hook, and then threw the line out for him, teaching him to jig it slowly. All the warmth and generosity in Tom's nature was writ large in his relationship with his son. Isobel felt a deep sense of satisfaction. This was where Tom belonged.

A final fish and they headed back to the tent to cook the catch. Tom strung the gutted trout on sticks of green aspen and placed them at an angle above the fire to bake. Isobel watched with admiration as Wynona led the boy through the bush showing him which plants could be eaten and those which were best avoided. Chayton wanted to know the names of the animals that had made the footprints he could see in the mud along the shoreline.

Tom often explored the country on his own, sometimes taking the boy with him and then always returning with Chayton on his shoulders. One day he returned with a young buck slung across his back. They feasted on fresh venison for several days. Wynona harvested wild garlic from the bush and then showed Isobel how to slice the raw meat into thin strips, rub it with garlic and salt and hang it on poles to dry in the sun. Within three days, the flesh became dry and black and could be stored for future use.

And so the days went by in relaxation, wandering, new learning for Chayton and some productive labour. By the end of three weeks they had several sacks of dried venison. It was time to head back to the farm.

She wished her husband could have experienced this strange liberation. How could she arrange her life so that she too could live in this unexpected realm of elemental freedom? But as long as her son George lived, even though he was now in an institution, she could not leave Scotland. But she could encourage her children to follow in Rob and Tom's footsteps. She vowed that she would do that, beginning with Hermione and John. Maybe, ultimately, she could join them and lay her bones under this endless sky.

As they were preparing to leave, Tom told her Wynona was pregnant again. She held him close and told him how deeply happy she was at the news. She had grown to love Wynona and Chayton and could not imagine her family without them being part.

Chapter

43

WHEN THEY ARRIVED HOME, THEY FOUND THAT ROB HAD GONE TO WINnipeg. There was trouble in Oak Lake. Some of the undertakings that the Indian Commissioner had made had not been forthcoming. He was expected to be away for a week.

They settled back into the daily routine. The gardens needed weeding which Isobel was delighted to do. The cattle were almost ready to be driven to market and slaughtered. Tom decided to wait until Rob returned even though John was quite able to assist him in driving them to Virden. The rains seemed to be regular, promising a good crop.

John had struck up friendships with the McIvors and others in the neighbourhood and he and Hermione had started talking about staying through the winter. It did not yet seem to be a commitment to moving permanently, but they clearly wanted to experience the full measure of a year on the prairies. Isobel encouraged them to stay. She said she could certainly handle travelling back to Scotland on her own. Train and ship travel was now commonplace and posed few dangers.

Then Rob returned, several days before he was expected. He had alarming news. A strange illness had broken out. It was spreading rapidly, infecting many hundreds in Winnipeg. Some were dying within a day of falling ill. He thought it best to try to get out of the way of its spread.

No one knew what the sickness was or how to treat it. It was clearly highly infectious. It had started in the eastern seaports, likely transmitted from Europe through new arrivals. The speed of its spread was such that orders had gone out in Winnipeg closing all the schools and forbidding people to assemble in groups larger than three. Rob was sure that isolated as they were from the big cities, they had a good chance that the illness would pass them by.

Then a week after he had returned, they heard that a family in Reston, whose son had been studying in Toronto, had come down with high fever which rapidly led to severe dehydration. Then a day or two later, both the son and a daughter had died. Fear ran through the community with the realization that the two had attended the church service in Reston just days before becoming sick. Two days later four other families showed signs of the infection.

Rob decided the community needed help. He rode to Virden, the nearest place with a doctor. He learned that there was no recognized treatment other than attempting to reduce the patients' high temperature and ensuring they drank plenty of water. The doctor also recommended that the community set up a central location where the sick could be cared for so as to limit the spread of infection. He was unable to come with Rob because of the demands the illness was making on his time in Virden.

The only location that was somewhat adequate was the temporary church in the barn in Reston. But there were no beds and water had to be carried from a nearby well. The family who owned the barn moved away to protect themselves from infection but agreed to allow those caring for the sick to use their house for accommodation. Within a few days, seven people turned up needing care, bringing their own beds with them. Two family members agreed to stay to care for them but more help was needed.

The risks were high. Infection was clearly spread by contact and anyone who undertook to help in the care of the sick put themselves at peril. It also seemed necessary for those who volunteered to stay on location for the duration of the infection. They could not return to their homes without the risk of infecting others.

Isobel told the family that she was going to volunteer to move to the barn. "I have had a full life. No one is really dependent on me now. I have a strong constitution and I am sure I will be alright," she told them. They protested but she was determined. John Simpson offered to go as well. Hermione was horrified but overcame her fears and supported his decision. She would stay to help Agnes with the children. Rob and Tom decided that the two households should remain apart for the duration. That afternoon Rob drove Isobel and John to Reston along with food, beds and bedding.

"God be with you, Mother," Rob told her. "You must take great care. I will come as often as I can to see how you are doing. I won't be able to go in, but will stand here in the yard and we can talk from a distance."

When he came by two days later, Isobel told him that John had fallen gravely ill. Three people had already died and had been quickly buried. A few who were sick seemed to be recovering which appeared to mean that not all those infected would perish. She said that she felt none of the illness' symptoms but looked very tired.

A few days later, Tom called from the top of the garden to say that Chayton was ill but that they did not want to take him to Reston. Rob and Agnes begged him to change his mind. "He will get the best of care from Mother," said Rob.

"No, Wynona is adamant. She will only let him go if she goes with him."

"But Tom, that will imperil the child she is carrying. Even if she got sick and recovered, there is no way of knowing what the effect would be on the child. You have to help her understand that," Agnes pleaded.

Tom looked distraught. "Alright, we will both take him there. But I will only leave him if I can be sure he will get the best care possible."

"Tom, don't take Wynona. Why expose her to any more danger? I will go with you," Rob said.

Wynona finally agreed and Tom carried the boy, his body wracked with fever, to the carriage. Wynona stood, her face a mask of agony as the carriage drove down to the main road. Agnes wanted to go to her, to hold her in her grief but knew that she could not. Rob and Tom returned by nightfall. Chayton stayed in Reston.

Rob decided to travel daily to Reston. More people had died

but John seemed to have pulled through. A few days later he was ready to return home. He wanted to stay to help but, though the fever had gone, he was too weak to be of use. When Rob went to pick him up he wanted Isobel to return as well. But she would not. "If I have resisted this infection so far, then I must be in some way immune. It is far better for me to stay and see this out than have someone else take my place who may not be resistant. Besides, as long as Chayton remains here, I stay."

Life had been reduced to survival. The essential chores had to be done – the animals fed and watered. But no new work was initiated. No one seemed to be able to see beyond the next day. John was being nurtured back to strength by Hermione. So far, no one else in the household seemed to be infected.

Chayton, too, seemed destined to survive. Some days later Rob learned that he was recovering and might be able to return home in a few days. When he did, Isobel had decided to return with him. The illness was tailing off. No new cases had come in for some days. To date, nine people had died but almost twice as many had recovered.

Rob went to inform Tom. He had not seen either Wynona or Tom for four or five days. This was not unusual as they had decided that the two households should keep apart until the infection passed. Rob walked up to his brother's house and called from the garden that he had news of Chayton. There was no reply. It was mid-morning so they must be up and about. He called again – silence. He was gripped by a foreboding that rapidly turned to panic. He ran up the steps onto the porch. Then he smelled it – the odour of death. He recoiled.

But he had to find out what had happened. Or should he first inform the family? No, he had to know. The door was unlocked and he entered the kitchen. No sign of them but the odour was stronger. His heart racing, he made his way to the bedroom. There, on the bed, lay Tom with Wynona beside him, her head on his chest. He watched for a moment but there was no movement. He realized that the stench was overwhelming and he ran to the porch, retching as he went, losing the contents of his stomach over the rail. He had to grip the railing to prevent collapsing. His body shook uncontrollably.

What to do? They were beyond help. He stumbled back towards his farm but had to stop and sit down to try to compose himself before seeing the others. He was breathing deeply, the air finally free of the odour. He sat for many minutes but the agony only grew. He had to find Agnes.

As he turned the corner of the barn he could see her in the garden, weeding.

"My dear, what's the matter. You look terrible," as she stood moving quickly towards him.

"Tom and Wynona – they're dead."

He collapsed into her arms as she struggled to hold him upright.

"What? How? Where?" she cried as she gripped him hard.

"They must have caught the infection and died very quickly and we knew nothing," he said in anguish. "I haven't seen them for days. They are beyond help."

Agnes began to moan. "Oh, my poor dears. How could this have happened? Are you sure? I don't believe it. They were so strong. How could they be cut down so quickly?"

"I don't know, but they are dead – of that I am sure," Rob said grimly. "What will we do now? Poor little Chayton. And the unborn babe?" he said, another wave of grief sweeping over him. "Lost as well."

"I must go up and see them," Agnes said.

"No, you can't," Rob stood, suddenly resolute. "They must have been dead for three or four days. The risk of infection will be huge. We have to consider carefully what we do. But the first thing we must do is get Mother from Reston. She must be part of any decision we make."

"Should we tell Hermione and John?" Agnes asked.

"We must but we must warn them to stay clear of Tom's house."

Rob and Agnes wept through the whole time it took to get to the make-shift hospital but by the time they arrived, Rob had regained his composure and was ready to support his mother. This time he walked straight into the barn, telling Agnes to wait in the carriage. Only a handful of beds were now there. His mother was sitting beside the bed of one young man. Chayton was nowhere to be seen.

"Rob," she cried, her voice expressing both delight and alarm. "What is it, Rob?" She had caught sight of his face now. "What has happened?"

"Mother, please come outside," he said, gently taking her arm. Once outside the door, he turned to face her.

"Mother, dearest – our Tom is dead and Wynona too. The illness took them before we even knew they were sick." He took a broken breath. "They have been dead for several days."

Isobel shuddered and Rob had to catch both her arms to prevent her from falling. "Oh no, dear God. Oh no. Not my Tom, not my sweet boy! How could this be? And Wynona too. Oh, this is too cruel, too cruel."

Agnes had stepped down from the carriage as soon as Rob and Isobel approached. She and Rob held Isobel who began to wail her agony, the keening of her grief breaking across the silent prairie. Someone came to the door of the barn and another to the porch of the nearby house. They stood in silence knowing that this could only mean one thing. It had been a sound all too common in the weeks past.

Gradually, the sobbing that convulsed Isobel's shoulders receded. Rob and Agnes walked her to the porch of the house and found a chair.

"Mother, I found them together, on their bed. They must have died very close in time. I have not had a chance to recover the bodies."

"But Rob, we must be very careful. The infection may still be strong," Isobel said, her customary clarity returning. "How long have they been dead?"

"I should think for at least three days."

"Rob, the doctor from Virden arrived here this morning. He says the sickness is dying out across the country. Perhaps he can advise us on what to do with their bodies."

They sat longer, holding each other. The other inhabitants of the house had respectfully retreated inside. "Where's Chayton?" Rob asked. At this, a small face peered around the front door. Isobel immediately beckoned to him and gathered him in her arms, holding him tightly. The boy's eyes were wide with enquiry but this was not the time or place to tell him what had happened.

Rob got up to find the doctor. His face was grave when he heard the news. "I am terribly sorry to tell you, but if the bodies have lain unburied for several days, the risk of infection is severe. You only have two choices. Either one of you takes the risk, retrieves the bodies and moves them to a grave with no exposure to anyone else, or ----." he hesitated, "you burn the house around them. I would strongly advise you to choose the fire."

Rob chose not to discuss the doctor's advice with his mother. They collected her belongings and those of the boy, bade a sad farewell to those who had been working at the barn and made their way to the carriage. Rob then drove to the home of Rod McFarlane. McFarlane immediately came out to the carriage. He stood, looking up at Isobel, his hands on her arm. "I am so sorry. This is devastating. I will come with you." Rob waited while McFarlane saddled a horse

It was a late summer day as they drove east, the sun high and warm, the fields green and flourishing. Magpies played mischievously on the road. Prairie dogs stood curious in front of their holes on scrub land. Everything belied the deep grief held within. And yet, even so soon after the discovery, there was a quiet comfort in knowing that the world continued to turn, to grow and flourish under a generous sun.

When they arrived home, Chayton was keen to cross the fields to see his father and mother. Agnes managed to distract him into playing with his young cousins. Rob took McFarlane aside and told him the advice of the doctor and the dilemma he faced. Together, they approached Isobel, Agnes, John and Hermione who had gathered on the porch. Rob told them the choice but said that he wanted to retrieve the bodies. He would dig a grave at the edge of their garden and then carry them by himself.

Isobel would hear nothing of it. "My dear, I cannot allow you to put yourself at such risk. It makes no difference to them now. But you cannot risk leaving Agnes and the children alone. And I do not want to lose yet another son to this dreadful sickness. We will commit them to the flames. Their souls are now beyond damage. The Lord has received them and what is left is only decay." Her voice trembled as she spoke but there was a steely resolve nonetheless.

McFarlane stepped forward. "I have no family. No one is dependent on me. I will bring the bodies out for burial."

"Thank you, but you will not," said Isobel with total firmness. "There is no point now in putting anyone's life at risk. We will follow the doctor's advice."

"In that case, we must get at it," said Rob, a controlled determination in his voice. "John, will you help me collect what we need to make an intense fire? When everything is ready, we will come down." And then he realized they would need another step and he turned to the minister. "Will you lead us in a farewell service?"

"I do not want Chayton to be anywhere near when this happens," said Agnes. "I will take him and the other children over to the McIvors until everything is done."

"Yes, but he should be here for the service – then you can take him to the McIvors. He will not understand it now, but in the years to come he will want to know he was part of the farewell to his parents," said Isobel.

Rob and John headed to the barn, hitched Pete and Harriet to the wagon and filled it with bales of straw. The others sat quietly on the porch. Agnes and Hermione went to prepare food. No one talked. The setting sun daubed its canvas with multi-toned red and pink. The trees traced the course of the Pipestone. It seemed just yesterday to Rob that he and Tom had come across this place, had decided this was where they would put down roots and exulted in pointing their plough for the first time into the pristine turf.

As they drove the wagon south towards Tom's homestead, he

unexpectedly remembered that bitter, blizzard morning when he had thought he had seen smoke rising from the grove of trees that now surrounded Tom's house. An involuntary shudder coursed through his body. Now it looked so peaceful, yet it concealed such tragedy. He was too numb to think any further.

When they returned, the rest of the family walked past the barns and up to the place where they could see Tom's house. Rob carried Chayton who, when he saw the house, cried out for his parents. Agnes took him from Rob's arms and sat with him and Elspeth and James. Rob and Hermione came on either side of Isobel.

Rod stepped forward and began the solemn service for the dead.

"I am the resurrection and the life. He who believes in me shall not die...." Rob could not hear the rest of the words, his mind tracing the multitude of vivid images of Tom from the past years. His grief was somehow bitter-sweet – his agony that his brother and Wynona's lives had been snuffed out shading into gratitude for all Tom had experienced since they embarked from Abbeylane on this wager.

His ears brought him back to the present as he heard his mother quietly say:

'If I ride on the wings of the morning, if I dwell by the farther-most seas,
Even there your hand will guide me and your strength uphold me.'

Agnes arose slowly with James in her arms. She took Chayton's hand. Hermione picked up Elspeth and the two women along with John walked swiftly towards the McIvors. Rob and Rod strode to the condemned house.

Isobel stood silent, steadfastly looking at where her son and his wife had lived and now lay in death.

Minutes later the flames began their work.

Bibliography

BOOKS

Brown, Joseph Epes, *The Sacred Pipe: Black Elk's Account of the Seven Rites of the Oglala Sioux,* University of Oklahoma Press, 1953

Elias, Peter Douglas, *The Dakota in the Canadian Northwest: Lessons for Survival,* Canadian Plains Research Center, University of Regina, 2002

MacBeth, R. G., *The making of the Canadian West: being the reminiscences of an eye-witness 2d ed.* William Briggs, 1905. Schofield, Frank Howard, Story of Manitoba, 1913

Shirra-Gibb, R, *A Farmer's Fifty Years in Lauderdale,* Oliver and Boyd, 1927

Wiebe, Rudy Henry, *War in the West: Voices of the 1885 Rebellion,* McClelland and Stewart, 1985

DOCUMENTS

Bulloch, Ellen Guthrie, *The Pioneers of the Pipestone,* Reston, Manitoba, 1929

Clinkskill, James, *Reminiscences of a Pioneer in Saskatchewan, 1882-1912,* The Western Producer, 1970

Kavanagh, Martin, *The Assiniboine Basin: a Social Study of the Discovery, Exploration and Settlement of Manitoba,* Teacher Training College, Hammersmith, London

Klippenstein, Lawrence, *Manitoba Settlement and the Mennonite Reserve,* Manitoba Pageant, Vol. XXI, No. 1, 1975

Lauder, L, *The Elphinstone Story,* Valley-Dale News, Newdale Manitoba, 1962

Lothian, James, *Collected Letters from 1871 to 1908,* Manitoba Archives

Lothian, James, *Note Book, 1908,* Manitoba Archives (MG8 B2)

Lothian, William, *A History of the Pipestone Church,* The Reston Recorder,1924

Lothian, William, *Correspondence,* Manitoba Archives (MG8 B3)

Parnell, C., *Campbell of the Yukon,* The Beaver, June 1942

Richards, Irene Lawrence, *The Story of Beautiful Plains,* Historical and Scientific Society of Manitoba, Series III, No. 8, 1953

CPSIA information can be obtained at www.ICGtesting.com
Printed in the USA
LVOW07s1911080714

393352LV00003B/75/P